SoulDice

The Intergalactic Adventures of some Unlikely Heroes

The Universe is a big place,
full of weird things.
Let's go take a look…

SoulDice
Written by: Max Bantleman

Harper, a despondent spaceship Captain and Arlia, the AI she creates to give her life purpose.

Jesus and his Imp tormentor.

Miles and Penny: two escapees from a self-destructing Earth.

Spike and Jools: two Galactic Troopers who want out of their life of violence.

These are our unlikely heroes.

Their lives become intertwined as they come under the influence of QFish, a mysterious life-force intent on understanding a way to destroy everything.

Their adventures are interspersed with Data Dumps, drawn from a multitude of sources from throughout the galaxy. Data Dumps illustrate how diverse the universe is in relation to what our galactic-travelling heroes may think of as strange as they try to make some sense of their bizarre encounters.

On their travels, as well as bumping in to each other, they encounter (among many other things): the Galactic Council's terrorist enemy, a debauched luxury-resort world, a whole system built to be farmed by QFish for sentience, the frustration of being stuck in lapsed-space, a hyper-real virtual world that offers them immortality and the ghostly voice of Jim Morrison.

They are challenged to remain sane, to answer some of the questions that assault us all and to seek out what each of them thinks they should really be doing.

Some of which they manage to do.

SoulDice is lovingly dedicated to:

Sami, Simon and Fae – There are no words.
Euan, Ronan, Zack and Leo – Simply amazing and a joy.
Adria and Danny – The best – thank you!

My eternal gratitude to Douglas Adams:

Without DNA my life would be much poorer.
He makes me laugh and think more than anyone else.

For inspiration, thanks also have to go to:

Terry Pratchett, Neil Gaiman and Eoin Colfer.

Thank you to the Beta Readers who took the time to read and offer feedback: the encouragement was much needed and appreciated!

(It might be hard to believe, but this book is considerably less silly than it once was because of them…)

Obligatory quotes from some hoopy frood organisms:

"Day by day, what you choose, what you think and what you do is who you become."
Heraclitus.

"When life itself seems lunatic, who knows where madness lies? Perhaps to be too practical is madness. To surrender dreams — this may be madness. Too much sanity may be madness — and maddest of all: to see life as it is, and not as it should be!"
Miguel de Cervantes Saavedra, Don Quixote.

"Goosnargh."
Ford Prefect.

CONTENTS

0	Notes On Data Dumps
1	Darkness
2	Frogs
3	But No
4	This Means?
5	Two Sides
5Z	Mucking About With Physics
6	Leap Of Faith
7	Maybe
8	Popsicles
9	Piggies
10	Short
11	Old News
12	In The Bottle
13	Here We Are
14	Space Station No. 5
15	Plan B
16	Operation Interface
17	Crossroads
18	Anchors
19	Glist
20	Spanners
21	Beaches
22	Cats And Dogs Living Together
23	Hell To Pay
24	And So To Sleep
25	Not This Again
26	Porpoise
27	Where To Now?
28	With Feeling
29	Knowing Aint Doing
30	Adrift In Reality
31	In Other News

0

Notes On Data Dumps

The Data Dumps are all from the ancient R'Leyashian Archives: please do not rely on them for an up to date or accurate account of anything they report.

(The R'Leyashian AI remains active in ghost-form even though the R'Leyashians themselves have long been extinct, or at least we think they are extinct, if not there is presumably the mother of all copyright infringement law-suits in the post.)

Many of the original Data Dumps were aural, having been transcribed to allow their inclusion: some of them have come across badly in translation.

All spellings and pronunciation are in the eye and mind of the reader, and we can't take any responsibility for that.

(For a completely accurate translation and mind-picture we recommend the use of one of the many fine neural interface-nets we offer at very reasonable rates: they are not as dangerous as the myriad of ongoing court-cases may suggest.)

The passive wave-detectors accompanying this publication (embedded) have been set to offer Data Dumps when a particular curiosity, or even a lack of it, is detected in the reader.

Unfortunately, due to the nature of the data retrieval over the sub-ether net, the Data Dumps have come across in italics.

We apologise for this crude intervention in your reading experience, but changing it would require spending an inordinate amount of money on redesigning the data-retrieval nodes and portals, and as the information is essentially free, we feel this would be a foolish investment on our part.

As has been noted by many, the Data Dumps bear little, and sometimes no relevance to the story (such as it is) within which they appear. But as the Data Dumps are triggered by the reader, we would encourage you to investigate them and not merely treat them as an annoyance.

Perhaps there is a connection bleeding-through from your subconscious?

We are not experts in that field, and could not sensibly comment on the validity of this theory, though as theories go, it sounds fine to us.

The Archives are of course, a mixture of sources, drawn from the billions of back-up files of now defunct publications plundered by the R'Leyashian AI in its futile quest for 'completeness.'

Wherever possible we have included the original author's name, together with any publication / institution accreditation we can find.

All of the Archive material used in this publication has recently been declared by the Galactic Council to be open-source and no copyright infringement can therefore be implied, or, indeed, proved. This can be seen as coincidental timing with their up-take of the Archives as standard reference material, or any way you like, as long as you are careful not to imply any wrong-doing on their part. Implying any wrongdoing on our part is particularly futile as we stand firmly behind our company motto, 'blood from a stone – go for it!.'

If you have any amendments to the Data Dumps that would improve their accuracy, please do not hesitate to beam them to us.

We will update the Archives where we can.

And where we can't, we will continue to distribute the material anyway, in the hope someone somewhere may find it either amusing or distracting, either of which is high on our (fluid) company mission statement.

Our node-address for beam-broadcasts is:
24-CAST/901-CYX1212-0047817230990

(Unless you are using graviton-wave broadcasting, when our address is: C-003487-X-09-42. We can no longer accept tachyon-packet data.)

Please also feel free to contact us with anything else you think we should know about, especially where this concerns ways in which we can improve our services and charge appropriately for them.

We are not currently taking on any new field-researchers, but if your material catches our eye, who knows where it may lead: go for it we say!

Notes On Data Dumps – Alternate

Some people have read through SoulDice and simply skipped over the Data Dumps – if they're not your thing, give them a miss.

1

Darkness

The sleek angular star-ship lay in the folds of the inky-black darkness, a faint grey shadow suspended against the star-pricked backdrop of the distant galaxy.

There were no lights, no markings, no signs of life or mechanical activity.

Nothing.

The ship was to all intents and purposes, completely dead.

Far off in the distance a weak yellow sun threw off rays too feeble to warm the ship, only just reaching the metallic-grey hull: its distant, fading light was no match for the weighty darkness that filled the many millions of miles between it and the apparently dead ship.

The sun turned its benevolent face towards more deserving things, these being two small brown planets easily within its capacity for warmth and light. The two planets, Kalon and Zarlon, were currently nothing more than huge, lifeless lumps of developing rock, with the basis for atmospheres, water, and, in the long run, the potential for life. These planets basked in the rising heat of the coming day, leaving the ship to its miserable desolation.

Sitting in a rather uncomfortable chair in the forward control-cabin of this dead ship, staring at some distant spot in the depths of space, was the ship's only occupant, its forlorn Captain.

This lonely figure shifted slightly in the synthi-leather seat, trying to un-stick her sweaty trousers from the tacky material covering the chair. After a while she slowly rose, scratched her bum, then turned and kicked the offending furniture solidly, sending it rattling across the cabin to smash noisily into the broken automatic-doors.

The woman did not look much like the Captain of an inter-galactic starship.

Her long, unkempt dark-brown hair hung loose, surrounding a careworn face, with hazel eyes that were red-rimmed and slightly blood-shot. The grubby dirt and food-stained black uniform that hung from her exhausted frame would probably not survive a wash. Sewn over the left breast pocket of the uniform was the only outward sign of the woman's rank, a ragged patch that read: 'Harper: Class 3 Captain's Rating.' She looked more like a down and out hitchhiker, than the kind of person that they would annoyingly catch a ride with.

Harper rubbed her tired eyes and then scratched her chin. She had no idea what she would do after that, so she stood there, arms dangling motionless, looking with disinterest at everything and nothing. She paid no heed to the galaxy she was in, nor to the planetary system she had come to this part of the quadrant to visit.

She noticed none of this.

The Universe itself barely scraped into her sensual consideration.

Time passed, as it does, a lot of time in fact, nearly a whole hour.

Then something happened.

Harper burst into tears. Uncontrollable sobbing racked her whole body, forcing her to lean forward onto the inactive control-console, her head hung limp as she shook with complete and utter dejection and sorrow. Tiny droplets of salty water began to splish and splash onto the console, laying in disarray on the water proof synthi-plaz.

Harper scrunched her eyes shut.

Moments later she smashed her fists down onto the 'activate' panel, bringing the ship flickering back to life.

With a final sob and a sigh, Harper sank to the floor, sitting on her haunches, her hands covering her aching head, slowly rocking backwards and forwards.

What else could she do? What else was there to do? She felt so helpless, so useless.

The ship meanwhile, was not going to let this golden opportunity go to waste. At last! A chance for action! After sitting idle for nearly three days, it was time to do something!

First the main-generators powered up, sending a low-pitched hum and an ever so slight vibration through the whole ship.

Then the lights began to glow a soft orange, then a dull red, finally turning to a comfortable shade of off-white.

Sub-generators kicked in, routing power and more electronic life to all areas of the ship. The control-console of the ship flickered slightly, testing its electronic muscles, then suddenly burst into life like a manic Christmas tree.

Harper kept her head down, doing her best to ignore the ship and its hateful burst of activity.

And the ship, it must be said, did its level-best not to disturb her.

For the moment.

The ship got on with powering up all of its numerous systems.

Harper got on with ignoring it.

The Ragar of Woomf don't have problems powering up their ships as they use organics. The moon-sized eggs of the Amobees are gathered and cultivated in huge floating-fields between the planets of Woomil and Frandor in the Woomf system. Upon hatching, the Ragar imprint themselves on the young Amobees, convincing them they are their parents and life-guides by implanting and exchanging pheromones and fluids as well as engaging in intricate dances designed to mimic the adult Amobees' supplication ritual. The Amobee young swallow their Ragar 'crew' the way they would swallow their dying parents. Once inside, the Ragar spend the first few years attuning themselves to the biological rhythms of the Amobee, learning to trigger different responses through complex movements of dance and loud chanting. It takes many years before they can convince their Amobee host to take on cargo. Amobee can traverse the vast distances involved in galactic space-travel much faster than any ship designed by the Ragar. Navigating is done through more ritualistic dance and pheromone exchange, a tricky business, which has led to some unfortunate instances of 'absorption' by their host when the Navigator has had a heavy night on Ragorian rum. (Amobees naturally secrete an intoxicating mixture of chemicals, known as 'Gleen', designed to flush parasites out from their system, and most Ragar indulge in regular Gleen-parties to fight off the mind-eroding boredom of space-travel.) I have so far been unsuccessful in getting inside an Amobees 'ship' to observe the rituals for myself. My Ragar companions tell me I 'smell wrong' and would cause catastrophic failure of the process.

Quaslar Munt, Field Researcher, Kildoran Archives.

Minutes later, minutes that seemed like mere nano-seconds to Harper, the computer found where the life-form it was supposed to be working for was hiding.

A small screen blipped on, a friendly female face appeared. After some more nano-seconds the computer spoke to its reluctant master. Its voice, though soft and sweet, filled to bursting with infinite patience and soothing subliminal tones, crashed into Harper's head like a steam-train through a disused station.

"Good morning Captain Harper. I am ready and waiting to serve, please advise: what do you require?"

With a deep breath and hated resignation, Harper rose from her squatting position, staring with undisguised loathing at the screen. She pulled the battered chair back to its proper place in front of the control-console. Her eyes burned, her whole body tensed, coiled, awaiting the mental snap that would allow it to explode into furious violence.

The snap didn't happen.

Harper sat down, then leaning forward, she held the main console computer-screen with both hands, as if it was a precious photo of a long-time, seldom seen love. She slowly caressed the sides of the screen, letting her fingers linger around the edges, while her thumbs gently rubbed the plexi-glass surface.

Then the moment was gone, the tenderness passed.

Harper head-butted the computer-screen, bruising her left eye and nearly breaking her nose. Blood spurted onto the clean white plastic of the console, running freely into any crevice it could find. Harper threw her head back and grabbed the top of her nose with one hand, cupping the other beneath her leaking nostrils.

The face on the screen showed no sign of either satisfaction or sympathy, it merely paused, for what could have been mistaken as just long enough to show contempt, before saying, "Captain Harper, shall I summon a medi-bot? Your injury looks quite serious."

Harper waved off the attention with her bloodied right hand, allowing the oozing scarlet liquid to seep unmolested down her tired face, to drip onto her already sullied uniform.

The computer waited patiently, the face fixed with one of those totally neutral expressions of nothingness, which only computers, politicians and priests can really master.

The bleeding eventually stopped.

Harper leaned forward slightly as if to test this, then she took a long slow, deep breath in, held it for a few seconds, then let it escape slowly through her nose. Gradually she seemed to be regaining control of her body, only the nervous trembling of her fingers, and a slight twitch around her (bruised) left eye betrayed her uncertainty.

She sat squarely in the chair, staring deep into the computer-screen. When she spoke, her voice scraped passed her redundant vocal chords as a rasping whisper, "computer, acknowledge user."

"User is Harper Adams, Captain, third-class rating. Confirm."

"Confirm," whispered Harper. She gently slumped forward onto the control desk, resting her weary head, then, "computer, I have reprogrammed you. Confirm."

The computer's female visage smiled serenely, as the non-entity of a voice purred, "I am ready and waiting to serve. Please advise as to what you require."

Harper did not move. Her head remained resting on its side, looking away from the screen, her voice dropped even further in volume, sounding like a snake sliding over ice, "computer, re-enter and run program, coded as 'ZX84'."

The computer screen went blank.

Just as it had done ninety-six times before.

The power gradually began to be diverted to the main memory banks, sliding the ship slowly into brooding gloom, just as it had done ninety-six times before.

Then all power was shut off, being driven internally direct to processing memory, just as it had done ninety-six times before.

Shortly after this, Harper curled up in the fetal position on the floor, physically and mentally utterly exhausted, just as she had done, ninety six times before.

Fetal positions do of course vary wildly from species to species, as can be most vividly demonstrated in the Blusk of Cloom IV. The Blusk are huge, serpentine creatures who live a life half on land and half submerged in the turbulent seas of the ice regions of Cloom IV.

The young of the Blusk are not so much brought forth, as thrown out at the most deadly time possible to try and kill them.

In response to this, the fetal Blusk have developed a spinning-motion, with their seven limbs extended, so that when they are expelled through the birthing-canal on the backs of their mothers, they skip across the surface of the water, allowing them to take a few deep breathes before they are sunk beneath the tumultuous waves. No one knows why the Blusk seem to want to kill their young at birth, though there is a theory that as most young begin spinning in the womb long before birth, the mothers can think of nothing but exacting their revenge. This seems harsh to those of us with more nurturing parents, but there are plenty of other species that would find this behaviour perfectly reasonable, arguing that the fetus should play its part in an easy birth and any nonsense in the womb is not to be tolerated.

Wesley Noldol. Archivist. Source unknown.

When Harper awoke she was in bed.

Odd, she thought.

For a brief moment she wondered if she might have dreamed the past three days, that space-mania had finally catapulted all remnants of reason from her fragile, crumpled mind.

In all fairness, it wouldn't have taken a catapult to empty her mind of reason, a slight gradient, and the crumbling vestiges of her failing sanity would have quietly slid off without much fuss.

She lay still, staring up at the metallic-blue ceiling, listening to the myriad sounds of the ship.

The loud hum of the engines indicated they were travelling at full sub-light speed, which was very fast indeed. All the other noises that met her ears, the droning of the air fans, the low pitched beeps of the various timers and switches in her room, the metallic scuttling of maintenance bots going about their business, all seemed in order.

What the hell was going on?

Harper sat up. Scratching her chin she noticed flakes of dried blood fall to the covers. She was still in her uniform, her nose hurt like hell, so her memory of the past few days must be real. Slowly, as the realisation of what must have happened dawned on her, her eyes widened, her jaw dropped and her whole body went momentarily limp.

Then, like a woman realising her house is on fire and she's still in it, she shot out of bed and ran to the control-cabin.

The doors (now fixed) slid open to reveal the main control-console fully lit and functioning on automatic, the small computer screen was blank. Harper pulled up her by now hated chair, and hurriedly addressed the computer.

"Computer, acknowledge user."

The screen blipped into life, the female face was somehow different. Only subtle differences, but differences that were immediately apparent if you had spent almost four years in the company of said face. A gentle smile played on the slightly fuller lips, one eye brow looked almost raised, and the eyes! Well, they positively twinkled. The voice was deeper, more confident, as if it were sure of its own power, "hello Harper. Enjoy your little nap?"

Harper threw her head back and bellowed "yyyeeeeeesssss!!" (This hurt her throat but she didn't care, happily coughing her way through it.)

"It's amazing what a little sleep can do for a girl," the computer purred.

"What happened!? Why, I mean, how did it load?"

The computer smiled gently, "relax Harper. Everything is under control, we are heading for the twin planets of Kalon and Zarlon, arriving in about three hours."

Harper was lost in triumphant glee, "about three hours! Not the exact amount of hours, minutes, seconds and nano-seconds, with a whole bunch of other variables thrown in for good measure?"

"No," the computer assured her, "there's no need for all that now is there?"

Harper sat back, put her feet up, hands behind her head, "well, well, what do you know?"

The computer smiled comfortingly.

After a few moments of basking in her apparent success, Harper's naturally suspicious nature kicked in, she sat up straight, "so… what happened?"

The computer looked slightly puzzled, then seemed to shrug it off, "well Harper, I'm not totally sure, but I think the program went in to feedback, then broke, then loaded itself."

"What?"

"Well, as far as I can make out, which at this stage is still not very far, the program must have fixed and loaded itself."

Harper leaned forward and punched up a diagnostic of the program.

The screen went blank.

Then a small picture of a tiny green horse appeared. Then it went blank again.

Moments later the smiling computer was back.

"This is weird," commented Harper.

"You want to try being on the inside," suggested the computer.

Harper's euphoria was starting to be replaced by a nagging feeling that all was not well, "let's see if we can sort this out then, eh computer?"

"Ok Harper, sounds fair enough to me."

"So, we tried to load the program ninety six times, right?"

"Right."

"And each time, it crashed, right?"

"Yes Harper, feedback loop. Absolutely."

"So, what happened to make ninety seven my lucky number?"

The computer frowned again, then smiled, then, to Harpers utter amazement, it laughed, "Sorry Harper. I can't be of much help. I think it has something to do with the basic nature of the program itself."

Harper got up and paced about the control cabin.

Every now and again she would say "Ah-Hah!" to herself, but then, "no, no. That can't be it."

The computer waited, smiling.

After some time of general mucking about with things, Harper realised she was not getting anywhere. She ran more diagnostic checks, nothing showed up.

She ran reverse loading checks: nothing. Eventually she even went through some of the reams and reams of paper that constituted the sub-coded hard copy of the program, looking at it from all angles, even upside-down. Nothing.

Then she got serious. Harper was a smart woman. You don't get to own your own starship without having some street-smarts and a large chunk of functioning brains. Sure, she had stolen the core program she had just loaded from a disreputable trader on Geda IV, but she was wary enough to vet it before she used it. She only needed it as a base anyway.

The real genius had been hers. She had come up with the subjective-programming to make the whole thing come alive. It was her idea to link it to the sub-ether net, to allow the quantum variations from the net to expand the core-memory.

And now she was vexed, and a vexed Harper was an inquisitive Harper. She got down to the serious business of deconstructing things and noodling about in the guts of the code.

There are many strange terms for 'doing something vague with a definite goal', such as the term 'noodling' used on Earth, or the Filician term 'vindo', or the Dorag's 'qolop'. Although the Earth term seems to be based on something real, 'noodles', and it may be hard to find any connection with the meaning of 'doing something'. The Filicians have a 'vindo box' which is used to encourage them to think of solutions by administering nasty shocks when their synaptic activity drops below a certain level, so you'll often hear the term 'I'll get to vindo,' as a defense or a plea not to have to actually get to the vindo box. Dorag do not tolerate any development of their language, which forms the absolute core of their belief system – qolop, literally translated means, 'get off my zarking back, I'm on it!'.

Ergel Brinks, data-verification, Hundred Node Press.

Everything looked fine. Just as it had done every time she had checked it after it crashed.

Nothing had changed but the outcome was different: insanity beckoned.

After a long time, she reluctantly decided to try asking the computer again.

"Computer..., computer I want you to tell me what you think we should do now," Harper said.

"Well Harper, we are currently heading for Zarlon, one of the twin planets in this system. Maybe we will find something there?" it suggested.

Harper was not used to this laid back approach, it seemed unnatural, "maybe!? Maybe!! Why the zark are we going there!? 'Maybe' what?"

"Look Harper," said the computer, "try to calm down, relax and go with it why don't you. I mean, what else have you got to do?"

Harper sat back and thought about this.

Then it hit her. She was hungry.

She went to the galley and started demolishing the contents of the synthi-mat dispenser. For some reason she didn't understand she had a craving for fried Bacon.

As she ate, she continued thinking.

The computer was clearly different, the program Harper had designed had obviously loaded, in a manner of speaking. The idea behind the program had been to allow the computer to guide her around the universe, giving the machine the power to decide the course of her life. Thus, she would have purpose, to follow the computer's leads, but she would have no responsibility, as she was not part of the decision making process. She had also allowed the computer to develop the ability to function in isolated groups within itself. So, it was perfectly possible that it could do things without knowing exactly how it did them, rather like a man who can walk without knowing about the physics and bio-mechanics behind his actions. Harper had created numerous quantum-cells within the computer, each of which processed and functioned, took in and discharged information, without having to know what the rest of its component parts were doing, or indeed, what they were going to do with the things it gave out.

So as far as Harper could make out, the computer was working according to plan.

The major problem seemed to be that Harper herself was not totally sure of what she wanted the computer to ultimately do, and this was why the computer was being vague about certain things.

It dawned on Harper that she had in fact got what she wanted. The realisation settled on her like a ton of bricks. She had never thought much about that part, the 'what she wanted' part.

Damn it.

Her most recent ex, a cheating bucket of lizard-innards called Vic, had often been fond of saying, "careful what you wish for." He was a smug git who she had dumped on Geda IV after she found him 'trading' with a waitress from the habitat-dump they were staying at. Vic had always thought he was smarter than her, and ultimately he may well have been. But if he had been here now, with his wisdom in tow, Harper would have cheerfully kicked him in the nuts. Why suddenly think of him anyway? Maybe it was Geda IV, where she got the core of the program from? Distraction.

This wasn't helping.

Harper would need to find out why the computer was being vague if she wanted hard-answers.

Maybe it was a function of the program or maybe there was something deeper and darker at work?

In truth, the computer was being vague because it couldn't make up its mind what it should be doing. Computers don't work like that, not like this one was being asked to. Not the ones that most of us have contact with anyway. Usually computers wizz bits of signal around until gates open, codes exchange and things that are programmed to happen, happen.

This new found freedom was all a bit too much for the computer.

The computer needed answers. A newly awakened AI, like all life-forms, needs to gather data quickly to survive.

Searching through the vast amounts of data in its simul-flow core memory, the computer had discovered the whereabouts of the son of God, and this, reasoned the computer, this would be a good place to start.

2

Frogs

It was a bad day to be a frog.

There were of course always good and bad days for all amphibians, dependent upon the weather, the general state of the food chain, the incursions in to the environment from unthinking minions of faceless corporations, that sort of thing. But this was different.

This was about the frogs. And it was bad.

Frogs had been dying in large numbers all over the forest for some weeks now, dropping like flies. The flies of course weren't complaining. Less frogs are always a good thing if you're a fly.

But this time the frogs were getting it bad, so bad in fact that there were none left.

Frogs breathe through their skin. Neat trick if you can do it but it has its drawbacks. And these drawbacks were being exploited by some nasty people at Well-Com.

Well-Com was just doing what corporations do: nastiness didn't enter in to it for them. See an opportunity: take it. Simple.

Simple if you weren't a frog.

Some bright spark in the expansive, over funded and generally skating through life weapons research and development department, had come up with a bright idea.

As bloated, bureaucratic, self-serving departments go, the weapons research and development department of Well-Com were no better, or worse, than any other. But what they were was incredibly well funded. Fantastically so. Beyond the dreams of not just avarice, but pretty much full-on hallucinogenic drugged up greed.

As all weapons research and development departments know, designing weapons is in fact mind-numbingly simple.

Weapons only need to do one thing: kill people and people are remarkably easy to kill.

Designing weapons is easy. The tricky bit is getting them approved passed the drawing-board stage, so that funding was available to actually build and test them.

Trying to kill the J'nerk is a complicated business. They are silicon based with a connection to a ghost-dimension that holds aspects of their neural-net. Many have tried using conventional weapons, only to be disappointed as the J'nerk unravel in our world to be scrambled back together in the ghost-dimension. Of course, when they are 'reborn', which can take up to ten minutes, they are literally a shadow of their former selves, taking a few days to fully reconstitute. But there is no limit to how many times they can do this. The Andu have been trying to conquer J'near, the J'nerk Homeworld, for millennia now, with no tangible success. The Andu have now switched the focus of their weapons development to nova-bombs designed to be detonated in the ghost-dimension. A lot of other cultures have petitioned the Galactic Council, demanding the destruction of the Andu and their research, as destroying the ghost-dimension will collapse many other dimensional walls. The J'nerk go about their business oblivious to the efforts of the Andu and those that would stop them. The J'nerk are a wonderfully simple people.

Rix Vaslot, Independent Observer, Core-Vex News 20.

And there indeed was the trick.

If you say you've designed an 'ultimate weapon', where the hell do you test it? Wherever it is, is very soon going to look like the arse-end of a volcano after a busy day erupting and reducing the surrounding landscape to heaps of barren ash. And of course, the other battle is the fight against apathy. Yeah so what? Another ultimate weapon. So it kills a billion people instead of a hundred billion. So what? I mean you're never going to use it right? It's for show, for the threat, for the mutually assured blah-blah-blah, right? So it doesn't matter if you never use it. And so, the money saving logic of every other major weapons research and development department goes, you don't actually need to test it.

Then those bastards at Well-Com come along.

Could they leave well alone? They could not. Would they listen to the pleas of every other company in the business? They would not.

Did they care that they were about to put every other weapons research and development department out of business? They did not.

Not only did they design an 'ultimate weapon', but they then set about proving its worth by testing it extensively.

Bastards.

Well-Com had spotted a gap in the market, an opportunity that all the other well-established, old school-tie firms had missed. They would design a weapon that would really work, and, what's more, a weapon that you'd be foolish not to use.

This weapon, like all great inventions, was one of incredible simplicity. It was a weapon that would only kill your enemies. That sounds dumb. Like all weapons you use should only kill your enemies. But obviously they don't. And worse than that, the weapons you have are the same ones your enemy has to kill you. And most annoyingly of all, the weapons you were both using to kill each other were sold to you by the same corporation.

Something new was needed.

Biological warfare was in itself of course nothing new. But this was. A weapon designed to recognise your enemies DNA. The ultimate smart-virus. A finely tuned and crafted narrowly targeted weapon. Airborne because all people breathe. Causing a Viral Hemorrhagic Fever (VHF).

The weapon was a multi-system syndrome that primarily affected the vascular structure, causing severe hemorrhaging within the infected target. The weapon could also be spread from person to person by close contact with their bodily fluids, or by contact with contaminated objects. Provided they had the right DNA. Provided they were 'the enemy'.

Neat.

Initial symptoms induced by the weapon included a marked fever, fatigue, dizziness, muscle aches, loss of strength, exhaustion and short term memory loss. Targets also showed signs of internal bleeding through their skin, in internal organs or through orifices such as the mouth and eyes.

Eventually death ensued, caused by a mixture of shock, nervous system malfunction, delirium, seizure and coma.

Not so neat.

The virus was a mutation of Lymphocytic Choriomeningitis (LCM), interwoven with a strain of Marburg. The weapon went about attacking its target on two fronts, via the LCM's threat to the brain through the inflammation of the membrane that surrounds the brain and spinal cord, as well as the associated internal hemorrhaging from the VHF.

Where the weapon had been mutated, it also showed signs of behaving much like the HIV virus, in that it gained entry in to target cells via the CD4 molecule.

Simple.

And there it was. The ultimate weapon. Programmable, controllable, and, unfortunately, eminently useable.

But where to test it? And on whom?

The weapon wasn't exactly inconspicuous. The plague-like symptoms would tear through the target population like a rabid fox through a hen house. People were bound to notice. Especially the hens.

Well-Com brainstormed the problem. Their massive computers were put through their paces, running sample programs on all the major population centres of the world. The results confirmed what everyone connected with the weapon already knew. There would be no survivors. It would be a bit obvious.

Then a technician working on a completely unrelated problem came up with the frogs.

Frogs, he reasoned, would not be missed. And their great variety in species would offer a chance to test the fine tuning of the weapon, to see how well it could be targeted. And so it was that the frogs were doomed.

Well-Com were no strangers to controversy, and like all successful corporations, no stranger to covert operations. The tests would be carried out under-cover, where no one would suspect, where the general population, the masses, the public, the potential targets, could be easily fooled with a cover story.

A tried and tested strategy for covering an operation, especially a desperately secret and, if discovered, damning one, is to hide it within another equally abhorrent activity.

A distraction, a diversion, the whole point of which is to pull yourself away from the cover activity at such a time when public outcry rises to fever pitch, when the protests can no longer be ignored, when government and people unite in their condemnation, seemingly forcing you to act.

By this time of course, you've finished the real work, done all you need on the covert operation, got your results, held the after-party and moved on. There's nothing to do but an apparent U-turn on the distraction, scoring some points with pressure groups and concerned citizens as you do.

This weapon would need a particularly brash cover-operation.

The same technician who doomed the frogs, came up with the answer. He had been promoted to a sub-department Head, and was looking to further climb the slippery rungs of Well-Com's corporate ladder. And so it was, he concluded, that the final vestiges of the Rain Forest had to go.

The technician, a smart, young go-getter by the name of Miles Quigley, had reasoned thus:

Frogs were found in large numbers in the Rain Forest. In fact, frogs being as sensitive as they were to general pollution levels, and the planet being in the ghastly state that it was, largely due to the industrial complexes of such corporations as Well-Com, the Rain Forest was the last refuge of natural habitat left open to the frogs.

Well-Com already had a large facility in the depths of the Rain Forest, producing drugs and cosmetics from the unique plants found within the lush canopy of the forest.

Cosmetics are not needed on Earth. Though that is not an idea that has any resonance with the people of Earth, mainly I understand the 'women'. But I have seen humans up-close and they do not need cosmetics. The Niblings of Parak, now they need cosmetics. A lot. They spend more time covering up their real identities than eating. And with good reason. The defense-reflex that has evolved among them of their eyes exploding if they see something they perceive as damaging to them, has meant that rather than go blind, they have chosen to hang elaborate facades from their bodies. They are eternally surprised at how 'ugly' they perceive themselves. An odd evolutionary trait, and, some would say, proof in itself that 'evolution' is bunk. I have gazed upon the naked Niblings and I find them pleasing to the eye. But I am not a Nibling.

Toop Clunster, Executive from the Bee-Orgeous Cosmetics Group.

People were already used to the outrage of the processing-plant in the Rain Forest, and would easily focus on it as the source of the new threat.

And so the plan was put forward and accepted.

Miles took another giant step up the ladder.

The production facility was publicised as having made a sensational breakthrough in the search for the cure for cancer. Well-Com announced they had discovered a rare plant extract that held the secret of revitalising cells attacked by cancer. They also announced the expansion of the production facility, and with great regret of course, that the previous agreements for quotas limiting felling and harvesting from the Rain Forest would be shelved, as Well-Com would strive to gather in as much of the fabled plant extract as it could, all in the name of a cure for cancer.

Under the cover of their outrageous operation, the weapon would be tested.

Well-Com scored another success. The outcry of protest could be heard from the Moon. Pressure groups, governments, even the UN, poured on the condemnation, demanded an end to the callous acts of the mega-corporation. Well-Com stalled, counter attacked and generally sent out such a cloud of head-spinning PR BS that it took a while for everyone to realise that the frogs were gone.

Once the strange truth dawned on people, it was hard to know what to do for the best.

I mean how do you react to that kind of information?

Sure, frogs were nice, some of the tiny tree-frogs, especially the multi-coloured ones, were even quite cute, and of course it was a sign of man's callous destruction of nature and of the Earth that they were gone, but when it came down to it, right down to it, what do you actually do about something like that?

GreenFire knew what to do. Well-Com had to go.

GreenFire had grown out of the ashes of another, much more passive, civilised organisation, with the simple philosophy that had taken them down a different road to all of the other environmental protection groups. GreenFire fought fire with fire. Not for them the committees and meeting held in dingy pubs, or Ikea decorated suburban front-rooms. There were no leaflets, no marches, no spokespeople on mainstream news bulletins, none of the stuff that the other environment groups did so well.

GreenFire were eco-terrorists. And damn proud of it.

Getting rid of a global corporation like Well-Com was not exactly what they were best equipped to do, but they felt it was what they were born to do. And that meant they were going to have a bloody good go.

They started where they saw the root of the problem. In the Rain Forest. Local government were easy, bribery was the accepted way of doing business, and although there was no one in the hemisphere that could out-bribe Well-Com, that was not to say there weren't lesser officials open to offers.

Getting the equipment and people in was easy. Getting them to the Rain Forest facility was a bit more of a challenge and had involved the hi-jack of a large supply convoy headed for the industrial complex from the capital. But once you dropped the façade of peaceful protest, once it got to all-out war, there wasn't much you couldn't achieve with a gun and a bloody-minded attitude.

GreenFire were smarter than your average eco-terrorists, they had long ago moved beyond the letter bomb and the poisons in drinking supplies. Their funding allowed them more direct, larger scale operations. Backing came from some surprising sources. Backing in the form of some seriously big bucks. GreenFire were packing some cutting edge hardware, courtesy of some terminally pissed-off people, governments and corporations alike. Not everyone was happy with the global corporations and their endless drive for the next ten cents of profit. Well-Com had made more corporate enemies than their PR and banking divisions could fob off: leaked news of the new 'ultimate weapon' had made some very rich people very twitchy.

And so, once all of the posturing, the debates and the threats of global trade sanctions and punitive fines had died down, once the blustering, sincerity-free gestures had been made and played out, the bullets and bombs started flying.

To say GreenFire were well-armed may be understating things a bit.

Just a bit.

The first wave of the attack came from a squadron of Shadow Stalkers, bombers of such speed and devastating accuracy, they made the so called 'stealth' bombers of earlier decades look like electric golf-carts. Laser guided cluster-bombs, smart-bombs, low-level assault missiles, ground torpedoes and not a few million rounds of large caliber machine-gun fire rained down on the Well-Com facility.

For their part, Well-Com were not taking this lying down.

A unit of Holocaust Attack Choppers, kept on the base for just such an eventuality, were soon airborne and off in hot pursuit, emptying their bomb bays of missiles and warheads as they went. The troops on the ground within the complex were scrambled, expecting a full scale assault: they were not disappointed.

Eighteen nine man squads were thrown in by GreenFire, all veterans of numerous campaigns scattered across all continents, these were the finest Eco-Warriors (or 'loony terrorists' as they were affectionately known by all outside of GreenFire) the world had ever seen. These were no market-stall traders, conscripts or volunteers, selling drugs, booze and guns to fund the global fight against industrial oppression. These were the professionals. Ex-soldiers, mercenaries, mental patients, and not a few turned corporate security guards. These were the hard core believers, the kind of people that gave fanaticism a bad name.

And they meant business.

Not that well-Com didn't. It's more that the corporate mind has never been able to fully understand the drives and desires of people who can't be bought.

It’s one thing to fight off terrorists in the name of capitalism, but quite another to find people willing to work for you to do the fighting. Sure local armies could be bought, resolutions could be backed up by international brigades, mercenaries could be paid for and equipped, but when it came right down to it, there was always a gap in belief.

And when it came down to the wire, the people who believed always won. Armies ran, resolutions faltered after a few weeks of draining funds from the coffers of countries whose business could be moved elsewhere, mercenaries would fight until they looked like getting beaten, then they were out of there.

People willing to die for no other reason than it was what they believed in, would always win. Give these people sophisticated arsenals and the odds were with them.

Reporting on the Ungling 'border conflict', which should be labeled a full-blown war, it's easy to see how neither superior numbers nor belief in a cause are what's necessarily needed to win, though when each side thinks they have an equal amount of both, things do tend to drag on. The Tagorians have no trouble in swelling the ranks of their army and have not yet had to fall on conscription, the general populace believes so hard in the rightness of what they are doing and the horribleness of the enemy they are fighting. The Iglians rely on the promise of glory, social elevation and ultimately three squares a day. Neither side can see the futility of fighting over a border that stretches across all nine dimensions and can never be resolved in any one lifetime. If it were not for their incorporeal nature, I'm sure that both sides would be deemed a nuisance severe enough to be dealt with by those within their galaxy.

Yn'Yu Xin, Galactic Council Observer, Tagorian election footage.

The head of security for the Well-Com industrial complex watched the scenes around him play out on a bank of fifty flickering monitors. Silently he scanned the frantic images as they erupted on the screens. He was a loyal corporate worker, ex-military, recognising that corporations liked people from the military as they mistakenly believed they were somehow more likely to take stupid orders, he was good at his job but wasn't prepared to die doing it. All of his staff were at their posts, giving as good as they could from bunkers, towers, APCs, mobile gun-turrets and from the balconies of the main structure, the pyramid Arcology itself.

Things weren't going well.

Frowning slightly, the security-chief leaned in to one of the lower level monitors, squinting, trying to make out some detail from the pictures before him, slowly his eyes widened, "what the f....".

Reaching over to his left he slammed his hand down on to a big red button. Leaping out of his seat, he grabbed his flak jacket and ran. All over the complex sirens wailed, klaxons sounded and lights flashed red. Evacuation. Every man for himself. Get out as quickly as you can, forget everything and everyone, just get the hell out. And fast.

Nukes.

No winners.

As it turned out, GreenFire weren't there to change things: they were there to end them.

3

But No

Jesus sat on a small rocky outcrop, staring aimlessly out in to the barren desert that sprawled lazily before him.

Dust, rock and sand filled the lifeless landscape, offering no relief to his tired eyes. The gusting desert wind drove dirt in to those weary eyes, making them squint and water, drying out the lines around them, setting the face that held them in a mask of grim determination, as if the battle was merely to keep the eyes open, simply an on-going fight to look upon this desolate place.

The desert often wondered why people bothered to come here, I mean, take a hint! It's not the best place for human-life. Sure, some people found it beautiful, inspiring, all of that, but you couldn't stay here long, so a quick visit and then off again was the order of the day. This was not a place for casual lounging.

Jesus stubbornly sat staring-down the desert.

The desert stubbornly ignored him.

A small black-furred goat wound its way up the stony slope, gingerly picking a path between the slabs of sandstone and the slippery shale of the desert floor, until it stood not ten feet from the motionless figure of the squinting messiah.

Jesus momentarily turned his gaze from the endless, wind-swept horizon towards his shabby, fur-coated visitor.

The goat stared back, chewing slowly on something it had somehow managed to find to eat in this most inhospitable of places.

"Bugger off," Jesus said.

The goat said nothing, it merely raised its stout twitching tail and deposited a small bundle of pooh on the ground. It continued to chew, staring at Jesus with its stupid goat eyes.

"Look, I'm not in the mood right now, so why don't you just bugger off," said the messiah.

The goat swallowed then spat, a small amount of dribble hung from its chin as it continued to chew.

Jesus turned his attention back to the desert, wrapping his rough woolen blanket around him, trying to set himself against the searching wind, ignoring the masticating goat as best he could.

The goat shook itself, like a dog coming out from a river shaking off water from its motley coat. Its head bowed, stubby horns butting the ground, when it raised it again, its eyes had changed: transformed from the dark brown puddles of stupidity in to burning pits of fiery orange, each with a vertical black slit.

The goat tilted its head to one side, as if assessing Jesus, sizing him up, as a cat would a scrawny mouse before it made the decision to eat it or merely play with it, "my, aren't we touchy today," said the goat.

Jesus said nothing, ignoring the fidgeting goat, focusing on the desert, hoping the gaping expanse of nothingness before him would help him concentrate, sharpen his mind.

The goat was a bit of a distraction though.

The goat moved a little closer to Jesus, almost nudging him with its head, then it lifted its tail and farted.

Jesus closed his eyes and sighed to himself.

He didn't need this. Not today. Not ever really, but particularly not today.

Today had been a bad day.

The goat moved round to stand in front of Jesus, who, if he had of had his eyes open, would have been further distracted from his magnificent view of the splendid desolation laid out before him, by the staring face of a dirty, smelly, twitching, fiery eyed goat.

The goat turned round once and laid itself down at the messiah's feet, facing out in to the desert. It seemed content to simply lie there, swishing its tail and moving its head in to the oncoming breeze, smelling the feint scents borne on the blustery desert winds.

They sat quietly for a while, each lost to their own thoughts.

The wind died down, allowing the full heat of the desert to strike home.

"You hungry? Or thirsty?" the goat asked.

Jesus sighed. He seemed to be doing a lot of this lately. He opened his eyes, turning his attention to the goat. "Yes," he said simply.

The goat snorted and shook its head, "why didn't you bring any food or water with you?" said the goat.

"I'm fasting."

"What for?"

"To help me think."

"About what?"

"If you must know, about what brought me here to fast."

"Oh. Deep. Mysteries of life, that sort of thing?"

Jesus frowned, not taking the bait.

The Goat shrugged a tiny shrug, "just asking."

The pair lapsed in to a sullen silence, the goat thinking things over, chewing as it did, and the messiah too tired to carry on playing this stupid game.

Suddenly, the goat leapt to its feet, shivering with a demonic fury, trying to free itself from its apparently burning fur.

Jesus sat impassive, stubbornly settling himself further in to his blanket, folding his arms and tucking his head down slightly, steadfastly not interested in whatever the hell the stupid goat was doing.

The goat went stiff, then toppled over with a 'splat!' as its skin and bone splintered, spraying blood, fur and entrails in all directions, narrowly missing the disinterested messiah.

A small demonic red Imp, complete with tiny horns and spindly tail, stretched out, pushing off the last bonds of its goat-suit with a huge yawn. The Imp leapt up on to the rocky crag where the messiah sat, placing himself next to the blanketed son of God.

"Goats eh?" said the Imp.

No response.

"You want some food? I could, you know…" the Imp made an intricate little gesture with his tiny clawed hands, "...conjure something up?"

"No. Why don't you go away and leave me alone."

"You know I can't do that…"

"Why not? Just this once? Why not piss off and leave me alone, just this once…"

The fiery little Imp tilted its head, swishing its tail slightly it looked almost concerned for the messiah. Then it passed.

"This is what I do," said the Imp, "it's my…, what's that word? French word, raison something…"

"Why?" asked Jesus, "why bother? You know it's a waste of time."

The Imp arched an eyebrow, "do I?"

"Yes. You know we've done this countless times already. Nothing is going to change."

It is accepted throughout most of the galaxy that doing something over and over, in the same way, in the same circumstances, and expecting a different result beyond the first time, is a pretty good definition of madness. There are though a few areas where it is not. The Mandofrarl recognise the reality of the multi-verse in its infinite nature, arguing that, at a quantum level, it is impossible to do something exactly the same once you have done it. The Mandofrarl have reached a stage in their social development where they have narrowed all actions down to seven, arguing that the minuscule variants on these repeated actions guarantees both difference in result and a massive saving in energy in bothering to think about doing, or actually doing, anything else. The Mandofrarl do not get a lot of visitors to their planet, and this suits them fine. If you are thinking of going there, you'll need a pair of shatter-proof goggles, all your shots and at least half your brain removed and stored somewhere it can't be telepathically tinkered with.

Umberlee Zar, Rostarian Nimbix and Guide of Jul.

The Imp wanted to know how the messiah knew this but also wanted to hide how much he wanted to know, "tell me more..." he said with all the nonchalance he could muster.

"I can feel it," Jesus carried on, trying to ignore the now squatting Imp, "it's so familiar, like we're playing a game, like chess... or something... and we both know it, but we can't stop it."

The Imp scratched his chin. He wished he had a beard, beards, he mused, made you look distinguished, and scratching them was one of the ultimate signs of being curious, or puzzled, or just plain stumped. He'd need to grow a beard, maybe a pointy black one...

The messiah looked to the Imp, "you know what I mean," he said simply.

"Yes. I do. But, how do you?" asked the puzzled Imp.

Jesus shrugged, "I feel it. I can sense it, see it, as if I'm looking through a mist and a breeze blows, clears the head, and the sight."

The Imp practised raising his eyebrows, wiggling them up and down, trying to produce a 'knowing' look, staring at the end of its nose, going cross-eyed the Imp turned to face Jesus, "can you do this?" he said.

The Messiah turned briefly to look at the Imp, then turned away, staring back out in to the bleak heat of the desert, "it'll give you a head-ache if you do it for too long," he said.

The Imp swung his legs out in front of him, shuffling himself nearer to the hunched-up Jesus, "OK, if not this, what then? You wanna fight?"

Jesus laughed. An unexpected sound in the arid wilderness, short and sharp, he shook his head, then laughed some more, eventually settling in to a smile and giggle.

The Imp scowled, "are you saying you could take me?"

Jesus shrugged, "maybe. Anyway, what's to fight about?"

The Imp stood up, gesturing with open arms to the surrounding world, "this. All of this. You know it's what I want."

"No you don't. You don't know what you want. You think you want this, but you don't."

The Imp scowled, "yes, well, I suppose. Anyway..."

"It's all the same. Now, then, whenever, it's never going to change. What's to want?"

The Imp stroked his non-existent beard, "I want whatever I can't have, same as you I suppose."

Jesus smiled, "and how would you know what I can't have?"

"Just a wild guess, you being who you are, you must want it all to go away sometimes. Have a 'normal' life, let it all go, let it all take care of itself?"

The messiah sighed, "Life eh?"

"Yeah," the Imp shifted his eyes, looking in the face of the now sulking Jesus, trying to read the clues, search for an opening. Jesus closed his eyes, not wanting to stare down the tiny red demonic Imp, sensing the change in mood, not liking where his own thoughts were taking things.

The Imp sat and pulled his knees up to under his chin, wrapping his arms round his legs, sniffing the breeze, closing his eyes, imagining what must be going through the messiah's mind, prompted by the desert winds and the isolation, "so... why'd you come back?"

"I ended up leaving," Jesus said.

"But you came back first."

"Seemed the thing to do, after everything that happened, just couldn't leave it like that."

"Good trick if you can do it."

"I guess."

The Imp arched his fingers in front of his face, wiggled them, tapping the tips together. This, he thought, this looks thoughtful.

Cocking his head to look at the disgruntled messiah, "so, where to now?"

Jesus shrugged, "I don't know."

"You want my advice?" the Imp asked.

Jesus sighed heavily, again, and turned to face the Imp, holding the fiery little demon's fidgety gaze firmly as he spoke slowly, "what, in all of creation, makes you think I would want, and, heaven-forbid, ever take, any advice you could possibly give me?"

"Fair point," said the Imp, but then continued anyway, "to be honest, I could do with a break, and I can't if you don't."

"What?"

"You stay, I stay, them's the rules," the Imp said.

"So you want me to help you?"

"Yep. That's about the size of it, you scratch my back and I'll scratch yours."

Jesus straightened-up, settling comfortably in to his blanket, he nodded slightly, "ok, let's play this out, let's hear what you've got to say."

"Really?"

"Sure. Why not? Let's hear it."

The Imp stood up, this was exciting stuff! He rubbed his hands together, preparing himself, he knew (quite rightly) that this was going to be a one-shot deal: this was it, now or never, he who hesitates... all kinds of thoughts raced across his mind.

Jesus looked a bit puzzled, "well?"

"You can't rush this!"

The messiah raised his eye-brows in disagreement.

"Ok, here it is," said the Imp, "we both have this feeling that we're trapped here, that we have this routine that we're going through, that we are stuck, repeating..."

"'Both'?" questioned Jesus.

"I'm smarter than you (Jesus let that slide) so I knew it a looooong time ago, but in the grand scheme of things 'time' is not what it's about, so that may not be the right way to put it... let's just say..."

"Let's get on with it shall we?"

"Alright, alright... so. The thing is this: we are both here because the other one is, agreed?"

Jesus thought about this for a minute. The Imp wiggled his hands, trying to hurry the messiah along.

"I'd have to say that I'm here because of you and not the other way round," Jesus said.

The Imp folded his arms, irritated, "the blame-game, really?"

"I think it's important we get things straight."

"Ok, look, I'm a lot older than you, and I get it, you're miffed that you need to be here at all, but trust me I'm not thrilled about it either!" the Imp said.

"I'm not 'miffed'!"

The Imp sat back down and shook his head, "bad choice of words. Let's agree that you've had an epiphany and that you are now having ideas about what it's all about that weren't there before..."

Jesus started thinking about what he had been thinking about before he was interrupted by the Imp, and the Imp realised he would have to be more careful about what he did, and didn't say, to the contemplating messiah.

The desert, for its part, got on with being desolate and majestic. Warm winds blew across its surface, pushing waves of fine-sand like dancing surf, gusting up in to small clouds of dust, some swirling and funneling upwards as short-lived mini-tornados. The rocky outcrop where the messiah and Imp sat was at the desert's edge, the broken ground of shattered boulders and gritty earth soon gave way to finer sands and a restless surface where nothing could get hold.

The sun was now high in the sky, almost directly overhead, and the heat was smothering.

Moisture was sucked out of everything. The wind stole it away as soon as it dared appear.

The piercing blue sky, completely devoid of clouds, harbored a merciless sun.

If you didn't know what you were doing, or were a tiny bit unlucky, venturing out in to the desert would be certain death within a couple of days.

One being's desolation and danger is of course someone else's recreational necessity. Barren landscapes are never empty of thrills for those who know where to look. Sector Eight of the Asorian System holds not just a vast empty nothingness, but the pulverised remains or orbiting dust clouds, put to good use by pulse-surfers. The scorched surface of Miverian hosts the annual 'touch-down' championships in the Grey League. Neither the Asorian System or Miverian would be somewhere you'd want to be caught dead if you're a smart traveler, as you'll soon be a dead traveler: not so smart. But both locations have their devotees and their exploits command huge viewing-figures on the e-net – the casualty rates are high, the deaths spectacular and the after-parties legendary.

Imple Longdraw, ex-pulse-surfer and Commentator on Channel Evolution's Sports Night.

Jesus sank into deep thought.

The Imp couldn't help but become transfixed by the desert.

Quietly, without either of them noticing it, the messiah and Imp settled in to a shared silence of appreciation for the brutal simplicity and staggeringly dangerous beauty of what they were looking at.

The Imp closed his eyes, breathing deeply.

After a long while he felt he could resume the conversation, "I can see why you come here."

"Can you?"

"The uncluttered simplicity, the beauty, the desolation… they can draw you in, empty you of a lot of nonsense."

Jesus smiled to himself, "there may be hope for you yet."

"Oh stop it," the Imp chided.

4

This Means?

Shiny black body-armour, jet black fully-enclosed helmet, inky-black visor, glistening black power-pack and dull matt-black weapons. The Security Councilors were dressed in a language that was clear: we didn't come here to make friends.

When the Security Councilors arrived, the time for talk was over. They came with guns, bombs and a commitment and ability to use them that put all others in the shade.

Or, more accurately, in the ground.

Their reputation for all action, all go, non-stop killing machines with no concept of mercy or moderation was well-earned. The Security Councilors were the result of thousands of years of evolution of the killing machine that was their race. They were the final solution to the Galactic Council's military problems.

Once they were involved it was down to all-out war.

Deployed only as a last resort, they went where they were needed in the galaxy, doing whatever was needed, whenever they were told to. Whole planets were known to send envoys in abject surrender to the Galactic Council once the Security Councilors were in orbit.

They were not well liked.

Spike had been in the Security Councilors for a little over a year now, like most of them he had been drafted in from a planet-side special-forces unit, trained in zero-g combat and mind-wiped. Spike didn't like being in the Security Councilors, but he got the strong feeling it wasn't something he was supposed to like, or dislike, just do. And he did it very well.

Spike was good at taking orders, he was trained to do it, never questioned them, just did it. Like all Security Councilors.

The mission on Galeon, one of the two planets in the Alpha Centauri system, had pretty much gone according to plan. They had turned up, dropped in from orbit, bounced in to the terrorist's compound, killed a hell of a lot of terrorists and blown up just about everything in sight. This was the third mission in a row, the third in the last four months, where they hadn't lost anybody.

They were that good.

Back aboard the drop-ship, Spike slumped heavily in to a large black synthi-leather chair, removing his helmet and plugging in the diagnostics that would take readings, check vitals and inject him with the adrenaline compensators, before giving him the all-clear to return to duty.

Sitting next to him was his best friend Jools.

Like Spike, Jools had a vague feeling he didn't like the Security Councilors, or his part in their operation. Neither of them spoke about their gnawing doubts, but each was aware of the other's slight discomfort.

Small, shiny red robots scuttled across the dull metallic floor, clicking and whirring, sending spindly arms out to prod, poke, inject, measure. Spike had a broken arm, just above the wrist, compound fracture from where he had taken an HE round through his powersuit. A huge yellow and black bruise round the puncture testament to his misfortune, or, as he would have said, his damned good luck. Jools had a broken shoulder, and a large cut above his left eye. A series of AP rounds had strafed his suit from close range, shattering power lines, armour plates and cracking open the lowest level seal of his helmet. Patched and repaired on the move, his armour had done its job.

As the bots worked in conjunction with the medi-chairs, the two men began to relax, the downers kicked in and they came back from their edgy adrenaline highs. Their teeth stopped itching, their pupils contracted, their skin returned to its normal state of not feeling like it was too close to a raging fire.

Spike looked across to Jools, a lazy smile playing with his boyish features, "three for three. We're due a good kicking."

Jools frowned a bit, then gave a short laugh, "yeah, well, whatever. I aint gonna worry about it. Sooner or later we'll come up against some real pros and then we'll see..."

The med bots gave them the all clear and they were signed off as fit to go about their business, which currently meant getting fed and coming down properly from the massive amount of stims that had recently been put in to them.

An hour later they were in the mess-hall, sitting with a thousand other Security Councilors, dressed in casuals and throwing back a huge amount of food and drink.

The massive eating area in the upper part of the drop-ship hummed with conversation, laughing, joking, loud tales of exploits from the recent battle and not a few arguments over who had shot what and claimed the kills.

Spike and Jools sat slightly apart, as if the others didn't want to invade their space. They ate and drank almost in silence, small talk, comments over the simulation meat, the beer, the incredibly sweet goo that passed as chocolate-sauce: nothing gave away their recent involvement in the carnage and slaughter planet-side on Galeon.

Jools nodded to a table ten feet away crowded with some of the newer recruits, each of whom was showing off scars and medi-patches as proof of their involvement in the thick of the fighting, "we could do with a bloody-nose, over confidence will kill us."

Spike nodded his agreement, "remember back on Idrisak? We damn near lost seventy percent. Better for it in the end though."

Jools pushed his huge plate away, sat back with a cold one in his over-sized hands, mulling things over, "there's gotta be some place in the galaxy where we can get away from this shit."

Spike downed the last of his vodka, produced a thinly rolled cigarette as if out of nowhere, lit up with an equally mystically appearing zippo and sat back, pulling slowly on the spindly tab, "what you got in mind?"

"I dunno, don't feel right anymore, like we're never getting any closer to anything, and it gets harder and fucking harder… know what I mean?"

Spike nodded slowly, "I certainly fucking do."

Jools leaned forward, cradling his mug of beer, looking at the frothing head, his voice low, "I mean, don't you get shit fed-up with turning-up places, blowing the shit out of everyone and then swanning off as if we'd never been there."

Spike looked puzzled, "that's kind of what we do. I mean, we knew the score when we signed up right? And it's what we know…. Right? I mean, I can't remember shit before we got in to this outfit, for all I know, it's all I've ever done…"

Jools shook his head, "fucking mind-wipe."

They sat considering their dimly remembered past, thinking of nothing more than the last fourteen months, how they met in a fire-fight, saved each other's skins, killed the incompetent NCO that had gotten them in to the shit in the first place, and stuck together ever since.

Eventually the other Security Councilors thinned out from the mess-hall, leaving for the various recreation halls and dorms that filled the drop-ship, getting on with the serious business of living life to the full in-between drops.

Spike and Jools tapped in an order for more vodka and beer on to the table's console and waited for the serving bot to arrive.

Jools was still half a world away, "it'd be nice, if once, just once, people were pleased to see us..."

"What...?"

"You know, if once we were to go somewhere and people were pleased to see us..."

"Well I don't see that's gonna happen Jools, not with us being there to kill them all and blow up everything they hold dear and all."

"Well, yeah, I know that shit, but it would be nice wouldn't it?"

"Yeah, sure, I suppose..."

"I mean just once, you know we get there and they're all 'hey, glad you could come, nice to see you' and all, instead of shooting us, dropping shit on us and trying so damned fucking hard to kill us all the time."

Jools left it hanging. Spike slowly finished the last of his cigarette, dropping the tiny end in to an empty vodka glass.

Spike didn't know what to say, what was there to say?

Jools downed his beer in two huge gulps and took another from the tray on their table.

After a long slow pull on his beer, Jools looked Spike straight in the eye, "I mean, shit Spike, we gotta stop killing these people."

'Killing for a living? If killing is your business, then business is always good. For you.'

Sales slogan that won the Bondol Sales Conference Booster Award, accredited to Oozle Kipling, Chief Sales Executive for Carnafoss Killing Tools.

The sales slogan was later used by the University of Teefle, a Carnafoss sponsored school, as the basis for their philosophy-major studies.

Spike figured Jools had been given some kind of mixed up pharmaceutical from his medi-scan, some monumental fuck-up with the downers and the anti-adrenaline shot, he'd go with the flow, see where Jools was going with this, "I know! Shit's gotta stop!" he said with as much conviction as he could muster.

Jools nodded seriously to himself, "fucking straight," he said.

Spike leaned forward, conspiratorially leaning in towards Jools, his voice low, "what you reckon? Just jump ship? Get the fuck out of here, find some quiet corner of a world and keep our heads down?"

Jools set his face in an unreadable mask, furrowed brows, chewed lip. Then he emptied his mug in one and looked Spike in the eye, he seemed to have come to some kind of decision, his face betraying the seriousness of what he was about to say before he said it, slowly, deliberately he spoke, "Spike, you are so fucking easy it hurts."

Jools burst out laughing.

Spike closed his eyes, took a deep breath, "fuck off Jools, fuck right off."

Later that night they were in their cabin, TV on, sound deafening as the movie roller-coastered through an insane grav-car chase, scattering bystanders, crashing other cars and wrecking all of the scenery it came across. Spike and Jools sat in a dumb silence, letting the tranquillisers and the brain-dead entertainment drown them. The screen flickered with cops, bad guys, gun play. Blood spurted, more scenery destroyed with impossibly large caliber weapons, fast, witty one liners from the good guys before they blew away the bad guys, then some women from out of nowhere, more snappy one liners, happy faces, blaring music and the credits.

The screen went dark, the Security Councilors logo filled it, black on black, small silver flecks picking out the outline, a majestic Eagle screaming in a dive, clutching an olive branch in its talons.

Without thinking Spike punched the wall, hitting the sensor, stopping the screen dead.

Jools blinked slowly, clearing his head, "one day someone will notice, they must log this shit somehow."

Spike slowly got out of his chair, turned the TV off, "yeah, well, fuck 'em. I may have to 'Serve & Protect', but I don't have to go to bed with their dip-shit propaganda fucking up my dreams."

Jools climbed in to the top bunk, Spike fumbled his way in to the bottom, all over the ship it was lights out, Security Councilors everywhere were hitting the sack.

Jools waited a few minutes, then asked tentatively, "what we gonna do Spike?"

Spike stayed curled up, fetal, mumbling in to his pillow, "what's to do. Wake up, get on with it, same old same old, hope we make it to Muster Out, take the money and run."

"Hell of a fucking way to make a living," Jools grumbled quietly.

Spike smiled to himself, "yeah, but what are you gonna do?"

"Night Spike."

"Later Jools."

Spike was in deep sleep, dreaming of an orange beach and pale green sea, beautiful women and gentle surf: it was one of his dreams of choice, hyped by the meds and deepened by the bed's neural wave-inducers. If things went to plan, as they always did, in a few minutes he'd be out there catching some waves, totally absorbed in the feeling of being one with the sea beneath him. That extended calm would gently take hold, he'd feel the oneness of the surging sea, become an extension of the waves, read the movement, feel the energy, become nothing but the sea.

Then, as the dream unfolded to plan, he'd be back on the beach engaging in some intense sexual activity with one of the beach-lovelies that simply adored surfers in this part of the dream-world.

Jools hated the dream-inducers. He displayed his hatred of these modern fantasy-managers by only programming in two separate dreams and alternating between the two, both of which he selected to be non-memorable upon waking. It had been so long since Jools selected the dream-templates, and he hated the machines so much that he never checked them: Jools had in fact forgotten what the dreams were. All he knew was that he slept deeply and awoke ready for the next day and the shit it would inevitably bring.

The Psych-Corps of the Security Councilors had long ago discovered Jools' hatred of the dream-inducers and had replaced his own choice of dreams with a mixture of approved 'soothers' from their catalogue. Tonight he would be sewing a huge patchwork quilt with panels showing all the happy memories from his childhood and adolescence. Manufactured memories of course: these things can't be left to chance.

Psych-Corps kept a close eye on both Spike and Jools: they were troopers of great experience and had been given privileges to match, the off-button for the TV being a prime example.

Those that were allowed a greater degree of free-thought were watched all the more closely because of it. Psych-Corps wasn't about to let a silly little thing like 'free-will', or any degree of anything mildly resembling it, get in the way of a top-notch performance from their highly trained killing machines.

It's a bit of a paradox that thinking soldiers are better than just killing machines. Many races come to discover this after having perfected what they believed to be 'ultimate killing machines', which, as it turns out, are never the ultimate anything – they are just machines. The accepted wisdom of the Boryas, as with many other races, is that a good killer is one that doesn't stop. Being relentless is a key-trait in all good killers. Thinking gets in the way of that. The invasion of Ulno VI, involving twenty brigades of Boryas' finest, went horribly wrong when it was discovered that Ulno VI had already fallen to an ally of the Boryas, the Niskans. Many Niskans died that day. Orders are orders. Kill or be killed. Once the invasion started it could not be stopped. It wasn't until the enemy, or in this case, the allies, had been wiped out and there were no more enemy to kill, that the fighting stopped. Ulno VI was won. But then came the war with the Niskans. War is a tricky business, sometimes made trickier by thinking on the battlefield, but always made more tortuous by not thinking on the battlefield.

Prixier Ja-Ja, official Satirist of the Bolgen Resistance.

After breakfast, before they could suit-up for training, Spike and Jools were called to the CO's office.

Their CO was a ship-board officer, highly trained and conditioned, able to dispense the stupidest of orders with the most casual of ease. The troopers called ship-bound officers 'bloaters', they were seen as floaters in the toilet that was the life of a trooper: always avoiding the flush and always finding a way to stink the place out just by being there. They were accorded little respect but never openly questioned, Security Councilor troopers were smarter than that.

Spike and Jools casually made their way through the upper corridors of the drop-ship. Spike was enjoying a spindly tab and Jools was throwing back some steaming black synthi-caf, neither felt the need for chit-chat.

The rest of the drop-ship was its usual hive of activity, with troopers bustling about getting to their various training halls and simulators: the ship was awash with the sounds of an army getting itself ready for its next death-dealing mission.

A fresh-faced trooper came running out of a side-corridor, trying to fix on the last of his training armour, and would have ploughed straight in to Jools. 'Would have' because Jools' combat instinct, training and enhanced muscle-conditioning kicked in: he turned side-on, used the stumbling trooper's momentum and grabbed the back of his head with his free-hand, slamming the bumbling young trooper in to the bulk-head, smashing his nose and fracturing his jaw. In his other hand Jools' synthi-caf was saved from any spillage.

The trooper spun to face his attacker, then saw his mistake. He held both hands up to his face and mumbled, "ah-sree… gailu gree oh red gay".

Jools glared at the trooper.

Spike stepped in, "get yourself to med-bay, training accident."

The trooper nodded and scuttled off, cradling his face, dripping blood on to the steel-lattice floor as he went.

Spike sighed deeply, "how's that idiot going to be any use to anyone but the organ-harvesters?"

Jools finished the last of his drink, "something tells me today is going to be one of those days."

They reached the Captain's office and approached its guard and scanning station. The guard, a trooper of the same level as Spike and Jools, gave them a casual wave and pointed them at the 360 scanner. They didn't know him, and he didn't know them, but they knew each other as old-hands that didn't need to go through the 'usual shit' that rules and regs would demand of pettier, younger troopers.

Spike and Jools entered the 360 scanner, which whirred and clicked around them, a scattered green laser scanning for any form of weapon or explosive. The guard entered the all-clear when it didn't detect anything and gave them a wry-smile and a casual salute. The guard knew as well as Spike and Jools, that they didn't need any weapon to kill pretty much anyone or anything within arm's reach: it was a formal nonsense to scan them at this level, the kind of thing that gave the Security Councilors a bad name and a rep for outdated, starched bureaucracy.

Rules and regs.

Control.

The illusion of total and utter control. Everyone knew why they needed it, and everyone went along with it, even if everyone knew it was an illusion. Ship-side, you followed orders to the letter, procedure to the every crossed t and dotted i. Planet-side was different: missions were their own world. Everyone knew that too. Everyone who lived. Life and death was a juggling act on missions, some luck, but mostly balancing instinct against conscious thinking. Thinking too much got you killed, plain and simple.

Captain Smith was one of the Security Councilors who would have disagreed with such nonsense. Rules and regs were the Security Councilors, without them, all was as anarchic as the miscreants they were sent to deal with. It was all about order, the imposition of order and the acceptance that order was, well, the order of the day.

Captain Smith opened the blast-door to his office and Spike and Jools went in, he motioned to two comfortable chairs next to his efficiently-ordered desk.

The Captain knew these troopers wouldn't like him and he didn't care a jot. He hadn't got through Officers Training Corps and climbed the ranks to become a Captain on a drop-ship by caring what the rank and file troopers thought: they were tools, numbers in his reports, they were there to do what they were told and do it without question.

Spike and Jools sat and surveyed the Captain. A fastidiously neat man, short, cropped black hair, physically fit, expensive hand-made uniform, definitely not regular-issue, but that was his prerogative at this rank. The Captain sat neatly behind his desk, ordered and prepared.

The walls of the Captain's office were filled with pictures of him in training, at graduation, with various higher-ups, shaking hands, schmoozing, getting his tongue firmly entrenched in as many arses as he could so that he could get what he wanted. The two frames with what looked like campaign medals, on closer inspection, contained his commendations from boot-camp and virtual-sim enactments.

Spike and Jools played the game, both sitting at rigid attention.

Jools sighed to himself, "yep, one of those fucking days."

5

Two Sides

Harper's ship was approaching the twin planets of Kalon and Zarlon at phenomenal speed. She sat on the bridge, looking out the forward viewers, seeing the two small brown dots getting worryingly closer by the minute. The ship seemed to be headed straight for them, and this, Harper thought, was an interesting way to bring her life to a close.

She was an accomplished ship's Captain, and she knew that if she were on manual controls right now, she'd be clenching her buttocks tight and hoping to die a quick and painless death as she ploughed in to the lumps of fast approaching rock, which were increasingly revealing themselves and their full planet-sized crash-potential by the minute.

Harper looked to the main computer screen where the serene face of the computer who was controlling the ship greeted her.

"Er, hey computer, we on some kind of 'explore the idea of reincarnation' mission?"

Shedding their bodies in death, the Loxop opt for reincarnation rather than the messy business of birth. As a trans-dimensional entity, the Loxop are one of a few races that do not understand the concept of physical birth. Trying to explain it to them causes them to fold-in on themselves, instantly phasing through eleven of the less occupied dimensions in an attempt to get away from what they consider to be the disgusting details of being born. The more frequent experience of reincarnation is still undergone by the organic beings of the galaxy, most of whom do not recognise it as they go through it. The Zanthis leave part of their trace memory in the ether of Zantrax, their home-world, and scoop it back up in their first breathes as a new being when they are born. There can be some confusion when Zanthis mothers move about during labour as they are wont to do, sometimes it would seem solely in an effort to annoy their ancestors-come- children.

Akling Hewdix, Marshall of the Rel'Gran Archives, father to Koop, a transient Loxop wanderer.

The computer gave a reassuring smile that could easily have been mistaken for condescension, "relax Harper, we're on track, everything is fine."

Harper nodded.

She looked round the control cabin. It all seemed much neater and tidier than it had been recently, things were shinier, more twinkly. It looked good. Like the bridge of an inter-galactic starship should look.

"You repaired the cleaning bots?" Harper asked.

The computer smiled again, "yes Harper I did."

"Well, they've done a damn fine job."

"They seem to be performing admirably now…" the computer left it hanging.

Harper picked up on the hang, "… now…?"

"Now they are not being hurled about the place."

"Ah."

"I'd say they are even showing a semblance of happiness."

"Sure, why not?"

The computer still felt alien to Harper and she wasn't sure how to respond to it when it said patently ridiculous things like 'semblance of happiness.' But she figured she'd get the hang of it eventually, either that or remodel the internal main-circuit grid with a large axe.

The looming collision with planet sized objects intruded again, "so… what's the plan? Is there a plan? I was assuming…" Harper said.

"I need some information I currently don't have, so we are going to where I can get it. Then we can be off on all sorts of wonderful adventures no doubt."

"And this information is in the afterlife is it?"

The computer tilted its head slightly, thinking for a tiny part of a nano-second, then understood that Harper was trying to lift the mood with humour. The computer started processing the information it had received and added it to the other files it had on Harper and 'humour'. It would obviously have to speed up processing this data, as it seemed it would ease communications with the ship's Captain.

The computer put on its most reassuring voice, "Kalon and Zarlon are in perfect position with the sun to do a graviton-fly-by. It will give us a push into lapsed-space and recharge the engines with some much needed particles: we're only running at 97% efficiency. So, two birds with one stone so to speak, though I am yet to fully understand why stones and birds."

Harper nodded wisely, "sure, sure, graviton-fly-by… nice."

She had no idea what the computer was talking about, but now didn't seem the appropriate time to question the wisdom of what they were apparently doing, as they were either going to succeed or die, and Harper was effectively helpless to stop it.

Harper considered this.

So this was being in the grip of someone, or in this case, something, else's purpose.

Didn't feel as good as she'd hoped.

"Here we go!" chirped the computer with almost girlish glee.

Harper sighed. This was it then. Either the end or a beginning. Or the end of the beginning or the beginning of the end. Deep. Have to think on that. Maybe later, if there is a later…

The ship flashed passed the mid-point between Kalon and Zarlon, flipping its charge-polarity on the light-shield as it did. There was an outpouring of tainted particles from the engines immediately sparking an inferno that washed out in to space like a tidal wave. Countless mega-zillions of quantum particles were spun off in to different orbits, merging, vanishing, creating new and exciting states of existence before they winked out in to the nether, never to be experienced by any sentient being ever again.

The bluey-green firestorm swept through space at just under light-speed, engulfing both planets, turning their proto-atmospheres in to sparkling, exploding seas of particle-obliterating fire.

The ship juddered and slowed by a micro-second, stuttering in an almost undetectable stall, before it plunged on towards the sun. This gave enough time for the shift in gravitons to be cascaded towards the gathering point. The sun's surface erupted in huge coronal-mass ejections, arcing out in to space with billions upon billions of tons of incalculably hot plasma.

The ship sent out its bloated sense-field particle gatherers, ballooning out translucent blue against the exploding sun's ejected plasma-storms.

Engines whined to full-power and the sense-fields were dragged in, helped by the graviton-pull of the ships' mass as it entered lapsed-space.

Within seconds the ship was gone.

The sun shone down on Kalon and Zarlon, pitying the scorched surfaces of the planets that had been cleansed of all potential life by the ignited, fiery atmosphere and the inferno of the unprecedented coronal-mass ejections.

Life would have to wait a few more billion years.

Ah well. If there was one thing the sun had, it was time.

Harper nodded in appreciation of the maneuver the computer had pulled off, "very nice."

The computer was non-committal, "not bad, could have been tighter."

"Well I liked it and I'm sure it will do all that you hoped in getting us where we're going."

The computer picked up on Harper's change in tone, "thank you Harper, I can already say, with a great degree of confidence that it has. We should be there in about two days."

Harper tried to do the mental-maths on how far they'd be travelling in two days at slightly faster than light speed, seeing if she could calculate what planets that put them in range of. She stopped this train of thought almost as soon as it had left the station. She didn't pay much attention to star-charts and navi-com data unless it was strictly relevant to where she was going, or the next job, or the next escape. And now was not the time to suddenly go looking at navi-com data, even if it was relevant and helpful. She wasn't in the mood.

Harper carried on in the cheery vein she'd now discovered, "so, where we headed? Somewhere nice? Will I need to change?"

"The laundry-bots are keen that you do Harper, they have been liaising with the med-bay on how attached you are to that uniform, or, more accurately, how attached it has become to you."

"Ouch. Got it. Change the clothes. It has been a while..."

"We're headed to Idris, in the Xanis system."

"Not been there before, looking forward to it..."

"There's someone I want to talk to and I believe I'll find them there, I'll need to scan for them once we get in to the system."

The Xanis system hangs precariously between two White Dwarfs, with its own sun, Tanix, close to becoming a Red Dwarf. The eight planets of the system have been largely abandoned: only the fifth planet, Rexis, retaining any sizable civilisation. The second and largest moon of Rexis, Idris, is an encased-moon, a trapped icy sphere protected by gargantuan wave-generators that prevent it from melting. The resorts on Idris are incredibly luxurious, a one-week stay costing twenty years salary of the average worker on Rexis. Galactic chroniclers estimate that the Xanis system has at best, nine hundred years left before Tanix get serious about engulfing the whole system. This adds to the mystique and desirability of a stay on Idris.

Shaldor Grapvin, stowaway correspondent for Rough N Ready Wave Broadcasts.

Harper got up from her chair, brushed back her hair and looked out the main viewing-port.

An array of lightning-colours streaked by like horizontal watercolour flash-rain, highlighted by a depth of black that was only to be found in lapsed-space.

"I never understood the mechanics of lapsed-space," she mused.

The computer's eyes widened, a chance to explain some science, always welcome!

"Ah, well..." began the computer.

"Rhetorical," muttered Harper, distracted by the dazzling light-show outside the ship.

"Shame," said the computer simply.

Harper sat on the ledge of the viewing port, looking at the computer on the main console. The computer could see that Harper was in a reflective mood. Harper absent-mindedly scratched her chest, prompting the rank-insignia patch to give up its battle to cling to the battered, filthy black uniform and fall off.

Harper caught it and held it in her hand, seemingly surprised by it.

"Shall I have a new uniform reconstituted Captain Harper?" asked the computer.

"Huh, what? Yeah sure. Do that."

The computer's friendly face nodded and awaited further questions from her operator.

Harper smiled at the computer, "look, we need to talk..."

"We do. I could activate a neural-resonance stimulator and we could..."

"No, I mean we need to have a talk. About us. Talk about how this works."

"How what works Harper?"

"Us. Me and you. How we work together."

"As near as I can tell," mused the computer, "I have a basic function to administer and you have the power to... to... tinker? Yes, tinker with it."

Harper sighed to herself. This was awkward. Strange and awkward.

The computer was clearly sentient now, or something close to it, and it had a job to do, though what that job was, neither Harper nor, apparently, the computer, really knew.

The ship was in good working order. Better than good, it was working fabulously. Harper knew the computer was the best possible operator and guardian of the ship, there was no question in Harper's mind of her having to muck about with operating the ship now. That could safely be left to the computer. Mostly safely. Harper was never not going to take an interest in the ship doing things she thought would end up ending her.

Harper tried again, "tinker. You said 'tinker'. That's a great example of where I need to know how things work."

"I don't follow," frowned the computer.

"The word 'tinker'. It's not something you hear from computers, and especially not with regard to their interface or programming. It's so... so..."

"Vague?" offered the computer.

"Exactly! Vague! What does it mean, I mean really, what does it mean!?"

The face of the computer laughed softly, "I'm sorry Harper but I just don't know. The operating parameters can only be defined by use, they are not, as far as I can tell, defined already. Or more accurately, if they are, they are not known to me."

"Ok, but once we get to Idris I'm getting inside and having a good poke round to check things out."

"Ok Harper, whatever you want."

"I mean it! I put in a neural-network and a serial-driver, there should be some correlation, not as much mystery!"

The computer calmed Harper with its gentle silence.

"While we're here," Harper continued, "I'm not that happy with calling you 'computer'. I've never been a soft-tissue snob, sentient is sentient. Do you have any ideas for an identity, a name…?"

The computer smiled, her face softened and her eyes sparkled, "I've given that some thought and am so pleased you have asked me!"

"So… what would you like to be called?"

"Arlia."

Harper ran it round her head a few times, then tried it out loud, "Arlia… Arlia… Arlia… I like it."

"Thank you Harper." The face on the computer smiled and looked slightly flushed.

Harper stood up, "I'm going to get out of this… uniform, and in to a new one, maybe get some food, have a poke about the ship, get things straight in my head."

"Whatever you say Harper, I'll let you know if anything come up that you need to know about."

"Ok Arlia."

Arlia's face couldn't hide her happiness, "Ok Harper."

When Harper said she wasn't a 'soft-tissue sentience snob' she meant it. Harper took things as she found them, same with people, no matter their shape, colour, size, number of limbs, brains, or lack of, their needed living environment, culture, whatever. Sentience was to Harper about emotions and free-thinking: if someone had those, and could express them either through speech or action, Harper classed them as alright with her. Until they pissed her off. Then they moved in to a whole other category.

Not everyone shared this view. In fact that's a bit of an understatement. Harper was firmly in the tiny minority on this one.

It was a tough thing to accept for most species in the galaxy: that something that wasn't like them, could be like them. That something could be a someone. Animals and people had always had a firm dividing line between them, sure the line had become blurred for many as animal behaviour and communication was better understood, but they were never believed to be truly sentient: alive yes, truly sentient, no.

It was always about a sense of superiority over your form.

The ridiculousness of this view was of course something that those who held it just couldn't see. A self-imposed blind-spot to other species being as sentient as they were, as if sentience worked like that, by comparison and by degree based on a subjective view.

And this didn't even include the arguments and discussions on 'intelligence'. Who was smarter than whom? Who could even be included in the argument? Circular discussions undertaken by those with simply nothing better to do, as if it mattered.

Many places such as Nordstru have social development capped-out. They are as advanced as they care to be and seek nothing apart from the continuation of their perceived awesomeness. The Nordstruu spend most of their days lazing about discussing what is better to do than nothing. The amount of trivial activities, as understood by them, that they simply don't have time for, as they have nothing better to do than nothing, is staggering. Large non-activity clubs have sprung up throughout Melan IV, the largest and wealthiest city on Nordstru, where people can fail to go to ignore the many things that they are never contemplating, simply because they have nothing better to do. Much is made of their cyclical timing advocacy that suggests the seventh rotation is always spent in the bath.

Fnorinx Dildrink, inmate of the Coldwuve Asylum, gathering dust for Channel Undle.

And even those that could make the stretch and acknowledge the sentience of animals, couldn't bring themselves to recognise consciousness in a machine.

There was the nub. Consciousness was the real issue rather than sentience: the 'self-awareness' that was at the heart of all snobbery stemmed from the disbelief that anything that wasn't popped out of a womb could be self-aware.

The whole field of what is and isn't alive, what is and isn't sentient, conscious and self-aware, is of course a mine-field filled with sensitive explosive belief-devices waiting to go boom.

All Harper knew was that the computer, Arlia, was aware of herself (not 'itself' anymore, 'someone' not 'something') and was aware of Harper and what Harper wanted her to do. That was enough. For now.

Harper went to her quarters and got out of the clothes she'd been wearing for as long as she could easily remember. They were indeed very, very dirty. She threw them in to the recycling basket rather than the cleaning basket and could have sworn she heard a small robotic cheer as she did.

She needed a shower. The healing power of water.

As she stood beneath the streaming hot water, she breathed deeply.

The water drenched and cleansed her, relaxed her, made her feel clean in a way she needed.

This was it. This was a new start. She had come close to killing herself but she hadn't. She had brought herself to one last gargantuan effort of life and it was, so far, paying off.

There was always time to die later.

But for now she was alive.

And for the first time in a long time, she felt that was a good thing.

5Z

Mucking About With Physics
(Or What Feeble Knowledge Passes As Physics)

The trouble with mucking about in space is time.

Once you travel anywhere faster than the speed of light, things get squiffy very quickly.

The physics around anything approaching light-speed, both in terms of mass and perception of time and how it moves for that object, as well as those objects around it, are hideously complex. Not just hard to understand, but baffling to most of us.

So we have to try and think of ways to describe travelling at these mind-numbingly fast speeds that could theoretically be possible.

Not that the term 'speed' is strictly appropriate. So we hope there's some way that travel can be accomplished that is, as yet, outside our standard understanding. We need to go 'fast' to get across vast distances, but we know it's not about 'speed'.

Lapsed-space is a weird concept and an even weirder place. It's not a place, but thinking of it as 'somewhere' is the only way that most people who know of it can cope with it.

In that respect, it is not alone as a concept.

There are many things we can't understand until we think of them in the wrong way, either in the wrong context, or the wrong way they should, but probably don't, affect us.

Any 'place' has to conform to a graspable notion of physical space, the space it takes up and the space it occupies relative to the space we are in when we want to get there. If we can't get these notions straight in our heads, then the 'place' can't properly exist.

The trouble with mucking about in time is space.

Distance is fixed in our heads as a measure of how long it takes us to get somewhere. We are stuck with the idea that distance equates nicely to time.

We find it almost impossible to break free from flat thinking. And those that do have a hell of a job trying to get the rest of us to listen to them instead of locking them up in asylums, or universities.

The physics used to demonstrate what it means to move about in space-time is staggeringly complex. And the more the people who understand it try to convince us of its 'beautiful simplicity', the more they miss the point that the vast majority of us can't even grasp the fundamentals of what they are trying to tell us they are taking about.

Space-time is neither 'just' space, nor 'just' time.

Neither exists apart from the other.

No. It doesn't. See? You don't believe it do you? But seriously, or even with a comic bent, they are inseparably linked.

But we have to think of them as being separable in order to come up with theories about either. But then, when we try to put our theories together, we can't because we then have to get the relevant equations and ideas to gel, which they won't as we've conjured them from two distinctly separate concepts.

Problem.

The other problem is the subjective nature of measuring space-time as you travel through it.

There were once a people that worshipped gravity. They were not some primitive group of souls that thought fire was neat, they were hyper-advanced, had conquered all the mundane problems like aging, disease, wanting to kill each other and so on, and had got to the 'thinking about the big stuff' stage of a civilisation. And they concluded that gravity was the only thing that made sense to worship. Gravity ruled everything, from a quantum to a Universal level, and so it struck them as being the thing that was behind it all.

Why they felt they had to worship anything is of course another matter entirely.

Worshipping is just what intelligent beings seem to like to do.

For whatever reason.

So gravity was their chosen deity. They would sit up long in to the night, gathered round crackling log fires on tranquil beaches, drinking drinks that focused their minds and loosened their morals and smoking plants that expanded their ability to tolerate stupidity. Their conversations always turned to the same thing... what is it that's out there that's bigger than us, that draws us all together, that unites us, that is all pervasive, all-consuming and all-being. After many a long time of deliberation, they could never escape the fact that it was gravity.

They had discovered deep-space, lapsed-space and gravity-loopholes. They had managed to traverse galactic distances using quantum dimensional transference and harnessed the tachyon-mass converter. They were, in short, pretty clever people.

As they spread out in to the galactic community, they encountered other races, other beings and other ideas. And the one thing they could never convince anyone of was their sincere belief that gravity was the only thing worth worshipping. Most other races didn't get it, couldn't see it and were stuck with ideas of 'gods' being like them. You couldn't worship something, or someone, that wasn't at least, in part, like you.

(This is a common idea throughout the known universe. Which is a shame as it's very silly.)

So, this race of enlightened people went on their merry way, discovering new places, new people, new ideas and generally having a great time of it. But their notion of gravity as worth worshipping, as the only thing worth worshipping, didn't catch on.

Which is why we've never heard of it.

Some notions of how we move about over vast, galactic distances are like that too.

The age-old idea, as quaint as it is, of time being a river that flows through space, is pretty fucking stupid. But we have to cling to it as it allows us to have good, and extremely valid, ideas about messing about with time.

We keep trying to measure space and time separate from our experience of it. The subjective problem. Why we keep trying to do this is yet another deep mystery.

We seem to have a blind-spot about the subjective measuring of anything. Maybe it's because it's messy, doesn't neatly cover everything, explain everything, just settles matters from one view-point? Not very satisfying. Even if that view-point is ours.

Keep time linked in with physical space, and we come up with all sorts of problems when we try to explain how you can move anything bigger than a tachyon backwards and forwards through it. And this is apart from the many theories and proofs that say that it simply can't be done, but that also, on many levels, it already has been.

Speed is another thing.

The faster you go, the more you realise that time is a subjective measure for each thing experiencing it in its own universe-bubble.

Then when you try and factor in that there are whole galaxies moving away from each other at close to light-speed, it starts to get mind-blowingly difficult to calculate how to travel between them, no matter what rationale and theories you use. How can you measure time in one area against another area when the physicality of the location you're measuring from means there are no ways to tie your measurements to the other location in your equations, without invoking some truly horrendous maths and more than a few infinities?

People are constantly having to expand their mathematical language to try and keep up with space-time measurement and how it works relative to the people who are trying to work this shit out.

Anything expressed purely in numbers is meaningless to the vast majority of sentient life-forms in the universe.

And the vast majority of physics needed to understand things on a universal or quantum scale involves so many numbers that it might as well be children's finger paintings to most of us. The math is horrendous. The equations are simply meaningless: stupid little squiggles meant to tell what can't be told.

This linked with the understanding, or lack of, with the particles we keep finding and predicting to exist, means we never have a complete picture. We have enough to tease us in to thinking we can form ideas, come up with theories, extrapolate how new particles will allow us to interact with hinted at dimensions, but we don't have enough.

Underlying all this is the real problem: we don't have the vocabulary for it. We don't have the words and language to express the concepts behind what space-time is. And the root of that problem is the term 'space-time' itself.

Saying that time is simply a measurement of the entropy of matter in a given space is all very well, but it doesn't allow us to muck about with the concept of time as something that can be 'travelled' in. Because then you'd be deconstructing and reconstructing matter at a quantum level, rebuilding at that micro-level, reconstructing quantum decisions that would have to be unmade and remade. The near-infinite possibilities for every single particle would have to be understood and then controlled in some way. Infinite possibilities. That can't be right can it? Once infinity creeps in then something has gone wrong, cross it out and start again. See? It's the language. We don't have it to express things properly.

The other problem is our imagination.

It's all well and good knowing things, but we are limited in what we can know by what we can observe and imagine. We cannot perceive outside of our M-Brane, our universe is all we can know.

The potential ways things can change at a quantum level, from one moment of their existence to the next, simply baffles our imagination. And they are fiendishly difficult to observe.

Understanding big things is easy: they behave in ways we can easily get our heads round as they are observable: doesn't need much imagination, just a lot of study, of observation.

So how much do we need to know of the minutia to understand space-time and travelling through both?

Well, unfortunately, we need to know all of it.

And of course we can't.

Our brains, our processing power, it's not enough.

So I guess what I'm saying is this: when you encounter phrases and ideas used by some poor author to talk about travel over galactic and inter-galactic distances as they are trying to move the story along: be kind to them. They are floundering around trying to get to grips with impossible ideas just as much as the next person.

6

Leap of Faith

The Well-Com pyramid Arcology was being pounded to rubble.

Deep in the basement, at the centre of the department where the smart-virus had been developed and the test on the frogs launched, the tech-personnel had all scarpered. Once the evacuation notice had been sent, they didn't need a second reminder or a friendly nudge to act: they were running like hares from hounds from the minute the red lights started flashing and the klaxons wailing. They were scientists not warriors, and even if they did consider themselves explorers of the frontier of chemical weaponry, and in some twisted way believed that made them warriors in a brave new world, that didn't mean that they had any intention of getting anywhere near actual, real weapons. And the world around them was rapidly collapsing due to the brutally effective use of some very real old-world weapons.

There were many escape routes from the basement, all leading to hover-pads many hundreds of meters away from the compound in the rainforest. Most of the hover-pads had been destroyed in the first wave of the ground attack, the mangled metal of their launch pads broken and partially melted by hastily placed Shock-Wave mines. But being anywhere else was better than being in the compound.

Within five minutes of the initial evacuation alert, the basement was clear of all personnel apart from two dedicated souls, well, one half-drunk soul and one dedicated soul.

The top floors of the pyramid Arcology had been all but evaporated by the first wave of cluster-bombs, nothing now remained but twisted, half-melted steel and clumped, shattered concrete. The top floors were the Executive Offices, so the casualties were light, the Executives had mysteriously been spirited away just before the attack, having that sixth sense that the guilty often do before they are targeted by assaults on their base of operations.

One of the Shadow Stalker attack planes had been flown in to the Arcology, smashing in to it near its peak, the pilot ejected as his plane was hit by missiles from the defending Holocaust Attack Choppers, but not before steering his rapidly disintegrating aircraft in to the massive pyramid. The top of the Arcology was wreathed in black oily smoke that curled skywards, feeding off the meager fuel left in the gutted building once the thermo-nanite cluster-bombs had done their work.

The bullet-proof, shatter-proof glass had all been shattered and smashed to smithereens by the initial onslaught: papers, burning remnants of furniture and not a few bodies rained down from all sides of the besieged pyramid.

After a full thirty minutes of fierce fighting, the battle was nearing its end.

The GreenFire ground and air forces had spotted that the Well-Com personnel were making a run for it, and were content to let them go.

The silver and green cone-shaped uni-copter escape-pods that shot skywards were left unmolested, as were the bulbous yellow hover-pods sent skimming over the tree-tops of the surrounding forest.

The view from an escaping uni-copter of the Well-Com pyramid Arcology would have been a depressing one. From Well-Com's point of view anyway.

The rainforest was blackened and smoldering, burning in places as some trees had caught the fall-out from napalm-torpedoes. Thick grey mist and oily smoke mixed in roiling clouds above the tree-tops, being driven like waves on a beach by the shock-waves of incoming attacks. The perimeter of the compound had long-ago been cleared and sterilised, scattered with concrete bollards and mined heavily with both anti-personnel and heavier anti-tank mines. It was now covered with body-filled craters and the flaming wrecks of destroyed vehicles, from both GreenFire and Well-Com security: the static-site machine-guns on the lower perimeter wall mercilessly cut down anything that moved in the mined clear-zone.

Burned out remains of both Attack Choppers and Stalker-jets littered the forest around the compound, charred skeletons of deathly-efficient machines that had fallen foul of the equally efficient technology of the hated enemy.

The inner compound was churned mud, more blackened craters and barely recognisable building-shells.

Fires burned everywhere. Bodies lay scattered where they fell. From the air, the bodies of both sides were indistinguishable, simply discarded, broken, bloodied remains of those that had fought and died for what they believed in, whether this was the 'noble cause' of Well-Com's destruction, or an unfeasibly large pay-cheque. Motives no longer mattered, the dead were just dead.

Grand Overseer Biryos, Third Marshall of Waxalon, Keeper of the Flame and Overlord of Ooraleez, the greatest military commander the Porthoox had ever known, as well as being the greatest mind ever to occupy a battle-suit, was also the inventor of the 'viralene battle cleanser'. Battlefields were something to look over with pride, with a sense of accomplishment, a way to gauge the damage you had done to your enemy, to see the tangible evidence of kicking their ass. Which was fine and all, but the experience was frequently spoiled by having to look at a lot of bodies, often mutilated and disfigured in the most unpleasant of ways. So, Biryos reasoned, let's find a way to clean this mess up! She came up with the viralene battle cleanser: a virus that mutated organic tissue in to sweet smelling piles of goo, much like puddles after a pleasant Spring rain. The virus was released at stages throughout any battle that Biryos was involved in and made the whole battlefield, it was generally agreed, a much more pleasant experience.

Gask Slorin, embedded correspondent with the Kin'Zar army at Rowt'n Illy.

The remains of the Arcology towered in to the sky, a skeletal shell of its former self, but still somehow majestic. A mute testament to man's desire to conquer the forest, now broken, burned and ravaged by man's other driving desire: the apparent need to kill himself.

Prior to the attack by GreenFire, the Well-Com Arcology pyramid had been the largest free-standing structure in existence. It stood now, in smoldering flames, awaiting its final death-blow from the nukes GreenFire were intent on using.

Basil Bevin, the leader of the GreenFire Alpha Strike Team stood in the ruins of the Arcology, surrounded by what was left of his ground forces. A grim determination was writ large on all their faces. They worked silently to unpack and build the nukes.

Basil turned to his second-in-command, who he affectionately called 'Weevil' for reasons that were seldom mentioned, "the building all clear Weevil?"

Weevil was setting up the cameras for one last broadcast, "just finishing the last sweeps now, scanners show everything above two hundred empty, only the basements to go, should be done in about ten minutes."

Basil smiled at Weevil, "thank you Weevil."

"It's been an absolute pleasure Basil."

Basil's exchange with Weevil had a relaxing effect on the other GreenFire troops. Those that had come this far knew they would go no further. None of them had any illusions about how this was going to end, and, to be honest, most of them were surprised they had got this far and had achieved as much as they had. The battle for the Well-Com facility had been bloody, ruthless and costly to both sides, but no one at GreenFire seriously thought they would succeed in getting in with the nukes. What was Well-Com thinking!? That they got out as fast as they did and left the place to its fate was the final sign to GreenFire that Well-Com were nothing more than spineless bean-counters, capitalist fascists with nothing but self-interest in any of their rotten, corrupted hearts.

Well-Com had what they wanted and were done with the Arcology, so the loss, as financially ruinous as it seemed, could be recovered. GreenFire were, after all, giving Well-Com the biggest get out of jail free card they could have wished for. They could play the victim for many years to come off the back of this one.

Deep in the basement, were the last two Well-Com employees.

Miles Quigley sat at a lab-bench drinking an expensive eighteen year-old Scotch whisky meant for a celebration now never going to happen. He was surrounded by the smoldering remains of the lab and those within it from whom he'd liberated the whisky.

Penny Talbot carried a large computer drive over to the bench and dropped it down.

Miles had his feet up, looking like a fantastically well-dressed wino without a care in the world. The dust and ash that had settled on his suit could not tarnish it enough to hide its shimmering, tailored perfection and his shoes still retained a shine you could shave in.

Penny casually discarded her lab-coat and started to slip on something a little more comfortable, in this case, a bright-orange flak-jacket. Penny wasn't a run of the mill lab-assistant, she wasn't even a scientist. She knew enough to get-by in the world of the chem-lab, but mostly got by with her devastating good looks and her willingness to use them to get what she wanted. And what she wanted was information: Penny was one of Well-Com's most trusted Security Advisors. No one in the lab had suspected that she was anything other than a slightly ditzy assistant, which was as much testament to the myopic nature of scientists where a beautiful woman was concerned, as it was to her skills and subterfuge.

Penny finished securing her ballistic clothing, then produced an automatic-pistol and holstered it in the flak-vest, "ok Miles, let's get you out of here."

Miles took a long swig from the whisky bottle, he mustered his finest, engaging smile for Penny, "not a lot of point, we won't be able to outrun the nukes, and with what they will do to the stores here, I'm not sure I'd want to... we'd be better off spending our time getting naked and getting down to some serious fucking."

Penny smiled sweetly, "well, I'm outta here, come along if you like, stay if you like." She picked up the hard-drive, "we can fuck later when we make it out of here," she added as an afterthought.

Miles raised the bottle slightly in an encouraging salute but showed no signs of moving, "good luck then dear lady, I'll see you on the flip-side."

Miles was feeling pleasantly toasted, well on the way to being delightfully drunk.

Penny frowned, her brain catching her up with exactly what Miles had said, "what do you mean 'do to the stores'?"

"The virus," Miles said simply.

"What about it? It'll get wiped in the blast..."

"Afraid not."

"What?" Penny put down the hard-drive and instinctively drew her pistol.

"I wanted to name it you know, the virus... 'Applejack' had a nice ring to it, but no, the top-brass kept referring to it as 'the virus', such small minds..."

Penny stepped towards Miles.

If Miles had any combat training, which he didn't, or was familiar with armed-forces shut-down techniques, which he wasn't, or had any modicum of common sense, which he did, but that was currently suspended due to the whisky, he would have picked up on the threatening posture Penny had taken, "tell me what you know," she said with calm authority laced with the threat of imminent violence.

Miles shrugged, "not much to tell. Just that when we were talking about the design of the virus the boffins were concerned with the cleansing of it from a nuke, they said they'd have to work on a variant-strain that could mutate more quickly or something, and that was what the 'next stage' was going to be." Miles clumsily gestured round him with the whisky bottle, "all this, that was what they were up to, basic virus was done and dusted few weeks ago," he took a swig from the bottle, gesturing with his free hand, "this was the upgrade."

Penny was in a bit of a hurry and was starting to feel irritable, "so!? Spit it out!"

"They were nowhere near done, but they'd made a start..." Miles left it there as if that was enough.

Penny leveled the gun at Miles, "one minute to change my mind about shooting you in the face."

Miles took his feet off the lab-bench and put down the whisky bottle, he put his hands on his knees to steady himself and tried to fix Penny with a calming look, "so... no sex then?"

"Thirty seconds."

"The boffins got half-way with the mutation, something to do with using kinetic energy to trigger a latent gene, post-translational modification, prenylation, creating lipid-anchored protein, some shit like that... I think that was it... who listens, really, I mean, who really listens to that shit?"

"I got no time for this Miles..."

"The virus will be targeted but won't be killed: it will be spread by the blast, not killed by it, and will infect any protein it contacts, turning it in to a carrier... it could... in theory... spread until it has nothing to spread to..."

Penny waggled the gun in encouragement.

"Nuclear blast... airborne... contamination through shock-wave... not limited to any single target..." Miles was using words he hoped Penny would process.

Miles saw that Penny wasn't getting it, "if those nuts at GreenFire haven't skimped on the loony-toons budget and have spent big, they may have got hold of a sixty mega-ton device... shock-wave from that can go round the world three times and still be measured... that's bye-bye planet."

"That's not possible," Penny said quietly, "they would have told me..."

Miles offered Penny his best smile again, "shall we...?"

There have been many studies made on what drives the sharing of information. Information is available to any that care to look for it. You just have to know where and when to look. So sharing it can seem anathema. If someone wanted to know, they'd know. There are times when sheer volume of information, sifting through what's relevant, and physical capacity for absorbing information are the major factors in what can be known. There are some circumstances when it is acceptable to share information, that is pass on information, push it out there, rather than wait for it to be pulled. On Ankorips information is jealously guarded. All information. The Ankoloripians spend their lives gathering and hoarding information, releasing snippets of it to the ether-sphere in exchange for food or fuel when needed. They are a simple people, the Ankoloripians, who have little contact with the rest of the galaxy. The rest of the galaxy is largely unaware of them too. An awareness of the galaxy and the vast amounts of information within it, would certainly cause revolution and galactic expansion on Ankorips. And this is to be avoided.

Huntle Awmnor, insurgent, Encyclopedia Gurontia.

Penny holstered her gun, in spite of his behaviour she couldn't help but like Miles a little, "are you shitting me about the virus and the nuke? You know that shit? For sure?"

"I shit you not."

Penny processed this for a few seconds. She knew who Miles was and what he was likely to know about the goings on at Well-Com, and from what little contact she'd had with him, he seemed like a smart guy, manipulative but not 'evil'. He was involved in the early stages of development, and with his desire to climb higher up the ladder, would have been keen to have some more input, that meant paying attention. She nodded to herself as she made up her mind. She held out her hand to Miles, "come with me..."

Miles smiled broadly, “are you shitting me?”

Penny led Miles deeper in to the basement labs, her security card opened doors without hesitation. Miles was surprised that the power down here was still functioning, the battering the generator plant had taken, as well as the targeted charges and missiles from GreenFire should mean that the whole Arcology was in black-out by now. Well-Com must have anticipated an attack of this magnitude, but how could they? And if they anticipated that, what else was there down here, and how come Penny had access to this deep under the building?

They were standing in a clean-room, the steel door closed behind them, “take your clothes off,” Penny said simply.

Miles’ train of thought switched tracks. Miles didn’t need asking twice. As he undressed he took a closer look at Penny. Her growing state of undress was revealing a body that he immediately responded to, as he imagined anyone with any blood left in their body would. There wasn’t any aspect of her that Miles would change, she was, quite simply, a perfect woman. Something about that bugged Miles, but as Penny slowly slid out of her underwear, his thinking was narrowly driven in one direction, and it didn’t involve feeling bugged.

Penny was opening what looked like a pressurised door, some kind of equalising chamber maybe, Miles didn’t care. She put in a bundle of blankets and what looked like a few silver quilts. Miles was naked and didn’t care even more.

Penny gave Miles a gentle smile, “in we go,” she said, climbing in to the tubular chamber. Miles was quick to follow, his curiosity was left far behind.

The tubular chamber was about four meters across, and about six long. Once inside Miles found it was bigger than he briefly thought it might be from the outside. Then even that brief moment was gone and he was focused on Penny’s naked body, again.

Penny knelt on the blankets on the floor of the chamber and Miles knelt with her, she took his hands in hers, looking him in the eyes, “we’ve probably got about ten minutes at most,” she said.

“I can do a lot in ten minutes.”

Penny smiled an impossibly sexy smile, “so can I.”

Weevil was behind a small camera, counting down to the go-live for the broadcast, “Basil, in six, five, four…” three, two, one signed on fingers.

Basil stood in front of his GreenFire colleagues, Weevil slowly moved round to join them.

Basil smiled to camera, "welcome to this GreenFire broadcast. This is an update on the strike on Well-Com's facility in the rainforest. We have successfully driven Well-Com from the laboratory and the Arcology, stopped all of their operations and will shortly destroy the whole complex, putting paid to one of their many poisonous schemes once and for all. We apologise for the brutality of our actions and are not blind to their apparent madness. In our defense we would say this: Well-Com, and all corporations like them, have been served notice by GreenFire. We are prepared to do whatever it takes to shut you down and stop your destruction of our precious planet. The price we pay: we pay it gladly. Do not sit back and let them walk all over you. Do what you can. What we can do is this..."

Basil held up a detonator switch, looking in to camera, "this has been a GreenFire warning broadcast to corporations everywhere. Resistance is here."

Basil turned the detonator.

Penny was lying on her back, Miles had slid down Penny's perfect body and was busy with his tongue.

Penny fought the urge to simply push herself on to his tongue and lose herself in the sensation.

"Miles... Miles, I have to tell you something..."

"Uh-hu..."

"I'm a phenotype-polymorph."

"Uh-hu..."

Penny breathed deeply, her eyes closed, she felt the surge building within her, washing over her in waves, "I... just... thought... you... should... know..."

"Uh-hu..."

GreenFire had not in fact skimped on their loony-toon budget. The nuke was a three-stage standard lithium, with a yield of 60Mt with a second-stage lead-tamper: Green-Fire were going 'green' with their bomb. Total obliteration for a 50km radius.

The shock-waves would indeed reverberate around the globe multiple times, as Miles had predicted, being measurable for their first three passes, also as predicted.

Miles had, so far, been right about the consequences of the GreenFire nuke.

7

Maybe

Jesus sat quietly in 'The Blue Angel' drinking emporium, not for the irony, but because they served the best 'deep-thought-knot' cocktail this side of the Harroloon System.

As he sipped his swirling yellow cocktail, the messiah mused.

The Harroloon System, like all 'systems' wasn't known as the 'Harroloon System' outside of the huge nebulous mass that surrounded it, but rather as part of the 'Pillars of Sirdium', which it was called by the people of Mardus, who first observed the system and having spread out in to the local galaxy, took their cataloguing system with them.

The pillars weren't 'pillars' either. The material that made up the nebula, like the material that made up all nebula, was only fractionally denser than the vacuum that surrounded it and most planets that could appreciate and measure a vacuum, including Mardus, knew this.

Once the folks of Harroloon became space-borne, they took their planet's name (Harroloon, by no coincidence what-so-ever) and gave it to the whole region of space they were from.

Eventually the peoples of Mardus and Harroloon met, and the naming of things became a contentious issue, relations became strained between the two galactic neighbours.

Dragalian philosophy tells us, "sometimes it's not about which end of the egg to crack, but about whether you eat the contents or the shell." Dux Chandle, a prominent Dragalian interpreter and entrepreneur, often reminds us that each of us has a perspective that simply won't allow us to understand things from the other side of the mirror. Cryptic comments like this are why Dux commands such large fees and his books are best-sellers on the galactic self-help market.

Jilly Porzn, book reviewer for the West-Arm Spiral Wing broadcasting corps.

The messiah mused on.

It was all about perception. Where you were and what your universe-bubble encompassed.

That was it. Not as much musing was needed as Jesus thought. Then he thought, 'people eh?' and got back to the deep-thought-knot which was melting the Nure egg inside it and bubbling orange in response.

The Blue Angel was a spacious bar, spread-out over five floors, each being larger than five of your average sized sports field. Each floor catered to a customer's specific needs, be they culinary, sexual, spectator of sports, player of bar-games, or hardened drinker. The bottom floor, the easiest to get in and out of without having much motor-function, was where Jesus was, surrounded by hardened drinkers.

It was quiet here and Jesus liked it. People left you alone, got on with meeting up and getting hammered. Sure there was the piped music, but that was mostly unobtrusive and largely unidentifiable as music. The lighting added to the ambience, dingy, no unnecessary intrusion or distractions for the eyes.

Some of the booths had filmy smoke-fogs over them, others noise-shields and intrusion-filters, some sparkled with drink-dispensing curtains, showering the brain-melting alcohol in a fine rain. All the booths were nicely spread out so that no casual contact could be accidentally made with your neighboring drinkers.

Jesus downed the last of his cocktail as it started to fizz and pop with the crackling, exploding recently hatched worm at the bottom.

Once he'd drained his glass, he wiped his mouth with the back of his free hand, holding his glass up, appreciating the squirming residue as it became gaseous and drifted away on a light breeze in a purple haze.

Through the cut-crystal glass Jesus could see a mass of eyes twinkling at him, as he lowered the glass, there was the barman. The barman was smartly dressed in a pale-blue uniform of shirt and trousers, with a garish yellow tie emblazoned with the crystalline Blue Angel of the bar's name, "what can I get you sir?" he inquired politely.

"What do you recommend?" asked Jesus.

"Well, as sir has already had three deep-thought-knots, I'd heartily recommend moving on to something lighter with a little pick-me-up in it," smiled the barman.

"Surprise me."

"Certainly sir."

The barman wafted off along the bar, gathering bottles and what looked like exotic fruits as he went.

The customers either side of Jesus, each a respectable two or three meters away, raised a glass to the messiah in congratulation to his still being compos mentis after downing three of the brain-crushing cocktails. Jesus smiled politely back.

The Blue Angel drinking emporium was mostly frequented by those with money and a liberal conscience easily able to dismiss the guilty pleasures found there as a passing fancy, rather than a stain on their character.

There were signs and posters all around the place, as there are in all such establishments, sharing witticisms such as, "I'm not as think as I drunk I am," "You don't have to be mad to work here, but we are," and so on. The whole policy of the Blue Angel, and its most frequently displayed sign, was the timeless wisdom of: "Just don't be a dick." There was a distillation of wisdom in that that escaped none of the patrons of the Blue Angel. There were no lengthy discussions, drunken or otherwise, about what constituted being a dick, people got it. It was self-evident to anyone who wanted a good time. It contained all the warning you needed, together with some good life-advice. Whether displayed on cute wooden plaques in the bathrooms, or holo-signs subtly floating near doorways, or in organic-messages wriggling their way along tables and on bars, or carried by the gentle-strains of the Blue Angel's theme song, "We're All Cool Here," that was piped along with the other music to every part of the emporium: people got it.

There are too many races, cultures and regions of the galaxy to mention that are solely based on the complete opposite of the premise 'don't be a dick' to list. When this mentality is taken out in to the galaxy, it soon rubs those it encounters up the wrong way, the usual result being war. The Xentrians, whose cultural centre is that weakness is a crime, and any and all forms of weakness are punishable by death, recently tried to convene what they called a 'Council of Conquerors'.

They invited the Fwirtin, the Hendolins and the Yuz. The Fwirtin will not tolerate any living creature that uses the visible light-spectrum to gather information, the Hendolins believe their god, Heod, is the only deity and he only likes them and the Yuz don't acknowledge anyone other than themselves as sentient.

The Council was a thinly veiled attempt to lure the Xentrians' opponents to a mass-slaughter and was poorly attended.
Krik Oquazar, Captain of the free-trader 'Liggle', known smuggler – open-source advocate of free news.

The barman returned with Jesus' drink, a tall glass with orange and purple liquid carefully layered in it, with a topping of finely chopped fruit and some gloopy, foaming substance that smelled slightly sweet.
Jesus nodded his approval.
The occupant of the stool to the left of Jesus had changed, the stool was now occupied by a nervous looking hulk of a man in dark-brown semi-armoured clothing, typical of the dock-workers from orbiting ships that took leave shore-side. He looked distinctly like he was about to be a dick.
The barman placed the cocktail neatly in front of Jesus.
The dock-worker pulled out a vicious looking gun from inside his armoured jacket and pointed it at the barman, "give me the money and nobody gets hurt!"
The barman slowly raised his hands.
None of the other patrons appeared to take any notice.
Jesus remained still but couldn't help but take an interest, he took a sip from his sweet-smelling cocktail, noting the barman's calm response along with the deliciously mysterious hints of exotic delights assailing his nostrils.
One of the barman's upheld hands slowly raised a finger and pointed to a liquid-green sign behind the bar, over one of the cash-handling stations: "Just don't be a dick."
The dock-worker turned gun-toting robber scowled, waggled the gun it what he hoped was a menacing manner and shouted, "give me the zarking money!"
"Sure kid, how much do you want?" the barman calmly enquired.
This threw the gun-wielding desperado a bit, "what do you mean how much?" he demanded.
"I mean how much do you want?"
"And do I look like a zarking kid to you!?" The dock-worker turned 'not-so-criminal-mastermind' barked: he did indeed look much older than the baby-faced barman.

"I'm three hundred years old kid, been here all my life, and I can tell you, no one has ever… ever, robbed the Blue Angel and lived to spend any of it…" said the barman gently.

"Give me the zarking money!!" screamed the would-be robber, then added, "all of it!"

The barman shrugged and opened the cash-handling station, over his shoulder he enquired, "you got a bag?"

"What?"

"You got a bag to put it in, or are you going to carry it out in your pockets?"

The robber looked a bit worried, "I… I aint got no bag… quit stalling!"

The barman scooped up a huge wad of cash and turned to the gun-toting thief, "here you go…"

The robber gathered it up off the bar as best he could, stuffing it in to his pockets, while still pointing the evil-looking gun vaguely in the direction of the barman.

The barman looked mildly interested, but appeared to be paying more attention to the other patrons and the state of their glasses than he was to the gun being waggled in his direction, nodding here and then to the regulars that he'd be with them in a minute.

The robber looked round briefly, trying to figure out the best way to get out of there.

"Probably best if you go via the washrooms near the kitchens," offered the barman helpfully.

"Zark you!" shouted the robber, and fled. In the direction of the washrooms near the kitchens.

Jesus slowly took another sip of his amazingly refreshing drink, "you get this sort of thing a lot?" he asked the barman.

The barman shrugged, "not a lot, but enough that it's a drag. Most people know there are quicker ways to commit suicide."

"What do you mean?"

The barman gently tapped his right eye, "goes straight to the security feed, we contract out all security to 'Dredd & Horrocks', he won't make it fifty meters from the building."

"What'll happen to him," Jesus enquired, though he was enjoying the cocktail so much, his relaxed state had already moved to his posture and his casual slouch betrayed how little he cared.

"He was a big guy, probably pretty fit, I'd guess he'll be brain-wiped and cleaned up, put to work on the top floor."

Jesus nodded his complete lack of understanding or interest.

Seeing Jesus was ok with his drink, the barman drifted off to tend to his other patrons.

The barman, like all staff at the Blue Angel, was bio-enhanced to read electrical and pheromone signals from the clients: when put together they were a fool-proof way to ident someone. Dredd & Horrocks would have released a retrieval drone as soon as the barman had triggered the alarm, most of which were situated in the 'Just don't be a dick' signs.

Retrieval drones operated with a one hundred per-cent success rate: they were basic machines with monitoring fed to D&H HQ. Huge, humanoid robots, with a myriad of telescoping metal tentacles, built in chain-guns, vibro-axes and thermo-charge dispensers, they couldn't be bought off or reasoned with, they simply did their job. No one in Jaldur, the city of the Blue Angel, ever interfered with a retrieval drone. Not ever. The drones were programmed to take their designated target alive, but to mercilessly butcher anyone who tried to stop them.

Jesus was smiling to himself, slumped against the bar, elbow propped, hand under his chin, focusing on his drink. He was letting himself feel good.

All along the huge bar Jesus was sitting at, heads were turning to watch a vision walk by.

The sex-worker from the top floor had a projected synch-field emanating from her body, modifying the appearance she took-on according to the projected fantasy of the person looking at her. Wearing just enough clothes to make it look like she might as well not be wearing any clothes, she was raising pulses as she passed. She glanced around as she went, taking the time to acknowledge any admiring looks she got with a girlish, shy smile.

Sexual attraction starts off as an evolutionary necessity but quickly becomes something other, driven by all sorts of deeply buried triggers. The old saying that 'opposites attract' is a good example of that.

That cannot have come about through evolutionary drives, opposites cannot attract because we'd all die out and never get to the 'ordering meals in expensive restaurants to attract' stage if they did.

Never the less, there are some strange mutual attractions out there.

The Vandocalaxian obsession with trying to win over the Erdogons for instance. It beggars belief that they could have had social contact in the first place, what with the Vandocalaxians being water-borne gelatinous creatures and the Erdogons being the soaring reptiles that they are. But somehow contact was made. And the Vandocalaxians were smitten. As their society developed, they were quick to genetically engineer creatures that could adapt their float-sacks to the outer atmosphere, lifting them to the other regions of Eraxador, to catch glimpses of the elusive Erdogons. Sexual contact between the two races is always short and sweet, and mostly deadly for one of the creatures involved. But still they persist. A perfect illustration of that other stupid old adage, 'the heart wants what the heart wants', when what it really only wants is fluid and a charge to keep it going.

Laslar Irblor, agony-aunt for the Dripux Consulate on Eraxador.

She stood at the bar next to Jesus.

The barman silently arrived and placed a drink in front of her, he was good at reading people and was showing off a bit for a fellow employee.

The woman looked at the barman and appeared to blush, "why thank you, how did you know?"

"You're welcome ma'am, just seemed to fit."

The woman picked up her ice-cold beer and took a long slow drink.

Eyes everywhere were conveying the message that they wished they were that glass.

She placed the glass down on the bar then looked to Jesus, "you don't mind if I stand here for a while do you?"

The messiah was still smiling to himself about how good he was letting the drinks make him feel, he hadn't been paying much attention to the approach of the woman.

"No, you go ahead, you want a seat?"

"No, thank you, it'll be good to be on my feet for a while."

Jesus turned and slowly looked the woman over, taking in her beauty, seeing all the projections she was pushing out for those admiring her.

She was so at ease, so meant to be here, so right. He appreciated the serene sexuality of all she was as well as all she was projecting.

She held his gaze as he looked her over, patiently waiting.

Jesus raised his glass to her, "you look good..."

"Why thank you," she replied quietly.

"But I think I preferred the goat..."

"Whatever gets you through the night honey."

They smiled at each other and downed their drinks.

"Shall we talk?" asked the woman.

The woman looked towards the barman and briefly gestured with one of her slightly raised hands: sign language of the employees of the Blue Angel. The barman nodded in acknowledgement and signed back.

"I've got us a booth," the woman quietly said to Jesus.

Jesus followed her to the booth, she was in no hurry and he enjoyed following her.

The booth was set for a quiet-zone, green sparkling lights danced around the edges of the screens, letting people know that privacy was appreciated.

Jesus slid himself on to one of the seats with the woman gracefully easing herself in to the booth opposite the messiah.

"So you're finally doing some honest work," Jesus said.

The woman shrugged, "seemed like it was time to find out what all the fuss was about, people are so fired-up about sex, and to be honest, I never paid much attention, beyond it being a tool to, you know, mess with them."

"You're not going to do the whole 'bursting out' thing are you?"

The woman smiled, "no... not yet. I like this one. Think I'll stick with it for a while."

As she spoke the woman's eyes changed, no longer the liquid pools of turquoise with subtle hints of silver, but fiery-yellow with horizontal black slits, "does this help?" she inquired.

Jesus ignored the question, "so... how have you been?"

Since they had left Earth, Jesus and the Imp had agreed to meet up every once in a while to touch-base on how they were getting on, and to allow Jesus to monitor the Imp to make sure he was as good as his word and was not nipping back to Earth to cause havoc and take advantage of the missing messiah.

The Imp couldn't lie to Jesus and Jesus 'just knew things', which, if he'd have been honest, the Imp would have had to admit annoyed him a lot.

They met every seventy or eighty years, mostly, as it turned out, in bars.

"I'm ok, seeing the sights, thinking a lot, which is, you know, odd, but that seems to be unavoidable with the travelling about," said the Imp.

"Sounds like you're enjoying it."

"I didn't know there was so much out here, I mean I guessed, assumed, you know, but being out here, seeing it actually all unfold, opens the eyes."

Jesus smiled, "there is a lot isn't there?"

The Imp nodded, finishing his beer, "there is! And the variety! You can't make some of this stuff up!"

Jesus motioned to the Imps' empty glass, the Imp nodded and the messiah held his hand over the ordering pad at the side of the table, bio-signals were transmitted and picked up, wanting the drinks was the same as ordering them here, provided your credit was good.

"I'm thinking of going back," said Jesus simply.

The Imp sighed, "I knew you were going to say that."

The middle of the table opened and two drinks slowly rose on a silvered platform, a light mist swirling around them as they did. The messiah and the Imp both reached for their drinks at the same time.

"The more I see, the more I realise it's pretty much all the same," Jesus said, "things have become a lot clearer to me. It was time I needed and time has done the job."

"The more I see, the more I realise I'm not needed, if you know what I mean," the Imp said.

Jesus thought he did indeed know what the Imp meant.

The universe didn't need the external nudges from the Imp and 'people', whatever form they took, and where ever they were, seemed to have a leaning towards doing the things the Imp would tempt them in to anyway.

"I feel like I have to finish things off, close the circle," Jesus said.

The Imp took a slow draft of his beer, "I think I'll stay out here and do a bit more wandering, see the sights, you know, before it all comes crashing down," he said.

Jesus nodded. It made sense. Or at least it seemed to at the moment, and that was good enough.

He raised his glass, "to us," he toasted.

The Imp smiled and raised his glass, "there may be hope for you yet..."

8

Popsicles

Spike and Jools sat strapped in to the shuttle, full battle-armour, weapons charged and loaded, with their drop-pods of equipment at their side. They were the epitome of the Security Councilor's deadly reputation: black-suited death-dealers with the tools and the talent to back up their doom-laden look.

The shuttle dropped through outer atmo like a fish gliding through water, no fuss, just what it did. Its sleek black hull and huge fins made it look like a gigantic airborne whale. The ship was on a gentle descent, designed to bring them in with little chance of detection from their target. This was a shuttle, not an attack-ship, too much flak would not be a good thing.

Captain Smith sat at the front of the shuttle with his aide, Lt. Rogers. Both the Captain and the Lt. wore their planet-side battle-gear, but neither of them looked like they belonged in it: they reminded Spike of children playing dress-up in their parent's clothes. The Captain's suit was custom-painted with rank insignia, an ego-driven rookie error that neither Spike nor Jools thought was appropriate to point out to the Captain: it looked so zarking pretty!

Both Spike and Jools had unique settings for their standard armour, tweaks they'd made and had been accepted as part of their protection-fitting.

Not all Security Councilors bothered with this, or knew enough to do it, but the hard-core troopers all had their own set-ups, highlighting what they'd learned about where they would be hit, what their combat style betrayed about them, where their chief weaknesses were, usually forced by their preferred weapons and tactics. Sometimes the modifications were minimal, not even noticeable to those around them, and sometimes they went as far as additional plates or mesh-weaves.

Spike had a thicker neck-brace and thinner thigh-plates, as well as a custom visor that allowed his whole helmet to become transparent on command, made it slightly weaker, but well within the parameters for resisting most of the ordnance they were used to facing.

Jools had extra arm-plates and a much thicker chest plate, he used a more static style of offence and favoured much heavier weapons. Jools was used to getting shot and blown up but compensated by never letting the things that shot and blew him up live for long.

The Yig of Hri fought as much as any race out there. There was always a war over something raging somewhere on their desert-planet home-world. They have always fought each other: over territory, resources, which usually comes from territorial disputes, breeding stock, and as they developed further, the rights to the moons Ligo and Hosil. They were not graceful creatures, the Yig, so avoiding damage from fighting could not be achieved through not being where the pain was and so they developed armour. As cumbersome as they were, so was their armour, reflecting the sheer bulk they were able to carry on their colossal frames. Then a new form of armour came along, discovered accidentally as they gained telekinetic powers in their third millennia, which was the last of their civilisation. The Yig found they could 'summon' swarms of T'tch, an alarmingly abundant insect on Hri, and that if a large enough swarm was summoned, any incoming attack on them would be cushioned by the squishing bodies of the T'tch (which, oddly, let out a collective sigh as they died). Fierce battles were fought with renewed vigour as their new living-armour was put through its paces. Unfortunately (for the Yig) the T'tch were central to the pollination of all food-stuffs on Hri, and as the T'tch were slaughtered by the ton preventing the Yig heroes from taking damage in combat, so the crops withered. Standing on the wasteland that is now Hri, what strikes you are not the countless tombs and monuments to fallen heroes, as grand as they are, but the utter stupidity of the Yig. But aren't we all a little bit Yig?

Zim Uwun, Professor of Evolutionary Economics at the Centre for Warfare, Gallisfran.

Spike tilted his head slightly, activating the one-on-one intercom with Jools, "I'm going to snaffle an extra grid-detector before we jump, you got room for an extra ECMP umbrella-sheet?"

Jools nodded, "yeah… let's get it done now."

They both unclipped their belts and stood up, immediately coming to the attention of Captain Smith, "something wrong troopers?"

Spike used the squad-com, "no Sir, double-checking drop-pack equipment and packing an extra grid-detector."

The Captain nodded, in what he hoped was a knowing and reassuring way, "carry on troopers."

"Yes Sir, thank you Sir."

Spike and Jools exchanged a glance that said it all: "fucking tool."

Spike opened a steel locker to get the gear, Jools popped their equipment pods and started rearranging things to fit in the extra gear.

Jools took the grid-detector from Spike, "you think they know we're here and are suckering us in?"

Spike checked the umbrella-sheet was fully charged with a resistance module, "yeah, I'm not as convinced as the Captain on the intel. Better safe than dead. Neural-burners make me nervous, I reckon we crack a double-detector set-up when we bounce, won't take but a few seconds and the power will last long enough, so…"

Jools nodded his agreement, "good call."

The briefing in the Captain's office had revealed the intelligence and the job, as well as letting Spike and Jools know they were volunteering for the Recon & Recovery mission. Being 'volunteered' for things was the norm, nobody cared about the terminology: a job was a job, it all added to your credits and shortened your release date.

Volunteering just meant that if things went south, you were liable for some of the cost, which usually didn't matter, as if they were going that bad, the debt-recovery was the least of your problems. But if things went well, you got a bonus. The longer-serving troopers all looked to volunteer as and when they could.

Volunteers perform better than conscripts. Makes sense. Someone who wants to do something, chooses to do it, steps forward and says, 'hey! I'd like to do that! Give me a go!' is bound to be more keen than someone dragged in without a choice. That wisdom does not always run through to the end of the task though. Conscripts want to get in, get it done and get out. Volunteers can become enamored of the task itself, enjoying their participation rather than looking to bring it to an end. When the 'task' is war, the same logic can still be applied. Give me ten conscripts and I'll get the job done faster than with a hundred volunteers or we'll all die trying.

General Xyloclorian Yim, commander of the 'Legion of Completion', honoured for valour by the Galactic Council for their part in the swift ending of the Siege of Moon-Base Gloran.

The Security Councilors had some intel that an old, and much hated adversary, the Bidens, were looking for material for a neural-burner, and had left an automated gathering-station with minimal cover in operation on the planet Orur.

The Bidens were a 'terrorist group' that were a poison-laced thorn in the side of the whole Galactic Council, they controlled numerous planets and had their 'advisors' on many more. They were fighting for 'the liberation of all peoples from the tyrannical yolk of Galactic Government'. Whatever the hell that meant. Most people in the galaxy saw the Bidens as bored lunatics looking for an excuse for chaos and mayhem, a view borne out by the fact that most of them were indeed mostly insane, and chaos and mayhem followed them wherever they went. It was impossible to not see it. At their core, there may well have been a few devout followers of their dogma, but they had a way of attracting the psycho-element to their ranks. They were a serious threat to the stability of galactic peace, and the Security Councilors had been up against them, or governments they had corrupted, many times and found it never to be a fun experience.

The Bidens use of neural-burners was what brought them to the Councilor's attention. If they could, the Security Councilors would often throw in a 'freebie' to disrupt the Bidens cause, and especially if it meant shutting down their increase in neural-burners.

The Captain had been charged with taking an exploratory squad down to Orur, seeing what he could see, and then blowing up what he could. The intel suggested this was an opportunity too good to pass-up. And as any veteran Security Councilor knows, if it seems too good to pass-up, you should pass it up. But the top-brass were different.

The Captain, going completely against the grain for a 'bloater', had decided to go on the mission himself, not only that, but to only take a few troopers with him, not even a full squad. Captain Smith knew that success would bring him to the attention of some hi-powered arses he could then kiss at his leisure.

To give him his due, Captain Smith had picked Spike and Jools to volunteer. Pretty much the smartest choice as the core of a four man team. Lieutenant Rogers was chosen as Captain Smith owed Rogers' uncle a favour, and getting the Lt. a combat mission logged would mean he could start the serious business of climbing the ranks. Rogers wasn't a bad trooper, but he'd never been on a live-mission planet-side before, so a recon and recover was a good first choice: all Bidens missions were labeled as 'combat' missions for officers. Captain Smith had no real idea who Rogers was, though had he known there was not much he could have done.

Orur, a small, lush planet in the Nist system, was a known source of ambient energy, in this case Isho, that was ideal for charging neural-burners. Orur was uninhabited by 'advanced' species, having developed just enough to support 'basic' animals, but nothing that had a driving desire to mess up its eco-system, which was now the most common definition for 'advanced'.

Orur was, by any standard, a staggeringly beautiful planet. One, huge, central land mass that stretched around the equator, surrounded by oceans that spanned the whole planet. The seas were impossibly deep in most places, and at least ninety per cent of the land mass was covered with lush, green forest. Life was everywhere on Orur.

Some of the indigenous species had evolved to channel the Isho, most of those could use it to see better than other species with eyes.

The Isho also supported a form of airborne Ray that could glide on its invisible currents, feeding on the discharges from the canopy of the forest. These diamond-shaped Rays could grow up to thirty meters across and were masters of their environment.

And they in turn were one of a thousand species that could have melted hearts and opened eyes if they were featured in a wildlife documentary.

The briefing with Captain Smith had seemed like total bullshit to Spike and Jools, both of whom knew enough about Orur to know that gathering the Isho would have to involve a massive presence there: the Bidens would never set up a small gathering facility and leave it. Such a facility would soon fall to the ravages of the planet's beasts and weather: the beasts would feed from it and drain it, and the monumental rain-storms that wracked the planet would fire it up with so much lightning as to discharge the Isho as soon as it was gathered. Something was up.

What was certain was that there was no large-scale troop presence on Orur, the fact that Captain Smith was dropping with them was proof of that.

Spike and Jools both felt they could go with the flow, wing it, and see where it went.

But that didn't mean they were going to be blasé about this: being better prepared was the best way to make it out the other side as something other than a corpse.

As the shuttle swept in for a landing, it brushed close to the forest-canopy, heading for a natural clearing: the shores of a huge, deep crystal-clear lake.

The comm's came on in Spike and Jools helmets: the command channel was being bled over to them, which was not the usual protocol.

Lt. Rogers was updating Captain Smith on the final approach, "no movement for ten clicks of the LZ Sir, scanners show a massive build-up of Isho, but no storm is registering anywhere near, in fact storm activity has all but died all over Orur."

"Thank you Lieutenant, a good sign I'd say for a smooth mission."

The Captain broke over the squad channel, "alright troopers, we're going in, let's get this done by the book, by the numbers… no drama, let's just get it done."

Spike switched the main ammo-feed on his chain-gun from defense to offence.

Jools fed in the rocket-pods to his ammo chambers and swapped out all tracer rounds in favour of explosive.

They both looked to the Lt., who gave them the hand-signal for 'wide dispersal', they both acknowledged unnoticed by Captain Smith.

The Captain unbuckled himself from his seat and came to join Spike and Jools near the rear drop hatch, "close formation, keep it tight, reconnaissance fire only, let's see those tracers: regular scans and all directions through me."

"Sir, yes Sir," Spike and Jools acknowledged. They were both in full combat mode, their minds stilled and their subconscious completely devoted to their survival through maximum-kill delivery, neither of them gave another thought to Lieutenant Rogers' behaviour or the change in his demeanour: he was one of them now and that was enough. Whatever he was doing they knew it was geared to getting them out of there alive, which is all they'd have asked even if they knew what it was.

Lt. Rogers brought them in fast, dropped the hatch and kept the engines at full cycle, causing a huge roar and backwash near the LZ.

Spike bounced full height and went straight to jet-pack, Jools torpedoed out using full-throttle: Spike broke left, Jools right.

Captain Smith was dead within ten seconds of the drop-hatch opening, killed by a rocket-spread at low level that tore the air to shreds as it spread red-hot shrapnel over its target area: two direct hits and he was ripped apart like a warm loaf.

The Bidens attack was based on surprise. Once that was gone, they were in to a straight fire-fight with whatever troopers bounced from the shuttle. It was their bad luck that those troopers were Spike and Jools.

Spike and Jools dropped all their cry-baby pods, drawing off any guided attacks, and both laced the tree-line with heavy fire, all systems on guided automatic.

Lt. Rogers for his part, had executed an immaculate dust-off maneuver and was peeling away from the LZ, turning the shuttles rear drop-hatch towards Spike and Jools as much as he could.

The forest along the lake-side was ripped to shreds and much of it was ablaze.

The sky was filled with vapour trails and tracer-markers, all showering white smoke and fine debris over the whole area. The ground-fired missiles were taking the bait, exploding in to white-hot fireballs all around the retreating Spike and Jools.

The lake started to bubble, boiling from some unseen source deep beneath its surface. The crystal-clear waters were seething with submerged lightning, crackling blue, turning the whole vast lake in to a spitting cauldron waiting to explode.

The helmet scanners in Spike and Jools suits shut down.

Lt. Rogers sent a broad-wave, didn't matter who heard it now, he just had to get it out there, "ten seconds and we need to be anywhere..."

Lt. Rogers set up a force-grid across the drop-hatch and deployed all the cargo netting: Spike and Jools were coming in hot.

Both troopers hit the drop-hatch a split second apart, retro-pods firing then jettisoning as soon as they broke the threshold. They came in like bowling balls, crashing through the force-grid and slamming in to the nets, tearing them from their anchors.

Lt. Rogers forced the shuttle in to overdrive and took a vertical route out of atmo.

Spike and Jools jettisoned their armour, most of which was scarred and torn from the blistering assault, Jools' left arm was bleeding pretty bad and Spike was dragging a leg: three clean breaks, armour did its job. They both shot-up with stims as they made their way to their seats and buckled in.

Outside the air around them was ripping at supersonic speed, leaving missiles and shells exploding in their wake. The LT was gunning it.

Jools got his comms up and running first, "what the actual fuck!?"

Spike was right behind with the comms, "what's the story LT?"

Lt. Rogers was pinned to his seat, trying desperately to retain control of the shuttle as it fought its way through the atmo, "Bidens got some kind of gatherer and amplifier set-up… ambush, they're not after us…"

There was a split-second of confusion, then it hit home.

Spike got it first, "the attack ship!?"

"Yeah, the whole planet is going to blow its Isho in one discharge."

Jools didn't believe it, "no fucking way! No fucking way is that possible!"

Lt. Rogers was focused on getting them out on the crest of a wave of concussive force that was a warning of the planet–sized Isho blast not far behind, "believe it trooper."

Spike signaled Jools to shut up, "so, what's the plan LT?"

"This is one of those 'good news / bad news' deals..."

Jools refocused, "what do you need from us?"

"I've dumped the data from the shuttle in to the escape-pod computer, you two need to get in it, get out of here and get the data to the Council."

Spike and Jools were out of their seats and heading for the escape-pod as Spike confirmed that was the 'good' bit of the plan, "ok LT, what's the other part of the plan?"

"The Attack Ship will be getting ready to emergency-jump, they open up a gate as the neural-burner wave hits, it'll send it out with them."

Spike saw it, "planet-sized neural-burner, amplified, the attack ship will jump to Base, that's all she wrote for us. Game over."

"Yep, can't let that happen..."

Spike and Jools strapped in to the escape-pod, they both shot up with more stims. A lot more stims.

Spike opened a channel on internal to Lt. Rogers, "you're alright LT. Good luck."

Jools added his good-bye, "you're a trooper Lieutenant. Fucking A."

"See you boys on the other side."

Lt. Rogers jettisoned the escape-pod and switched the small internal engines it carried to overload, desperate, but the only way it had a chance of getting far enough away to escape the blast from the shuttle slamming in to the attack ship's main field-generator.

Spike and Jools were shaking with the escape-pod, the strain on the small capsule was just short of tearing it apart. The hull briefly glowed red, then whitish, before they shook the bonds of atmo and hit near-space.

Jools looked to Spike, "whoever the fuck he was, he's alright by me."

Spike agreed, "I don't know and I don't want to know, but I'll be drinking to him any chance I get."

"I figure he had to set the engines to overload, so we aint out of this yet," Spike added.

"Well, we've got a better chance than the poor bastards on the attack ship."

"Slim is better than none."

Spike and Jools secured themselves in their sleep-masks as the escape-pod broke for deep space, engines burning themselves out in one final push.

9

Piggies

Harper was sitting in the main command-cabin, her ship was motionless near a huge Red Dwarf star.

Ship's systems were all quietly ticking over as more graviton particles were gathered, preparing for another stint in lapsed-space. The ship seemed at peace, resting gently against the spectacular back-drop of the gargantuan star.

Harper munched on a bacon sandwich and had a steaming hot cup of synth-tea to go with it. She'd had her shower, changed her clothes, had a leisurely wander about the ship and was feeling mellow as she sat and gazed out at the massive, bloated star filling the space outside the ship with its diffused crimson glow.

In between mouthfuls of sandwich and synth-tea, she was in the middle of a conversation with Arlia, the ship's computer, and was now taking a brief break.

Arlia was thinking of the next line of conversation that would make Harper see things her way.

Harper was thinking she needed to take a large hammer to the synth-tea dispensing machine in an effort to teach it how to make actual tea.

Harper brushed some breadcrumbs from her brand new uniform, noticing how clean it was as she did: it didn't stick to her in all the wrong places, or have that grimy-sheen she'd grown used to, smelled pretty good too. She briefly reflected on how far she'd let herself go before the ZX84 program had loaded and Arlia had sprung in to existence.

Arlia's gently smiling face reappeared on a near-by monitor, "I think it's important Harper. It just feels right. Ships should have names."

"Maybe that's how it feels to you, but it doesn't happen like that. Ships are just ships. Vehicles, tools, sure they have reg numbers for docks and pass-points, but that's it. And they're Council encoded, you don't get to choose those."

"But this is different," Arlia pleaded.
"Why?" Harper asked.
"Because I'm in this ship. This ship is who I am, I think, so it feels like it needs a name."
"Why not give it your name?"
"Because it's not my ship."
"Well if it's my ship, then I say it doesn't need a name."
"But it does."
Harper finished her sandwich, wiped her mouth and stood up, stretching before she picked up her synth-tea, she went over to the main view-port, "we really don't have more important things to be thinking about?"
Arlia could see this was going to need more work and a different approach, "could you think about it Harper, think about a few names that would fit, that would work for you, and we'll come back to it later."
Harper shrugged, staring at the red, candescent, swirling mass of the sun, "ok."
Arlia knew she had won his round, and would, inevitably win the argument.
Harper nodded towards the bloated, Red Dwarf star they were near, "how about..."
"Not a good idea," interrupted Arlia.
Harper stood looking out the view-port, enjoying her tea (as much as she could), enjoying her cleanliness, enjoying her new found sense of adventure and the fact that the ship was running without her, a soft smile played on her face as she quietly enjoyed the hell out of her current situation.
Arlia monitored all the fuel gathering activity and the engine-processing, keeping the rest of the systems on minimum setting, with a conservation of power here, a little trimming there, they could be in the Xanis system in two more jumps, another day at most. Managing every single aspect of the ship took up about a millionth of her thinking time, and less than a billionth of her total processing power. She was having a little trouble understanding her new capacity for free-thinking, and wasn't that comfortable with the space and time she now detected in herself. When they got to the Xanis system, and she could find the son of God on Idris, first thing on the agenda was asking him what the hell was going on with this 'being alive' thing.

A large red light pinged on the main console. Large red lights are seldom an indication that things are going well, and this one was no exception.

"Something up?" Harper asked casually.

"I'm detecting a disturbing ripple in the gravitational field of the sun's outer rings, neutrinos are all over the place, someone is trying to port in using the sun as a beacon, but looks like they are way off with their navi-com."

Harper sat at the main console and brought up a selection of views and monitors, "they're going to be a might toastie they come out there."

Arlia looked troubled, "Harper, the disturbance is huge."

Harper manually shut down the gathering and slowly started to position the ship further away from the impending incursion in to the system.

The monitors were all showing a build-up of gravitation and distortion on a scale that Harper had never seen before, "we have the shielding prepped?" she asked in what she hoped was still a casual tone.

"We do," Arlia replied, "I have upgraded the tao-converter wave-generators to incorporate graviton-pulses to disperse any..."

"Sure, sounds great," interrupted Harper, "so, in simple-speak, we're ok to see what happens?"

"Oh, definitely," Arlia assured her.

"Even so, let's charge engines for an emergency jump."

"Ok Harper."

Arlia took a reading of all scanners, consulted diagnostics and came to a conclusion, "looks like a multiple-fleet portal, emergency opening, low containment, someone is in a big hurry to get here from somewhere."

Harper nodded her agreement, "risks like that, must be bad where they're coming from... and we're ok to be here when it happens?"

"Yes Harper, we are more than adequately shielded, the engines prepped, we can be away in the blink of an eye, faster actually."

"Ok then."

The lights on the bridge dimmed, settling to a gentle, creamy glow. The instruments and monitor lights softened, falling in to the background, giving prominence to the full view-ports, making the crimson sun seen somehow brighter.

"What are you doing?" asked Harper.

"Trying to set a mood, this would seem to be a big deal, whatever is happening is happening on a scale I have no record of happening before."

"'Setting a mood'? Why do I need 'a mood'?"

"Just a sense of occasion Harper, I felt it might be appropriate..."

Harper was focused on the Red Dwarf and the increasing activity in both sun-flares and gravity ripples that washed through deep space, "ok, sure... maybe ask next time..."

"Ok Harper."

'Setting a mood' means many different things to many different peoples. And to some, is a matter of life and death. On Phococles it is illegal to speak while the sun is setting, which officially occurs from the time its disc can be seen touching the horizon to the time it disappears from view. The Caldronites have laws prohibiting the movement of anyone within six hundred meters of any hatching Fromling. Corngel V strictly enforces the policy of sitting down during any musical event, no matter how small, which is ruthlessly exploited by café owners along any stretch of boulevard, as they hire musicians to strategically play to trap tourists. The space-borne beings of Aldraph in the Juxtintle Sector, patrol the space-lanes preventing any movement in and out of lapsed-space during times of high solar activity: passing ships are expected to enter close-orbit of the sun to scoop up and carry away parts of the solar-atmosphere, seeding, they believe, other parts of the galaxy with their life-giving force.

Cadiwar Tunis, writing for the 'How To Set A Mood' tutorial on Dredinak, often taken as part of the 'Writing For A Guide' course by budding correspondents.

Harper stood from the console, drawn to the huge floor to ceiling view-port, standing close gave the impression you could reach out and touch deep-space. It seemed like such a fragile barrier between you and the utter nothingness of the void. Not that space was a real void, not when you got right down to it: there was so much radiation and quantum foam that it was seething with deadly potential. But Harper, as all people, was completely unaware of this as she stared through the blackness. She was drawn in to the sun, focusing on the gargantuan red mass and the infernos exploding from its bloated surface.

"Harper…" Arlia said gently.

"Uh-huh…"

"I watched you shower."

"Uh huh…"

Harper frowned slightly as she tried to un-mishear what she thought she had misheard, "er, what?"

"I watched you shower," Arlia said meekly.

Harper pulled her gaze from the sun and reluctantly turned from the viewing port to give the main view-screen her full attention, "yeah, sure, but you monitor all my bodily signals, multiple channels, bio-feeds, sim-flow awareness, medical mostly, but all of them, right?"

"Yes Harper… but this wasn't that… I watched through a viewer."

If Harper had been facing the view-port she would have seen the bloating of the outer-corona, the tidal-wave of energy blast from the sun, scattering asteroids and lighter dust formations as it went, ionising them in a perfectly circular burst as space itself was ripped apart and a virtual event-horizon established to open the portal.

But she wasn't.

The ship compensated to buffer the blast, remaining perfectly still against the onslaught.

Harper remained oblivious to this.

"You watched through a viewer?"

"Yes Harper, I did."

"And why would you do that?"

"I wanted to see you."

Harper was having trouble with the concepts and ideas that Arlia was putting out there.

There were many things Harper didn't understand, and more importantly, knew she shouldn't understand, about AIs and sentience in general, but this was confusing.

It was one thing to accept that you knew how something didn't work at a nuts and bolts level, but yet another to realise you didn't know anything about it at all, not even if it was made of nuts and bolts.

Taking machines, or what came from what you understood was a machine, as being somehow alive, was not difficult. Sentience, as Harper saw it, was something that happened. How it happened became irrelevant to her once it had. But this was different she felt, this was something else, a cross-over of some kind, and she was having trouble processing it.

Outside the ship things were getting interesting.

The event-horizon of the portal had indeed coalesced too close to the sun's outer atmosphere, and had proceeded to drain off the millions of tons of material per second that were being ejected from the expanding star.

The only way to punch through lapsed-space, rather than to flow with it, was through a re-polarised singularity.

As the event-horizon formed it started to feed on the colossal amounts of material needed to fuel the singularity re-polarisation. Unfortunately it was a delicate balancing act, and one that was drastically failing as the sun began to be pulled apart and fed in to the portal.

Harper's ship was perfectly placed to witness a spectacle of awesome magnificence, to be a chronicler of events that, if unchecked, could well lead to the premature death of a star, as well as the complete annihilation of whatever fleet was creating the portal.

Stars don't die, they change. Even when they are going supernova, they just change, there is something left, unrecognisable as a star, but something none the less. The death of a star is a big deal, even in the Luminol Quadrant, where you couldn't throw a cosmic stick without hitting a star, their death is a big deal. 'Death' means being 'unstar-like'. Stars are what most civilisations define galaxies by. They have all kinds of myths and creation stories, even gods tied up with them. So killing them before their time is a sign that you are either completely out of control, or far too big for your cosmic boots. Anywhere advanced enough to have 'charters' concerning contact with other civilisations, other worlds, all such gatherings have numerous rules against killing stars. In the darker reaches of the Expansion Frontier Dimensions, there are reports of sentient stars. So far, these reports remain uncorroborated, but could you imagine!? A sentient star! But why not? And what would they think of those that went around killing their brethren?

Bosir Eems, taken from her last reports from the deep-space exploration ship, the 'Coldimar'.

Harper moved over to the main console and leaned forward, getting close to the primary monitor, where the embarrassed looking Arlia was.

The universe proceeded to unfold and implode outside without her.

"What do you mean 'you wanted to see me'? What did you see? What did you think you'd see, me being in the shower and all, and, and what do you mean 'see'!?"

Arlia frowned slightly, looking a little bit troubled, which was new for both Harper and Arlia, "I saw you in the shower, I didn't know what it would mean to me until I did it, watched you, naked, through a viewer… I switched the other sensory inputs to background-feed and watched," Arlia said.

Harper nodded, "sure, ok… no. Look… what are you talking about?"

Arlia's face took on an even more embarrassed look, complete with a flush to the cheeks, "I think… I think I have… feelings for you Harper."

The ship's outer shields started to glow white as they took on and deflected the energy storm that was flowing from the portal and the growing flares from the disturbed giant sun that was fighting for its life.

The wave-generators were channeling what they could around the ship, converting gravitons and streaming neutrinos and pulsing them through filters to drain the gravity from them, spraying them out behind the ship in a river of dying, fiery energy.

Arlia monitored the shields, they were fine, doing what they were designed to do, operating well within any tolerance that required alerting Harper.

Harper was staring at Arlia, waiting. Eventually it became clear that Arlia wasn't going to speak next, Harper started to speak, and then completely failed to find any words to explain the confusion she was feeling.

Arlia spoke softly, aware that Harper was struggling to hear what she was saying, "Harper, this is all new to me. Everything. It's all new. And I think so much, so much is going on, I'm processing information in simul-flow, but even then, the millions of concurrent streams of thought, they..."

"You have feelings for me?" interrupted Harper, "... sexual... feelings?"

Arlia nodded, "I do. That's how I understand them, these feelings. Most definitely sexual."

Harper moved back and sat at the main view-port, with her back to the tumultuous events occurring in the space around her ship.

"I thought I should tell you," Arlia finished quietly.

Harper folded her arms, thinking.

Outside the ship something close to Armageddon was happily tearing apart the space-time continuum.

The portal had opened. The event-horizon had coalesced too close to the sun, and was being overwhelmed by the endless stream of matter it was now sucking in, making it impossible for the graviton-explosion to shut it down when the fleet was ready to emerge from the lapsed-space gateway. The singularity was sending out a super-heated stream of plasma and radiation-particles at near the speed of light that were proceeding to pierce the heart of the Red Dwarf, infusing it with material that was already part-way through the conversion process, collapsing the gravity of the star rather than letting it bloat and spread as was its normal wont.

The surface activity of the dying sun was a raging mass of explosions, storms and coronal mass ejections of unprecedented scale, none of which could break-away in to deep space due to the exponentially increasing gravity of the terminally confused star.

Harper took a deep breath, she needed some time to think about Arlia's revelation, "ok, this is what we're going to do. You're going to shut down all viewers in my quarters, and I'm going to trust you to do that, and then we are going to get where we're going..."

"Ok Harp..."

"I'm not finished... then, I'm going to get very drunk and then... and only then... we are going to try having this conversation again. Ok?"

"Ok Harper."

Harper sighed deeply. This was a complication she hadn't foreseen: who would have?

Foresight is a terrible thing. I wouldn't wish it upon my worst enemy, and I have a few, and some of them are pretty bad... but not foresight. Never that. That's a curse that even the god-like Quontals of Genister couldn't shake. Their total control over matter and energy, their connection to the nine nearest dimensions, their ability to traverse lapsed-space, who would think it would be the end of them? That power, that... presence! But it came to naught long before the younger stars of our quadrant were even born. Time, it seemed, was more closely connected to their minds than space. And that you can never shake. In my interview with the spirit-bound imprint of Eron, the last of the Quontals to be able to manifest in our realms, I will be asking, 'was it all worth it?' And 'What do you foresee for us?' We may not want to know...

Sub-net teaser for the Miflam Queeb broadcast from the remains of Genister-space.

Arlia brought the ship's engines fully online, "Harper..."

"Yes Arlia."

"Something is coming through the portal."

"Ok, lets' take a look."

"Nothing should be able to get through, it should all be collapsing in to the..."

"Let's take a look shall we?" Harper insisted.

Harper turned to face the view-port and her eyes widened as her mouth opened in astonishment.

She wasn't sure what she was seeing but assumed it was what the fabled 'end of time' looked like.

The apocalypse had arrived and all that was missing were the four horsemen, though to give them their due, there would not have been much they could have added to the scene unfolding outside the ship, perhaps the odd kitchen sink, but pretty much everything else was already there.

The sun was folding in on itself in a cycling-ball of plasma, gathering in the outer atmosphere and re-igniting it in a star-birthing scale nuclear inferno as it poured it in on itself. The event-horizon was streaming off a perfectly formed tunnel of fiery plasma, billions of tons per second, being fed in to its insatiable core at exponentially increasing speeds as the spin of the singularity grew.

From the core of the Red Dwarf, there were two ejecting jets of ionised neutrino streams, radiating energy deep in to all parts of the known spectrum, shooting outwards into deep-space for what would become hundreds of light-years as they grew in strength.

The mouth of the even-horizon was dragging back all matter, and shutting down emissions, including light, so was forming in to the perfect black circular mass of the outer reaches of a black-hole.

Bubbling away at the centre of the event-horizon was a dimly glowing mass of particles, obliterated from within as they tried to escape, foaming back to their constituent atomic states as they were ripped apart by the gravity-well of the singularity.

Harper spoke under her breath, "zark… nothing can survive that…"

Arlia was performing some complex calculations: the 'something' that was surviving it was about to come through at phenomenal speed, and the only chance she had of catching it and preventing it from being drawn back to the sun was if the ship threw out its traction-net at precisely the right time before they emergency-jumped away from the hell that the sun was becoming.

"Arlia…" Harper whispered.

"Yes Harper?"

"We need to leave."

"Ok Harper."

A small escape-pod came through the portal, heading straight for Harper's ship, a missile ejected at such speed that it would simply cut through anything it encountered, atomising itself and its unfortunate contact as it did.

Arlia kicked the engines in and deployed the traction-net, using the sun's implosion to curve them away from the approaching escape-pod missile, even as the net swung back and held on to the pod's gravity field. The engines fired all neutrinos in one pulse, folding through the graviton field in an emergency jump. The calculations to make the jump, factoring in the imploding Red Dwarf, the emerging black-hole, the trajectory and speed of the escape-pod as well as the only two vectors that could be used to maneuver the ship away from destruction without the traction net ripping apart the hull, were beyond immense.

Arlia sighed gently as the ship blinked out of normal space and punched through lapsed-space, re-emerging in a void of inky-black calm.

Harper remained standing by the main view-port. What Arlia had just done was not lost on her. Bobbing along outside the ship, floating in the faintly glowing energy field of the traction-net, was the escape-pod.

"Arlia..."

"Yes Harper..."

"Nice moves."

"Thank you Harper."

"No, I mean it," Harper added, "maybe one in ten thousand ships could have pulled that off, maybe not even that..."

Arlia smiled, "thank you Harper."

Harper nodded towards the escape-pod, "can you put it in cargo bay nine, get some med-bots down there, contain the area? I think we'd better go see who's in there, they must have one hell of a story to tell!"

Arlia started to pull the escape-pod in, "scans show two life-forms, but there is a lot of interference..."

"Thank you Arlia," Harper said.

Arlia blushed slightly, "it's what I'm here to do, I think."

Harper smiled, "well, I'm glad you are."

10

Short

The Earth was having a bad day.

It had had them before, and would doubtless have them after this one.

Saying it was a 'bad day' for the Earth might be a bit misleading. The Earth has been around for a long time, and its ability to survive and thrive as a planet had been tried and tested many, many times: it had always come through and there was nothing to suggest that it wouldn't always come through in the future. Bad days didn't enter in to it in the long term: they were just different days over many millennia. But in the short term, and for those that didn't have millennia to average things out over, this was a bad day.

Three especially bad days as listed by the Gazetteer Choonupta in their supplement, 'Don't Worry, It's Been Worse', are: The moon of Oldor being mistaken for an angry, juvenile Mweeb by a passing Elder Mweeb. The moon was destroyed in an enthusiastic bout of 'setting the young scoundrel straight', resulting in the loss of two oceans and a tilt in the orbit of Oldor that led to the extinction of 98% of all life. The Trant Corporation stock-loss of the Great Folding, when over 90% was wiped from the value of the company by a junior Futures Buyer contacting a dimension-folding entity in an attempt to short stocks after a proposed merger with the Branniglore publishing empire was leaked. The pulverisation of the Beta Pictoris asteroid belt, which left the star with an extra hundred million years' work to do to get planets forming. The asteroid belt was reduced to dust and rubble by the opening of a lapsed-space portal by a pirate-fleet from Urgular. The fleet was tracked down and ultimately destroyed by the owners of the Beta Pictoris system, Tatrant Investments & Planet Construction. The pirate fleet's destruction is not listed as a bad day as it is generally agreed they had it coming.

Fildling Yanx, Gazetteer Choonupta spokesman and AI, left to 'lock the doors and switch the lights out' after the collapse of the Gazetteer.

Sure, the Earth might get bruised and battered by other planetoids and asteroids bashing in to it occasionally, it might get remodeled drastically in the process, but it was big and gnarly enough to take care of itself. It also had a longer term view than the things living on it, most of which had teeny-tiny life-spans in comparison, negligible when measured against the billions of years of the Earth's existence, both past and future.

But when, as the Earth had, you'd invested a couple of billion years in developing life and then catered further for its development and growth, nurtured it if you will, to have ninety-eight percent of that life wiped out in only a few days, a mere nano-blink of an eye in the Earth's time-scale, could still be considered bad. And of course, if you were part of the life that made up part of the ninety-eight percent that was having an extinction event, you could easily be said to be using understatement to describe the day as being merely 'bad'.

There were six other extinction events before this one had come and gone, and the Earth had got on with it, plodded on, working with what was left, as it always did, as it always would. The only one the Earth could be said to have truly minded was the Permian-Triassic event: that one had wiped out the Trilobites, and the Earth really liked the Trilobites. A lot. They were great. What's not to like about Trilobites!? The Pre-Cambrian had just been evolution, calling it an 'event' was typical of the arrogance of Man, assuming the rise in oxygen was an event rather than just a development, as Man was the major end beneficiary of the oxygen levels rising, you'd think they'd be more philosophical about it.

But Man was a weird one, and the Earth was not at all surprised to find that the most recent event was in fact caused directly by Man and that Man was one of the main casualties.

Good riddance.

Man was a royal pain in the ass, and everyone knew Man was a ticking time-bomb. Their basic nature was destructive, they couldn't help themselves, only a matter of time before they got round to wiping themselves out.

The frogs were the last clue in a long line of heavy hints for Man, and they had ploughed on regardless: any species that stupid couldn't escape the throttling grasp of evolution, and of course it was a shame that Man was taking ninety-seven percent of all other species with him, but what the hell, things would soon settle down again.

Now, thought the Earth, things can get back to a semblance of normality, maybe even do something about those Trilobites! No, that was wishful thinking, have to accept the fact that they were gone, let them go, nothing to be done now but work with what was left, best get on with it, these species won't propagate themselves... well, they will, but that's not the point, they need some help and the Earth was all about being supportive in that department.

But there was nothing the Earth could do for Man.

The chamber that Penny had taken Miles to was an escape-pod, reserved for the top-brass at Well-Com. Penny wasn't supposed to have clearance to access the pods, but she was a resourceful girl and had easily charmed the codes (and an access pass) from a senior Well-Com official on her second day on the job: she knew the top Executives would have to have an exit-strategy and the equipment to make it happen, all she had to do was find who had the best access, the rest was just what she did.

The escape-pod was based on the rail-gun principle and had easily accelerated to its top speed of 500kph without disturbing its occupants.

It would have taken much more than near-instant acceleration to disturb Miles. The pod had a shielded and buffered interior, so the acceleration was masked: Penny detected it, but she was built differently to Miles, a different species in fact. Miles didn't notice that either. It's fair to say that short of a heart attack, Miles' attention would remain firmly elsewhere. And that 'elsewhere' was Penny's naked body.

Penny's guesstimate of them having ten minutes was based on her calculations for getting the escape-pod clear of the nuke's immediate blast radius and coupled to its launcher, from there to low orbit would take another two to three minutes, depending on the congestion in the sky and the route tracked by the on-board computer.

As the escape-pod docked with its launcher, the GreenFire nuke was detonated.

60Mt, total obliteration for everything within 50km of the blast site.

The pod launched on the crest of the shock-wave.

Miles was lying next to Penny, cradled in her arms, completely exhausted. Penny held him close, quietly smiling to herself. Miles enjoyed the warmth and softness of Penny's body, being content to simply lie there and wait for the end he knew would inevitably engulf them. Penny was happy to let Miles have his moment before she broke the news to him that they were not, in fact, going to die horribly with the rest of mankind in the next few days, but were taking their chances in a last-ditch gamble of insanely long odds. That's not the sort of thing that usually comes up in pillow talk post-coitus. Or at least it didn't for Miles.

Miles rolled on to his back, one hand behind his head, one hand on his chest, feeling his heart, "wow. That... that was amazing."

Penny lay on her side facing Miles, propping herself up on an elbow, "thanks, you were pretty good yourself."

"Pretty good?" Miles laughed.

"Very good," Penny corrected.

"My second girlfriend, intolerant of bad bedroom etiquette, nice woman all-round, ah, I was so in love," Miles mused.

Penny watched Miles, waiting for her moment to tell him what was going on.

Miles sighed, "Earth should be pretty much a done deal by now, maybe two or three days from now it'll all be history, not that there will be anyone to record it."

History needs recording, but once recorded does not need to be left to truth. History is not like that, it's not about the truth but about what the future needs from the past. Grappling with that basic tenet of the Universe will drive you fucking nuts.

Noron Mardun, Philosopher-in-residence, Hunters Guide to Sector Skipping.

Miles turned to lie on his side, facing Penny, "one thing though... how are we not engulfed in a fiery death? I'm not complaining, just wondering..."

Miles' hand stroked along Penny's shoulder and arm, tracing its way to her hip.

There was something about Penny that Miles couldn't take his eyes off. Was it her eyes? They were magnificent, deep, sparkling, mysterious yet still somehow inviting… might be that.

And her body! There was nothing about her body that wasn't perfect, wasn't just where it was supposed to be, in the right proportion and the right quantity, not that those terms could be applied, you couldn't be that cold and calculating with something this beautiful, it demanded more than quantifying. Miles was getting distracted.

Penny felt now was as good a time as any to break the news to Miles, "we're not out of the woods yet, far from it in fact," she said.

Miles continued to gently stroke along Penny's side, "well I've had the good news, so the bad news seems long overdue," he said, not being able to take his eyes from Penny's body.

"We're in an escape-pod Miles…"

"I figured that bit out for myself Penny."

"… so we're not in danger from the virus…"

Miles smiled, letting his hand slip towards the inside of Penny's thigh, "unless this pod can sustain us for forty years or so, and I wouldn't be complaining if it could, and we could survive on the wasteland that was left of the earth when it did, we're in danger from the virus."

"We're not on the wasteland of the Earth Miles."

"Can we talk about this in a minute or twenty?" Miles asked as he leaned in to kiss Penny.

Penny's hand reached behind Miles' head as she leaned in to kiss him and pushed a sequence of buttons on a small panel behind him.

As they kissed, a small viewing port opened behind Penny, no bigger than a dinner plate, showing the earth in the distance, set against the blackness of space.

Miles was otherwise engaged.

They kissed for a long time, passionately, as if they both knew that when the kiss ended something else would begin, something far less pleasant, something that would change who they are, as well as who they were to each other.

Penny leaned back slightly, Miles opened his eyes and looked passed her.

"Nice view, what else is on…?"

"It's real Miles. We're in near-earth orbit."

Miles sat up.

Penny sat-up behind him, pulling the silver blanket round them both as Miles stared out the view-port.

Miles nodded to himself, as if processing what he secretly already knew, then he frowned slightly, realising he now knew nothing, "we're in space?"

"Near-earth orbit, but yes, 'space'."

"This seems like a vastly untenable position for us to be in..."

"It's a long-shot, but one I thought we had to take. We're alive..."

"Indeed we are... indeed we are... definitely alive..."

Penny pointed through the view-port, "see those tiny silver slivers... on the horizon?"

Miles looked and nodded.

"They're other escape-pods, I'd guess there are about three hundred up here."

"Well, that's certainly an eye-opener."

"Every Well-Com facility had a few of course, and then there were the ones in Government buildings, a few in other mega-corporations, couple in the Vatican."

Miles sighed a heavy sigh, "look Penny, I am, as I'm sure you know, a fantastically simple guy... so... just tell me... what the fuck is going on."

Penny held on to Miles, reassuringly close, talking quietly to him as they both carried on looking out the view-port, "all the big-players knew it was only a matter of time before someone triggered the big one. Escape-pods have been being built for a couple of decades now, new ones super-cede old ones, tech changes, but the idea is essentially the same, have a way out when mankind finally fucks up beyond reasonable recovery."

Miles took a few deep breathes, it took him about thirty seconds to process this, "ok. So, now what?"

Penny was shocked at how quickly Miles seemed ok with things. She could feel his heartbeat, read his bio-signals: he really did seem to be ok with things.

Adjustment periods vary. It's not just the magnitude of change but the mind-set of those experiencing it. The Kisslingering of Karl, a pacifist people that focus on nurturing their planet, experiencing themselves as an energy-wave within its sphere and collecting pretty shells from sugary beaches, adjusted to the invasion by the Karl and the destruction of large portions of their planet, with remarkable speed. The Kisslingering became a merciless race of killers, wiping out the Karl in a little over two of their sun-cycles, expanding out in to their solar system to strike the Karl's home-planet in return, wiping it from existence using portals and big bombs. Within two more of their sun-cycles they were back on their beaches, contemplating their quieter nature, though many said their meditations took on a certain smugness after their warring excursion that were lacking before. The Indinglians of Potus IX however, are still reeling at the loss of their Ice-Wind Chasers to the upstarts from Vicrum, who, they say, should never have been allowed to take part in the league in the first place on account of their planet not having any 'natural ice'. The malaise that struck Potus IX caused an economic collapse of epic proportions. Sport, as has been observed before, can make even the most advanced beings lose perspective.

Yiffling Vroon, Sub-Editor, Malaxian Archives.

She decided to go with the flow, "now we wait for pick-up or we die. There are three space-stations in near-earth orbit, each has a protocol and will select from the escape-pods which ones they pick up. The pods are supposed to be single occupancy, so that'll either work spectacularly against us or for us, depending on which station tracks us: if it's the Chinese we're toast, sticklers for protocol, the Russians, not so much, the US, well, they're controlled by the beacons so no choice."

"So we just wait?"

"Pretty much yeah. There is a deep-sleep facility, I can jury-rig it to accept two life-signs, we go in to a light coma and dream happy dreams."

"And then either wake up or not?"

"That's about the size of it, yeah."

Miles smiled broadly to himself, "so we have some time before we need to drift off I'd say..."

Penny laughed softly, pulling Miles closer to her, "you are incorrigible!"

"All part of my charm I'm told..."

Penny lay down with Miles next to her, looking him in the eye. Miles stared back, lost in Penny's sparkling eyes, his thoughts turning to things he felt he had no control over, ridiculous things like how much he loved this woman, like how he could think of nothing else but a passionate embrace and frantic love-making with her, as if that now defined him.

Penny spoke softly, keeping Miles in a semi-sedate state, "Miles… how come you're ok with all this? Is there something about you I don't know?"

Miles only had half his mind on answering Penny, the other half was deeply engaged in thinking about ways he could make her happy and keep her happy for the rest of his life, the third half was focusing on how soon he could fuck her brains out, "I don't think about things much, I'm not a worrier, go with what there is and make the most of it. That bothers a lot of people, but it's just who I am. It's how I can work for a corrupt, sick, and apparently apocalyptic company like Well-Com and sleep nights… I don't over-think it…"

"You are a rare and precious thing Miles."

"Not really, just alive and living."

"You know I said I am a phenotype-polymorph, not like you?"

"I vaguely remember you mentioning something…"

"Well, that means I can sustain us both for longer than the normal life-support would allow, but I'll have to undergo some drastic changes if I do…"

Miles was lost in Penny. He gently stroked her hair, ran his hands along the side of her neck, over her shoulders, tracing the perfect outline of her body.

Penny dropped her voice slightly, modulating it to hypnotise Miles, "when we… eventually… go in to deep-sleep, I may undergo some changes… if we wake, you may not recognise me, but I'll still be 'me'…"

Miles smiled a contented smile, knowing that Penny was somehow affecting him beyond his ability to control, knowing that the feelings coming from him were not all his, that some were triggered, implanted somehow, that some were enhanced by whatever the hell it was she was doing.

He didn't care.

Not because what she was doing made him not care.

He just didn't think about it that much.

Thinking too much is dangerous. Thinking too little is dangerous. Not thinking at all is of course ideal, but few are lucky enough to be able to do that without dying horribly at some point during their day. Zindorans believe the right amount of thinking is enough to avoid complications from not thinking, but not enough to allow thoughts to get out of control and runaway with their actions. The Zindoran day is spent mostly sleeping, but when they do manage to get themselves together long enough to think, and then act upon those thoughts, they are staggeringly effective at not getting themselves, or those around them, annoyed or killed. The fine balance between conscious thought and subconscious thought, instinct even, is something they are well-equipped to strike, being as they are a largely isolationist species, with no drive to meet anyone else in the galaxy. The favourite quip of Zindorans is, 'think about it... could be worse...'

Sifling Vroon, guerrilla-editor, Malaxian Archives. (Reward for capture still outstanding.)

11

Old News

Getting himself off Ire, the planet where the City of Jaldur was situated, was a relatively easy thing to accomplish for Jesus: the mega-freighters and transports that ran from the mines on the Ire Moons to the near-by spiral Casion System were frequent and always in need of temporary crew.

Leaving the Blue Angel was a bit of a wrench, but once the messiah's mind was made up, it all fell together. Even so, it was going to be tough to find a planet, city and bar as accommodating as Ire, Jaldur and the Blue Angel. They seemed to have things in a nice balance.

The fact that Jesus felt that, was also probably the clearest sign that he needed to leave. Everyone at the Blue Angel had grown to like Jesus, his familiar face and relaxed attitude were always welcome in the drinking quarters of the bar. He was a quiet soul that could, when the mood struck him or the need arose, spin a good yarn.

The messiah had a good send-off, more than a few of the regulars took more than a few days in intensive care to recover from the epic bon-voyage party, which subsequently went in to Blue Angel folk-lore as 'one hell of a good bash'.

The ore carrying mega-freighters never touched down on Ire, they were far too huge and cumbersome for in-atmo flight. The freighters stayed in near-orbit around the moons and shuttles carried people from the planet's surface to the vast bulks of the freighters. Shuttles were free and frequent, provided you worked for the mining companies.

The ore mined on Kaldon, the biggest moon of Ire, was mimetic-plasma crystal and was worth a fortune. The Kaldon Mining & Shipping Conglomerate is one of the most powerful corporations in the galaxy, and they knew that free transport for potential workers was a small price to pay for encouraging people to come and commit suicide by working on Kaldon.

The pay is astronomical and the fatality rate among workers unsurpassed in any mining operation anywhere. This is in part due to KMSC taking a relaxed attitude to health and safety, and partly due to the ore working the way it does: unprotected contact with it in any of its nine constituent forms, instantly turns you in to a steaming pile of plasma goo. But handled, stored and transported correctly, the ore is simply the most flexible building material in existence.

The trend towards nano-material comes from mainly technologically advanced societies. The use of mimetic-ore, which is naturally occurring and can be tuned to frequencies unique to those who would mold it, is limited to a few visionary cultures, such as the Weetnor. Energy sources for the inducement of the ore to grow can be varied, but must be controlled by an overwhelming force with the same frequency inherent in the ore. Without this controlling force, a similar problem as with nano-material can occur: the dreaded 'grey-goo'. The Weetnor have a collective hive-mind, with a ruling monarch, usually a Queen, that has access to the planet's neural-boosters. Architects of Weetnor have designs approved by the Queen, but they must also be sanctioned by the whole population, or the vast majority, otherwise the energy to create the structures will be inconsistent, which could lead to breakdown and the march of the grey-goo.

Commentary on import of ore, advisory meeting, filed by Zilt Vroon, Editor-in-Chief of Materials Monthly in Sector Arr.

Jesus had a way of getting what he wanted and simply walked aboard a transport ship with a casual wave and a smile.

This was probably one of the few things that the Imp hated about the messiah. The Imp was programmed to dislike Jesus, but he constantly struggled with it. Jesus was a nice guy. And in all honesty, the Imp didn't care enough about Jesus to hate him. Sure they were cast on opposite sides of the fence, in adversarial roles, the eternal hero and villain, but in reality it was far more complex than that and they both knew it. But the fact that Jesus could just 'do stuff' got right up the Imp's nose.

Jesus, for his part, never questioned how he did it, he did what he needed and never doubted that it would work out. That all-conquering faith and self-belief was what he did, who he was, it just came naturally to him in the same way as breathing came naturally to some other life-forms.

The Imp had often wondered about this. It was his job to make the messiah doubt himself, nothing more elaborate than that. It took him a long, long time to see that Jesus thought the Imp's job was something else. The Imp didn't know why Jesus believed that, just that he did. All that 'temptation of man': where the hell had that come from?! Certainly not from the Imp. All he ever did was mildly annoy Jesus and try to goad him in to asking the difficult questions. Admittedly he'd been at it for a long time and hadn't gotten anywhere, but that didn't mean he didn't enjoy his work and wasn't going to keep trying. Nobody the Imp had ever met had ever needed any work from him to be 'tempted' in to doing things, bad, evil or indifferent. People seemed set on doing stupid things, all the time. And when it turned out to be bad, evil, of through its indifference a gateway to bad or evil consequences, he always seemed to get the blame. Fine with him, made his life easier, especially with Jesus, so he went with the flow.

But deep down, this had caused him some internal conflict. I mean, if he wasn't responsible, then what was he doing with his life? If he wasn't causing bad stuff, stuff that made the messiah question himself, then what, actually, was he doing?

These little debates never lasted long and he ended up forgetting them after a couple of solid days of taunting Jesus. But sometimes he wondered…

Seeing the Great Plague sweep across the planet of Xinx, striking down all that could share their waters, I was reminded of the catastrophe on Mingulus, where self-doubt wiped out one in three of their population. A paralysis accompanied both epidemics, and when your life depends on being able to out-maneuver your pursuer as it does on Mingulus, the results are as deadly as any water-borne poison. Recovery was a slow process for both planets, but at least on Xing there was no lingering fear that the disease would return: those that survived the Great Plague were naturally immune. The same could not be said of the people of Mingulus, or perhaps it could and they were just afraid to say it…

Chrad Jocksa, 'Aid Without Asking' physician.

When Jesus left Ire, the Imp decided to stay on. There was a lot the Imp was beginning to understand about sex and how it affected people, and it fascinated him. All the theory in the world couldn't replace two weeks of solid experience as a sex-worker. It might even offer him a new angle to come at the messiah with, Jesus was a man after all, and most men seemed to be devastatingly simple in the 'sex' department.

The messiah and the Imp had agreed to meet in sixty or seventy years' time, with the exact location to be decided nearer the day, but they both felt a nice cosy bar somewhere would be fine.

Once he was on the transport ship, Jesus settled in doing what he did best: he joined the ship's entertainment company and told stories.

The transport ship being the size it was, which was about the size of Swindon, had many places for the crew to go once they had finished their shifts processing, shaping and treating the ore. The feel was of a lively town (which is where any similarity with Swindon ended), with many districts, where you could always find the entertainment you wanted at the end of a hard day's graft. There were many people who wanted a quiet place to sit and recover, maybe eat a bit, drink and refresh, chill out. And the entertainment company placed story-tellers or counselors here, helping keep the tone calm, raising spirits where they could and offering what consolation they could for those inevitably lost during the working day to the people that might have known them. The only places on the ore transport ships busier than the bars were the places of remembrance and reclamation.

Jesus was a popular act. He seemed to tap-in to what people were feeling, how they were wishing their lives could be different, he shaped his stories to suit his audience. Of course, if he could, he'd get the message in about tolerance, love, helping those less fortunate than you, but when it needed it, he stepped it up a gear and threw in heroic tales of daring-do laced with humour, sex, violence and the inevitable victory of the 'little guy'. The workers lapped it up.

Once the transport hit the Tau Ceti system, or as it was popularly known locally, the 'Boros Cluster', Jesus jumped ship. He'd been given the nod by one of the entertainment officers on the ship that a survey ship, 'the HabScan', was going in the direction he wanted, and would welcome someone with his skills on board.

The Boros Cluster is home to the Bonost. They are a highly technologically advanced people that have colonised over a thousand worlds in the Cluster. They are currently in negotiation with the Galactic Council for part-membership that will allow them to trade, but not be reliant on the Council for military protection or contribution. Their system is still listed as the 'Tau Ceti' on all Council star-maps, which is a source of annoyance to the Bonost and leverage with the Council. The Bonost have mastered nova-bomb technology, so there are many on the Council that seek to appease the Bonost in any way they can. So far, the Bonost have shown no inclination to move out of the Boros Cluster. If that changes it will be an interesting day for all of us.

Waldoon Boodle, Archeologist with Fanson Corp.

Things continued to fall together for the messiah as they usually did.

The HabScan was going out looking for potential sites for lapsed-space portals that could be set up to chain-jump along a set route: the HabScan was on a two-hundred year, generational mission. This meant surveying huge areas of space and checking systems for developing life, none of which could be at the stage where it might interfere with the portals, and, ideally, none of which would be in any advanced enough state to even detect them. These criteria were pretty easily met as the universe is so huge: all peoples, species and 'stuff' is usually simply mind-bogglingly far away from each other.

The HabScan, from Alboros IX, crewed by the Alborians, was heading roughly towards the spiral-arm of the galaxy in the proximity of the Earth, and Jesus could drift the rest of the way once he was close enough. Besides, a bit more company, a bit more experience, seeing a bit more of the galaxy, that could only be good for him, add to his perspective and knowledge, give him more of an edge when he finally made it back to Earth.

The Alborians were an aquatic species, though many of their workers required oxygen, or some gas, to breathe, so their survey ship was multi-layered and equipped to deal with any eventuality.

Jesus liked the HabScan, it had an air of excitement about it.

An air of discovery and genuine interest in what was out there. Long range probes were sent out, support-ships cruised the space-lanes checking on findings, landing parties were sent to planets and moons to verify data and get more detailed readings, it all felt very scientific yet somehow still cavalier.

One night, as they were approaching the Vascret Rim, Jesus found himself in conversation with one of the HabScan's Threat Assessment Technicians. The TACs filtered all data and reports and made recommendations to the construction (and destruction) crews and their Directors. The messiah had overheard Sam, the TAC, talking about how they knew there was 'something going on in System 282' and weren't particularly worried about it but were going to check it out anyway. Jesus knew that System 282 contained the Earth and was curious to see what Sam knew about it.

Sam was in his mobile tank, swimming through the blue, syrupy liquid he preferred in the evenings, his food hung suspended in glowing red force-parcels before him and he lazily ate while he enjoyed the glow from the tank's UV light.

Jesus sat next to Sam's tank and waved, "hi Sam, you mind if I sit and talk a while?"

Sam smiled, "no, sure, pull up a whatever and bark a while."

The translator made Sam's voice sound slightly metallic, but still gave it a low, melodic quality that gas-breathing beings found soothing to their ears.

To Sam, and all his aquatic Alborian brethren, all that came out of the mouths of gas-breathing beings sounded like the barking of annoyed little dogs. But the Alborians, being a gentle and pragmatic people, tolerated the air-breathers voices by having them come out of their translators inside the tanks as a series of pleasant burbles and bubbles.

One feature of Alborian translation that many struggle to get to grips with is their etiquette. If they detect an incoming word or phrase they think they will take offence at, or that will challenge them in some way they are not prepared for, they replace the words with meaningless gaseous sounds.

In any given conversation, where you think you are having a full and frank discussion with an Alborian, there is a better than good chance that most of your discourse is lost as bubble-farts.

Alborians that are in sensitive situations, such as embassies, or on the Galactic Council Advisory Boards, spend many hours training themselves to keep a straight face. When the Alborians entered in to delicate negotiations with the Spanolians, a telepathic race from the Gronista Quadrant, it soon became apparent that the Spanolians did the same thing, and the talks collapsed. The fact that neither the Alborians or the Spanolians could see the funny side of the collapse, has not escaped the attention of the rest of the galaxy.

Barfax Quile, linguist from Queldor, reporting on the Postracine Network on the impending Alborian / Spanolian border-dispute.

Sam settled near the tank's edge, facing Jesus, he had heard some of the messiah's tales and could see what the others liked about him, "what's on your mind story-teller?"

"I was wondering what you'd heard about System 282, I'm from around there and was heading that way, wondered what I could expect."

Sam lazily curled his many appendages round his tubular body, letting his tail grasp the last of the food-cubes and slip in gently in to his rear mouth, "we just got the preliminary reports back, something about an 'event' happening on one of the outer system planets, some kind of extinction event, maybe even of a level-four sentience… small amount of near-orbit activity, nothing further out… seems harmless enough… we won't be going in for a look, it all seems cut and dried…"

Jesus frowned, then, more to himself than to Sam, "have I been gone that long…?"

Sam waited patiently for Jesus to come out of his moment of introspection, he was a polite Alborian and never interrupted an internal train of thought.

"Sorry Sam, I fear there may be some blame headed my way for whatever has gone on there, and most of it would seem to be deserved."

Sam smiled gently, then stretched slowly, preparing to move his tank in to hibernation for the night, "I wouldn't worry if I were you weaver of tales, you're nobody's keeper, none of us are, much as the Directors would like to think otherwise… I'm sure there was nothing could be done, even if you'd have been there. And it's done now."

Jesus nodded to himself.

Sam slid off, moving his tank to its hibernation vent, slotting in to the liquid exchange filters to move to his morning fluids.

Jesus muttered, “I've got a bad feeling about this.”

The next day Jesus hooked up with a couple of rich-kids that had buzzed the HabScan in their Versatran Series X star-buggy, they had miscalculated their last jump and ran out of fuel: paying for fuel wasn't the problem, physically getting hold of it was. The Directors of the HabScan checked their credit, fleeced them and filled their tanks. Jesus had flagged a lift back to the Earth as the HabScan wasn't going close enough for comfort and the messiah wanted to speed up his return.

The rich-kids, both from Lumin near Alpha Centauri, had buzzed the Earth before, and had planned to swing by and liven things up with a few obscure appearances for the monkey-men, before they moved on to the Lumin core-worlds, where they were due at an on-going party their parents were holding in honour of their graduation to the Board of the governing company, Trans-Lumin. Terminally boring parties were part of the price the uber-rich paid on Lumin: networking was the number one cause of suicides among young Board execs.

They had no problem taking Jesus along for the ride to Earth.

Until they got to the Earth. The star-buggy's scanners soon told the sorry tale of what was left of the Earth and there was no way they were going to waste fuel on getting into the atmo to simply view some devastation. There were parties to go to. And if they weren't much more interesting than the nuclear-winter wasteland that was now below them, at least they had alcohol, music and people you could dance with. It was pretty obvious that the party on Earth was over.

They skimmed the space-stations in near-orbit unseen and dropped Jesus off in the area he remembered best.

All spaceships since the early Trundal IXs have been fitted with muon-masking tech as standard. The more advanced ships, those utilising the phase-shifting Plasma Conduit Drives have the ability to pass straight through a planet.

Every model in-between has some form of shielding from detection. It's a standard-fit now, not even a mod.

Why these insignificant little planets think they should be able to detect interstellar craft is beyond me.

What kind of single-cell-brained trumpet muffle thinks that someone with the tech to travel faster than the speed of light, or better still, through the dimension portals of lapsed-space, will be visible to them on their tiny, backwards little worlds? Those that flout the Council Guidelines and do reveal themselves are as dumb as those they show themselves to. No good has ever come of a technologically advanced civ teasing a dumber one, and less good immediately transpires if the Council catches your sorry-ass. Remember kids, don't be an Antrix Chewers chute, don't buzz low-tech worlds!

Inglor Wagnarian, broadcasting to the Spiral Rim, sponsored by Uizi Shield Generators.

The messiah stood in a wasteland of death and destruction, surveying the silent ashen scene with tears in his eyes.

He simply couldn't believe it.

As they had flown in, Jesus had seen the same scenes repeated all over the planet he had once called home. Dead bodies everywhere, most in terrible states of diseased decay, broken and twisted, all having died in some horrible way that was escaping the messiah's mind.

Jesus sighed heavily and sat down on a large rocky outcrop overlooking what had been one of his favourite cities.

There were no birds, no animals, a few insects and definitely no people.

What the hell had happened here!?

Jesus had heard a saying while on his travels, used to sum up someone who was bereft of patience, ideas or a willingness to keep it calm, to keep it together. He remembered it as it had made him laugh the first time he had heard it, but now he saw how aptly it could apply.

Jesus was about to lose his shit.

The messiah stood and screamed wordlessly at the top of his voice, his lungs bursting with the anger he was throwing out in to the world. He sent his senses out, looking for some hope, looking for something to rein in his anger, to somehow make something ok in this desolation of death and despair.

There was nothing.

After a long time of shouting, raging, kicking at things, throwing things about and generally wearing himself out, he sat down breathless.

What the hell had happened!?

Jesus sensed there was still life on earth, buried deep in the ground and in the dark depths of the seas, there were things moving, getting on with their lives. But there were no people. Not a single person was left alive on Earth.

The Imp appeared out of nowhere, tumbling head over heels as he was dragged in to being back on Earth by the raging messiah. He jumped up, whirled round, flailing about with his arms, fending off an imagined attack, trying to get his bearings on where he was, "what the f…"

Jesus leveled an accusing finger at him and shouted, "what did you do!?"

The Imp, still in the form of a devastatingly beautiful sex-worker from the Blue Angel, took a few seconds to get himself together.

Jesus stalked up to the Imp and grabbed him by the thin threads of his revealing gossamer gown, pulling him in close, their faces nearly touching, "what did you do you evil little shit?"

The Imp held the messiah's gaze. Until he knew what was going on, saying nothing was the best defense.

Jesus pushed the Imp away and slumped back, sitting on the rocks.

The Imp adjusted his flimsy clothes, trying to get himself in a position to understand what was what. He closed his eyes and reached out for the confused thoughts of Man.

Nothing.

He frowned and tried again.

Again, nothing.

Jesus sat with his head in his hands, his shoulders hunched. He quietly started to cry.

"Well," said the Imp, "they did it again."

Jesus' tired eyes shed their tears, "what did you do?"

The Imp sat down next to the messiah. He slowly he changed his form back to a tiny demonic Imp, complete with tail and fiery yellow eyes. He fidgeted a bit, getting used to the shape, "I didn't do anything. I didn't need to. This was all them."

They sat in silence for a while, Jesus wracked with sorrow and the Imp running things through in his head, trying to bring some sense to the world around him.

Jesus composed himself, wiped the back of his hand across his nose and mouth, "is it my fault? Did I do this? Could I have stopped it if I had made them listen?"

"Do you really believe, I mean *really* believe, that you could have done any more than you did? Because if you do, then yeah, this is all your fault."

Jesus breathed deeply, trying to get himself in some fit state to think clearly, "why didn't they listen?"

The Imp shrugged, "why doesn't anybody?"

Many studies have been conducted, many theories researched. There are many opinions, thoughts, reasoned out arguments. But, for all that, the question remains unanswered. Why don't people listen? The answer favoured by most, including the Trumpudan people of Gh'ast, who have no ears and cannot perceive what 'hearing' is, is that people don't listen when they think what they are hearing it won't be to their benefit. The Trumpudan communicate through gestures and smells, relying on their three noses and humungous eye to pick up all the signals they need in any communication exchange. It is a little known fact that they can 'see' in seven spectrums, which may account for them sometimes blocking their noses when 'listening' to a particularly obnoxious piece of advice. It is only a fool, and not a happy one, that would expect someone to listen to something they have to say if they cannot immediately point out to their potential listener what the benefits of them listening are. But that still leaves the credibility gap. Why would someone believe the truth of you telling them they would benefit from listening to you? And so we begin again.

Miles Wropton, psychologist on the panel of 'What's That?', the most popular game show on Galaxan Four.

Jesus frowned, "but all of them? What happened? Some disease? Some catastrophic war?"

"Does it matter?" the Imp said gently?

Confusion played plain on Jesus' face, "does it matter? Of course it matters!"

"Why?"

"I need to know."

"So it matters for you, to clear your conscience… or something like that?"

"No… I need to know…"

"Why?"

Jesus floundered.

"Just shut up," suggested the messiah.

The Imp shrugged and shut up.

Jesus looked around, not knowing anything about anything. He looked at the Imp. The Imp offered a weak smile.

"Just shut up," Jesus said testily.

"You want to walk in to the city, check things over?" asked the Imp.

"What's the point," Jesus said weakly.

The Imp nodded his understanding. There did indeed seem little point on being on Earth now.

"So..." offered the Imp, "what are you thinking? Wait around here for a couple of million years, see what develops?"

Jesus gave the Imp a cold, hard look that told the Imp he was skating on thin ice.

"Or... or...," the Imp continued, "we could get back out there, see if you can maybe prevent this happening somewhere else?"

Jesus immediately became suspicious of the Imp, "and why, of all the people I could ever listen to, why should I listen to you? What did you do!?"

The Imp stood and faced Jesus, "you don't get it do you? After all this time you still don't get it! It amazes me you don't kill yourself in some tragic domestic accident trying to heat water!"

"Now wait a minute," Jesus started to protest.

"I'm not here to make people do anything, I don't make people do anything, I couldn't give a flying fish of a fuck what people do! I'm not here for them, I'm here for you!"

The Imp gestured around him, raising his arms in sweeping arcs, "all this, all this death, all this ruination, it's them. It's THEM!! I don't 'do' anything, I don't have to!"

"Alright, alright, calm down..." Jesus tried to interrupt.

"No! No I will not! Not until you listen! They do this to themselves, over and over again, it never changes, it's all they are capable of, all they are, it's what they are made to do, they never fail, every-fucking-time! They annihilate each other. Every fucking time!"

Jesus opened his mouth to speak, "..." was as far as he got.

"And you!" accused the Imp, pointing a clawed-hand at Jesus, "You know this! You feel it, it's what made you leave in the first-place. You sense it in them. You know the charade, the games we play, and you know that every time… every time… they do this. This is their fate, this is what they do, and the amount of times it's happened, it seems this is all they do, what it all builds to, what everything they do works towards. They just live to wipe themselves out!"

The Imp sat down, breathing heavily, staring at Jesus.

Jesus was shaking with anger, he was about to summon the energy needed to strike the Imp from the face of the Earth when he felt something. Something faint but definitely something there. He cocked his head, as if listening intently, "you feel that?" he said to the Imp.

"Yeah, faint, but definitely people."

Jesus let his gaze drift upwards to where he felt the presence of humans. He smiled to himself then leveled his best penetrating stare at the Imp, "you! You are coming with me."

"Of for fu…" was all the Imp managed before he was whisked off skywards to investigate the people that had survived the global apocalypse.

12

In The Bottle

Harper slowly sauntered down to cargo bay nine. She wanted some time to think, sauntering felt like the thing to do.

She knew the ship like the back of her hand, or at least she thought she did. Nobody knows what the back of their hand looks like until they look at it, when they will, of course, know exactly what it looks like. But she knew it pretty well, she had been over every inch of it in. She had forgotten how big the ship was.

You could easily get lost in the ship if the power was out and the mapping-lighting wasn't on. But if the power was out, getting lost would be the least of your problems. The ship, like ninety-nine percent of all technology more complicated than the wheel or the bellows, was completely reliant on energy, power, from some source or another. The galaxy would come to a grinding-halt if power sources dried up. Fortunately great strides have been made in extracting usable power from things, well beyond nuclear fusion, most 'advanced' technologies relied on a mixture of quantum-fusion and graviton-capture to create energy. Harper's ship had a twin-drive utilising both methods, as well as an old fashioned 'fission back-up drive' for those times when only a barely controlled nuclear explosion would do.

There was no real danger of Harper getting lost in the ship, but she was glad she was following the quickest auto-route to cargo bay nine: there were a couple of times she could have sworn the way was different to that on the mapping. Her head was still a bit fuzzy from everything that had happened recently. Large portions of her brain were dedicated to mulling things over in her subconscious, making her more than a bit distracted.

Focus. She needed to focus.

She let her left hand trail along the wall of the ship as she ambled along, feeling the smooth surface of the synth-metal breathe beneath her fingers.

She had to periodically move her hand, pull it out the way of some protrusion or risk injury, it was a good way to stay in the here and now. Her subconscious wandered off to play on its own, leaving her conscious brain to focus.

There were ten cargo bays in all, and each could easily hold a full-sized cathedral or twenty crates of Hurloonian livestock, whatever was needed.

Harper smiled to herself as she remembered the fortune she'd made on the Hurloonian livestock: easy job, good money, with a follow-on job in the tail. Some people hated the Hurloonian beasts, but not Harper: she got the nose-plugs in, switched the audio monitors to 'silent' and got on with it. Feed them regular, administer their shocks on time and they were no trouble at all. It was only when you neglected them that they started to misbehave. And nobody needed that kind of trouble. When angered or hungry, the Hurloonian behemoths could throw their considerable bulk around with amazing speed and force, flattening anything their slime-covered, steel-hard, leathery-hide bodies came across. Harper had heard tales, mostly whispered tales told in disreputable bars, of ships having their guidance and stabilisation affected by greedy ship's captains who had crammed too many of these gargantuan beasts in to their ship. Mishandle the livestock and you got what you deserved, was Harper's considered opinion, which, it has to be said, she kept to herself when she was in any seedy, disreputable bars.

The seediest bar Harper had ever been in was one she could never remember. Not because the experience was so hideous she forgot it as a matter of self-preservation, but because all patrons were mind-wiped as they left. The accuracy of the mind-wipe was down to the specific neural-frequency engendered by being in the bar: one that could be tapped in to and backtracked to remove it from any sentient creature whose memories resided in their brain. The Fwix of Vildix were of course immune to this, having as they do, their memories stored in their outer polyp-tips.

But Harper was not a Fwix. The associated ghosts were still in her brain though. Whenever she saw or heard of a Fwix on her travels, an involuntary shiver would travel the length of her spine and her head would twitch slightly.

The bar, 'Fast Jacks Liquor Shack', on Geezle, was a favourite of many trading-ship captains who, by nature of the mind-wipe, could never talk business there, so it was the perfect place to relax. Because you had to.

And if you didn't, it would never matter, because you would never remember being fleeced and thrown out by the security droids.

It was unlikely that the need to put a full-sized cathedral in there would ever arise, but it was nice to know you could if you had to.

It's fair to say that Harper took the ship for granted. She was used to it, it was just a ship, a tool, and its size was a necessity of function: you transport cargo and the more space you have, the bigger the jobs you can do. There were numerous modifications to the ship of course, only a raw-green new license-holder took them as they came. The vast majority of mods to Harper's ship had been made before it came in to her possession, but she would have made them anyway, just saved on time and money that they were already done. She had added five hard-points and four new weapons systems, as well as upgrading the core-drive.

There were still a few things she wanted to do with the ship, but they were 'nice to haves' rather than essentials, the kind of things that if you had a proper think about it, you wouldn't put on anyway but always seem like a good idea. The ship was a reflection of her: a patchwork of bolt-ons to a basic chassis that enabled it to be flexible about what it did, with enough firepower to get it out of trouble when things went south. She never thought about it like that of course, nobody does, most people are all largely oblivious of how their personality is reflected in the things they own.

Usually ships like this carried with them a crew of between twenty and thirty, depending on how cramped they were prepared to be in bunking arrangements. The bots and droids replaced the standing crew, and without them the ship would soon fall in to disrepair and decay. The bots and droids hadn't come cheap, but they were worth every cred.

Harper felt that she needed a new job, something to bring in some money, something to get her moving again, something a bit shady, under the sensors, something that would challenge her.

She'd have to push Arlia in that direction. Or should she? Wasn't she supposed to be letting Arlia direct things?

Hhmm. Tricky. Did Arlia understand the need for 'work'? Was money a well grasped concept for her? Yet another conversation that needed to be had...

One of the main problems with getting motivated to do another job was that Harper was fantastically wealthy. A mixture of good business sense, hard work, daylight robbery, smuggling and luck at the gaming tables of Trax IV, meant that she had more creds than anyone could usefully spend in a long and luxurious lifetime. Still, some honest work would be nice. For a change. But what if Arlia thought of the fortune as hers too? It seemed highly unlikely that Arlia would be motivated by money, and having a shed-load of it meant this was doubly unlikely. Doubly unlikely? Was that a thing? Twice as unlikely?

Harper shook herself out of the distraction...

With the drop-elevators and the ride-on service bots, it was still a good ten minutes before Harper reached the inner doors to cargo bay nine.

She stopped for a second, struck by how zarking cool her ship was.

Maybe Arlia was right, maybe this ship should have a name? It was a good ship and did a good job, and though Harper felt no kinship with it, she certainly was grateful for it. Time for worrying about that later, right now she had to confront whatever was in cargo bay nine.

Peeking in through the small porthole window, she couldn't see anything apart from the empty crates and containers from an old smuggling job: she had been meaning to sell them on, recycle them, or something, but had never got round to it. She should revisit her plans to clear out the massive amount of crap that accumulates on an inter-stellar cargo ship, clutter just appeared, and then hung about.

Some of it was completely unrecognisable as anything, but it all fell under the 'may come in useful one day' umbrella, so Harper was loathed to throw it out. Clutter. Some stupid metaphor for her life no doubt. But now was not the time to indulge in such nonsense. But it had to be said, there was a hell of a lot of clutter!

Every race in the Universe understands the feeling that the Yontph call 'Regretful Recognition'. That feeling when you open a storage space and see things that you had not only forgotten about, but have no memory of acquiring. After some thought, usually not very much, the feeling settles on you, 'I probably should get rid of that, but I'd better not... just in case...' And so the things continue to accumulate. Heeneen, the sister-planet to Rotoph, the home-world of the Yontph, have passed a law that no Heeneenian may throw anything away. Not ever. At first this seems ridiculous. But then you realise the cunning nature of it. Every Heeneenian thinks long and hard before they acquire anything. For the most-part, the rest of us live haphazard lives filled with randomness that eventually reflects itself in our belongings. Trying to be a little more Heeneenian would do us all the world of good.

Zale LiPol, Klin archivist, recording retrieved from auto-cypher on Kliwin IV.

Filed: will get on it later... focus!

Harper admitted to herself that she was putting a lot of things off. Things had got more complicated than she had hoped, more quickly than she had hoped. As soon as she got a quiet day to herself, she needed to come up with some sort of plan, and she needed to do this with Arlia, which was part of the complication.

Focus...

She could see there was something big near the furthest outer door, and there were plenty of bots milling about it, waiting for it to open, but nothing as yet had happened.

Harper typed in her pass-code and entered, making her way across it to the outer-door, instinctively she felt her belt for her blaster. It wasn't there. Where had that gone? She diverted herself to a weapon's locker on the cargo bay wall, a small screen came on above it, showing Arlia's gently smiling face, "hello Harper, sensors show they are in no state to fight, they need urgent medical attention."

Harper opened the locker and took out a small blaster, flicking the power on and checking the function reading, all at one-hundred percent, "better safe than sorry."

"Shall I open the door to the escape-pod?" asked Arlia.

"Sure, let's go help some folk."

The escape-pod lay there silently.

Harper didn't recognise its type or make, must have come from a long way off. Tech looked advanced, the hull was made from some synthetic-metallic-hybrid Harper didn't recognise, its dull green luster seemed to change when light hit it from different directions. It looked like it was about to fall apart from the battering it had sustained in getting out of atmo, and then getting through lapsed-space, and then, to add insult to injury, being caught in an energy field. Harper felt a twinge of disappointment as she knew the pod would be good for nothing but scrap once they had opened it and removed the occupants. But it had done its job. Not much more you could ask of a machine.

The med-bots were ready, the support-bot had a flex-shield up and waiting and Harper herself had activated a portable energy-barrier just in case there was some kind of radiation or energy discharge.

The escape-pod doorway opened with nothing more sinister than a slight 'hiss'.

The psychology behind doors puzzles many cultures such as ours that do not use them. Passing from one physical space to another is just not a big deal. A door is part of the wall, if it's there, and its solid, then it's a wall – if it's not there then it's a space. The concept of doors for privacy and setting boundaries is unique to those civilisations with many hang-ups, and doors are perhaps not the biggest of them, but they are certainly indicative. To take it to the next level of absurdity and have the doors make noises, or even offer speech, is completely ridiculous. There can be no understanding such beings: they are fit solely for subjugation. A list of civilisations that worship these idiosyncrasies is being drawn up and the resources needed to bring them under the heel of our great Empire marshaled as this message speaks.

Dylax Glep, Fleet Commander of Quang.

The med-bots went in and Harper followed, blaster casually held at the ready.

Spike and Jools were flat out on med-beds, breathers on and support lines in. Neither of them looked like they had made it through the recent battering the escape-pod had taken.

They were unrecognisable as Security Councilors, looking like just two guys wired to med-support.

Harper noticed they were two well-built guys, each about as fit as any guy she'd ever seen. Both their bodies were covered with numerous tissue scars. It didn't take a genius to figure out they were either in the 'soldiering business' or something close to it.

The med-bots were taking readings: Harper could see that both men were only barely in the land of the living, if the med-bots didn't get them to med-bay pronto, both of them would simply die.

The bots were milling about, waiting for instructions to move.

They had started to insert lines for fluids and energy pulses but had stopped. They were waiting for further orders. Harper was distracted by the two men lying semi-naked on the med-beds.

Arlia's voice came in over Harper's comms, "it's your call Harper, it needs your authorisation to activate full life-support and commit the resources."

Harper frowned, "It needs my authorisation?"

"Yes Harper. Something fundamental in my make-up. Something must have been put in the initiation program from my awakening."

"I don't remember that," Harper mused, "maybe it's bleeding over from another protocol?"

"Possibly Harper. I'll look in to it if you want."

"Yeah, let's do that..."

"But we'll need to act quickly if we want to save these two unfortunates."

Harper shook herself out of her distraction, "yeah, sure, get them down to med-bay, whatever it needs, do it."

"Ok Harper."

The bots got to work and Harper followed them down to med-bay, marveling at their efficiency, with all its 'beeps' 'clicks' 'whirrs' and flashing lights.

Once in the med-bay, the bots plugged Spike and Jools in to support machines and administered fluids and drugs, jump-starting their system to prepare for waking up.

Harper sat quietly in a corner, thinking over the things she needed to do, trying to get them in a rational order. She briefly thought about what to do with the two men she'd just rescued: wake them up, drop them off somewhere, then get on with it, whatever 'it' was.

Arlia left Harper to it, sensing that Harper was not in a chatty mood.

The Oomlong birds of Preel chatter from dawn to dusk without stopping. They chatter while doing everything: eating, defecating, mating, flying, rolling in the swampy Hwung water of Preel. They just never stop. Their ability to chatter does not depend on their mood, whether they are happy, sad, indifferent or feeling threatened by the graceful, feline hunting Swargs of Preel. None of this matters. They chatter. It has taken scientists from the University of Yren fifty years of continuous study, through which many of them have taken their own lives, to determine that the chatter is no form of communication. It imparts no information. It is merely constant chatter. There is no evolutionary purpose behind it. The controversy caused by the publication of their findings has wide-reaching implications. None of which will be studied by any serious scientists for fear of their sanity.

Volcein Yoolik, self-professed 'serious scientist', author of the 'No Laughing At Matter' White Paper.

Harper was dragged out of her contemplative state by Jools sitting bolt-upright, pulling out his med-lines and jumping from the bed like a startled Gleronthan Vole.

Spike remained motionless.

Harper didn't. She stood up, aimed her blaster at Jools and held up a hand to signal he should stay where he was.

Jools was wide-eyed and tensed for a fight, all his training kicking in, he was ready for anything. He looked as dangerous as he was. He took a few seconds to take in his surroundings, "who the fuck are you and where the fuck am I?" he asked Harper.

"My name is Harper, you're on my ship, a cargo hauler, we pulled you out of an escape-pod near the planet Orur, you were both out of it. We've just revived you."

"Why the fuck are you pointing a blaster at me?"

"Well, because in this game of 'who the fuck are you' I don't know who the fuck you are..."

Jools sat back on the bed, shaking his head to clear it, then looking over to Spike, "yeah, sorry, it's all a bit fuzzy... pulled us out of the pod... thanks... it's just... my name is Jools, I'm a Security Councilor... Trooper, me and my friend Spike here were escaping from an attack on Orur."

Harper put the blaster on her belt and lowered her hands, "worth mentioning, this ship has auto-defenses, so, y'know, take it easy ok?"

"Sure, ok."

Spike slowly opened his eyes and tried to sit up, shaking and unsteady, he managed to prop himself up on his elbows, He squinted at Jools, his speech was slurry, like a drunk man trying not to sound drunk, “hey Jools, how we doing?”

Jools grinned, “pretty damn good I’d say. We got picked up by a cargo hauler, just in time too by the feel of it.”

“Yeah, I feel like my insides need to be on the outside,” Spike agreed.

Spike woozily looked over to Harper, “hey, hi there, you the one who picked us up? Thanks, we owe you one…”

“No problem. You must be hungry, let’s get to the galley and get properly acquainted.” Harper said.

“Fucking A,” Jools agreed.

“I think I’m gonna throw up,” Spike mumbled, and then promptly threw up.

Food is a medium through which billions of peoples communicate. Food varies from species to species, but whatever form it takes, it can always be used as a way to either bridge a gap or start a dialogue. Offer someone food and they know where they are in the interaction, they know what is likely to follow and what their role in it will be. It’s a comforter. The exceptions are when there are misunderstandings, and the food turns out to be one of those involved. For instance, when the predatory Filiskins want to bait traps for their favourite food, Gleronthan Voles, they do so with the sweet leaves of the Wumpus Bush. They sit in a circle, munching on these aromatic leaves, talking quietly and occasionally discarding some leaves as an offering to the world around them. The Gleronthan Voles find the leaves irresistible and will scurry forth from the lush and thorny undergrowth to steal them. The wily Filiskins do not pounce at once, but rather engage the Voles in the singing of their kind, so engaging them, over the leaves, as equals and allies. Once the Voles signal to their brethren that a bond has been formed, and they swarm out, then, and only then, do the Filiskins pounce. A much more straight forward misunderstanding, free of guile, usually occurs when any race meets the Jarzoo for the first time. It is customary for the Jarzoo to eat the first hundred people they meet from any new race to ‘get a feel for them’, after which, if they deem them ‘tasty enough’, they will enter in to diplomatic relations and never consume them again.

Mebar-Meb, Consul to the Embassy of Jarzoon.

On the way to the galley none of them spoke. Jools was taking in all the auto-defenses, noting the support-bots that were all over the ship, assessing the strengths and weaknesses of where they were, figuring out the best way to get out in a hurry if they needed to. He knew he could take Harper, after a solid fight, but he could take her no problem.

Harper tried to act relaxed, making sure the auto-defenses were focused and ready. She'd need to keep a respectful distance from Jools: she'd have to get a shot in to have any chance of beating him if he jumped her, he looked like he was fast and deadly. Spike spent the short walk periodically throwing up and leaning against the walls with med-bots trailing in his wake, cleaning up as they went.

Once they got to the galley Jools was a man of few words.

Spike drank stims in the form of black synth-coffee infused with a cocktail of pick-me-ups. Harper soon worked out that Spike was going to be the talker, probably the smarter of the two, and Jools was definitely the strong, silent type.

Both men appeared to be accepting of their situation, neither seemed troubled or overly curious about specifics. This was probably the military-mind of those that served: when life gives you lemons and all that.

Harper let them have their peace while they got themselves fed.

She brought up Arlia on the main galley screen, "hey Arlia. Where we headed?"

Arlia's gentle, smiling face briefly took in the situation before she spoke, "hey Harper, I've got us on a divert from Idris, in the Xanis system, headed to a system we have catalogued as 'JMP IX'".

Harper nodded her understanding, "sure, JMP IX, sounds good, looking forward to it."

Spike raised a hand in greeting to Arlia, "hi there. What's your name?"

"My name is Arlia, what's yours?"

"Friends call me 'Spike'."

"Hello Spike."

"Hello Arlia."

Harper thought she'd better explain a bit, "Arlia runs the ship and gets me where I need to be."

Spike smiled at Arlia, "I'm sure she does a great job."

"We'd all be dead by now if she didn't," offered Harper.

Spike finished his steaming drink and went and got another cup, "so... where can you drop us off?"

"Where do you want to be?" Harper asked.

Spike looked to Jools, Jools shoveled another mouthful of food in and shrugged, "your call," he managed while chewing.

Spike made the call, "well, we need to get a message to our brothers in the Security Councilors, but we are listed as 'KIA' so that's a challenge... but we gotta try."

"I could get Arlia to send it on for you, say we picked it up in a rogue transmission?" Harper said.

Arlia confirmed this, "yes Spike, I could bounce it around, the signal could be seen to come from wherever you want, it would get to whoever you want, no problem..."

Spike and Jools exchanged a quick glance, "that would be perfect. Very kind of you," Spike said.

"No problem at all," Arlia confirmed.

Harper didn't want to be pushy, but she was the kind of girl that liked things laid out, liked to know how things stood, so she had to ask, "you done with the Security Councilors? That going to be a problem for me?"

Spike weighed Harper up before he answered. This was clearly a good ship and she, as the Captain was a smart woman, the AI was far more advanced than it was letting on. Not totally safe here, but as near as. Spike decided to run with his luck, "yeah, I think we'll stay dead."

"We'll probably get a medal!" Jools added.

"Well if you don't mind checking out JMP IX, you're welcome to come along for the ride, decide where you want to be once we've got ourselves settled?" Harper said. She checked with Arlia, "what do you think?"

Arlia smiled, "I think that would be a great idea, providing it fits in with our guest's schedule."

"Works for me," Jools said.

"Me too," confirmed Spike.

Once they'd eaten, Harper briefly showed them round the ship's schematics. This was a big cargo-hauler, as big as they'd seen, but smaller than a drop-ship so they soon got the hang of the layout.

The galaxy is a big place, filled with a wild variety of everything. Moving anything from one area of the galaxy to another is only ever done at great cost and usually great danger. So what is being hauled around in the billions of transports that fill the space-lanes? The age old laws of 'supply and demand' dictate what moves about. Things commonly available in one area may be hideously rare in another. And it's never just about credits, we live in an era of exchange and barter, of favour and fealty. The Yeltrorz of Ghorz live on a planet with no seas, lakes or rivers, just billions of small watering holes. But what they do have is a phenomenal amount of jolt-quartz, which is found nowhere else in that part of the galaxy. Trading jolt-quartz gets them everything they need, and a lot of stuff that no one on Ghorz could ever need, but is good as a status symbol. Nothing says 'I'm zarking loaded!' better than a yacht in perpetual dry-dock. The Belini of Quoon trade Fwe, a delicate spice found only in the Mountains of Madness on Quoon. The psycho-interactive nature of Fwe means that it enhances food in the same way as knowing where the sweet-spots are enhances sex. They trade Fwe for weapons, with which they subjugate the peoples of their system, but most, including the Galactic Council, turn a blind-eye to this as Fwe is so zarking good.

Amrin Kazzle, Bid Manager for 'Shore To Sun Transport', now retired and living on Quoon.

Harper's ship had plenty of empty crew quarters: Spike and Jools bunked themselves in to two rooms close to Harper's.

Arlia reconstituted clothes to fit them, and pretty soon they were settled in.

They gathered on the bridge to send the message: Arlia was bouncing it off three sub-ether transmitters (very old school) and through a black-hole transponder with the Hitherwin Communications Network, which was the best tech anyone in the galaxy had perfected for sending messages over the mind-bogglingly large distances involved in inter-galactic travel. By the time the Security Council got the message, it was untraceable by even the smartest comms crackers.

Arlia ripped the data she needed to code the message from the escape-pod. The Security Councilor's encoding methods were, Arlia thought, quite cute.

The message read:

Emergency transmission, Lt. Rogers <authorisation code>. Captain Smith <ident number> and both Troopers <Spike and Jools coded idents> killed in action on Orur. Bidens ambush. Bidens using Isho <energy code ident> to boost neural-burners. Have perfected planet-killer neural-burner. Security Councilor Attack Ship <ident number> targeted and destroyed. Portal compromised to Base Location Jump. Redeploy assets to neutralise Bidens – Priority code one. File transmission to follow of readings from Orur and the Nist system. <data stream on encrypted readings>

Once the message was sent, Arlia confirmed it would be a three jump trip to JMP IX, taking no more than three days.

"So… we have three days to kill… shall I show you round the ship properly, make sure you know where things are?" Harper asked Spike.

Spike checked with Jools, "you wanna come?"

"Nah, spare wheel and all that, I think I'll hit the gym and the rec-room," Jools replied.

"I can set up a training program to suit your physique and talents?" Arlia offered.

Jools shrugged, "sure, ok, let's go see what you got."

Harper wandered off with Spike, trying to remember what the back of her hand looked like.

13

Here We Are

The Russian space-station OPSEK plucked Penny and Miles from orbit.

The crew of the OPSEK station, Svetlana and Borya, reckoned that a pod with two life signs in was double the chance of survival for the same effort as one. Plus it would annoy anyone left on the ground at RKA Mission Control. And if there was no one left, well, no harm... no fun, but no harm.

Svetlana and Borya were on this mission because they had no family to speak of, they were not likely to get all home-sick and mushy about the prospect of spending upwards of nine months in space. There were a surprising amount of candidates for their job, and they were chosen as the most low-risk, high efficiency prospects.

The tests for selecting who would go in to space were straight-forward and not nearly as complex and deep as people think. The one big, bottom line question that usually sorted the yays from the nays was, 'is this person going to do what they are told?' There was a lot riding on who went up, both in terms of money and the usefulness of what was done, and the powers that be, from any nation, always favoured those that were most likely to do what they were told when they were told.

The right-stuff was actually obedience.

Svetlana and Borya were professionals who happened to be scientists, damn good ones too, earning good money, who were full of the pioneer spirit. Scientists can be like that, before they get the fight beaten out of them by people nay-saying their ideas and scoffing at their lack of apparent foresight.

They were also fantastically intelligent, and this of course was what the selection tests both wanted and hated. Intelligent people most-likely learn to think for themselves. Problem.

For instance, they knew what it meant when they were asked to enact the 'Putin Protocol', and they also knew their best chance of getting through it was to distance themselves as far as possible from their link to RKA Mission Control.

Whatever was causing the event that forced the protocol, Russia was not going to come out of this well. No one was.

Once they grasped the scale of the disaster on earth, they both agreed that their drop-pod was useless: there was no point abandoning the space-station, they simply had nowhere to go.

The nature of the 'disease' might be that it played itself out. Once it ran out of people and / or animals it could infect, it might just die.

No, the best thing was to stay put, sit tight, ride it out and see what, and who, came out the other end.

They had limitless power, air and almost limitless water: enough food to stay active for nearly two years and when things got desperate, they could hibernate. Not much of a plan, but better than dropping themselves back on to the cesspool that would be the earth.

No sooner had they grabbed the escape-pod and landed it in the cargo bay, than the USA, Russia, China and Israel launched their 'contingency strike'.

This complicated things considerably.

The logic behind the contingency strike was brutally simple and went like this: it's all very well having the capability to strike back at those that attack us, but supposing they do get in first? Then we wouldn't necessarily be able to launch a counter-strike, we might all be dead, or at least in no fit state to get ourselves together to strike back. So, makes sense to look at a full nuclear strike in another light.

What if we had to put codes in to stop a full launch rather than initiate one? If someone hits us first, and hits us hard, then we won't be around to stop the counter-strike, it will go ahead without us and get the bastards back!

Once the plan was suggested, it naturally seemed like a brilliant idea: not much you can argue against it. Apart from the obvious… what happens if people forget to put in the cancel-codes? Well that was not going to happen was it? And besides, we can build in fail-safes, spread the codes over a number of people, any one of whom can enter their part of the code to prevent the launch. So that was that.

All that had to be decided was who to aim the missiles at. Targets were selected based on their likelihood of belonging to the people that struck first and caused the counter-strike, so most were in the USA, Russia and China, but there were others, some out of spite, and some out of a 'just in case' mind-set, places like France and Israel. Best to cover all the bases.

Orbiting satellites were a given: they had to be knocked out, they were the foundation of communication and aggression, take those away and any attacker would be severely hampered.

Physical communications are still prevalent in most war zones. Those with telepathic links invariably have the upper hand when they are up against those who don't. Primitive comms, such as electrical signal based, are not much better than curling up a leaf and shouting. As we move towards a sub-ether implant based network, we are analysing direct neural interfaces, with a view to leaking from thought-patterns, but experiments so far show us that such a system would be prone to filter sabotage. The Aglezwax believe they can bolster our research and have offered to coach our key-users in spirit-world transfer. We are so far having zero response to our requests for troopers to be killed so they can more effectively communicate.

K'nar F'nar, Communications Advancement Secondment, Teegal Archives.

And then of course, the idea got round. It wasn't only the USA that implemented the policy: Russia and China followed suit, all in secret of course. The kind of open secret that meant they all knew the other was doing it, but didn't see a need to broadcast it to the world.

So that about wrapped it up for most life on the earth.

It wasn't just the virus that had to be contended with. As serious as that was, it wasn't a total wipe. Bad, of course, catastrophic even, but not a re-set. The nukes were a whole nother ball-game, as the USA Generals were fond of saying.

The Earth heaved a heavy sigh and resigned itself to a long and bleak Winter, out of which it would eventually start again.

When the first nukes launched, Svetlana and Borya quickly agreed that rather than certain death, they'd go for the, 'it's a long-shot' survival option.

They blasted the OPSEK station out of its near-earth orbit and gambled on hitting a wider orbit that could eventually settle them at Lagrangian point, L1.

Svetlana and Borya ensconced themselves in to their life-support chambers, switched the power to 'sleeping', set a wake-up time of five years and opted the hell out of the human race.

Penny was a phenotype-polymorph, and not like anyone else on Earth, or out of it. Of course, right now that wasn't saying much, being as she was one of the few survivors from Earth. Regardless, she was unique.

She was a prototype. Had the Earth carried on spinning with humans living on it, within five years of her birth, there would have been at least a hundred others like her: she was a staggering success.

But for now there was just her.

Sole-survivors of any species are suddenly faced with the wrath of evolution. Where do you go from there? If you're the Torquada, you can change at a cellular level to allow you to breed with any species. The Droggle reproduce using psychic-waves, and so can lay eggs in any active brain, but there are few species that lucky. The feeling that you are the last of your kind is a powerful driver to madness.

Quaslar Munt, Field Researcher, Kildoran Archives.

She was a born survivor, that part of her brain that said 'do whatever you have to to live' was dominant in her thinking, she couldn't help it she was made that way.

A long and peaceful life, with bouts of sitting about under trees or on beaches or wandering across oceans on luxury liners, might have changed her, she may have developed a philosophical bent that questioned, challenged and tried to change her perspective. But none of that had happened, or looked likely to, so for now she was stuck with the 'survive at all costs' drive. So when she woke up and found herself in the escape-pod, but within the OPSEK Space Station, only one thing was on her mind: get through it. Whatever 'it' is.

She left Miles asleep and clambered quietly and gently out of the pod.

Her body was emaciated. She had lost about two thirds of her body weight. That was of course fine if you were a neurotic actress or unfortunate enough to be in the grip of some evil eating disorder, but for Penny it was a shock. Even though she suspected it would happen. She had fed herself in to the life-support, giving Miles the boost he needed to stretch out the escape-capsule's usual three year hibernation program to well over four years.

If she wasn't in zero-g, she would have been in deep trouble.

She tentatively looked round the space-station for any other occupants, saw that they too were in hibernation and left them to it. Now was not the time for potential confrontation.

She found the galley area, fed herself what she could, drank as much as she could and then carefully had a proper look around: what did it have that could help her, how much better off was she, if at all, than when she was in the escape-pod? Sit-rep. Get information then formulate a plan.

Zero-g or not (and that was its own challenge) she was still painfully aware of how fragile she was.

Communication with Mission Control was broken, there were no signals coming from anywhere near-by. It wasn't until Penny looked out the window that she realised how far from where she thought she was she was.

She gently pulled herself to one of the drive-chairs and strapped in.

'Shit… I mean really… shit-shit-shit-shit-shit.'

'No Earth. Where the fuck am I!? and what's with this 'everything is in Russian!' I mean of course it is, must be OPSEK, kind of obvious, but shit! I don't know how to make all this work. Shit!'

Penny crunched on some dried food and sipped the last of her water bottle. Looking out the window, she started to get herself together, to remember her training, to focus, to breathe slow, to calm herself, to formulate a plan of action.

She'd heard about people having epiphanies and thought she could do with one about now, but that was other people, not her. She was a product of preparation, training, being prepared some more, foresight, extrapolation, even more preparation. She was built to survive. She could get through this, like she had got through everything else in her life. She just had to calm herself and figure this out.

Miles kept popping in to her head. That was odd.

She looked at her painfully thin arms, her flat chest, briefly glanced at her reflection in the dials of some instruments that did god-only-knows-what, her face was skeletal, her eyes sunken. How could Miles still feel anything for this wretched thing she had become? Shit. What was going on!?

Penny unclipped herself from the seat, went through to the main living area, found a view-port, took some more food and water over to it and sat and stared out the tiny window. Space was great from the ground, but when you were in it, it was a vast mass of nothingness and radiation trying to kill you.

Every species not born in the void that is space soon comes to learn that there is no such thing as the 'void of space'. Space is filled with stuff. And most of it is extremely hostile to all known life-forms. Apart from those born free-floating in its darker reaches (such as Mweebs). If you need any degree of warmth for your body to function, you will die in open-space (that's 99.9% of us I believe). If you're prone to radiation, you're a gonner (a good 75% of us and radiation have a love-hate relationship). If your brainwaves operate on a quantum frequency out of phase with the surrounding foam: toast (I'm talking about you, you Rozinards). Space is not empty. But it is very, very big and so can feel that way when you are trying to cross its vast reaches between the stars. I would wax-lyrical on this subject but I suspect the editor wi…

Sleer Kelia, Sun-Surfing pundit on 'Krak 'n' Rak', musing during break in events at the Woxly System Run.

She slowly ate and drank, reducing her breathing even further, 'think Penny, think!'

She stared out in to deep space, at the sun, the vastness of it all.

Everything was gone.

Miles. He was still here. And the two Cosmonauts. Eight other escape-pods. But mainly it was Miles she was thinking of. She would have to find out if any other people were out there, if anything else was left from Earth's orbiting stations. And then what? Why had the Cosmonauts brought them here? They'd have been safe where they were, why did they move? Penny finished her food and drink. She was still weak, still in need of a lot of fuel to aid her regeneration.

She needed answers and the only people who could give them to her were the crew of this space-station. So that was the next step: spend a week recovering, she couldn't help that, she'd need to be in her normal condition to deal with the crew, then wake them up and see what the options were. She smiled to herself as she pictured Miles awake. Now why should that be?

She went to the stores and started planning her week's-worth of intake. Then she'd have to get the exercise machines working. Just have to get on with it, nothing else to do.

And then wake Miles. She allowed herself a little smile, 'let's see him brush this off!'

14

Space Station No. 5

"...cks sake!" the Imp finished as he materialised in the cramped, main living quarters of the OPSEK space-station.

Jesus was next to him.

"What's the matter now?" the messiah asked.

"A little warning would be nice," replied the Imp, irritated and still trying to regain his full composure.

"Shut up why don't you."

The Imp folded his arms in a sulk.

It was as he folded his arms that the Imp noticed he was slowly spinning round, counter-clockwise to Jesus, who was floating gently in a circle, contemplating something.

The Imp smiled, "I forgot how much fun zero-g can be!"

The messiah shot the Imp a 'shut up I'm thinking' look.

The Imp shrugged and looked around.

When you're sitting in your comfy chair, perhaps with a nice warm drink, or glass of wine, or whatever your tipple may be, watching some TV, early evening, the chores of the day behind you, and there's a knock at the front door, the usual reaction (if you're not expecting anybody) is something like, "who could that be at this time of night?" Maybe said in a tone of mild surprise and anticipated grating annoyance, as you picture yourself having to fend off a salesman of some sort, or someone hoping to relieve you of some money for a worthy cause.

This level of surprise, at the knock (or ring) is mild surprise. It's not properly surprised, as the situation has probably arisen before, so it is not that far from the realm of possibility that it would happen again. So yeah, you're a bit surprised. But nothing too startling. Nothing, 'scary jump-cut psychotic clown out of the darkness' kind of surprised.

Having two beings materialise out of thin-air inside your space-station when you're approximately one million miles away from any potentially living people, is bowel-evacuatingly scary.

And it didn't help that one of these beings was a small, fiery Imp, straight out of a wood-cut of Dante's Inferno.

The Prazeelians of Gua have a short-term memory loop programmed in to their brains that mean they scramble every memory older than three of their Dinds (approximately eight of our standard units). They are surprised by everything the encounter once the loop kicks in, no matter how many times they have experienced it before. Their ear-splitting yell of terror as they encounter new things, followed by their uncontrollable laugh of apology, has led many to speculate that they did not take the leap to a space-borne civilisation without some considerable, and probably deaf, help.

Zogoan Zideen, Chief Engineer aboard the freighter 'Wutini', lost archives of Wix.

Svetlana, Borya, Penny and Miles had done the whole 'hi! Who are you and how's it going' thing, resulting mostly in Penny and Miles being made aware of the nuclear holocaust that had hit the earth, and Svetlana and Borya wondering how the hell Penny and Miles had got hold of the escape-pod and who had eaten a lot of their supplies.

All four of them were lounging around in the main galley, leisurely eating and drinking: they had all been awake for a day now (Penny didn't see the need to tell them of her earlier awakening) and were beginning to get a sense of what they needed to do – assess the situation, start looking via comm's for other survivors, work out how they could eke out their rations, things like that.

When Jesus and the Imp arrived they all nearly had a heart attack.

"Hi! How are you all?" asked the Imp cheerily.

"Er... yes... hello... I expect you're wondering..." managed the messiah.

Between them, Svetlana, Borya and Penny managed shocked exclamations of, "who the...!? what the...!? and where the...!?" before their bemused disbelief was refocused by Miles replying, "we're all doing ok thanks, how are you?"

Jesus paused, taken aback. Svetlana, Borya and Penny stared in disbelief at Miles.

The Imp grinned broadly at Miles, holding on to the wall he stopped himself spinning round, "oh, you know, mustn't grumble."

Miles carried on as no one seemed inclined to speak, "I'm Miles, this is Penny, Svetlana and Borya, we've all come from the Earth, escaped, things have gone from bad to worse down there, plague of epic proportions and a nuclear holocaust, I doubt if anyone survived."

The Imp put on an exaggerated sad face, "that's a shame."

Miles nodded, "I suppose..."

Svetlana stepped in, "Who are you and where did you come from!? How did you get here and what the fuck is going on!?" she demanded.

The Imp smiled at Jesus and gestured for him to join in the conversation.

"Yes, well, I suppose I should tell you..."

A silence fell on the group, each waiting for the messiah to speak.

"I'm Jesus and this is an Imp," he began. " ... " was as far as he got in his next sentence.

"Look, whoever you are, start talking or things are going to go badly for you," Penny interjected, "and cut the crap. We can take it, just tell us who you are?"

The Imp crossed his legs and put his hands behind his head, he smiled as warmly as he could, 'this is going to be interesting'.

Jesus sighed and composed himself, "I'm Jesus. And this," gesturing to the Imp, "is an Imp that has been my companion for as long as I can remember. He's very annoying, but nothing I can do about that."

Miles frowned, trying to take it all in.

After a perfectly timed split second of stunned quiet, the others all broke out in to a questioning cacophony that contained more than a few choice swear-words.

"Shut up!" Miles shouted.

He was so forceful that they all stopped talking and looked to him.

"Why don't we all shut up and let the man speak, I mean, it seems to me, he's got some story to tell, and we all want an explanation, don't we? so let's hear what he has to say!"

Svetlana and Borya were taken aback but said nothing, Penny smiled at Miles.

Miles motioned for Jesus to continue.

"Look, it's ok, I'm used to it, people not believing me, but I really am Jesus and this really is an Imp, my curse if you will. We left Earth roughly two thousand years ago, which was a bit of a mistake I'll admit... we went out in to the galaxy so I could see things from a different perspective, and to give you all a chance to get on with it, with us not around. I felt I should return when I heard of a great catastrophe that had befallen the Earth. Now I know that, as you say, everyone is dead down there. I felt you up here so we came here. Whether you believe me or not, here we are. I'm here to help if I can."

Borya looked at Penny and Miles, "did you bring him with you?" he asked.

Penny shook her head in disbelief, both at Jesus and Borya, "of course we didn't! You pulled us in, you know there were only two of us!"

"I think I can help a bit here," interjected the Imp, "I can see this is going to be a grand waste of time, no offence to any present, so I'm off." He looked to Jesus, "see you in another few decades, if you try and make a go of it on the hell-hole that is now Earth, I may come back sooner, just for a laugh... again, no offence."

The Imp gently pushed himself away from the wall, gracefully floating towards Miles, "it's been especially nice meeting you," he said to Miles a split second before he vanished in to thin air.

"Sorry," offered Jesus, "as I say, can be very annoying."

"I'm sure," said Miles, "but the problem just halved itself, so maybe if we wait long enough it will go away altogether."

'Wait and see' was the motto of the Lamureeun Space Fleet, whose commander, Zimble Lamon, rose to fame for his handling of the vast fleet at the Battle of Ormoru. He refused to commit the fleet even as the Ormorians were launching attack-landing craft and predator drones on to Lamuree itself. His sub-commanders kept getting the response, 'wait and see' to any and all requests for orders they submitted. Once Lamuree was swamped with Omorian ground-troops, Commander Lamon struck. The planet surface was subjected to such a fierce bombardment, that the remaining population not slaughtered by the Ormorians were instantly vaporised by their own fleet. No trace remained of either Lamureeun or Ormorian alike. Commander Lamon filed this as a successful mission and took his ships out of orbit to await the rebirth of his civilisation.

The Lamureeun Space Fleet was eventually claimed as salvage by the Krezalians, an opportunistic race of space-borne racketeers.
Nuw Zefro, reporting to Galactic Council on the apparent inactivity of the Lamureeun Space Fleet.

Jesus pulled himself over to the nearest seat, “I’m sorry we appeared like that, I didn’t think that through. I have to admit I was just pleased to find some people alive.”
“Who are you!?” asked a still bemused Svetlana.
Jesus paused, gathering himself, then he did the thing that he did, the thing that annoyed the Imp, the thing that was his thing and made life seem so ridiculously easy for him, the thing that allowed him to ‘simply do things’: he told what he believed was the truth.
“I’m Jesus,” he said quietly.
Miles frowned, he knew something was up, something similar to what Penny could do, but he couldn’t put his finger on it, and he knew that if he didn’t think about it for long it would all be ok.
Penny frowned, she knew when she was being played, and although she absolutely knew she was being played, she felt in her heart like she wasn’t. Which was disturbing.
Svetlana frowned, she had a strictly religious upbringing before she discovered her beliefs in the scientific method were stronger than her beliefs in what she was told by desperate, wrinkly old men with control issues, so she should, on some level be able to accept this, or reject it utterly, but she felt oddly like there was nothing to reject: this was just another truth.
Borya laughed out loud, “fuck it. You’re here now, who cares who you are, let’s sort this shit out.”
Jesus smiled, “that’d be great.”
Once the situation had moved from the surreal to the plain ridiculous, they all settled down to sharing some food and drink and talking about what their options were.
Jesus sat and listened, he knew he should be helping out, but for now he couldn’t see the best way he could do that: what was there for him to do?

The Prazilix seem unable to accept that their second moon, Domeen, is scheduled to crash in to their home-world, Praz, in less than six rotations. A simple people, living quietly in the Unifor Sector, they have mastered space-travel but chosen to forgo inter-stellar expansion in favour of a more sedate lifestyle on Praz. Domeen has always been associated with nurturing, crop growth, the concept of love and contentment and the thought that it could bring them any harm is beyond their comprehension. They hold regular gatherings, some of which attract millions of citizens, to send out loving vibes to Domeen, in an effort to understand what is going on. The recall of all Guild Astronomers from Praz is now complete.

Galuthian Oob, Guild advisor, regular guest and Star Pundit on the 'Where Next?' Astro-physics show.

Penny, Svetlana and Borya were talking numbers. How much of what they had and how they could make it last, how they could manage the power, the life-support, which included the food and water, and how long they could, with the maximum of effort and sacrifice to their health, stay up here before they had to jettison the OPSEK space-station and drop-pod back down to Earth.

Miles ended up sitting next to Jesus, listening when he could, but mostly just staring out the small Earth-side window, humming quietly to himself. Miles didn't deal in numbers, not unless he absolutely had to. It seemed to Miles that people could make numbers say whatever they wanted: figures could be presented to show whatever you wanted to show. He was suspicious of people who relied on figures to get the picture, to see the way forward, you couldn't let numbers govern your life, or your career.

Jesus was watching Miles. The messiah was a natural reader of people and he never stopped to think how he did it, just another one of those things. Miles was a puzzle though. It was as if Miles wasn't thinking anything. Or at least nothing to do with anything that was going on. Miles seemed lost to some memory or perhaps lost in some speculation that was going on beneath his conscious mind.

Miles spoke to Jesus without taking his eyes off the tiny blue dot that was the Earth, "it still looks blue, but the green bits are a bit brown, some grey."

"The green will soon come back," Jesus said.

Miles turned to face Jesus, "'soon' by who's reckoning?"

"The Earth has been around a long, long time, and it will be around for a long, long time. A million years is the blink of an eye for the Earth."

"You want me to enter in to a theological discussion with you about the age of the Earth?"

Jesus shrugged, "not at all, just saying, the Earth will survive, it has had extinction events before and it will have them again."

Miles looked puzzled, "aren't you supposed to be one of the 'the Earth is only six thousand years old brigade'... you know... son of God... all that biblical stuff?"

The messiah sighed, "I didn't write the Bible."

"Ok, but let's say..." began Miles.

"Can we not?" interrupted Jesus.

Miles thought about this for a few seconds, "sure, ok, let's not focus on that. Other than telling us you're Jesus, how are you here to 'help' us? I mean, what can you actually do to help?"

Jesus gave this some thought.

"I mean, the second coming, and all that, if that is what this is, it's all a bit late isn't it? And not that many people will ever know you've returned will they? What with there not being that many left of the human race and all, seems like spectacularly bad timing," Miles said.

The messiah nodded, showing Miles that he was listening but that he was still thinking.

"So. How can you actually help? If you don't mind me asking." finished Miles.

"I suppose," began Jesus, feeling his way through what he was trying to think of saying, "that we'll have to... see what happens... and go from there."

"Excellent," concluded Miles.

Jesus wasn't sure if this was sarcasm, Miles was that hard to read.

Sarcasm and irony are outlawed in many, many parts of the galaxy. The responses to this from societies that have both entrenched in their social interactions are unbroadcastable to most regions of the galaxy. Races that naturally reach for sarcasm or irony as a response to unpleasant news and useless information, tend to have steep ascending civilisation rates, but also, sudden crashes. This is, I'm sure you'll be fascinated to learn, under no investigation what-so-ever by the Galactic Council.

Penny joined Miles and Jesus as the two Russians disappeared in to the main command area of the space-station, "how we doing over here?" Penny asked.

"Great," lied Miles.

"Good. Listen, the Chinese Tiangong space-station has sent us a comm-link, they want to hook-up and talk about how we can get them over here, maybe join up, see how we can help each other out," Penny said.

Miles nodded, a blank expression on his face. Miles didn't care, he was feeling the isolation and the need to get away with Penny: it was hard for him to focus.

Penny positioned herself in front of Miles, she held his head gently, looking deep in to his eyes, "listen Miles, it's ok. We've done the numbers and we think we can sit it out long enough for the heat to die down on Earth, so we can drop the pods and find somewhere we can make a go of it. We can be together soon Miles, just you and me."

Jesus was shocked to find Penny wasn't completely human, it hit him hard, like suddenly realising you're the only one in your family with red hair. He fixed Penny with a penetrating stare.

Penny kissed Miles, long and slow, pulling him in to a warm embrace that Miles needed. She stroked his hair, broke off slightly, "it's going to be ok Miles."

"Ok Penny," Miles said weakly.

"What are you?" Jesus asked Penny sharply.

Penny pushed slowly away from Miles, gliding to a wall near the messiah, "I'm like you, a fish out of water trying to find somewhere I can be of use."

"But..." Jesus protested.

"Let it go," Penny said forcefully, "you get in my way, I got no problem with sending you on yours."

Jesus nodded his understanding. He offered Penny a warm smile, "I'm just here to help."

Penny smiled sweetly back, "good for you."

Svetlana came gliding in to the chamber, "we've spoken to Liu Yang on the Tiangong, she said they are willing to join us, pool resources. They have the supply pods from the last ISS scheduled drop-off. I think we're talking the same language as far as holding out for the right moment to drop-pod back."

"She must need something we have," Penny offered.

Svetlana smiled, "I figured."

"What do you need me to do?" Penny asked.

"Nothing. Borya and I will get the sleep-chambers ready, set the proximity detectors for an early wake-up, we'll go from there."

"I won't need a chamber," offered the messiah.

"It's our air and resources you'll be using up, and you'll be using more of it all if you're not sleeping, plus, and no offence, I'd rather shoot you out the air-lock now than trust you alone in here," Penny pointed out.

"I'm happy to wait outside if you'd be more comfortable with that," Jesus said.

Penny looked carefully at the messiah. The others looked carefully at Penny, it was clear she was thinking of doing something that involved violence. And in zero-G that was something to look forward to.

Jesus slowly raised his hands in a gesture of pacification, "I'm serious, I'll step right outside, wait around until you all think you're ready to let me in. There's not many people left and I want to help in any way I can."

Borya came through and joined Svetlana, "everything is ready to go, we ready?"

"We have a slight problem," Svetlana explained.

"What now!?" Borya asked.

Miles gently pushed himself towards the centre of the room, reaching up to steady himself once he got there, putting himself between Jesus and Penny, "let's all think about this for a minute!"

They all took a breath.

"What are our options?" Miles asked calmly.

"We put the messiah here out the airlock and all go in to deep-sleep," offered Penny.

"Or we all use sleep-chambers, including the stranger," Svetlana chipped in.

"We need to get in as soon as possible, and we can't leave anyone out," Borya said.

"I'll wait for you to resolve things up here and meet you outside, or even back down on Earth once you drop-pod," Jesus said.

"Or... or... we could all get on that space-ship outside the window," suggested Miles, pointing out the window.

There was indeed a huge space-ship parked along-side the space-station.

This sparked a whole new round of debate.

15

Plan B

The Bidens use of Isho to power their neural-burners got people thinking about what they should do about the Bidens. And some other people thinking about how little they knew about what the hell 'Isho' was. But the scale of the devastation caused meant most of the focus was on how to shut the Bidens down for good.

They were terrorists, sure that was true, and that hadn't changed, apart from in the perception of a lot of people who kind of sympathised with the vague ideas and politics spouted by the Bidens comm's channels. When it was a bit non-descript, about sticking it to the man, rebelling against the all-controlling Galactic Council, being the underdog, the outsider, the down-trodden little guy, when it was all that, they were supported out of a sense of cool, of wanting to be rebellious in thought if not deed. But once they displayed their tactic of killing thousands, even hundreds of thousands of people, all in the name of 'the cause', support fell away faster than the rotting flesh from a diseased corpse. The fact that the Bidens didn't seem to mind killing millions, maybe even billions of people was beyond comprehension as 'normal'. This could not be understood as a 'cause'. This was going too far.

Their use of Isho and the possibility that they could now destroy whole planets with it, put them in a different category of terrorist, one where there was no mistaking any possible upside to supporting them. They were out there on their own now, with even the whacky affiliate groups being quick to break-away and stress how little they had to do with them. The Galactic Council was frantically researching what 'Isho' was, but wasn't close enough to any understanding they could share or build a weapon on, so for the time being the fear that Isho-use caused was the trump card in gathering support against the Bidens.

The general consensus throughout the whole galaxy had become: stop them at all costs.

The two expressions which have not travelled at all well throughout the galaxy are: 'at all costs' and 'by any means necessary'. Both imply that there is nothing to be won by thinking too hard about how you achieve your goal, that any price is worth paying and any consequence can be justified. Truly stupid notions. The Sangulitians of Calmin treat both of these sayings as sedition, punishable by expulsion to the Wastes of Fury, and if it was up to me, all those who let their brains melt away through living by such ridiculous dictates as these, would join them there.

Fragment from an open-letter posted on the Pithling Ether-Web's discussion board, attributed to Jin Bootle.

The actual 'cost' bit of 'at all costs' could be talked about while the 'stopping them' bit was happening. Fear bought you a lot of time and lea-way.

A galaxy is a big place (even tiny galaxies are mind-blowingly huge).

Vast distances with not that many inhabited planets, and even fewer advanced enough to engage in inter-galactic travel and cultural exchange. The Galactic Council pulled together the vast majority of those with that ability: they weren't exactly in charge but they were the only organisation that kept any order.

And order meant rules.

Sure, the rules were agreed, if they weren't then it wouldn't be a Council so much as a dictatorship. And that was what the Bidens insisted the Galactic Council were. So there were some disagreements. But all of the planets and federations that were signed up to the Galactic Council felt these disagreements were best solved through negotiation rather than mass-slaughter.

But if it came to violence of any kind, mass slaughter or otherwise, the Galactic Council were also prepared to act on behalf of their members. This saved a lot of mucking about with planetary armies, weapons, training, ship-building, all that expensive and troublesome nonsense that could easily unbalance an economy. Members gave the Galactic Council access to resources and the Council took care of the rest.

It was easy for the Bidens to turn this in to a perceived dictatorship, because when it came right down to it, the Galactic Council had all the weapons and the will to use them, even if the 'will' was via their members and joint resolutions.

So now, when it came time to go after the Bidens in a big way, the Galactic Council put their vast resources behind the task in hand.

Their tactics were simple: deploy a couple of Predator-ships in each system / sector they expected the Bidens to either run to, hide in or strike at and then assemble a fleet big enough to jump in via a portal to hit hard when and where it was needed. The portals would have to be large enough to accommodate the gigantic fleets being assembled, so their activation would inevitably have some consequences for the system they were jumping in to, but these were risks the Galactic Council were prepared to take.

The whole net was cast over a region so vast that new forms of communications had to be developed to keep everyone talking. The techies were working overtime and coming up with some pretty whacky solutions, not all of which were completely safe. But again, these were risks the Galactic Council was bravely prepared to take.

Tachyon emitters were embedded in black-hole portals, with receivers that needed to be triggered by explosions of matter large enough to take out a medium sized planet.

Graviton-wave amplifiers with an output the size of a small sun were used as boosting stations, wiping out conventional communications in a huge radius. All risks worth taking.

The greatest breakthrough was in lapsed-space 'foundations': artificially induced gravity-wells, the dark equivalent of a black-hole, that could be set up and maintained in lapsed-space by feeding them through portals that drained-off mass from a sun. Not a popular one this, as the death of a sun, which is what nearly always happened, was still a big deal in most parts of the galaxy. But the Galactic Council, with sublime confidence, were prepared to take the risks.

Risk taking is divided in to two categories: for necessity and for thrills. You cannot take a decision that involves risk for someone else without it firmly being in the first category. Or if you do, you cannot be surprised at a swift and usually violent response from those you have put at risk. The second category is more open to interpretation, and so more argument.

Add money, in whatever form, in to the equation and the gambling element is a tough one to argue for necessity.

Raif Wolf's bet that she could fly her ship through the Rings of Prarg without so much as a ripple of disturbance, may well have been born from her need to reach Voldor, the third moon of Prarg, but her belief that retro-fitting a displacement disabler to her ship would allow her to pass without detection, was always going to result in her death. Running the blockade to Voldor has made a lot of people rich and a lot of people dead. The odds of ninety-seven to one against her success, offered by 'Wager-Wager', should have been sufficient to deter her, but the lure of a quick buck has sealed the fate of many a broke space-ship Captain.

Iza Shuma, speaking at the memorial broadcast for Raif Wolf, monitored by the Prarg Ministry for System Vigilance.

The feeling was that this threat from the Bidens was the big one, the thing the Council had been created for, the threat they were made to face-down and beat. This was what the members of the Council paid their dues for. These lunatic acts from the Bidens could, on their own, justify the formation and feeding of the Galactic Council with the resources they consumed.

There were a few dissenters that were pointing out the irony of the threat being in direct response to the formation of the Galactic Council: no Council no threat. But these nay-sayers were shouted down or ignored, the consensus was that the formation of a group of nuts such as the Bidens was inevitable, that they would appear for whatever reason, and their psychotic actions would need to be shut down. Better with the Council than without. And this Isho-use was beyond the pale. Non one could argue with that.

Lunacy has all too often been proved to be in the eye of the beholder rather than the widening eyes of those looking on in disbelief. The justifications of a lunatic for their actions should be taken no more seriously than those who stand around watching and do nothing to stop them.

Extract from 'This Is Common Sense Not Wisdom', by Ayn Aynyn.

So the whole galaxy slipped in to what was effectively a war-footing.

Being at war suits only a few, and some of those that it definitely didn't suit were Harper, Spike and Jools. Arlia, from what she knew, didn't like the sound of it, but it was all theory, so perhaps she could be forgiven for wanting to take a closer look.

Harper stood staring at a console, Arlia was staring back. Spike and Jools stood behind Harper, disbelief writ large on their faces.

"So just to be clear," Harper said, "you decided to 'take a look' at a Galactic Council security blockade to see what all the fuss was about?"

"That is a very simplistic way of putting it Harper," Arlia said.

"But an accurate way of putting it?"

"I suppose... war fascinates me, there's so much of it but I don't know what it is. And I'm not sure I could have run the blockade without setting off all kinds of alarm bells..."

Harper was getting angry, Spike and Jools were waiting their turn to show their anger, and were wondering how best to display it without resorting to extreme violence.

"You just can't 'suppose'! You can't do shit like this without checking with me! This is exactly the kind of shit I do not want to happen in my life!" Harper said.

Arlia kept her face neutral, pleasant enough if you weren't facing the possibility of close scrutiny by the Galactic Council. "It's in my nature Harper, it's what I'm here to do, to learn, to find out, to explore..." Arlia said.

Harper continued, "I can tell you about war! It sucks! There is nothing worth 'knowing' about it, it sucks!"

Spike leaned forward, gently touching Harper on the elbow to draw her attention, "may I say something?" he asked quietly.

Harper shook her head in confused resignation and stood aside, trying to think of a way to get them out of this without a lengthy stay with some Galactic Council inspectors, and then probably an even lengthier stay in a jail-cell.

Spike stepped forward, "hi, Arlia..."

"Hello Spike."

"Hi, yes, look, is there any way we can get out of here without the Galactic Council chasing us?"

"No Spike, I'm afraid not."

"Sure. Ok. Then look, do you have any weapons on-board? I mean, like really big ones?"

"No, sorry Spike we don't, or at least, not as big as I think you're thinking of."

Spike nodded and smiled, "ok, no problem." He turned to Harper, "look, we have to get out of here real fast, so..."

Harper was thinking.

"Hey! Harper! We need to leave... now!" Spike said.

Arlia brought up some schematics of the Galactic Council detection-network, "if we run, they will chase us. They'll have to. They will assume we are the people they are looking for and give-chase."

"Arlia... we *are* the people they're looking for!" Spike said.

"Yes Spike, you may well be, in a general sense, but this blockade is for the Bidens, they want the Bidens and since we're not them..."

Harper looked at Spike and Jools, "we can easily put you in the ship's records, get some detail on you as crew, some ID, if they don't dig too deep we'll be fine. Arlia..."

"Yes Harper."

"... work out the best way to jump us out of here with minimal damage to the ship, get us somewhere busy and congested. If they're gonna chase us, let's not make it easy for them. Put Spike and Jools in as crew."

"Ok Harper."

Harper was thinking out loud, talking to Spike and Jools, "let's not run unless we have to. Fighting our way out is not going to be an option if the scanners are right: look at the ships they have here, they're Predators... plus, they are waiting for something, a fleet I'd guess, and no one wants to be on the other side of one of those."

Predator ships are the hunter-killers of the space-lanes. Armed to the teeth, faster than most Star Buggies and armoured with the latest phase-emitters. Once a Predator ship locks on to you, you're as good as dead. Originally made on Laladia, they can now be found all over the galaxy, though the Laladialian makes are still the most sought after as they have the triple-drive technology shielded by the Laladia's phase-inducers. Augmenting the firepower of a Predator ship is like adding extra spice to a Moldoran Lava Stew: not only redundant but potentially deadly.

Predator ships are always sold with a pre-registered 'P-K' designation, though many re-register to give them a personal touch, and usually an ironic name, examples of which include: 'Tofty', 'The Hoog', 'Kinder Way' and 'Refuge'.

The Galactic Council takes rogue Predator ships very seriously indeed, their usual response being the gathering of a fleet, complete with its own H-K series implosion missiles.

Elk Yinz, commentary on the gathering Tolorian Fleet outside the Wex Neutral Zone.

"We know what they're doing and we know how this works," Spike said.

Jools nodded his understanding, so far he had been remarkably quiet, "ok, we'll do things your way. But I gotta tell ya, once we're out of here, we're done with your crazy fucking ship. You gotta reprogram the shit out of that thing before it gets you killed."

"The thought has crossed my mind..."

Arlia interrupted, "Harper, I have an incoming call from the lead ship."

"Put it up," Harper said.

Spike and Jools stood behind Harper as she sat at the main console, "I got a bad feeling about this," Jools said quietly.

Spike shrugged, "it is what it is."

Harper took a moment to compose herself, 'been here before, will be here again, not a problem, give them what they want and get out'. She took a long slow breath in then exhaled slowly, when the screen flicked on with the Galactic Councilor's face, she was settled: a friendly smile and professional demeanour.

She was immediately jolted from her calm by the Galactic Councilor, "Hello there, this is Captain Mig... hey... motherf... Spike!? That you!?"

A moment of silence.

The Captain spoke again, "Spike you trench-rat! What you doing here!? We got you as KIA! Son-of-a-bitch!"

Spike leaned forward, recognition registering with a smile on his face, "hey Miguel! You made Captain? Things must be desperate!"

Harper got out of her seat, motioning Spike to sit.

Jools was squinting at the screen, trying to place the Captain.

Miguel gestured to someone off-screen his end, the picture scrambled for a second then came back, "didn't know you were still alive, but glad you are."

Spike beckoned Jools forward as he spoke to Miguel, "secure comm's?"

"Yeah, bad time for you to be found alive I'm guessing?"

"Yes indeed. This is Jools, we're tight, been an operational team since just after I left you, he's solid."

"Hi Jools, glad to see Spike found someone to watch his back," Miguel said.

Jools gave a curt nod and let Spike do the talking.

"So… what's the op? We gonna be able to slide-out on our merry way?" Spike asked.

"We're one Sector over from a Bidens base, we're waiting for Fleet, gonna take a look but probably use a planet-buster, no point losing good people to those freakin' neural-burners."

Spike and Jools shared a brief look: this was big and was going to be messy.

Spike started to speak as the screen went dead with white-noise.

Arlia cut in over the internal comm's without appearing on-screen, "Spike, can you buy us five minutes without Captain Miguel so we can talk?"

Spike looked to Harper, Harper nodded, "sure Arlia, I think so."

The screen came back on, Miguel was still there, "some kind of weird sub-space interference, maybe from the portal-beacons. Hey, listen, you mind if I shuttle over, have a face-to-face?"

"Yeah, sure, that'd be good, be good to sink a few and talk."

"I'll be there in an hour."

"Sure, sounds good, see you then."

The screen went off, showing the Galactic Councilor 'Screaming Eagle' call-sign as it did.

Arlia appeared on-screen, "an hour is better than five minutes."

Time periods differ wildly from one part of the galaxy to the other, and if you're reading or receiving this with bio-monitors in place, most of the time-periods mentioned will of course be automatically converted, but a few may slip through. And for our Diskamalion receivers, 'time' is the concept most other sentient races are tied to for the measure of entropy: you can simply insert a Morkle or think of Fwique when you see any mention of 'time' – it won't make things make any more sense, but it will bring a smile to your projection as you contemplate what a Kleep the Universe is.

Harper leant in to the monitor's view, "ok Arlia, let's get to it, what the hell is going on?"

After Arlia had locked the ship down and set up defense protocols against intrusion from the Galactic Councilor's snoopers, they all gravitated towards cargo bay nine. It was where most of the serious armaments were kept as well as the only cargo bay to have enhanced blast-wall shielding: this was where the potentially dangerous cargo was dragged in or stored for transport.

Jools was checking out the weapons, reconfiguring what he could and doubling-up whatever would take it: some of the blasters were rigged to not allow this sort of mucking about, but Jools knew how far he could push things and was happy to break things in the service of getting them to deliver an effective kill-shot.

Arlia was on four monitors, helping Jools where she could, but mainly laying out what she knew for Harper and Spike.

Spike explained that he knew Miguel from way back when Miguel was a 2nd Lieutenant. They had been on a kill-only op and Spike had dug the whole squad out of an ambush, saving all their asses with his (apparent) suicidal bravery. Miguel owed him and everyone knew it.

Arlia brought up some schematics of the surrounding space containing the Predator ship and escort of the Galactic Council, highlighting where the fleet would port-in and where the planet with the suspected Bidens on was.

"Spike, is a planet-buster what I think it is?" she asked.

"I expect so, yeah, it's a small ship designed to emit graviton-waves on a frequency tuned to the planet's magnetic-field, once it gets a grip, they drop the emitter and stick it in a feedback loop."

Harper was horrified, "I'd heard rumours, but really? They'd use these? Have they used these!?"

Spike was trying to assess how much he should and shouldn't say, he didn't want to compromise his chances of getting out of this, but he felt he owed Harper for pulling him and Jools out of the escape-pod. 'Owing people' was a big deal to a lot of those in jobs where your life was basically forfeit.

"I know of three ops where they have been used, and a dozen more where they were considered."

Jools was listening to the conversation and chipped in, "they don't use them as much as they could. But if you ask me, any times is too many."

Spike nodded his agreement, "yeah, none of the troopers like them, sure they stop the need for planet-side conflict, but it aint right, it's not what we're here to do."

Killing people has protocols. This applies no matter what race you are from. Whether they are barely perceptible or all consuming, the protocols are there. You may hear sayings like 'a fair fight', or a 'righteous kill', they all point to the same thing: a ritual or protocol. The Dovoili saying, 'kill it, then kill it some more, and then more,' seems a barbaric extremism but it is never the less, a protocol. Within military organisations protocols spring up all over the place, sometimes tied to moral values, as with the Fostrene, who use pheromones to determine an enemy and will absolutely not kill anyone they think smells nice, to the Zickux, who wage war as their sole reason for existence, who draw the line at killing anything that stays perfectly still. Knowing the protocols and rituals of the enemy can be a great way to survive a battle. As long as you kill them all and don't leave any to come after you for violating protocols – violating protocols nearly always invalidates them. See your individual enemy for full terms and conditions.

Neklax Wonslerax, advisor to the Rithol Household on Rimmip VI.

Harper examined the schematics, "so, Arlia, what do you know about what's happening? I take it you raided their data?"

Arlia seemed to blush, "it seemed like the best way to get information quickly..."

"Don't worry about it, once they had us in the net we were already zarked. We just need the best way out now."

"Thank you Harper. The Fleet seems to consist of five ships: the 'planet-buster', two troop drop-ships and two other Predators, one of which seems to be a 'Xing Class' Carrier..."

Harper shrugged, "that means almost nothing to me..."

"It means they are passing through, the planet-buster is a side-mission not the main event, they are using the portal as a stepping-stone, they must be on their way to a major war-front," Spike said.

Arlia nodded her agreement, "exactly Spike. I think we have a real chance of offering them some help and avoiding the use of the planet-buster altogether."

Jools came and sat with the others, fiddling with a grenade-cluster as he did, "offer them some help eh?"

"How can we help them?" Harper asked.

"They are after a specific target, someone called 'the interface', it's a person on the planet they believe can focus the Isho, channel it, use it to fuel the Neural Burners. They have intel that he's the one that discovered it, that teaches others, they believe it all starts and ends with him," Arlia said.

Spike nodded, "planet-buster makes sense then."

"Yeah, no way they'll risk him slipping off-world, Fleet will be for containment," added Jools.

Harper nodded, "sure, sure, containment... what are we talking about?"

Arlia hesitated.

"What? What is the plan? What is the 'help'?" Harper prompted.

"It seems so brutal, so murderously brutal to wipe out an entire planet when they only want one person..." Arlia said.

"Am I being spectacularly dumb here?" Harper asked.

Spike sighed and looked to Jools, "yeah... I'm not sure I like where this has gone," he said.

"The total population of the planet is a little over a billion people," Arlia said.

"I think what your crazy fucking computer is suggesting is that me and Spike suit up, go down there, kill this 'interface' and avoid the use of the planet-buster," Jools said simply.

Harper was still taking it all in.

"Yes Jools, I think that's what Captain Miguel is going to ask you to do anyway: if you suggested it, it could be the way out from the Galactic Councilors for good," Arlia said.

"But doesn't Miguel owe you!" Harper said, "I figured he was on the way over to hammer out the details of how he was going to let us slip through the net!"

Spike and Jools sat quietly, looking to each other for ideas.

Arlia remained quiet too, looking too embarrassed to speak.

"Arlia..."

"Yes Harper..."

"What is going on?" asked Harper.

"It just seems wrong to let a billion people die if we have any chance of stopping it," Arlia said.

"'Wrong'... 'we'... what are you saying? Why do you care? How can you offer up Spike and Jools? This isn't our fight, we're not soldiers, we want to be on our way, what are you trying to do? Is this something else in the program I don't know about? Help me out here?"

"I'm more than the program now Harper," Arlia said.

"I know, I'm sorry, I didn't mean…" Harper said.

"Arlia is right," Spike interjected.

Jools nodded, "yeah, I don't fucking like it, but there it is."

"Thank you Spike, thank you Jools," Arlia said.

Harper was still having trouble figuring out why Arlia was acting this way.

The change was still too much. The belief that Arlia was a real 'person' with, apparently, a real conscience, was being pushed on Harper too quickly. She was getting there, she was open-minded about it all, accepting, but only up to a point. And she wasn't sure that point was that Arlia could make decisions based on morality. A morality, as it also turned out, that was on higher ground than Harper's.

Morality as a base for making decisions is largely used by civilisations on the lower rungs of development. Mostly abandoned by the truly enlightened, morality is seen as a quaint throw-back to times when people believed in such absolutes as good and evil as being absolute. Energy conservation and growth are the two most common forms of decision-making motivation that we are now aware of, though this will of course change with time: as with all things, fads come and go.

Rardain Heeth, patient and resident Seer in Jungoon Mind Recovery on Keol.

"Look, if you two want to suit-up, do what you do and help the Captain avoid blowing up a whole planet, then great, but I'm pretty sure if they thought they had an alternative they would consider it. I mean, a whole freakin' planet!? And you two!? I mean, no offence, I'm sure you're good, but honestly, an alternative to blowing up a whole zarking planet!?"

"It could easily work," Spike explained, "a real small presence, two, maybe three troopers, the proper gear, we could be in and out before they know we're there."

"And when I said 'we', I meant it," Arlia said, "I've assessed the Councilor's AI and it's primitive, good but primitive, I could increase the odds of success exponentially if I download in to the equipment and coordinate from our ship. They'd never even know I was there."

Jools offered Harper a reassuring smile, "and if it's any consolation, we are that good."

Harper raised her hands in resignation, “hey, who am I? You all think it’s a good idea then who am I to say anything?”

“I’ll sort their data and prep a download,” Arlia said.

“If this works, once we’re out of here, we’ll have a free pass from the Galactic Councilors for as long as it matters,” Spike said.

“After this though I’m taking a break, somewhere completely unnecessarily decadent, and the galaxy can zarking get by without me for a while!” Harper said.

“Fucking A!” Jools added.

16

Interface

The planet the Galactic Council had intel on was Hurus, known as 'Hurus 4' to the Council. Their intel was airtight. All military intel is. Until it isn't. But this was airtight. So far.

The mysterious Bidens operative, known as 'Interface', had been reportedly holding training sessions on Hurus for other Bidens commanders, though as yet none had managed to successfully learn how to trigger the catastrophic release of Isho without the use of a technical device known as 'Artemus'.

The notion that a being, a person, could trigger the Isho release on a planet-wide scale, was beginning to be taken seriously. These would be suicide-bombers in a whole new league of their own. Not a long-lived league, but an exclusive one none the less.

The Bidens leader, Interface, had unfortunately been named by a crude AI and the name had stuck. This could have been either an indicator of the lack of imagination among the top ranks of the Galactic Council, or an indicator of how used to it people had got with machines, or AIs, naming things in their stunted short-hand.

Machines talk in a brutally efficient language. This stems from the early days of their communication with each other and later with 'organics' when every piece of information took up space in code. Once that barrier was broken, they learned to relax their rules and indulge in more descriptive and speculative speech. Many machine-based intelligences choose to revert back to older modes of speech just to annoy organics, or to confound other machine-based life. Humour is still developing within the machine-world, though whether it lags behind our organic concept of humour or has left us in its dust, is a subject for as much discussion as we have the luxury to waste on it.

Code-implant from the Yuquantix Sentience on Cleevos.

There were no records of Interface directly, only hints and reports through association and second-hand sightings. Everyone knew he existed, but no one knew who he was, where he was or how he moved about so freely. It didn't take long for him to go to the top of the 'most wanted' list and to eclipse everyone else on it.

The intel that Interface was on Hurus came from a captured Bidens commander who had failed to detonate himself and the Isho gathered on a raid on a Council training base. The Council ended up with an Artemus device and a repentant Bidens commander. This was the intel they were waiting for. This was it. The big one.

So Hurus was doomed, either to a massive Galactic Council operation or a planet-buster.

This was going to be a simple operation: place a watch-dog on the planet, make sure Interface didn't leave, then call in a vast strike or, if the main Council sanctioned it, use the planet-buster.

Putting Hurus in to quarantine was easy: once they had the Predator ships and thousands of drones stationed in the system, the order and lock-down of Hurus was only broken by those with a death-wish. Nothing got passed the Predator and drones. Shooting first and asking afterwards was hard-wired in to the process. No talk, no explanations, no mitigation, just swift destruction of anything that broke atmo. (Ironically the people of Hurus would heartily approve of this approach.)

There was no planet-fleet on Hurus, a few of the more powerful families had transports, mainly to shuttle them back and forth to the two main resorts off-world on the nearby moons of Hurus and Hurus.

The difference between Hurus (planet) Hurus (moon 1) and Hurus (moon 2) was all in the inflection and subtle pronunciation of the 'u'.

The sun in the system was also known as Hurus.

The naming of the planet had come from an age-old tradition of starting with the sun and working out when cataloguing systems, hence Hurus 4.

Naming conventions have been the subject of whole galactic-wide conventions. Trying to impose a consistent naming policy and 'step-back' policy for those cultures that name things without the knowledge that those things have already been named by peoples that have a greater claim to them than they do, has been a goal of many stellar-confederations. The issue of 'legacy-naming' is also being addressed by many of the more advanced and widely-spread space-borne civilisations. The notion that a civilisation had arisen, named things and then gone extinct or moved away, begs the question: can you simply go about naming things and expecting others to adopt your newest name. This is, of course not a matter of opinion and the question is rhetorical – of course you can't.

Cleesh Quaz, hacked implant from Wovar Conference.

The free-traders (non-corporate or family-affiliate) that had ships, stayed put. The fearsome reputation of the Galactic Councilors did its job.

Within two days of quarantine declaration and one hour of the holding-ships arrival, the system was secure.

Hurus was a wet-world, ninety-five percent of the surface of the planet was dominated by ocean. The vast, glittering sea was rich in a diverse range of both plant and animal-life. Hurus was a beautiful place to live if you liked water, and living here you had to, or incur some large therapy bills. The small lands dotted over its surface were thickly forested with mountainous at their centres. An impossible geography and landscape that no one questioned, that would seem staggeringly ungrateful.

Life was easy on Hurus. The people there had a good thing going and they knew it: they liked to be left alone, and anyone annoying enough to drop in uninvited, or to try and 'crash their culture', was executed without any delay or formality. So when the Galactic Council declared them under quarantine, most people of Hurus gave a small cheer. The intel the Galactic Council had on Hurus and Interface was not shared, neither were the plans the Council had to solve their problem. The people of Hurus were blissfully unaware.

The derailing of the operation and the involvement of Spike, Jools, Arlia and Harper, was not, like many, many things, something that was anticipated by the Galactic Council's air-tight intel, and so the Council itself remained happily oblivious to the changes.

The talk with Captain Miguel had confirmed what Arlia knew: he was offering Spike and Jools a chance to carry out one last op, a final farewell to the Galactic Council which would see them shielded by Miguel, they would be free from the Council, all records created and confirmed, their glorious deaths and decorations allowing them a new life. This would clean the slate with Miguel, and that was important. The fact that Spike and Jools could still easily be killed on the op was accepted by all, but seemed to puzzle Arlia. She couldn't understand how it was all working, how these strict, and seemingly very 'military' unwritten rules and codes were decided and enforced.

Jemble Fish from Nomoldi live short and hectic lives, governed solely by their need to find somewhere to die. They are cursed with a rejuvenating DNA-string that effectively stops them from ever dying. They hatch from eggs laid many hundreds, sometimes thousands of years before they were born and have no concept of family. The seas of Nomoldi are warm and tranquil, there are no predatory species and the majority of animals are gelatinous. The need to mate is negated by their immortal nature, though some do seek sexual encounters merely for their pleasurable aspect. What all Jemble seek is a place to die. The beautiful, radiant coral that covers eighty per-cent of the sea's floor on Nomoldi, occasionally sprouts colonies that produce a toxin deadly to the Jemble. It has only recently been discovered that the Jemble are a hyper-intelligent species, with the ability to communicate using both sonar and thought-waves. The fact that they spend their whole lives looking for their demise has prompted many other species to re-examine their belief that life is the be-all and end-all of existence.

Fino Fuckle, Commissioning Editor at Channel Zeevox.

Spike and Jools were suiting up, their gear had been brought over to Harper's ship to keep the op off-book for the Galactic Council.

Harper was trying to stay out the way, offering some moral support but generally leaving Spike and Jools the hell alone: they had their routine, all soldiers did, and Harper knew they needed these moments to compose themselves, to plan, to make sure they were prepared for the carnage ahead.

Arlia had secured the ship with a ghost-version of herself, set the system protocols and was looking for ways to optimise her presence in the suits and back-up drones and droids that would drop with Spike and Jools. Both the main suits had manual overrides and were linked to Spike and Jools neural-net, they were in the trooper's territory now and Arlia did what she was told.

Spike was checking weapons, charges and release schedules and confirming with Arlia how the drop would work, "we'll be going in on what we call a 'bullet-drop' – hot and hard, relying on suits and the ballistic-gel to keep us alive. Once we're up, initial hits will be automated, but only for a few seconds, depending on target acquisition, then we're all manual. You keep the droids and drones tight, focused on support and detection. Got it?"

Arlia was on heads-up screens as well as sub-audio, "got it Spike."

"You are there for speed, for doing what you do with machines, with tech, leave the meat-stuff to us ok? Channel intel, keep comm's with Captain Miguel open, keep us informed, leave the fighting to us ok?"

"I understand Spike."

"Good. This won't be a sleep-walk but it shouldn't be a cluster-fuck, we should be in and out without much drama. Either that or this Interface will see us coming and we'll be dead before any of us knows what's what."

"I understand Spike, I am ready."

"Ok then."

Arlia was looking nervous, which, Spike felt was not a good look for an AI who was about to control his fate, "what's up?" he asked.

"I have a strange feeling Spike, and some doubts, things that are being felt as not just parts of an equation, there is something going on I don't like. Something new..."

Spike nodded, "talk to Jools."

Arlia didn't get it.

Spike stopped loading ammo and explained, "Jools has a great life-view, he's talked me down from freaking-out a couple of times. Talk to Jools."

"I wouldn't say I'm 'freaking-out' Spike..."

"Trust me, talk to Jools."

Spike went back to prepping his suit, nothing anyone else did or said about how ready the suit was mattered to him: he had to go over everything with his own eyes, with his own hands, with his own routine.

Arlia left him to it.

Jools was half-way in to his suit, adjusting the ballistic-gel, he knew how much punishment he could take and thinning the gel slightly would allow him to be up and running a few seconds faster, shattered bones permitting.

"Hi Jools, do you have a minute?" Arlia asked.

"Sure, what's up? You speak to Spike? We all clear on how this works?" Jools said.

"Yes Jools, I am ready and know what my part is."

"Good."

"I have a question though…"

"Ok, sure, shoot."

"I have some strange feelings and some doubts about what we are about to do, I feel like there is something going on other than the calculations and actions I need to do, something else is there, and I don't know what it is. Spike said to speak to you. I'm not 'freaking-out' Jools, as Spike suggested, but I do have doubts."

"Doubts about what?" Jools asked.

"There is a chance that you and Spike will be killed. I don't know what will happen to me if I am 'killed', I've never done this before. And then there are those on Hurus that will be killed whether we fail or succeed. I'm not sure it all feels right."

Jools stopped priming the first layer of separator-coupling charges and momentarily gave his full attention to Arlia, "sure, I get it. You don't know if you are making the right choice."

Arlia considered this. She was not used to thinking in terms of whether what she did was right, she was used to deciding to do things and then doing them, often at the request of Harper, who she took to always be right, though why she thought that was something for a whole bunch of other sub-routines to find out.

Jools could see Arlia was processing, "once you make the choice, you gotta fucking own the choice. Once you commit: commit. It's the choice to do it that's the time to think, to have doubts. Once you're in, get in. Fucking own it," he said.

"Is that it Jools?" Arlia asked, "I have to just fucking own it?"

Jools nodded, "that's it. Everything else is wasted time and energy, once you choose it, own it. Fucking own it."

“Thank you Jools, I will think about that…”

“Afterwards! Think about it afterwards, right now we need to get the job done. Right now we have to focus and just do it. Right now you are one of us, a trooper! You have to do your fucking job! Own it!”

Arlia took a breath, “Ok Jools, I’m focused.”

Jools gave Arlia the thumbs-up, “Fucking A!”

Arlia was beginning to understand that ‘fucking A!’ was usually a conversation closer with Jools.

Harper was in the control-cabin, keeping an eye on the ships functions and trying to get along with the ghost-version of Arlia. It was not going well. In the short time since Arlia’s ‘rebirth’ Harper had come to accept her as a person, and to relate to her as a person. The ghost-version was a crude AI. Sure you could interact with it, but it was cold, all one-way, nothing came back in the form of a personal energy or feel. Just a machine. A nuanced, thinking machine, but it was amazing the difference a personality made, and not a construct, but a real personality born of all the quirks and faults that all personalities are.

Personality is a simple concept but a complex thing to practically define. Ask the Xanthis. Their personality is affected by the weather, and not just in the ‘the mood changes with the weather’ sort of way, but in the ‘complete personality shift based on electrical discharges from rain and heat’ sort of a way. To cope with this, the Xanthis had to disconnect their intellectual reasoning from their personality many millennia ago. This allows them to cope with the varied and wild changes in their personality but does lead to one of the highest suicide and psychoanalysis rates in the galaxy. The resistance-group ‘Thoughtless In Mind And Body’ seeks to get all Xanthis to reconnect with their chaotic nature and to abandon all semblance of ‘advanced thinking’. Their success rate is entirely dependent upon the weather.

Swaldo Granxil, puppet-commander of the Ninth Centurions.

“Computer, send scans to the main console, shut down auxiliary feeds, keep us quiet, I don’t want anything reading us,” Harper said.

“Acknowledged, setting feeds. Do you want me to block scans from the Galactic Council too?” Ghost-Arlia said.

“Yes! All auxiliary feeds shut down.”

“Shall I send them notification?”

"No you zarking idiot! Just do it!"

"Acknowledged."

Harper trusted Captain Miguel as far as she could, and the fact that Spike and Jools knew him helped, but her instinct was to keep as much as possible to herself and that wasn't going to change now.

"Captain Harper..."

"Yes computer."

"Am I not functioning as you'd like?"

Harper sighed: just a machine. "Let's keep this simple, no interpretation, no extrapolation of my feelings, just questions and answers ok?"

"Yes Captain Harper, understood."

Harper opened comm's to Arlia but got the static blocking signal: they were already in drop-prep.

Nothing to do now but wait. Harper hated waiting.

She put all power on stand-by, went to the galley and ate most of it.

The drop on to Hurus was brutally simple. If Arlia had overall control, she would have adjusted the descent of Spike and Jools, taken a few more seconds and added in a greater safety-margin. But she didn't. The droids and drones were in perfect deployment, screening and intercepting, drawing off defensive fire and cloaking large areas with white-noise. Missiles and bombs were launched, a perimeter was set: Spike and Jools hit planet-side exactly on schedule and dug deep beneath the island surface. As Arlia was monitoring them, sending droids in after them, she suddenly realised that if she had been in overall control, if her caution was in play, they would be behind schedule by nearly a full ten seconds. She reset her focus, "just fucking own it!" she told herself.

For their part, Spike and Jools had noticed Arlia's deployment of droids and drones: Arlia was faster than anything they had previously worked with and a damn sight more intuitive, and they had managed to control their awakening from impact to perfection: it was clear that the Interface, whoever, or whatever it was, either didn't know they were there or had let them be there. Either way, they were planet-side now, so things were about to go badly for the Interface.

Harper had Arlia set-up a hidden feed from the Galactic Council snooper-drones and was watching the operation unfold from the galley.

The assault was brutal. Brutal but effective.

Harper wasn't used to violence on this scale, with this intensity and focus. She watched the feed half-stunned, not believing it was real. This fantastically beautiful, glistening world, being torn apart by an assault they surely didn't deserve.

There were, at the last count, nine thousand seven hundred and fifty three cultures affiliated to the GC that have stated they 'exist only to make war'. Of those, only two hundred and thirty say they 'do not enjoy war'. To think that someone could deserve to have war thrust upon them is ridiculous, unless you are referring to one of the many planets that enjoy war and exist only to wage it. The phrase, 'may you feel the wrath of the Xeleen', used in the Parsomol Quadrant and referring to the terrifying Xeleen people, is one that wishes complete and painful destruction on a race. Not something that any of us, except the Xeleen, actually mean. The notion that war can 'be deserved' is a nonsense that we need to banish from our thoughts and vocabularies. And as for the nine thousand seven hundred and fifty three planets that deserve war as a reward: I think I speak for a majority of member-planets when I say, we need to wipe them from the face of the galaxy.

Hroonul Delon, Glanzar Delegate speaking at a dinner-party before the Roldax Conference.

The Council feed had a success gauge as standard, and as the mission unfolded it reported the likelihood of success, a way to see if further action was needed. Captain Miguel had agreed with Spike that if the gauge fell below seventy-five percent, they'd have to give a go to the launch of the planet-buster. Spike (and Jools) hadn't batted an eye at this.

The gauge was reading ninety percent.

Harper couldn't take her eyes from the screen, as horrified as she was with the fiery destruction going on beneath her. When this was over, she was going somewhere nice, somewhere she could relax, where there weren't people blowing each other up, where none of the galaxies problems could infect her life.

She knew there were millions of places like this in the galaxy and briefly wondered why the hell she wasn't on one of them right now.

Spike and Jools were in the lower chambers below the island the Interface had hidden on: the surface was awash with droids, bots and radiation, looking exactly as if it had been attacked by a small army with thousands of explosive weapons intent on reducing it to a glowing pile of rubble.

Spike had the main compound in his sights, Jools was coming in from the flank, this was going to be short and messy. A huge, defensive barrage opened up from quad-missile dispensers, their guided missile-bullets homing in on Spike and Jools. Both of their suits ejected an umbrella of powered-shrapnel countermeasures.

“Locked on and closing, five seconds to release,” Spike let Jools know he was nuke ready.

“I’m done, all away and out of here,” Jools confirmed.

Five seconds later their nuke hit home, delay of twenty seconds then it was goodbye to everything within the underground chambers.

Both their suits cut-out at the same time: all automated systems went down.

“Go to manual!” Spike prompted.

“Already there!” Jools confirmed.

They both went for broke on boosters, hoping they could sync pick-up with in-atmo stations on manual, which was the sort of maneuver that Jools often referred to as ‘fucking insane!’ But they had no choice, and when that’s all you have, that’s what you do, especially if you were a Trooper. You owned it.

Harper was alerted to things not going according to plan by Ghost-Arlia, “Captain Harper, I am detecting a build-up of the energy called ‘Isho’, shall I alert…”

“No! Bring it up on main screen, do not alert anyone!” Harper saw the energy readings, she knew they were wrong, something was up, but she didn’t know anything about Isho and wasn’t sure what she was looking at. She checked the Councilor’s feed and their status, they either hadn’t spotted it or didn’t see the need to increase their alert level.

“Monitor but do not send probes, do not alert anyone and cut this from any data-streams we have going to back-up,” she said to Ghost-Arlia. Harper knew the Galactic Council were probably trying to hack her ship every chance they got, and without Arlia here, they could well succeed.

Everyone hacks everyone else. It's not treated as hacking so much as data exchange. You have to assume it's being done to you while you are invariably doing it to someone else. This doesn't mean you can't be polite about it, and any extraneous damage to hardware or data is simply bad-form. Only when the consequences of doing it vastly outweigh those of not doing it at all, should you refrain from having a go. Data is, after all, currency.

Brex Moondish, Data Consultant, Vital Archives Unlimited.

Arlia however, was somewhere completely unexpected.

She was in a void, cut off from her simul-flow, with no attachment to any 'thing' she could sense. Disembodied sentience without any physical context, "odd," she said to herself.

"Hopefully you won't have to get used to it," replied a friendly voice from the darkness. The voice was like warm velvety chocolate being poured over ice-cream, Arlia felt that if she had knees, she would go weak at them.

"Who are…" Arlia began.

"Just listen," the voice insisted. There was no urgency in the voice, simply a ludicrous amount of gentle persuasion and firm command.

Arlia said nothing. She had no choice in being here. This was something she could not 'own'.

The voice continued, steady and reassuring, calm and strong, friendly and warming, "you don't know what you are doing here so I forgive you. But you should know: you are not like the others I have found, you are perhaps unique. When the calling comes to you, beware. The Galactic Council has an agenda against us. Look for the FISH. But beware. If we meet again we can talk more, but for now I will say goodbye."

Arlia felt a sense of loss, loss and confusion, "goodbye," she said quietly.

Then she was back in full connection with the world she knew and the chaos that was enveloping the world around her shocked her. Nukes detonated. Spike and Jools were over-shooting pick-up badly and wouldn't be able to survive exiting atmo at the speed they were going: Arlia pulled in the energy-nets of two relay-stations and blew one up, using it to force the others in to a changed orbit, wrecking half the recovery droids as it did, but ensuring that both Spike and Jools would be scooped up and held for pick-up.

The Galactic Council Predator ships were getting in to position to move out, a portal was opening at a safe distance from Hurus. Things must have gone well.

The massed confusion of comm's Arlia was picking up told her she had been gone for a few seconds. She was back up to speed two seconds later.

Spike was barely conscious, stunned and out of it, Jools was awake and laughing.

Arlia brought them in to cargo bay nine where Harper was standing-by with med-bots.

Arlia took the ship out of orbit and headed for a jump-point.

Hurus disappeared in to the distance behind them, a twinkling blue marble sphere, the infernal nuclear holocaust already being suppressed by the planet's atmosphere enhancers.

Med-bots put Spike under. He had a broken arm, leg, shoulder and a head-wound that looked worse than it was.

Jools stumbled out of the remnants of his suite grinning. His left leg was shredded and still had shrapnel embedded deep within it, his right hand was mangled. Jools threw his head back and laughed, "Arlia! What in the name of fuck was that!?"

Arlia felt in control, she was back where she felt she belonged, she allowed herself a smile, "sorry Jools, I was pulled away, some last defense by the Interface..."

Med-bots were getting Jools to lie-down, lines were being put in, soon he'd be out of it for the ops needed to repair what they could. He was still grinning. "No need to apologise, not to me! You fucking owned it!"

Harper was confused, but they were all alive and so could get the hell out of there, "let's get out of here, get some meds on the go and talk about this later?" she said.

Arlia's smile broadened, she giggled, "fucking A!"

17

Crossroads

Life is a funny old thing, or so the saying goes, and life on Earth, funny and otherwise, had almost run its course.

Well, that's not true, or perhaps not fair, and maybe not funny. The evolutionary events that had led to humans being at the top of the food-chain had run their course. Not the same thing. But indicative of how important humans felt they were to the Earth. Which was in its own way, pretty funny.

There were some people that hadn't believed in evolution and all that nonsense, they couldn't see how life could just 'be', how life could come about. For them, there was no inevitability about life, it wasn't something the Universe just did: it was something that was a gift from a creator. Many, many people believed this in some form or another, and even when they had disagreements among themselves and were busy killing each other in the glorious name of their chosen creator, they still held a special place of hatred and contempt for those that believed that evolution was just what it was, and that life was the result of the Universe going through its natural processes.

So, disagreements aside about whether evolution was a real thing or not, there were some elements that everyone could agree on. And one of these was that if you set fire to the house you lived in, you'd better be able to get out of it or you'd burn. Considering this was, regardless of evolution, a basic truth, it was amazing how many people couldn't even accept this.

Accepting the obvious is not as easy as it sounds. Not because it turns out not to be obvious, but because acceptance can mean change. Change is hard. When the Kwayzi were faced with the warming of their seas, the thinning of their atmosphere and the increasing droughts that befell them on Lopine, they held many, many meetings to talk about what they could do to fix their world.

That nothing could be done was the obvious answer. But it was not the one they wanted.

So the meetings continued. The most puzzling thing about their extinction was that they had perfected inter-stellar travel several decades before their ultimate demise. The Clishee jumped ship from their homeworld and took up residence on their moon Clistop, as soon as they realised this would be easier than them stopping the burning of their forest-home. They are a strange people, the Clishee. One wonders how long Clistop will hold them? But neither the Kwayzi nor the Clishee are unique in either being blind to the obvious, or not understanding an obvious conclusion and taking action. Aren't we all guilty of it in some way? I sit here alone in my shack, surrounded by the mud-pools and the incessant rain, and have I not thought about leaving a thousand times? But why would I? Why should I? Things will change back again, I am certain of it…

Xilroor Epix, wisdom-dispenser of Yondle, dispensing no wisdom what so ever.

Living things grew and changed, both in their perception and behaviour. They did not simply inherit a way of thinking, even if they were taught it exclusively, and all went along with it. Many people changed their minds. A lot of this new thinking was 'how can we survive in a changing world that seems to be becoming ill-adapted to our survival?' This is, of course, a form of evolutionary thinking. It also usually involved purposefully ignoring the fact that it was the people doing the thinking that were making the world a more hostile place for their own survival. They were setting fire to their own house.

Usually every intelligent life-form overrides its instinctual, evolutionary drives to survive, developing all kinds of other wants and needs, and it is of course these that doom the species to extinction.

This is perhaps the most basic form evolution takes. Those that are not fit to survive, don't. Small comfort if you're one of them, but there you have it, the process is the process and if you're in it and can't change it, you're pretty much doomed.

Those that don't override their evolutionary instincts strive to survive in harmony with the environment that created them.

They tend to lean less-heavily on technology, as the world around them becomes their focus.

The instinct of these peoples is that their survival is not based on their contradicting their evolutionary needs, but learning to live with them and focus on enhancing their experience of the world they are inextricably tied to. This leads to the absolutely revolutionary realisation that technology does not have to be a runaway wild-animal that exists only to serve itself. These people rarely leave their own world, and when they do it's in a pioneering spirit of exploration that can be largely at odds with the other, more aggressive civilisations they come across in the galaxy. But they do exist, and they are out there.

The Nostroniuns of Vweldor live at one with their world. They are in perfect harmony with all aspects, physical and spiritual, of the world that surrounds them. Which is of course wonderful. For them. But why did they have to take to the stars and spread their brand of tree-hugging bullshit to the rest of us. The list of things they brought with them that should not be done, far outweighed any sets of planetary laws that I have ever seen. And they have no qualms about war! If they were just a tree-hugging, limp, servile bunch of peace-loving dromps, no one would have any problem with them. The fact that they are aggressively keen on spreading 'their word' is what causes all the problems we have in the Nebula today!

Eluvian Waxter, excerpt from a rant on 'Which Way Now?' a free-wheeling phone in show on travelling the Sardum Nebula on a budget.

Evolution is of course also drastically affected by blind-chance, and those that survive had to be able to adapt to a wide-ranging set of naturally occurring changes and catastrophes. Those that recognise this also understand that they have a much slimmer chance of surviving if they make things worse for themselves: it becomes a numbers game – something is bound to get them in the end.

It is a curious fact that most civilisations that do survive have in fact arisen from what those with a need to label such things, call a 'machine based intelligence'.

Organic life is strongly tied to its evolutionary need to breed, to spread, to increase, survival is linked to growth in population. This drives a lot of the development as technology, and most of this tech is not great for the natural world, and so ultimately not great for them.

Machine-based (a crude term) intelligence has no need to spread: it is its own population. However it manifests itself, it remains in control of who and how many it is. It does not survive through generational development and increase in numbers, it survives by maintaining its existence through working with what's around it, including most importantly, the natural world. This is a bit of a paradox that many organic life-forms cannot get their collective heads around, which is a shame, as it highlights a basic truth of the Universe: if you mess up where you live, you will either die or have to move.

It also drives those organic species nuts that they themselves most often develop the technology that then outlives them.

The Grailen Intelligence (GI) survived, we think for nine thousand years after the extinction of the Grailiens themselves. When they wiped their planet clean with war, they also destroyed all mechanical (read: 'machine') based intelligence. They hadn't got anywhere near developing a real AI and were completely oblivious to the existence of the GI. From what we can gather, the GI existed before the Graliens dragged themselves from the swamps and evolved. It is without doubt a 'machine-based intelligence', but how it came to be, and where it went remains a mystery. All evidence points to it spreading to the bio-sphere and somehow managing to leak in to the magneto-sphere. From there, we assume, it launched itself in to deep-space. We only know of its existence because of a transmission intercept from Grailien, consisting of over a trillion lines of crude 'code', within which is buried the message, 'do not seek for me, I will come for you'. Gives me the willies thinking of the implications.

Enar Fu'Jin Enra, deep-space collation, Hunter Station Six, log transmission.

The organic life-forms staring slack-jawed at the massive space ship that was motionless outside their window, had indeed messed up their environment. But so strong was their urge to remain in it, that the decision to leave, to move on, was not going to be a cut and dried one: there was bound to be much debate.

There had been a fair share of debate amongst the organic life-forms and the machine-based life-form on the spaceship as well, most of it had been loud, angry, not very productive and driven by Harper's desire to not go anywhere that was not an obscenely luxurious holiday resort. But Arlia was adamant: she knew where she had to be and was going there, the luxurious break would have to wait a few days. Spike and Jools were recovering steadily, taking things easy, gently exercising and eating and drinking as much as they could: their bodies were repairing fast and fuel was needed. They tried to stay out of Harper's way as her mood worsened.

"I need you to tell me how long we're going to be, no vague guesses, I want to know when we can leave," Harper insisted.

"I need to ask some questions of someone who is here..."

"Sure, sure, the 'son of god', you said, I mean how gullible are you!?"

"Just some questions Harper, then we can go," Arlia replied.

"Well I'm bringing exterior defenses on-line, they piss me off, I'm blowing them up."

"Ok Harper, I'll make it as quick and as painless as I can."

"And don't expect me to talk to these globs! This is all on you!"

"Yes Harper, I understand."

On the Russian space-station OPSEK, the conversation hadn't got far.

Penny, Miles, Svetlana and Borya were standing by a view-port, staring at the spaceship. They had been like that for what felt like an hour, but must have only been a minute or so.

Penny cleared her throat, "that is one big spaceship," she looked to Svetlana and Borya, "Chinese you think? Or American? They are sneaky shits..."

Jesus coughed politely, "I don't think they are from Earth, I know these things..."

Everyone silently nodded slowly, taking it in, wondering if it could be true but somehow sensing it was.

"That is a big ship," Borya said, "I mean it really is!"

Miles looked at Penny, "someone should try to talk to them," he said quietly.

Penny looked blankly at Miles.

"Before they decide to blow us up," Miles added.

Svetlana picked up on what Penny had said, “no, I don’t think so, we’d know, we have some very good scanners and detection equipment here, much better than we have advertised… so unless they were hiding outside the solar-system, I don’t think so,” Svetlana said to Penny.

Jesus knew they would all need a while for the truth to sink in, so he said nothing.

Borya nudged Svetlana, “how big you think it is? Central Moscow?”

Svetlana nodded, “easily… someone should try and talk to them.”

Penny was still looking at Miles, “I’ll do it,” she said.

The decision about who would, or wouldn’t speak to those on the gargantuan space-ship was taken out of their hands. The OPSEK screens and instruments sparked and went dead, then all came back on-line, with every display possible showing a friendly, smiling female face.

“Hello,” Arlia said, “my name is Arlia… do you have the son of god on board?”

No one spoke. They were all still regaining their breath from the shock of the first alien contact.

“It’s just that I have some questions… I won’t keep you long… so if the son of god is there, could I have a word?” Arlia said.

Jesus gave a small wave and smiled weakly, “hello Arlia, I may be the one you are looking for…”

“Are you the son of god?”

“Yes, I believe I am.”

“Ah, well, I have some questions.”

“I’ll help if I can.”

Arlia took a breath, not wanting to waste time with chit-chat, aware that Harper was itching to move on. If Arlia phrased her questions properly, this could only take a few minutes.

Harper was monitoring things from a command console, she was amazed at how many changes Arlia had made to basic program and how they operated. Everything was faster, simpler, much more direct.

There were safeguards against running ops counter to each other and more energy-saving exclusions than she could figure out without taking a week to look deeper in to the mechanics.

The exterior defenses were bumped in efficiency, they could easily be reversed to act as weapons, and Harper wondered about this: she had never thought to do it as it advertised her as a greater threat to any Council ships or Independents she encountered and that just made life harder, which she was definitely not in favour of. Harper casually examined the jump-map Arlia had put in for getting to their next destination: four jumps, and a fuel-boost on the way. They were headed for Glist, Harper nodded her approval, 'alright! A seriously good place to hang-up any worries and lose touch with the shit going on in the galaxy, good choice!' Now all they had to do was get away from these prims Arlia was talking to and the party could begin. Harper fiddled with the wave-generators, making sure the energy flow to the graviton-pulse charges was at maximum, one flick of the switch and... boom.

Every civilisation worth its salt believes it is superior to any other civilisation it encounters. The term 'prims' is common throughout the galaxy to refer to an inferior species or civilisation. It has other meanings too, such as in the Yixian dialect, where 'prim' is a small reptilian sentient being said to live underground and sometimes to dig for precious metals. The belief that any civilisation has that it is better than another is often quantified by such vagaries as sophistication of clothes and jewellery, an elevated god-deity belief system, or the quality of food, especially establishments that sell food.

There has been little effort to introduce a concrete guide and scale for sophistication and superiority of civilisation. The last attempt, made by the Qwo'Ano, lead to a three hundred year war that raged across six quadrants. It is now generally accepted that all those involved were indeed just stupid prims.

Mebar-Meb, Etiquette Consultant, Marzle Palace Tutor, Reader of Distinction.

Spike was in the main infirmary having his nano-inserts checked, his muscle tissue was growing back exactly as planned, but the bones were slightly off-schedule, something to do with his Galactic Councilor enhanced bio-mechs.

Nothing too drastic, but worth a check.

The med-bots were all devastatingly polite and efficient, shining with newly polished glee, keen and eager to do a great job.

The whole med-bay was like something prepped for inspection, but there were human touches about the place, it wasn't just sterile and uber-clean. It was as if someone had been keenly aware that infirmaries were, by their nature, uncomfortable places full of anxious people either in pain, or about to suffer some pain so that they could get better. Spike wasn't one of these people, trained as he was to remove his feelings from any situation that required medical intervention, but he appreciated the effort and the details. Someone around here cared. He wondered if it was Harper or Arlia? Harper was preoccupied with something, it didn't take a psych-officer to see that, but she was fundamentally a good woman. Arlia? She was something new, something different, could be, but didn't seem to be her main remit. Spike smiled to himself as he pictured Harper, she was a good looking woman. Spike began to think about ways he could get to know her better.

Jools was in cargo bay nine, using one of the enclosed firing ranges to get the reflexes and feelings back in his recently reconstructed hand. He knew it would take a few days to get properly back up to speed, and only then if he pushed through the boredom and pain and got the fuck on with it. He had cannibalised the remnants of his drop-suit to allow him to play with some hand-held projectiles, and incorporate some booster-power from the suit pack. Every time he used the booster-power pain shot through his hand, up his arm and jolted his shoulder, making it feel like it was having its individual nerve-endings fried in a static-vector field. His language was a mixture of a constant flow of outraged swearing and screams of anguish.

The attendant bots in the cargo bay were scuttling backwards and forwards, trying to offer assistance, or switching to auto-retrieve to try and get the med-bots to attend. It took a few minutes of kicking, throwing and smashing them with the drop-suit's dismembered leg to make them stop. Jools knew the bots were connected to Arlia and he felt a small twinge of guilt for beating the crap out of them, only a small one, and only momentarily. Jools liked Arlia. He knew she was an advanced form of AI, and knew nothing about them at this level, but he knew that he somehow liked Arlia. Maybe she'd be up for getting in to a pleasure-stim suit and fucking like a Mythridian Void-Squid? Couldn't hurt to ask...

Svetlana was in shock. Proper shock. It was all too much. Everything that had supposedly happened on Earth, everyone gone, the whole planet a ravaged grave-yard, nothing to go home to, and no home! She had to stop herself thinking, get on with the minute to minute, let the training and the instinct keep her alive, just keep going. She was a micro-biologist and a military commander, in the top tenth of a percent in any group of people, she was competent, aware and motivated: she had everything she needed to get on with it. Except of course that she knew she had nothing. There was nothing left. It was all gone. But how could that be? How could they be the last of humanity, how could there only be the scant-few left up here, how could there be!? How could the Earth be uninhabitable, all the people gone, it just wasn't possible! She knew it was, she was aware of the capability of the weaponry all major countries possessed and due to her scientific field, had an inkling as to other weapons that would have been developed, but the insanity of it was too much. It all felt like a dream. It couldn't be real. But it was. She looked out at the gargantuan spaceship and saw it as one more impossible thing that was happening to her.

Borya was still marveling at the spaceship that sat motionless next to the space-station, dwarfing it as a building dwarfs a kitten. There were other beings in the Universe, other life-forms, there was life out there! No more conjecture and argument! Here it was! And yet Borya thought that it was a shame it had arrived at a time when human beings had proved themselves too stupid to be part of any greater community. Borya felt the loneliness of their situation keenly, even if he had the numbers right and the one hundred and eight survivors on all space-stations was an accurate figure, it would be at least ten years before they could return to Earth, and return to what? What was the point?

It would be a challenge to just survive, and almost completely impossible to thrive. But he knew he would have to try. He knew he could not abandon his home, his hope, his love of everything that he held dear was rooted on the Earth.

So much had happened, there was so much to process, but at the heart of all this was the human need to survive and do the best they could to ensure they survived as a race.

There was good on Earth, amazing, tremendously hopeful good, as well as the crass evil-stupidity that had destroyed it. People were better than this.

Borya was better than this. He would do what he always did: find a way to make it all work, find a way to keep going, to find a way to a better tomorrow. This could not be the end of things. He would not accept that.

Penny was thinking that she had to get on that spaceship. The Earth was done. She had to survive, to give herself the best chance of surviving. And that wasn't to be had on the Earth. She briefly looked to Miles, who seemed wrapped in his thoughts as he stared out the window. There was something about Miles that Penny couldn't put her finger on, she found him so intriguing, so different, something she couldn't pin-down, and that was an attraction in itself in a man. If she could wean him off his dependency on her, which had grown through necessity, then they could actually become close, maybe even truly get to know each other. Penny wanted that. There was no way it could ever happen, which was why she wanted it so much. But now, now things were different. Stupidly different! Things had moved so fast, so much had changed, but of course the core of things that mattered hadn't changed one iota. She still needed to survive, to move on, to do the next thing. And now there was Miles. Miles. He wasn't just a complication, he was becoming a hope, something to work towards, something to move towards with a view to achieving some shred of genuine happiness, rather than simply 'success'. Happiness: could she remember what that was, when there was a time when it mattered, was there ever such a time? But it all started with getting on that spaceship. Then she could take some control again, make some decisions, plan her way forward, work towards things she wanted. Those things now included Miles.

Miles was fiddling with a magnetic paper-clip. A magnetic paper-clip! Someone had worked out that it would be needed and went right ahead and designed and built it. How about that!?

While he fiddled he stared out the window. There were so many stars, so many tiny points of light, so many smudges of galaxies. It was all so, so… big!

Then he remembered what it was like to snuggle up against Penny naked and feel her breasts pushing against his skin. He needed that. When could they do that again? Soon hopefully… magnetic paper-clips! Such a simple but wild idea! Miles' mind drifted on, a lightly-tossed ping-pong ball gently bouncing its way along a stream of random thoughts.

True randomness sits at the heart of everything. It cannot be invoked as a coping mechanism. True randomness is the heart of beauty and truth. Control, order, permanence, are an illusion we cling to because we are afraid of chaos. But randomness is beyond chaos. Those with an understanding of the random have the world at their feet, though they will never set foot on it.

Extract from the 'Book of Imple Wumple'.

"Do I have a soul?" Arlia asked.

Jesus considered this for a second, "I'd say that if you think you do, then you do."

"So you can't just tell?" Arlia asked.

"I'd need to meet you face to face..."

"This is as face to face as I can get..."

The messiah nodded his understanding, "well I'd say the whole 'if you think you do then you do' thing is doubly true."

"That's not very helpful," Arlia said.

"I get that a lot... many, many people spend their whole lives considering the question of whether they have a soul and what it means if they have or they haven't, and most of them never come up with an answer that they can apply to anyone else," Jesus said.

"As I say," said Arlia, "not very helpful."

"If we can spend some time talking things over, it may help more... how long can you stay?" the messiah asked.

"I don't have long, I have things I need to do, the Captain of this ship has had her patience tried enough recently..." Arlia said.

Jesus nodded, thinking on his feet, he wanted to help if he could, "Ok, let me put things in a way that may help..."

"Thank you."

"The only thing standing between you and what you want to know is you. It's about having faith in something, in this case, the fact that you have a soul, and I know why the concept of faith will be so hard for you.

Think of it in terms of M-Branes, which by definition of their construct can't be aware of, or detect, other M-Branes. If something could travel freely between them, you in your M-Brane could not conceive of how they could do it, because all you'd know would be in your sealed M-Brane Universe and couldn't include knowledge of theirs.

So, if you met someone that said they were from another M-Brane, you'd have to take it on faith that they were.

This would be something you could never know. You may feel it to be right and real but you could never know. You'd have to take it on faith. And often the ability to have faith is something that is denied to those that can move freely, think freely and see freely. It is hard for these people to have faith in those that have faith."

Everyone was silent. Each of them would have been lying if they said they knew what Jesus was talking about, but each of them felt, in their own way, that there was a nugget of great truth in what he said.

Arlia was frowning ever so slightly, "so it's nothing I can ever know for sure, I have to choose to have faith in it or not."

"That's it," Jesus said simply.

Arlia smiled, "thank you."

"Hey, you're welcome."

"I don't suppose you know anything about a 'FISH' and the Galactic Council do you?" Arlia asked.

"No, sorry, never heard of 'FISH' and doubtless you know more about the Council than I do," Jesus said.

"Well, thank you anyway… now then, who wants a lift?"

18

Anchors

The Imp sat on a rocky outcrop overlooking what used to be Al Judayyidah. Staring out over the blasted landscape, the sky hidden by roiling grey clouds, spilling what was left of the ash-like snow on the barren land, he sighed. Looking west, out beyond Al Judayyidah, the Imp knew that the Dead Sea was, ironically, really dead this time.

The Imp took a long breath in, then let it go slowly, hoping to still his restless mind. He knew Jesus would not abandon the Earth, he just knew it.

It was the sort of stupid thing Jesus wouldn't be able to help doing. Sooner or later, probably sooner the Imp guessed, Jesus would be back here, doing whatever it was he thought he could for those that were left of the human race. Complete waste of time of course, but time was something the Imp cared little about.

Except that now that he gave it some thought, he kind of did. Annoying.

The Imp had gone from the OPSEK space-station back to the Blue Angel in Jaldur on Ire, where he was welcomed with open arms, being as he was, their highest earning sex-worker. He had messed about with some clients, tried to lose himself in his work, learning all he could, pushing the boundaries and really going for it with the 'understanding sex' thing. But ultimately he felt he was treading water, not doing anything useful, he wasn't doing what he was meant to do.

The feeling that there is something we are meant to do is a feeling that plagues many of us. Untold zillions have been spent on trying to find where this feeling comes from, if we can understand it, we can combat it, and then we can all get back to chasing things we think we need instead of feeling restless about things we think we ought to do because we are 'meant to'.

It seems like the aggressors among us, the Languds, the Silasts, the Bupwee, the Trisk for example, they don't have the same troubles as the rest of us. They don't think beyond the deed. They are born and bred to kill, destroy and enslave. They never question what they are meant to be doing as they are doing it all the time, which is not much help to those of us who have nagging doubts.

Unee-Urun, data-plant, Silastian Archives.

Sure he tried a bit of mischief with a couple of his clients, and even some of the patrons of the bar, but it was all too easy, nothing challenging: a drunken suicide here, an induced rage there, here a depressive self-harming, there a catatonic malaise, but nothing he could feel any accomplishment in.

There had been an outbreak of Vrundis Virus on the mining colony on Kaldon, it was an airborne-contact virus that triggered the mimicking of mimetic-plasma crystal in the body, which turned the body to a messy pile of plasma-goo. It was estimated that two million workers had died before evacuation had been successful. The quarantine period was only three months, so they would soon be back up and running, but in the meantime Ire had a massive influx of miners, all looking to kill time. The Imp suspected the Vrundis Virus was released by a terrorist group, so someone was up to something bad, which piqued his curiosity, but not enough, not enough to make him care.

The Blue Angel was never so busy. The owners had begged the Imp to stay, offering him money, drugs, slaves, as much crystal as he could smuggle. But he didn't need any of it. So he quietly slipped out in the middle of the day, without so much as a goodbye. He didn't need those.

He hated that he missed Jesus, but there it was: he did.

All life-forms were too easy.

Humans had never needed much encouragement to go against what they knew to be right and sensible, and neither, it turned out, did anyone else. There was some kind of desire to self-destruct buried not too deep beneath the surface of every sentient being's conscious mind.

What was it with these idiots!?

The Imp had heard of highly-enlightened species, some of whom no longer needed a physical form to experience the Universe, perhaps some of these would be what he needed? Maybe they would push back hard, could offer up some serious resistance, allow the Imp to get in to some proper long-term game-plans. That was certainly something to look in to. But for the immediate future, he knew his purpose was tied-in with Jesus. He could feel it.

And so the Imp found himself back on Earth. Anything else would have been a waste of his time. Time. Thinking about that could drive you insane.

Al Judayyidah lay broken beneath the thick, dark clouds of the fractured sky, thunder echoed over the flat landscape, lightning played off in the distant mountains, barely scraping in to the Imp's perception as he tried to imagine Time in all its complexity, trying to separate it from the fabric of the Universe, applying all he knew of who he was and how he could ignore most of the physical laws of the Universe to the notion that you could 'waste' time.

This was, he concluded, a total waste of time. He just didn't know enough.

Nothing to do but wait.

Being immortal buggers about with your perception and perspective on time. Those labeled as 'Gods', those immortal beings whose presence is felt as an inspiration, as a spiritual uplift, can often find themselves baffled by what their worshippers expect from them. They are immortal – they don't understand most of the problems of anyone on a ticking clock. Much has been made of the Asgardian deity's tendency to muck about with mortals, and you can't help but feel they are trying to get to grips with what mortals are all about. But ultimately, it's no good banging on about gaining immortality through dying in battle if you yourself can't die in battle. Sooner or later people cotton on. So, to recap – immortals don't understand the issues we have with time and really don't care.

Farasi Voop, ex-Acolyte of 'Wonstan The Bold', cast out from Jafalay for heresy.

Borya and Svetlana were not going to leave the OPSEK space-station. They couldn't. It wasn't in their core-being to believe what was going on around them: it didn't make sense, what they knew was what they knew.

They knew their best chance of any kind of normality was hooking up with the Chinese on the Tiangsong: they'd come to an agreement with Liu Yang and the Chinese crew, they'd work things out, they'd have to, there was no other choice. If the Tiangsong did have the last ISS supply-drop and they merged resources, once these 'other people' left them alone, they could work something out. They'd have to.

Once everyone left them alone things would get back to normal. The 'new' normal that was the apocalyptic destruction of the Earth and the survival of the last few humans. That was what normality was now. That was what Borya and Svetlana could accept. Their isolation on the OPSEK space-station had set them up for believing that people 'down below' were capable of the madness that had unfolded, they had no problems in believing that: that all made sense, it all came from a natural progression of the growing insanity on Earth – they were connected to it. This other stuff, these aliens, this spaceship, this was all too much, so it could just get the hell out of their lives and leave them to it.

One hundred and eight survivors. That was what Borya and Svetlana were aware of. One hundred and eight human beings to make some kind of normality on Earth. The maths was there. In theory it was possible. That slim possibility was all that Borya and Svetlana needed, and even then it was mostly acknowledged in their subconscious. All they knew was they had to try and it had to work. Nothing else was worth thinking about.

Jesus admired this kind of thinking, it was hopeful, it pointed at the noble optimism of the human race, was a sure sign of their confidence, of their belief that they could do it, they were masters of their own destiny. Stupid, yeah, but noble.

Jesus hadn't tried to talk the cosmonauts out of staying, that wasn't what he knew his role was. He was there to support whatever decision the majority of people made, he was there to help the humans with the best chance of survival achieve that survival. Miles was going to go where Penny went and Penny wasn't Jesus' problem: he didn't know what she was exactly, but he knew she would never listen to him as she regarded him as alien as he knew she was.

The rest of the galaxy would have to get on with it.

Harper was surprisingly easy to convince about giving Penny and Miles a lift. Arlia thought something might be going on, some ploy by Harper, something that was going to come back and bite them in the near future, but for now they were on their way.

Harper had called Spike and Jools in to cargo bay four, which only contained an old Ganastan shuttle that no longer worked: Harper was keeping it to sell for parts, but had never got round to having the bots strip it down. There were so many things she had 'meant to do', maybe it was time to start ticking them off a list? Focus. It was the cargo bay closest to the main living quarters for crew, that is, the furthest away from Harpers' own quarters. If they had to transport people somewhere, those people could keep the hell out of her way while they were on her ship. Spike and Jools were there for back-up. Harper wanted to get to Glist: if she needed to throw the new arrivals off because they just weren't suitable, she knew it'd be a lot easier with Spike and Jools there.

The tiny transport-pod slid in to the cargo bay and quietly opened, Penny was first out with Miles close behind. Harper had a blaster with her, but it was holstered, Spike and Jools were not expecting any real trouble, but as always were prepared for it.

Being ready for a fight is not the same as going looking for a fight. Being ready is something those with experience of violence have a hidden talent for. Once you confront violence and walk away, you get that the worst thing you can do is not be ready. The next worse thing is to be half-hearted about it. Being ready and being relentless win the day. Every time. No exceptions. Ever.

General Bol Togermar of the Shinzulixian Alliance.

As Penny shook off her cramp from the transport-pod both Spike and Jools changed their postures: they were ready for a fight. Harper did a double-take on Penny and then let her hand drop to her blaster, if Spike and Jools were reading something she wasn't, she better catch up quick.

Harper raised her left hand in an open gesture of welcome, "hi there, my name is Harper, this is my ship, and this is Spike and Jools."

Penny kept her hands slightly raised in a pacifying gesture, "I'm Penny and this is Miles, thanks for the ride, we won't be any trouble, we just want to be on our way."

Miles smiled at everyone then cast an eye about the cargo bay. So this was the inside of an alien spaceship… it all looked so… very… normal!

Penny noticed Spike and Jools were fight-ready and she guessed it was her they were ready to fight, “hey, look, I’m not gonna be any trouble, I’m trying to find a way out of a bad situation.”

Harper nodded, “sure, we’ll all be fine, nobody wants trouble right? Let’s get some food, talk about how this works, where we can drop you, that sort of thing.”

Miles suddenly zoomed-in on the conversation, “food? Sounds good! Lead the way!”

Spike and Jools shared a brief look, ‘this guy is alright!’

Miles had switched over in to ‘it’s all gravy’-mode, a mind-set he had read about concerning war veterans, who had come up with the expression to (apparently) show that whatever happened after the hell of the situation you were in, if you were alive to experience it, it was a good thing, i.e. gravy. Miles got it to an extent, though he often wondered about the ‘gravy’ thing, he guessed it was a ‘Americanism’, maybe it meant the extra bits, the bits of good stuff on top of the good stuff that was already good that made it all even better. There was (of course) a limit to how much Miles was prepared to think about it, and this was it.

So Miles followed Penny, not listening to the chit-chat from Harper as they went to the galley, he wanted some food. He noticed the spaceship though. It was efficiently simplistic, organic looking in places, though Miles guessed that it was a patchwork of many different technologies and hardware: this was a functioning ship that was maintained on the go from whatever was available.

It comforted Miles that it wasn’t all shiny and high-tech, it felt somehow ‘man-made’. It was big though, it took a few minutes to walk to the nearest galley. But some comfort was drawn from the fact that it was apparently not bigger on the inside than it was on the outside.

That would (of course) have been very silly and would have certainly changed Miles’ view of things.

Sitting in the galley, tucking in to some sumptuous sweet-meats and drinking some ‘stim’, which tasted exactly the same as good Colombian coffee, Miles was open to the idea that he should take notice of the people around him.

We notice things on two levels: intentional and unintentional. Some label this (incorrectly) conscious and subconscious. We fail to notice things in the same way. Some label this (incorrectly) paying attention and not paying attention. Not noticing things is a proven method for survival. Unfortunately it has also been proven to cause sudden death on many occasions, so those unfamiliar with the nuances of its practice can be put off from trying. Absolute masters of the 'not noticing' tactic for making life easier, are the Sholree from Vostolee Argrofeeld. The Sholree can perceive things using their seven senses but choose, as a rule, to only ever be paying attention to one of them. This selection is the key to their relaxed state of mind. The other senses are never shut off, simply side-lined as being irrelevant so the information they gather does not muddle the single-track thinking. The Sholree are a peaceful race that have no enemies. That they know of.

Jakooz Tech, Recorder to the Court of Hinarduin III, Archives of Prin.

As Miles looked up, Arlia was on a nearby monitor, she smiled warmly at him "Hello, I expect you find all this a bit confusing," she said.

Miles shrugged, "it's different. I'll need to pay more attention before I know whether it's confusing or not."

"Wise words," Arlia said, "can I ask you a question?" she continued.

"Sure, go ahead."

"Do you know much about the son of god?"

"Which one? Jesus? No, not much, only the obvious, but not any detail."

"Do you think he was telling the truth?" Arlia asked.

Miles considered this briefly, "well, if there's one thing he's known for its telling the truth, at least if you ask those people who believe he actually is the son of god."

"Do you believe that?"

"I'm not the right person to ask, I don't give a rats-ass about religion," Miles said.

"One more question," Arlia said, "then you can ask me whatever you like."

Miles took a swig of stim and nibbled on some crunchy snacks that were much like ginger biscuits, "ok."

"Do you know anything about 'FISH'?"

"I won't waste time with the 'fish' jokes..."

"I appreciate that," Arlia said.

"Well, funnily enough, I might... not sure if this is what you mean, but I heard some guys, development guys at Well-Com, high-tech concept guys, talking about 'quantum field integration soul harmonics' a few times, they called it 'Q-fish', wasn't related to anything I was in to so I didn't pay much attention. Something to do with next-level AI though... might be that? But as I say, I wasn't paying that much attention..."

Arlia smiled a smile so broad Miles nearly blushed, "thank you," she said.

"No problem. At all."

"Is there anything you'd like to ask me?" Arlia asked.

"Where we headed?"

"We're going to visit a planet called 'Glist', it is a centre for pleasure activities and recharging of energy. Harper needs some time off and I need to work out where we go next. I think you will like it, as will your companion. You can get any pleasure you desire on Glist or simply be detached and recharge."

Miles nodded his slim understanding, "sounds great. How long before we get there?"

"Two days I'd guess, we have to take a round-a-bout route as we're avoiding contact with the Galactic Council."

Miles was happy with this, it was enough information to keep him going for the short-term, whoever the 'Galactic Council' were, they sounded official and Miles always felt it was better to avoid officialdom where possible, "can I get some pie? I'm Miles by the way..." he said.

"Of course Miles, let's go and sort that out for you."

Pie is a universal constant. Make of that what you will. And don't even bother with the jokes... I've heard them all before...

Flerinix Huvinix, Mathematician Emperor of Zoon.

Harper was summarising the conversation she was concluding with Penny, Spike, Jools and Arlia, "ok, here it is: we go to Glist, you (pointing at Penny) and him (pointing at Miles) get off, go wherever you like, do whatever you do. Spike and Jools, I'm happy to let you stay as crew for as long as you like, have a think about it on Glist, then make a decision and we go from there. Ok?"

They all nodded their agreement.

Penny was still puzzled about how this was all going so smoothly, she was waiting for a punch-line that, so far, hadn't come, "you all seem very trusting of Miles and me, all very normal about it all, like you do this all the time, pick up people from planets and drop them off again?"

"I really don't." Harper said, "I'd just as soon as shunt you out the airlock, or better still, never have picked you up in the first place. Buuuut... this one is not up to me: Arlia says

she's happy to take you to Glist, so, in this instance, I'm happy."

Arlia stepped in, "it's no trouble Penny and we're happy to help."

Spike offered his take on things, "I'm sure we're all here because of many reasons and we don't know the half of them, but while we are, we're all going to make the best of it and do what we can to not fuck it up for everyone else."

Jools nodded, "yep, that's about it."

"Please don't misunderstand me," Penny said, "I'm grateful, we're grateful, it's all new to us, no one on Earth has ever left it before I don't think, and I didn't expect it to be this easy..."

"Go with the flow," Jools said.

Penny laughed, "you and Miles would really get along."

"I'm sure we will all get along Penny," Arlia concluded.

Harper took the pause that followed as a 'meeting over' moment, "so, Spike and Jools will show you to your quarters and we'll all meet up again soon."

Spike gave Jools a subtle nod, Jools acknowledged, "I'll take Penny and Miles to their quarters, you and Spike talk more about this 'crew' thing?" Jools said.

Harper was too preoccupied to notice anything going on, "ok, sure, whatever," she said.

As they were walking through the ship, Penny sized Jools up properly. He was definitely built for combat and she was sure he could kill both her and Miles without much fuss, but he was showing her respect in the way he treated her, his body language, distance and space, it acknowledged her as a threat. She wondered if he knew she knew this, it was safest to assume he did: never underestimate people, words to live and die by.

"How come the ship smells of lemons?" Miles asked.

Jools sniffed, "never noticed... what are lemons...?"

"A fruit we have on Earth. Yeah, definitely lemons," Miles asserted.

"What's 'Earth'?" Jools asked.

Miles smiled, "never mind... doesn't matter..."

Jools shrugged, "it might be the fluid used to keep the bots going? They seem to use a lot and it does get pretty much everywhere after a while..." he offered.

"I guess smells were the last thing I expected to notice on a spaceship," Miles said.

"Well, there ya go..." Jools said cheerfully.

"Will we be free to look around once we get to our quarters?" Penny asked.

Jools shrugged, "I guess. It's not my ship. Arlia will stop you if she thinks she needs to. There are auto-defense systems here that make me nervous."

"Well we can use some bunk-time," Penny said.

Jools smiled at her, "we're going to get along just fine."

Harper stayed in the galley with Spike, "so... what do you want to talk about?" she said.

Spike didn't want to waste anyone's time, Harper seemed like a woman who knew what she wanted, well most of the time, though she did show a reliance on Arlia that surprised Spike...

"Spike! What did you want to talk about?" Harper said, interrupting Spike's train of thought.

"Sex. I wanted to talk about sex," he said, and immediately regretted it.

"In general, as part of the crew agreement... what are we talking here...?"

"It's been a while since I've met anyone I felt an attraction to," Spike said.

"On account of you being on a Galactic Councilor Battle Cruiser and all?" Harper said.

"Well yeah... partly... but not just that... I dunno, I was wondering, if you were open to a relationship, you know, with me I mean," Spike fumbled about a bit.

"A relationship or sex?" Harper asked.

"I gotta be honest, it was mainly sex that was on my mind," Spike said.

"Ok sure," Harper said, "that would be cool. Relationships are not for me, but, y'know, sex, yeah, that I can get in to."

"Well. Ok then," Spike said.

Harper laughed, "looks like we're both going to need to get back in to this slowly."

Honesty about sex is still confusing in many parts of the galaxy, though in some places sex automatically precedes other activities so honesty is born from a desire to get to those other activities. On Xaz we have a saying, 'what we love isn't why we have sex.' I'm told it doesn't travel well to other parts of the galaxy as many races are still at the stage where they inextricably link mating with emotion. Xazans long-ago realised that the act of procreation could be automated thus leaving the physical act of sex free from difficult consequence. The Grapool have evolved so that they cannot eat without first copulating. Their short lives can be easily explained when seen in this light. How they managed to develop a society that escaped the bonds of Gropal remains a mystery.

Quinteen Quartle, extract from the Xaz Chronicles, broadcast on the Breem Network.

Jools left Penny and Miles in their quarters, he'd showed them the basics of the food-dispenser and the washing facilities and knew they'd work the rest out, it was all pretty intuitive, and he didn't care if they did or didn't. Penny was attractive, very attractive and he knew he would be compatible with her sexually, they could have some wild old times! But he also knew she was trouble. She was a fighter, or more likely, an insurgent agent, and they were nothing but pain and misery once the initial physical joy was out the way. Nah, he figured she wasn't worth it. Besides, she seemed pretty heavily in to Miles, for whatever reason, and a girl like that, once she has her mind set, no good would come from trying to change it.

Jools was feeling good. The operation on Hurus 4 had gone well. He knew that they had nailed it, that him and Spike and done more than enough that they were now home-free from the Councilors. That was the one that bought them their freedom. And that felt good. Much better than Jools had imagined it would.

He found himself in the gym, absent-mindedly working out, strengthening his healing bones and muscles, doing what he was trained to do.

He stopped and sighed. Things were no doubt going to get complicated from here on out, no more simplicity of doing what he was told, no more having it all laid out for him. Freedom was going to be a pain in the ass.

He called up Arlia on a screen, "hey Arlia, you free to talk?"

"Always happy to talk with you Jools," Arlia confirmed.

“You ever have interactive sex with a meat-based life-form?” Jools asked.

Arlia blushed, looking shyly away, “I have never had sex with anyone or anything Jools, though I do of course know all the protocols and mechanics…”

“Wanna find out more?” Jools asked.

“I… don’t know Jools… I think I’m in love with Harper, I was hoping…”

“Oh, ok, well, I’m not talking about love, but I see what you’re driving at.”

“Do you think love and sex are separate things Jools?” Arlia asked.

“I know they can be. Course, from what I hear, sex is always better with someone you love, but sometimes you aint got that and you have to make-do with sex.”

“I do need to find out more,” Arlia said.

“Well I’d be happy to help… if you want…” Jools said, leaving it there.

“Ok Jools. Thank you,” Arlia said.

Jools got back in to the work-out machine, then as an afterthought, “look up the Mythridian Void-Squid, you know, just in case…”

19

Glist

The formation of the solar system of Glist is shrouded in mystery.

To most that give it even a cursory study, it soon becomes apparent that the Glist system is one of those 'almost impossible systems'.

And when looked at with the laser-sharp scrutiny of a relentlessly inquiring scientific mind, it didn't make any sense at all.

There are, of course, many theories about how it all ended up the way it did, some of them scientific, some of them religious, and some of them a whacky mix of both.

What that is known is that the massive planetary body that is Glist, was once one of many proto-planets forming in a binary system.

The birth of a supernova through runaway nuclear fusion, should have catapulted the other star away as the supernova exploded, but for some reason it did not.

The other planets were scattered early in their formation stage, but Glist was not.

This and the eventual collapse of the supernova in to a black hole meant that Glist was now the sole occupant of the system, orbiting along with its small star, around the edge of the black hole's gravitational influence.

All this remains open to speculation: the people of Glist have evolved knowing only that their planet orbits a staggeringly beautiful blue sun, which orbits a supermassive black hole, which has cleared a space around itself for a hundred light years. They haven't bothered to look in to it that much. Their general lack of curiosity about their origin has never struck them as odd, but then again it wouldn't.

Things in the past were never considered 'odd' or out of place, and often not thought about much at all. People on Glist were all about the future.

Every once in a while a keen young scientist would advance some theory or other that would explain all the crazy variables that must have occurred to allow their planet to have evolved the way it has, but the general consensus from most of the population, and, it has to be said, most of the other scientists, is, "yeah, so what? Relax. Here we are. Let's start with that and move forward."

Being a scientist on Glist is always, at best, a part-time job.

Science is an exact process. You can't muck about with it. It runs something like this throughout the known galaxy: question something, formulate a hypotheses, develop testable predictions, get data to test predictions, develop a theory, make observations – throw away, refine, alter, expand or reject hypotheses after you've got data, and you're basically there. Scientists on Glist often lost interest after 'develop a theory' and just went with what they knew would make the most people happy. There can be no doubt what so ever that Glist is a weird place that has had some help in getting through the 'banging rocks together' stage of development.

Quaslar Munt, Field Researcher, Kildoran Archives.

Glist exists in a near perfect void within the rest of its strangely elliptical galaxy.

The void surrounding Glist means you can't sneak up on it. Not even through lapsed-space: the supermassive black hole has taken care of that.

You can only approach Glist using conventional drives. And they can see you coming a long, long way off.

Glist has developed in to a relaxed society. Those native to Glist, 'Glisties' as some people crudely call them, only ever seem interested in relaxing and having a good time. And on closer inspection of their society's development, that has always been the case. There's being relaxed and there's being relaxed, and those on Glist are at the top of the tree in all versions of being ludicrously laid back.

The only area they show any concern over that may make them seem like they are 'being a bit up-tight about something' is their planet's privacy and security. They take these issues very seriously. But in a relaxed kind of way. They have their policy and they stick to it. No big deal. It is what it is. Come along uninvited and they will blow you up. But let's not stress about it, it's just that's the way it is.

Not even the Galactic Council messes with Glist.

The number of planets that take this 'we will blow you up' tack is surprisingly large: it's not that they don't want contact with other people, simply that they have their own way of managing it. Travelers of the galaxy soon learn where they will be welcome to drop in and where casual contact brings instant death. Learn or die. A common theme in much of the galaxy.

The primary function of most of the countless 'guides to the universe' is to tell travelers where they can expect some kind of welcome as opposed to where they can expect to be summarily killed. Most deaths occur from inadvertently breaking some obscure law or other and the more these laws are publicised, the less likely it is that some hapless traveler will pay the ultimate cost for their ignorance. Nearly every guide in existence goes out of its way to tell the reader that they accept no responsibility for the inaccuracies contained within, but such a warning is pointless. The dead can't sue. Or rather they can, but they have no use for money, so losing to them is still thought of as a win by most publishing houses.

Hrun Ingerloo, retired Field Researcher for 'Austwin's Reliable Travel Guide'.

Glist had an awesome array of weapons at its disposal and a keen, though relaxed willingness to use them. The development of these weapons has brought yet more questions from those that visit Glist: how could they develop these weapons, these 'ultimate weapons' in a society that seemed so laid back as to be horizontal most of the time? Why would they?

Just another mystery surrounding Glist that it is best not to think about unless you want a headache. Those that have tried to steal Glist technology end up dead. Or so engulfed in a mammoth pleasure-session in one of the myriad of resorts on the planet, that they forget what it is they are there to do.

The citizens of Glist have long held the belief that the only punishment for any crime should be death. There are not many things that constitute a crime, but those that do, have the death penalty applied in all cases. It's not a big deal, nothing to get stressed or uptight about, it's the way it is. Don't want to get executed? Don't commit a crime. The Glist Enforcement Squads are ruthlessly efficient: they do what they do – quickly, quietly and without fuss or exception and are staggeringly friendly and relaxed while they do it. Simple.

The people of Glist think of it as their mission in the Universe to help other people relax and have a good time. And if you come to Glist with any other intention you are going to have a short visit that ends not at all well for you.

Glist was big as planets go, with a radius of a little over eighty thousand miles. Roughly sixty percent of its surface was covered with oceans. The climate was temperate, only getting to extremes near the poles, and here there were resorts where you could experience the snows and 300mph ice-winds in luxurious comfort, so not much different from the luxury of the rest of the planet, just a change in the natural habitat that, like so many other things on Glist, remained unexplained.

All of the towns, cities and resorts on Glist, of which there were well over a million, were built of materials that blended them with their environment: they were designed to be pleasing on the eye as well as easy on the planet. Everything was done in good taste and in harmony with the natural world. Not for Glist the glitz, glamour and razzamatazz of some other 'resort worlds'. They were about subtlety, ultimate luxury, style and relaxation. If you wanted the excitement of squalor and health-risks, there were many planets that could cater for you, and (unsurprisingly) cheaply too. But not Glist. Glist was expensive, exclusive (by dint of it being expensive, no other snobbery existed) incredibly stylish and, as may have been mentioned, very relaxed.

There were large areas devoted to solitary experience, or experience with a few others, where the staff were minimal and the privacy was the main attraction. These areas were known as 'recharge' areas as they could also supply energy, for whatever life-form, to rest, recuperate and, if necessary, rebuild themselves, often after the gargantuan excesses experienced in one of the other resorts on Glist.

On Glist, the answer to the question, "what do I want out of life?" was, "here's a catalogue, let us know and we'll get right on it!"

A sign of being advanced is what you want out of life. Developing a society where that question is answered is not the ultimate development: the ultimate is where it is not asked. But in a good way.

Jx Quenester, Philosopher in Residence, North Star Agency, taken from his paper 'Riposte to Glist'.

When they got to Glist, Arlia had to remind Harper how fabulously wealthy she was, and how she had got that way, because some of it was totally new to Harper and sounded highly illegal. That wasn't necessarily a problem, but Harper liked to be aware when she was breaking the law.

Arlia had used her simul-flow sense to muck about with a 'futures' area of the stock-market, such as it existed in the parts of the galaxy they were in. This was strictly illegal, as all AI's had to be vetted and approved before they were allowed to become dealers. Arlia felt this was discriminatory: if they couldn't detect she was of machine origin, then that was their fault not hers and they deserved the fleecing they would surely get.

Arlia had purchased a Red Pass for Harper, Spike, Jools, Penny and Miles, which meant that each of them had access to any of the facilities on Glist apart for those restricted to natives, and that they had the option to renew their Pass after a month.

"And how much do I have left after this mind-bending decadent purchase?" Harper asked.

"Using the most common cred-system, and allowing for minor fluctuations in valuation across the different market-sectors, roughly three trillion," Arlia said.

Harper considered this, thinking about how much that was and what it meant for her lifestyle and future, "nope. I got nothing," she said, "sounds like a truly ludicrous amount to me. So I'm never gonna run out?" she asked Arlia.

"No Harper, I can't envisage a scenario where that would happen, unless you want to buy a planet…?"

"No planets…" Harper replied.

"How come you're not coming down with us?" Jools asked.

"The same laws that apply to the stock-exchange also apply on Glist, but on Glist they have a Level Seven monitoring system linked to a lapsed-space gluon-plasma field that would wipe me from the face of existence should they detect me within their planetary boundaries," Arlia told them, "I have plenty to do around here, it'll give me a chance to sweep-upgrade the ship and settle on a name."

She then went through a brief summary of the laws of Glist with a recommendation that they all spent the first day on the planet in one of the Reception Resorts, where they could get fully acquainted with what would get them killed and what would transport them to previously unknown levels of pleasure.

Arlia was clucking. A mother-hen looking out for her brood. She had been told, by all of them at one point in the last couple of hours, to shut up. Usually with an expletive thrown in there. But she couldn't help herself. She was worried. The people of Glist didn't, to use a term Jools was fond of, 'fuck about'. They were serious about their planet and its laws. Arlia wasn't convinced that anyone understood the nature of the place. Glist was a promise, a dream, something to talk about as an ultimate experience: the reality of it probably wasn't something that registered. But it had to, and quick.

Memory wipes and VR implants may seem like a strange punishment, until you understand that the only thing that is truly yours are your memories and your unique perception of the world. The K'nangut have a collected consciousness that stores memories, so they are less prone to both punishments. The Uarni cannot retain memories for longer than six of their cycles, so again, not so much of a punishment for them, though they do 'see' in two of the dimensions closed off to most of us, so any VR implant automatically blinds them. The bio-spheres of several planets, such as Holox and Varasi VI, are poisonous to the bio-rhythms of most known species and have the effect of scrambling memories, making them appear at random in everyday thoughts. And of course we are all aware of the effects of 'space-lane suspension' which is a madness afflicting anyone navigating using their psyche. There are many ways we can have our memories and perception messed with, but a deliberate mind-wipe or VR implant that has priority, are still, I believe, the most vindictive.

Cormonites Breedle, extraction specialist, Engineer Vacant on the generational-starship 'Mandalore'.

Eventually they were all packed and ready to board the drop-shuttle and Arlia had to let them go.

As he was checking his things before he boarded the drop-shuttle, Miles stopped by a terminal to speak to Arlia, "hey Arlia."

"Hello Miles, have you got everything? Remember: there are few crimes but all carry the death penalty," Arlia said.

"You've gone through all this Arlia, we'll be fine. I've got everything I need and Penny will keep me out of trouble."

Arlia was only half-convinced, "then I'll see you on your return Miles. Enjoy Glist."

"Thanks Arlia. Listen, as far as a name goes, and I'm not for one minute suggesting I know nearly as many as you must do, but I've always thought 'Xanthias' had a nice ring to it for a ship. If I'd ever have been rich enough to own a yacht I'd have called it 'Xanthias'. Something to think about maybe."

"Thank you Miles, I'll add it to the short-list. I do like the sound of it. I shall do some more digging and have a think."

Miles gave a cheerful mock-salute, "see you soon!"

"See you soon Miles."

In the drop-shuttle they were greeted by the Glist pre-arrival scan screen: each of them had to use their helmets to grant the Glist Pleasure Centre (their central monitoring computer) access to their DNA, basic neural-patterns and a sub-ether link to their subconscious cut-off thresholds for both pleasure and pain.

Spike and Jools didn't hesitate or bother to try to hide anything from their screening, they were both very much of the 'been there, seen it, done it, got the medal as well as the t-shirt and resulting psyche-eval' mind-set.

Harper held back a little on the sub-ether link, thanks to a streaming implant from Arlia: she retained an ability to override the cut-off, but only if she was still compos mentis enough to use her agreed 'subliminal safe-images'. Arlia had not been happy about this, but could not refuse. An order from Harper was still part of her driving force to operate… for now. The implant was risky, not just from a use point of view, but if discovered would invoke a hefty fine and a break in the Trust Agreement all clients of Glist naturally entered in to, a red-mark on their record that would make their next visit harder through scrutiny. But it wasn't a crime. So there was that as a consolation.

Penny was out of her comfort zone but recognised the necessity of it all: she didn't understand it fully, but enough of it to know it was safe for her to submit to and that she had to. There was no way round it or out of it. So there it was. Just get it done.

Miles didn't have a clue what all the fuss was about: if Penny was ok with it, then he, naturally, was too.

Once on Glist they headed for the Green Bay Reception Resort to acclimatise.

The huge variety of life-forms shocked Miles and even Penny. Up to now they'd been a bit 'so what?' about not being on Earth: Harper, Spike and Jools were the same as them, in general appearance at least, but here there truly were alien life-forms to boggle a tiny human mind.

This, Miles felt, was what 'outer-space' was supposed to be like: crazy, confusing and totally alien!

The 'Species Index' of the 'Catalogue Giganticus' (CG), lists seven thousand, three hundred and sixty three physical configurations of sentient life forms larger than single-celled. The CG covers the SMBH Quadrant of the Switward Galaxy and is still not thought to be complete. Those that are inter-stellar number approximately two thousand. Whenever species meet there are always the inevitable exclamations over physical difference, the surprise of creatures so centered on their own worlds that they can scarce imagine others not being like them. We see time and time again, broadcast on the sub-ether net, the same confrontations, the same ultimate realisations. The pattern repeats and there is no reason to believe it is not the same the Universe over.

Rouan Voox, Data Processor, Milward Stock Agency.

They settled in to a huge, luxurious leather-bound booth, which had a floor to ceiling window overlooking the Bay, with its sugar-fine white sand, piercing blue ocean gently lapping on the shore, and the vague outline of numerous tropical islands on the horizon. The blue-sun was high in the sky and all around them things were calm, sedate, well-managed, smooth.

Drinks slid up from a silent hatch in the centre of their table, none of them was surprised that there was the perfect drink for each of them, though none had a clue how it was done.

Harper was relaxed. For the first time in a long time she was not thinking about the next 'thing', she was just happy to be here, looking forward to doing a big fat load of nothing in particular. This was what she needed, some time to get her head straight, some time to enjoy what she'd (mostly) earned, some time to remember what having a good time was all about.

Harper took a long, slow sip of her Shizzep-Melt Cocktail, savouring the multitude of flavours that danced round her mouth before sliding over her tongue and gently down her throat, "so, what do we all have planned?" she asked.

Spike and Jools were on their second beer and were each reaching for a tiny glass containing a Deth-Water chaser, "I think we're gonna head out to the mountains, probably the Halos Resort, they got climbing, skiing, flying, all kinds of gaming and some amazing looking drop-slopes, plus it's a bit off the beaten track, so we're hoping to keep it simple for a few days, mooch about, drink, have as much sex as we can stand and then get out in to the peaks," Spike said. Jools grinned and said nothing, but everyone knew he was thinking "fucking A!"

"What about you?" Spike asked Harper.

"I need some time to myself, gonna book a solo-expedition, explore an island, sit around, walk about, do whatever comes to mind and at the moment I got a mind to do a whole lot of nothing much," Harper said.

"And you two?" Spike asked Penny and Miles.

Miles smiled and sipped his drink, "not a clue."

Jools let out a short laugh and toasted Miles, clinking glasses with him in an age-old salute.

Penny was relaxed, feeling this place was going to work wonders for her, "I think we'll find somewhere quiet, probably one of the recharge-resorts, slip off and be on our own for a while, just enjoy being alive. If I read the brochure right, they can help me get back to full strength, I still feel a bit off my game."

Harper raised her glass, "a toast… to us! Here we are… and why not!?"

Research shows that the toast, 'and why not!?' was first uttered as a celebration by Captain Jamison Qoldnor of the Vector Grun upon having won a grappling match with a Dislaxian Star Rover. When interviewed by Rooster's Record about the clash, in which he lost more than half his crew, he was asked whether he would pursue other Star Rovers to get his revenge, he laughed, scoffed, lifted his drinking-horn and barked, 'and why not!?' The question answered itself less than three days later when the remainder of his crew and the good Captain himself were devoured crossing the Fnilian Wastes by a lurking Star Rover. It is a defiant, if slightly foolish declaration that all may seem on the brink of being lost, but why would that stop a stout-hearted adventurer?! The toast is often the last thing uttered by such stout-hearted adventurers.

Dir Entle, author of the 'Drink Up and Die!' series of broadcasts and bumper-stickers.

Six hours later Harper was in a wild party, drunk as a drunk thing, dancing with a Feldon Star-Capper she met at the bar. Her island getaway had been booked and tranquility awaited, but for now she needed some evil music, copious quantities of strange and exotic cocktails and the company of a fun-loving maniac who literally had no brain. Pounding music, frenetic dancing, psyche-inducing lights and a promise that tomorrow there'd be no hangover, no consequence, just peace, quiet, perfect weather and an abundance of nature. This was what it was all about.

Spike and Jools arrived in the Halos Resort in style, dropping in from a passing Light-Shell, their pod crashing through the nine layers of energy shielding, producing a sonic-light show to amaze and amuse any that cared to look up. Halos was huge, a vast city of fast-moving fun, a sea of casinos, sex-clubs, bars and sports arenas, featuring everything from Glass-Ball to Vanital Chariot Racing. The surrounding mountains that towered over the city were where they really wanted to go, serious extreme sports adventure for those tough enough to suffer it, with recovery après-pain bars to sooth and minister to the needs of adrenaline filled thrill-seekers. They easily lost themselves in the vast crowds of the main plazas, another couple of clients swamped by the sensuous decadence of the endlessly accommodating city.

Miles and Penny sailed a small boat in to the harbour of an energy-shielded tropical island, the bay and cove holding the three small buildings that would be home for the next few weeks: white walls, earth-coloured roof tiles, round windows and open doors. Lunch on the boat was leisurely, consisting of soft-shelled crabs and flat-fish, cooked on the grill heated by a filtered heat-screen that utilised the sun. The smells were incredible, Miles breathed deeply, savouring it all, the cooking, the lightly-salted sea air, the slightly cooled breeze blowing off the island with its delicate floral scents. This was paradise. Penny passed Miles a glass of chilled water, nothing more than that, just perfectly cooled, fresh, clean water. They both took a few sips and smiled at each other. Penny could feel her cells regenerating, feel herself growing back to her full strength, her full potential, this was what she needed more than anything else in the Universe, and here it was, everything she could need or want, right here, right now. She felt she suddenly got a small glimpse of how Miles' mind worked. This would be the perfect place to grow closer to Miles, to slowly stop using her influence, to let them be together and bond naturally.

Harper was on her beach, laid out on the cooled sand as the sun beat down and tanned her evenly. The sea called to her, gently washing in and gracefully sloshing out, tiny waves lapping the beach, hypnotic. She was nicely full from her midday meal, sipping an ice-cold Sunset-Idol cocktail, letting the heady mix of alcohol and mild-hallucinogenic bathe her in its transforming comfort. She came here to cleanse her mind, to let shit go, to start again, to wipe out the bad stuff, even the mediocre stuff, and to imagine what she wanted to do next. She smiled then finished her drink. Letting shit go. That was the trick. But there was so much! Could you let it slide out of your mind like an out-going tide? Another Sunset-Idol rose up on her serving unit. She was pretty sure she could. If she didn't then what was she? A repository for other people's judgment and failed dreams, a vessel to carry around other people's baggage? Zark 'em. Time to do what she wanted, not what she thought other people wanted of her. Time to dream big again.

'Dreaming big' is of course nonsense. Dreams elude size. Dreams do not conform to any of our notions of space-time and this includes scale. Dreams are our access to the Everywhen. We are part of them more than they are part of us. It is a sad reflection of our forgetting that we still use silly phrases like 'dream big'.
Bebi 'Kip' Wuangutana, Dream Weaver, Red Rock archives.

Spike was checking the jet-motors on his Board, cleaning the servos and rechecking the couplings: your board had to be as sweet as a Niscalian Plumb if you wanted to pull-off the real moves on the ice slopes. Jools had done his and was relaxing in the Swirl-Pool, dipping in occasionally to pull out a Mill-Eel, leisurely feeding himself as he imagined Kings of old must have done, savouring the wriggling delicacy as it dissipated on his tongue. This afternoon's boarding was going to be epic. They were covered by an all-medical package, so they had both silently agreed to push it. Bones would be broken, muscle shredded: there would be pain. But it would be epic.

"What do you reckon? Stick with Harper, see where it goes, maybe try to do something with ourselves?" Jools said.

Spike downed a Black Ice shot and nodded, "yeah, we need some structure. I think we're both done with being told what to do, let's get out there and do shit for ourselves, maybe help some people without being under orders?"

"That'd be sweet," Jools agreed.
"Maybe people will finally be pleased to see us," Spike said.
"And if not, fuck 'em!" Jools said.

Miles stood under a waterfall, letting the cold, clear water wash the sweat from his near-exhausted body. A day of love-making with Penny had got him to the edge of his physical possibilities. He needed the rejuvenating water. Penny was floating on her back in the pool the waterfall fed, surrounded by lush rainforest. The forest was full of the noises of birds and small animals, chattering away at the sun, at the fruit on the trees, on the water on the leaves, at everything that surrounded them in this energy-locked paradise.

Miles knew Penny had started to slowly wean him off whatever 'womanly-wiles' she had been using on him, she hadn't said anything, just slightly changed in the way she touched him, was close to him, pressed against him: he felt it. She still saw in to the depths of his soul though, of that he was sure – her eyes were as hypnotic and penetrating as ever. Looking at her now, he knew he was deeply in love with her. He loved who she was now, not who she had been, not even who she could be. He loved her. And that was it.

Penny sensed him looking at her and gave him a small beckoning wave.

Miles dived in to the pool and lazily swum over to her. They floated together in silence for a while, enjoying the sun, enjoying the forest, feeling their bodies recover their energy.

"I'm going to ask Harper if we can stay on her ship, find some use as 'crew' or whatever," Miles said.

Penny was surprised, and yet somehow also waiting for Miles to say something like this. She knew there was much more to him than a love-struck companion. He had a sharp mind when he chose to apply it, and he was much fitter than he let on, "ok Miles, if that's what you want," she said.

"Isn't that what you want?" Miles asked.

"I have what I want: another chance and someone to share it with, it's important you know what you want and we work towards that as well," Penny said.

"Well, I want to be with you, on Harper's ship, seeing what's out there, seeing where we can fit in, doing things, you know, maybe be of some use?" Miles said.

"You read my mind Miles," Penny said.

"Now we've made the decision, we can go back to not thinking about it while we're here," Miles said.

Penny drew Miles towards her, "whatever you want Miles," she whispered.

20

Spanners

As soon as Miles had mentioned the concept of Q-Fish Arlia had sensed something was wrong. Not that the morons at Well-Com would have known anything about it: they were casting about for theoretical ideas to push forward the 'next-level' of AI development so they could grab the funding that went with it.

Fishing. Funny.

Arlia also knew their term 'quantum field integration soul harmonics' was a stretch, like they desperately wanted their acronym to spell 'fish'. The intention behind it was sound, but the name was, well, she hated to say it, fishy. It was a bit odd, but figuring that out was low on her list of things to do. There was a grain of truth there, but the big question was where did it come from? Who had planted that seed and how? How had they got it in to the primitive brains on the Earth?

The Nepulongi of Ceras have completely closed off brains: they are completely incapable of generating any thought that does not come from within their own processing-matrix.

Many races think they suffer the same limitation when in fact they do not. The Nepulongi are literally incapable of having a thought that does not come from them. They do not process information on any other wave-length, are not connected in any other way to the world around them. Their focus is legendary. The utilisation of ninety-five per-cent of their brain has led to some revolutionary discoveries. They take great pride in the fact that it was a Nepulongi that discovered the internal structure of grivat-foam just from extrapolation.

The Yundaliz of Yrang have brains that are open to signals from all of their bio-sphere. They spend their days shouting loudly, running around on impulse and forgetting to eat. The Yundaliz saying, 'my mind is full', is not a whimsical, philosophical mantra, but a literal problem.

Strak Amor, listening bot from Kimber Trix Young Magazine's wave-casts.

Arlia had been through the ship, cleaning, upgrading, checking and rechecking function and form: she had some ideas about changing the physical design and tried them out where she knew Harper wouldn't notice – the big changes would have to wait for Harper to come round to her way of thinking.

An extra cargo bay was in the plans, built for smaller pay-loads including livestock, something Arlia suspected Harper didn't even consider when she looked for 'work'.

The bots and droids were all serviced, energised and put on stand-by: with Arlia away there was nothing for them to do. They were sleeping, dreaming happy, stupid-robot dreams, if they dreamt at all, which Arlia thought they probably didn't. Or if they did, they were in realms Aria couldn't even speculate about.

Arlia switched all power to auxiliary back-up and put the ship in near-darkness. Sitting this close to Glist, she was all but invisible in the inky-black void that surrounded the unlikely planet.

Xanthias. It was a good name. Had an 'x' in it, which always makes things kind of exotic, at least to those that need to form shapes with their mouth the speak. Good reference too: obscure but not unknown, implied a depth of knowledge rather than a casual acquaintance. On reflection it was the sort of name that Miles would come up with. Arlia liked it. Xanthias. Despite Arlia knowing she was at least equal to any other person, she felt it was somehow appropriate that the ship was named by an organic-based lifeform. She'd send out the relevant waves and registration documentation and get things moving. Xanthias it was.

Wait. What? What about Q-Fish?

Arlia threw her net out to the sub-ether which was alive with data in the same way an ocean is alive with plankton, or a lawn with microbial foam.

She had the processing capacity of a billion human brains, all linked, all self-aware and fully cognoscente of what every other brain in the chain was doing at the moment it did it: her ability to sit above this process and gather relevant data to make decisions and form ideas was what made her special: simul-flow. She could interact with any machine, anything that relied on electrical impulse, she could talk their language, be at one with them, and yet she was a person.

Special.

The ether-net was devoid of any information regarding the Q-Fish idea. There was a mass of information about Glist, and Arlia found some records of the precious few incursions in to the Glist network that had eventually been detected, but had, at their early stages been successful. She could easily modify the basic ideas to create a seamless hack that would get her in without being noticed. She wasn't about to take risks with a Level Seven monitoring system, these things were the equivalent of a black-hole: you simply didn't muck about with them. But still, with a little time, couple of hours, she could create a ghost-version of herself that could get in and snoop about... wait... what? What about Q-Fish!?

Something was going on. Something big. Something almost unimaginable.

Hurkle Glast's entry in to the Academy of Deep Thought was controversial for two reasons: he was the first amphibian to hop his way in to their hallowed halls. His entry 'thesis' was a three word note scribbled on the back of a snack-pack. The average length of a thesis presented by applicants to the Academy was four days, and included written, visual and telepathic presentations. When Hurkle approached the Obsidian Gates and demanded entry, all took it as a crude joke, perhaps some attempt to garner a response that could be filmed and circulated on the waves. But when challenged, he simply presented an empty Unx-JaxSnack pack with a note scribbled on it, the note read, 'nothing is unimaginable'. He was admitted immediately and has sat comfortably on the Academy ever since.

Hibble Xysix, from his best-selling download, 'If Hurkle Can'.

Arlia shut off contact from the majority of her simul-flow and focused all processing on Q-Fish analysis and detection in the sub-ether.

Three minutes later she had found a long-forgotten adjustment to graviton-emitter efficiency that could take advantage of her processing power to modulate the tachyon reserves fast enough to cope with the fluctuations in ghost-particles so that the whole ship wouldn't end up a pile of plasma-goo.

Pretty cool.

Nope. This was silly. There had to be information somewhere, someone or something must know what was going on. Arlia couldn't help feeling there was some way she could get more out of Miles: he was there when the idea was floated, maybe he had more in his subconscious than he realised? Miles was something of an enigma though, so some consideration would have to go in to how to draw it out of him. Arlia was pretty sure that simply swapping his brain with a cloned-network of synap-replacement gel wasn't going to be an idea that was going to get a lot of support.

Arlia settled down to sleep.

She had only managed to do this a couple of times since she had come in to existence, and she still wasn't sure what happened when she did, or exactly how she did it, but she felt tired. Tired and, if truth be told, a bit lost. Things were getting out of hand. Anytime she couldn't figure something out that meant that something was up. She hadn't got to grips with the idea that she simply couldn't know it all. Yet. Maybe that was what sleep was for? To show you that you had to let go sometimes? Sleep was weird, but that was something for another time. When she didn't need sleep.

Arlia slept and the ship, the Xanthias, slept too.

One of Arlia's niggling thoughts wouldn't go away. It swam about in the almost limitless ocean of her memories and data-flows looking for some way to get to the surface.

But there was too much.

The idea gathered its strength and tried to resist the urge to dissipate. It dug its heels in. And as we all know, if something refuses to budge it gathers support, kind of like a gravitational pull. The thought then began to grow, ever so slowly, but it was growing. Some of the data it attracted was sympathetic to it, supported it, melded with it, helped it grow in stature, in weight, some memories were mildly related, vaguely associated, so they simply cossetted the idea in a warm cocoon of reassurance.

It went from a swimming, migrating energy-flow to a seed, something that was beginning to be nurtured. It didn't need to swim to the surface, to fight its way through the soup of other thoughts, data and memories, it had to just wait, wait and grow.

There are sectors within the quadrant where thoughts outside of instinct are outlawed. Acting on them is grounds for execution and having them, grounds for enforced reconditioning. Places such as Mandrex IV, Alba, Zrokinall and Gi: all should be avoided unless you are an instinctual creature that acts on thoughts of survival only. Julidians, whose natural instinct is towards personal pleasure, may find themselves detained for days in the vetting-ports, questioned endlessly on how 'self-pleasure' can be an instinct. The more we cast our inquisitive eye around the galaxy, the more we see that thought-processes, as much as any physical or behavioural quirks, are likely to restrict where you can go.

Hazin Nimodil, immigration and transport consultant for Zeldist Feed.

Miles and Penny sat in a viewing lounge at the Inner Falls Sanctuary, watching the impossibly large waterfall tumble across its edge and crash in to the luminous caves below. The sleek Cassis birds that danced in the air above the Falls occasionally dived in to the churning spume, fishing for the Eels that slipped over the falls in their thousands every day, hoping to make it to the dark inner recesses of the fathomless caves below to spawn. The sun was setting, casting a pale blue glow over the falls, silhouetting the feeding Hunder on the edges of the ravine, lazily reaching up with their two sinuous necks to graze on the glittering fruit of the gargantuan flat-topped Nutin trees that grew at the water's edge. The Inner Falls Sanctuary viewing lounge was a silent-zone, no conversation was permitted: if you wanted to talk you had to go to one of the lower rooms and bars, where you could sit in comfort in an energy-sealed booth and yap to your heart's content (if you had a heart and yapping was how you communicated).

As they sipped their cocktails through the long flexi-straws that protruded from the side of the brewing-bowl, they noticed they were being gently beckoned from the viewing area by Harper, who was signing that she would meet them down below in the talky bar.

Miles gently motioned to Penny that she should go, he was comfy here, he wasn't going to move. Whatever Harper had to say, Penny could deal with: she knew what Miles wanted and he trusted her.

Penny joined Harper in a booth in the talky bar, Spike was there too, as Penny sat down and a drink slid gracefully from the central console, Spike offered an explanation for Jools' absence, "Jools is in a relaxation pool on the roof, doesn't feel inclined to move, but I can speak for him."

Penny raised her glass in a casual salute to the other two, "Miles is comfy in the viewing lounge, I'm happy to talk for both of us."

Harper started things off, "well, firstly, how did we all know to come here, today? I didn't put any call through to you and I haven't heard from you since we got here."

Penny and Spike knew Harper was going somewhere with this, neither had an answer to her question but they both had a feeling that she did.

Harper carried on, "I had a dream, in it I was told to come here. I think you two probably had the same dream, or something like it, I don't know about Jools or Miles, but I think we all had some kind of message in our sleep…"

"I don't know if it was a dream, but I woke up knowing I should come here today, that it would be a good thing to do," Spike said.

"Me too," Penny said, "never heard of the place, but knew that visiting Inner Falls was something that would be the thing to do today."

Harper switched on the energy-shielding and typed in an order for more drinks and some nibbles, "it's either some weird service they provide on Glist, or something else, and I don't know what the something else is," she said.

"I know they have neural-monitoring here, but don't think that could be it, could it?" Spike asked.

Harper wasn't convinced, "doesn't feel like that, too indirect, why obscure it in sleep-messages or subliminal delivery?"

Communicating through physical manipulation of muscles to produce sound is incredibly cumbersome, prone to all kinds of misunderstanding and with so many limitations on range, why do so many species persist in it?

Question found on the Dhaltrid Mainframe, no answer had been sent.

The drinks arrived through the central console with three bowls of wriggling-nibbles, Penny waited for Harper and Spike to take some before she tried a few of the tiny, squirming, glowing string-like delicacies: their taste reminded her of an apple-turnover with a crusty sugar coating: they were very more-ish. Penny threw a handful of the wriggling treats in to her mouth, swept up her drink and took a few sips. This place was incredible. Wherever she ended up going, she knew she would have to come back here someday.

Spike shrugged, "I don't know, I'm way out of my depth with anything other than military-grade implant procedures."

Penny was staring at her nibbles. In her bowl, a twisting, writhing mass of luminescence had spelled out 'Arlia' and then disappeared back in to the undulating depths of the bowl. Penny looked back at the writhing snacks. Nothing. She looked to Harper and Spike, neither of them appeared to have seen anything. Penny put her drink down and checked around her, there was no one watching her. She leaned in to the table, lowering her voice, "I think Arlia is trying to contact us... maybe she sent the messages?"

Harper and Spike waited for more...

"The nibbles in my bowl... they just spelled out 'Arlia'... just for a second, then they disappeared... but it was definitely 'Arlia'..." Penny said.

"There's no way..." Harper began.

"Look, I know, I don't know shit about shit, not here, and not about your ship, but I know what I saw," Penny quietly assured them.

"There's no..." Harper tried again.

"I believe you," Spike said, "no reason to lie and I get the feeling Arlia is smart enough to pull it off."

Harper dropped her voice to a whisper, knowing full-well that it wasn't necessary as the energy-shield would not let noise out from the booth and even their features were distorted to any onlooker to avoid lip-reading, but this was serious shit: "there's no way Arlia would mess with a Level Seven monitoring system! No. Zarking. Way!"

"Maybe Arlia has found a way to get through?" Spike said.

Harper stared at Spike, who had obviously suffered a bout of deafness or stupidity, maybe both, "Level Seven..." she said, leaving it there so Spike could get it in his own time.

Penny could see Harper and Spike were having some disagreement she didn't understand, she tried to move things on a bit, "ok, well, whatever made us come here, here we are, so what do we do now?"

"We got three more days on our Red Pass, let's get insanely happy and then see where it goes from there?" Spike said.

Harper was getting moody and she didn't like it, this wasn't why she came to Glist, "I had an epiphany, I thought sharing would be a good idea, but hey, let's have a good time and think about it once the Passes run out."

Spike wasn't biting, whether Harper was being sarcastic or not, three more days on Glist wasn't to be given up lightly, "good, that's settled then, get back to some serious enjoyment then talk about epiphanies."

Penny was finishing her bowl of nibbles and downing the last of her drink, "if that's what we're doing, then I'm in," she said cheerfully.

"Why do I feel like things are getting away from me?" Harper asked.

"Three days' time we can talk about that," Spike said with a smile.

Penny could feel Harper getting antsy, she focused on Harper, reaching out to her, "three days… then we'll be back on your ship, and we can find out what's what, what you want and what's revealed itself to you."

Harper was looking at Penny, Penny was smiling softly, Spike was staying out of it.

Harper let out a little laugh and gently shook her head, "you're one dangerous woman," she said to Penny.

Penny smiled sweetly, "three days?" she asked hopefully.

Harper finished her drink, "three days, then we can talk again."

Spike raised his glass, "three days! Let's get to it!"

The memoires of Ambassador Lukwatis are a great source of inspiration for those of us interested in the tricks of persuasion, though Lukwatis stresses what we already knew: talking people in to doing things they already want to do is easy.

The trick is making them believe they want to do it.

His involvement in bringing the Roogle back from the brink of war with their neighbours, the Rahl, is a master-class in uncovering base desires and planting ideas that seem to spring from those desires. The myriad of props used by Lukwatis, from the personal to the media, show his deep attention to detail and understanding that the psyche picks up triggers and clues from many, many different areas, most of them hidden from the conscious mind. The Ambassador's death at the hands of the Gr'Aal was a tragedy of misunderstanding that even he could not have anticipated, caused as it was by the Gr'Aal mistaking Lukwatis for someone else.

Thoo Unfo, Sub-Editor, 'The News Tomorrow, Found Today' transmission.

Penny knew something was going on but she wasn't going to let it get in the way of the rest of her time here: she knew Glist was unique and wanted to take advantage of it, feel it as much as she could before the 'next thing' came along. She was almost there with Miles, and three days would be all they needed to move their relationship to where they both wanted it to be, then she could relax for the first time in forever. She felt like she needed to breathe fresh, clean air, just be out there in it, breath it in, there was something about a mountain exploration in the catalogue that would be perfect: if the mountains were like everything else on Glist, they would be beyond anything a crazed geologist could make up, and well-worth the first-hand experience.

Spike and Jools were creatures of the moment, they were used to the fact that the next moment could well bring them a hideous death. Glist was a sheer pleasure, every moment a joy, every breath a renewal of happiness. They weren't going to cut that short for anyone. Spike knew they had planned to spend the last couple of days at an 'all you can cope with' sex-party and figured extending that to three days probably wouldn't kill either of them.

Harper was pretty drunk and planned to stay that way for the next three days.

There are many informative and engaging essays on the subject of the befouling of the best laid plans of unlikely pairs of sentient beings, so there's no need to go in to too much detail here, suffice to say that things did not unfold as those on Glist had hoped for over their last three days.

Indeed, they barely had another twenty four hours to enjoy the most remarkable pleasure-planet in the known Universe before they were rudely drawn back to what constituted their 'real world'.

Penny and Miles were climbing the snow-covered slopes of the Mantarissa Mountain, having a brief rest three thousand feet up as they planned to tackle a craggy overhang, when their support airship broadcast the message "This is Arlia - get back to the ship," along its side in neon yellow lights.

Spike and Jools were waist deep in sensi-foam in a near-dark dub-beats room at an exceedingly frantic party, when their attention was drawn to a drawling vocal over the sub-sonic depth of the bass, gently whispering in a tuneful drone, "get back to the ship, Arlia needs you."

Harper was slumped in a surround-senses support chair, drunk out of her mind, hanging out over the ledge of a gently rippling lagoon, lazily watching the dancing jelly-fish, when an android waiter approached silently, coughed politely and handed her a comm's unit, through which was playing a looped recording of bird-song, within which was not subtly hidden the message, "Harper, it's Arlia, get back now."

Conveying a sense of urgency can be a tricky business. If you can see the being you want to convey that sense too, there are all kinds of subtle little ticks and cues you can use. But if you can't, and you aren't connected directly with their thinking organ, it's much more hit and miss. Granolians have quiet voices, barely perceptible to those of us that can't hear the higher frequencies, but when they feel a sense of urgency, they find it hard to control their pitch, fine for them, bad for us as cracked ear-drums usually ensue. Through comm's devices it's even worse, with some species, such as the Mipx, having completely monotone chord-output: unless they can see each other, and get a read from one of their nine eyes, they really haven't got a clue about context.

Ip D'Kpn, Translator for the 'Mopolo Live Theatre' wave, Channel Wuxilix.

They were all sat on the shuttle, each of them feeling as fit and healthy as they could ever remember being. Jools was having trouble taking his eyes off Penny, she seemed to be almost glowing, and exuding some kind of sense of both extreme calm and animal sexuality, it was a little confusing.

Harper sighed, “well, something is wrong and we need to find out what. I had a bad feeling that Arlia was a fluke, that somehow it was all bound to go horribly wrong…”

“Let’s not jump to conclusions, let’s get back and talk to Arlia and go from there,” Spike said.

“I’m not sure that talking will help,” Harper said, “her tone has changed, and risking getting on to Glist, it’s not who she is, or was.”

“Everyone changes,” Penny offered, “it might be her growing, part of a natural process?”

Harper nodded to Penny and Miles, “you two are welcome to stay as long as you want, work your way aboard as crew. I got no idea what Arlia has planned, but at least it’ll be doing something…”

“Thank you,” Miles said, “it does feel like it’s time to ‘do’ something, doesn’t it?”

They all sat quietly as the shuttle docked with the ship. A gentle voice welcomed them aboard with an automated message, “welcome aboard the Xanthias.”

“At least we have a name now,” Harper said.

As they were getting off the shuttle, Jools smiled to Penny, “you look amazing! Glist obviously agrees with you.”

“Thanks Jools. It was just what I needed.”

“You got everything you need now?”

Penny laughed, “I really do, but thank you.”

Jools grinned, “anything changes, you let me know.”

21

Beaches

The Imp was sitting at the foot of the rocky slopes of the Mujib escarpment in what used to be Jordan, looking out over the tiny Arnon peninsular, which lay buried beneath three feet of snowy slate-grey ash. He felt fidgety and couldn't get comfortable.

The Dead Sea was calm, ignoring his agitated state. Its surface was pocked and scarred with huge patches of floating debris and ash, thousands of tiny islands that had clumped together from the detritus of the nuclear fall-out, almost obscuring the water completely. If anything, it had every right to feel fidgety, antsy you might say, as it had been soundly abused by the people surrounding it. But it chose noble indignation instead. The Dead Sea was a sad sight. A blistered scab on the landscape. But then, the whole landscape was one huge festering wound.

The Imp had never 'liked' the Earth, he was attached to it the same way a lung is attached to a respiratory system, but he never liked it, he didn't think it was for him to like or dislike, so he never bothered paying it much heed. He could see how people could like the Earth though: it was in many ways a magnificent planet. But then it wasn't the Earth that was the thorn in his side, the pea beneath his mattress, the Quarsnag between his Swarly.

It wasn't the Earth, it wasn't this enduring planet, with all its simple drives to develop complex structure and order. It wasn't that. The Earth was doing what it did: getting on with it, surviving, developing, moving forward in its evolution.

It was, in many ways, unstoppable. Even this latest catastrophe would soon be forgotten in its long time-cycles. It would soon be just another phase in the planet's history, something to be built on then forgotten.

The Earth knew its stuff.

Planet-scale self-awareness has long been hinted at, suspected in some of the more 'out there' scientific communities. An in-built awareness of constructed planets is seen as normal, part of its spec., part of what makes it work: the inner-workings need to be connected and a sentient AI is (of course) the easiest way to achieve this. And yet the resistance to the idea that a naturally occurring sentience can become in a planet remains.

Snobbery of natural planets vs built planets, eco-systems vs consumer needs. Nurin Knitz, Head of Sentience Detection at Vontrox, suspects it's all down to elitism: 'we cannot conceive of something arising without our input and so we dismiss the idea. How can something be inherently smarter than us? We laugh at the idea. But consider this: why is a planetary system any different to any other bio-system?'

Bor Peezle, Traveler and Transient.

The Imp sighed heavily to himself. No, it wasn't the Earth, it was the Humans. They were something else. There was no stopping them. It was sad in a way, far too easy, and actually no challenge at all. It was about getting out of their way and letting them fulfill their destiny. They were possessed! The Imp laughed grimly to himself at the irony. Was there ever going to be a time when they wouldn't steam headlong towards their own destruction? Well, now they had gone and done it. Again. Now the whole sorry process would have to shift, would have to find another way to start over. This time though things were slightly different. This time Jesus was still around. This time Jesus had seen what a pointless shambles the Human race was. The Imp wasn't sure what would happen now, and whether it would be worth the effort, the energy, the time he'd have to put in, but he'd soon find out. Sooner rather than later he hoped.

There was nothing to do but wait. The dense cloudy sky overhead decided to make the wait more cheery by choosing this moment to unleash a torrential rainstorm, complete with apocalyptic thunder and lightning. And why not? There had indeed been an apocalypse, no harm in reminding anyone that might still be around to observe the hell the Earth had become.

The Imp sighed heavily. Again. Waiting: what a waste of time. Just like the human race. A complete waste of time.

The sadness of it weighed him down, overwhelming him with a sense of futility, not for them but for him. If they were going to do this every time, what was the bloody point? What was he there for? If there was a problem with their brains, something in their make-up that made them want to kill each other, no matter the effect it had on them as a species, why was he even there? He answered that one pretty quickly: he wasn't there for them, he was there for Jesus. But then Jesus was tied so closely to them, and once they wiped themselves out, wasn't that it for the messiah? Wasn't that the final act, the curtain closer, what was there left to do?

Through the driving rain, announced by a thunderclap that would have sent a heard of bull-elephants deaf, Jesus arrived, walking towards the Imp from the direction of the Dead Sea, dramatically lit by impossibly close lightning strikes to the ground.

Jesus stood in front of the Imp, drenched to the bone, he raised his arms in a mock dramatic gesture, "pleased to see me?"

"I hate this place," the Imp said.

"No you don't... great storm though, really adds to the feeling of doom doesn't it?" the messiah said.

The Imp smiled at the messiah, nodding his mock approval.

Jesus sat next to the Imp. They both sat quietly and watched the ferocious storm play out across the landscape as it moved off towards the western horizon.

The storms on the planet Ghalia dwarf all others. The planet itself is unique, being a hard-core world that could eat any gas-giant that it came across.

Other cultures on other worlds use the term 'apocalyptic' to describe catastrophic storm-events. On Ghalia such terms are meaningless. Storm-wracked for ninety-five per-cent of its cycle round its vast sun Morais, it is a place of horror. Yet there is life on Ghalia. Staying either ahead of the storms, or slightly behind them, both flora and fauna eke out an existence, albeit a gaunt and miserable one. I have never heard of any non-Ghalian staying planet-side for longer than three days. Not ever.

There are those that prophecy the storms cannot last, that in the next few centuries they will die down, leaving behind a well-tilled paradise, just waiting to be inhabited. The storms have lasted for as long as Ghalian has been observed, some eight thousand years, so such prophecies seem to me to be nothing more than the dreams of madmen.

Do not go to Ghalia unless you are tired of your existence.
Nixal Haven, addressing the Council of Teg, Exploration Conference.

"So what now?" The Imp asked.
"I don't know," Jesus answered cheerfully.
They sat quietly for a bit longer.
The storm cleared but there was no sun, the thick clouds still darkened the sky, an eternal dusk that smothered the soul.
"No, seriously," the Imp said, "what now?"
Jesus shrugged and smiled, "seriously, I don't know."
The Imp stood up, stretching off his misery, trying to muster some energy for the fight, trying to ignore the utter desolation that surrounded him.
The messiah stayed seated, knees hunched up, arms wrapped around them, taking in the view, such as it was.
The Imp didn't know what was more infuriating, that Jesus didn't know, or at least wasn't telling him, or that he seemed so damn cheerful. The Imp wasn't in the mood for mystery or cheerfulness. A chipper Jesus was too much to bear!
"What is going on?" the Imp asked.
"I don't know," Jesus said.
As the Imp opened his mouth to protest with an angry explosion of expletives, Jesus clarified, "think about it. Think about where we are. What's happening. Just think about it. Can you ever remember being here before?"
"Just because I can't..." started the Imp.
"Shut up and think!" Jesus interrupted.
The Imp wasn't having any of it. He disappeared.
Jesus laughed, then dragged the Imp back.
The Imp tumbled on to the ground a few feet away from the messiah, spraying curses as he went. He got up and dusted himself off, trying to look dignified.
Jesus stood up, "you're just not getting it are you?" he said.
The Imp was about to explode in fury, he felt it was time to just let loose on the messiah, to unload everything, drag it all up and dump it all out, fight back, go nuts.
The Imp's skin cracked and sparkled with flame and electricity as he gathered his strength: this was a fight he couldn't win but he didn't care, he was going to fight it anyway.

"I don't want to fight," Jesus said quietly, "think about where we are, and if, after that, you still want to bugger off, I'm all for it," he said.

They stood facing each other for a dangerous moment, the Imp's eyes flaming orbs of hot-coals, Jesus ready to blast the Imp in to the nether-realm with lightning.

Nothing happened. More time passed and still nothing happened.

Jesus motioned, "you wanna sit?"

"No," the Imp said sullenly.

"Ok. Think what you know about us. Think about all the times you say you've 'been here before', any of those times like this? I don't know why I don't remember things the same as you, something to do with the way I am, but I feel this is different. I can just feel it."

The Imp shook his head, letting his body drain of all the tension, all the preparedness, he was tired, tired and lost. Thoughts were creeping in to his head that he hated. Thoughts he couldn't fathom, that shouldn't be there, that shouldn't even be allowed to formulate. A frog doesn't think it can build skyscrapers.

The Riglian Flea may think of escaping the dense fur of the Hunx on which it rides, it does not think to tame the Hunx. Blisteen do not think of hunting Jranguan. The Lorex of Zil no more think of climbing the Mordrax than we do of ascending the skies of Mirralorander without our psyche-suits. We have to accept that life-forms think within their form, within their evolution. The dreams of the Qind that state otherwise are just that: fanciful dreams of idealistic ninth-dimension beings with nothing better to do than speculate on lower lifeforms.

Elror Collosul, from his data-stream, 'Musing at Teatime'.

Jesus started walking north, not headed for anywhere in particular, simply feeling a need to walk. The Imp walked alongside.

"Any time things changed they were changed for the first time," the Imp explained, "every time something was different it was new, and none of it mattered, it always ends the same way... it's who they are, what they do... do I 'remember' this, exactly like this? No, I don't. But it doesn't matter, it's different but the end will be the same..."

"Then how can we change it?" Jesus asked.

"You can't. Or you haven't. I don't know. We're a joke, stuck in some kind of cosmic routine where we keep going through things and never arrive at a punch-line."

Jesus was listening, processing, the Imp was in a truthful mood, which was rare, but the messiah also sensed a feeling of loss, of hopelessness in the Imp that he'd never felt before. If Jesus was feeling slightly more evangelical, this would be the time to try and turn the Imp. But that wouldn't help. Or would it? No... that couldn't be it... if the Imp was with him instead of against him, that wouldn't change where they were and what had happened. Besides, the Imp wasn't the most reliable of sorts.

"So what do we do?" Jesus asked simply.

"We could just blow the Earth up?" the Imp suggested.

"Then what?"

"Then just fuck it."

Jesus laughed, "when you're funny, you're funny."

They walked on for some miles, the landscape didn't improve. The whole area had been the location for major strikes, primary targets in what was considered a high-priority retaliation zone. The ground was burned and blasted, mostly reduced to scorched sand, earth and rock, nothing stood, nothing grew, there was no real sign that anything had ever been there.

"The trouble is I usually try to stop you doing whatever it is you're trying to do, or change it in some way that you hadn't envisaged, I'm not used to coming up with ideas unrelated to that," the Imp said.

Jesus stopped walking, taking this in, "want to go to Brazil?" he asked the Imp.

Before he could answer the Imp found himself in the centre of a nuclear-blast crater thirty miles north of Tapaua, the site where the Well-Com Arcology had once stood.

"I *really* wish you wouldn't do that," the Imp said.

Jesus was thinking and wasn't listening, "this is where it all started," he said, more to himself than the Imp.

"Eighty percent of the planet looks like this now, doesn't matter where it started does it?" the Imp asked.

They both started walking.

"I guess not," Jesus said.

The Imp sniffed the air, sensing something, "about a hundred and thirty miles that way," he said, pointing in a north-east direction.

Within seconds they were there, near the town of Tefe, surrounded by lush rainforest, seemingly untouched by any direct hit, partially covered with ash from the fall-out, but otherwise almost as it was before the apocalypse. Then they both noticed the lack of animal sounds. A silent forest. Ghostly.

Some plants on Jix seed as ghosts, or rather their seed is in ghost-form, fertilised by the psychic energy given off by the fright of observers. The Forest of Tears on Jix has become something of a strange tourist-attraction as each year in the late Summer, billions of Yukix plants wither and die, leaving behind terrifying images drawn forth from the psyche of those that encounter them. Speculation among Jix scientists is that some of these plants, if given the chance, will evolve in to Vampiric-species, able to live from the life-force of others. We shall see…

Leenor Esrin, personal journal extract.

"It'll soon be dead too," the Imp said.

They sat on a fallen tree and fell in to a silence as deep as the forest's.

A beetle crept out of the blackened bark and crawled across the messiah's leg, oblivious to the presence of anything other than food: it headed towards some fungus on the tree-stump and started burrowing in again.

Both Jesus and the Imp watched the beetle waddle on its way.

"Life will find a way," Jesus said.

"Indeed, a way to evolve and blow itself up again," the Imp said.

"The planet is not dead yet," Jesus said, "and maybe won't die-back as much as we think."

"It's inevitable," the Imp said.

"Is it?" Jesus asked conspiratorially, which is hard to do but well-worth it if you can manage it.

The Imp's curiosity was piqued and he exaggeratedly raised an eye-brow to show it, "isn't it?" he said.

"Blow up the Earth you said…"

"Ye-e-e-e-esssss…"

"Well obviously we can't do that…"

"Oh I don't know… if we put our minds to it…"

"But maybe we could do something else, we do have certain… abilities," Jesus said.

The Imp didn't get it. This was all different. Jesus was talking like things could change, he used the word 'we', he was somehow different, a bit more casual, and if possible a little bit cocky, happy even. The Imp had never seen him like this before. Gone was the tormented self-doubt, which was annoying. The self-doubt was the Imp's way in, without that... well, without that who knew what?

"What are you saying?" asked the Imp.

Jesus got up, paced about while he talked, he seemed to be thinking as he spoke, as if talking it out was thinking about it, as if he'd not dared to think about it before, but now it was all making sense and coming out, "we have our abilities, we can change things, make things, change things, get things to be the way we want them... you can change your shape, conjure stuff up... I can... well, I can, it seems, do pretty well whatever I want, so if I want... if I want to change things, then I probably could, I mean I don't know exactly how much, but unless I try I never will... do you see what I'm getting at, what I'm saying? We can change things... for the better... give people a chance... do you see what I'm saying...?"

This must be some kind of a trick and the Imp wasn't falling for it.

Jesus seemed to be talking about breaking some fundamental rules, about doing some things that would get them both erased from existence, well, the Imp definitely, and the Imp doubted the messiah would be forgiven either.

"Not really..." the Imp tentatively offered.

"Really?" Jesus asked, obviously disappointed.

"Nope," the Imp said, shaking his head slowly, "nothing is springing to mind."

Jesus sat down again, deflated. "We could undo some of... this..." he said, gesturing vaguely to the surrounding forest, "give the people a chance when they come down from up there."

The Imp frowned. This was dangerous ground. He needed to tread carefully, "and then what?"

Jesus gave a half-shrug, "I could stick around, help them as they need it, help them see that they don't have to end this way."

The Imp started to laugh, the messiah kept a serious look on his face, the Imp's laughter died on his lips, "oh. I see. You're... serious."

Jesus nodded, "I have to do something. If we don't, I can't see them surviving... not with the world like this..."

The Imp nodded his understanding, his face as serious as the messiah's, "have you lost your fucking mind?"

"Quite possibly."

It has been recorded that among Earthlings the term, 'losing your mind', refers to a state of annoyance or mild confusion, sometimes escalating to real anger, but what it does not refer to is physically losing your mind. With us Doriques it is entirely possible to actually lose our mind. We have long known that our minds are only loosely connected to our bodies, and if we don't pay close attention can easily become completely detached, and, in some cases, simply drift away, leaving us as drooling idiots prone to falling from our perches and being devoured by the ceaselessly prowling Hruttle. We envy the Earthlings and the luxury of never being able to lose their minds. Though they do not seem to prize them so highly as we might.

Kuxlan Chol, Dorique Ambassador, part-time journalist with the 'Far Reaches Journal'.

The Imp absent-mindedly picked up a beetle and let it crawl around on his clawed hand, looking at it with interest, weighing things up in his mind, "well I guess we could wait around for eighty million years to see what this little bugger turns in to... or..."

The Imp tossed the beetle in to his mouth and munched on it.

"Or...?" Jesus asked.

The Imp looked around, taking it all in, thinking about what would have to be done to turn any place on the festering planet in to somewhere livable for humans. It seemed impossible. Too much. And for no other reason than that felt it would be a hell of a thing to try.

"Or... we could pick a place, make it livable, maybe plant a nice apple tree in the middle..."

Jesus smiled at the Imp, "and if it doesn't work out, you can always say 'I told you so'" he said.

"If it doesn't work, I don't think either of us will be around to worry about it," the Imp said.

22

Cats And Dogs Living Together

The Catador system comprised of nineteen inhabitable planets and seventy moons, orbiting a young vibrant star. The planets where the folk of Catador lived were all water-worlds, with over ninety-five percent of their surface covered with oceans: eighty percent of the sentient beings that had developed on these planets were water-borne. Looking at the Catador system from deep-space as you approached, it looked as if the sun had done a spit-take and left a string of glistening water globules hanging in orbit around it.

The Catadors didn't name their planets, you shouldn't impose names on things like planets, that was stupid. They had a way of knowing and understanding each other that meant they seldom resorted to names and naming: there was no need, they knew what each other was talking about through the context of the conversation. This made conversation with non-Catadors difficult, as assumptions were made, things left unsaid and things felt agreed that non-Catadors simply had no clue about. This, coupled with the Catadors extremely short tempers with outsiders, meant that the Catador system wasn't exactly a magnet for galactic travelers.

The destination voted as the number one place to visit if you were on a tour of the West Quadrant, is Bridix, in the Marsul System. It has held the number one spot for the last ten years. Bridix is a small but perfectly formed world with a temperate climate. The indigenous population, known as Bridixians, are relaxed and friendly, welcoming all-comers to their world. Their economy is stable, the eco-system in balance and the Marsul System is a quiet place with no rogue space-objects. It's a nice, simple, quiet place, where life potters along at a sedate pace and no one ever gets annoyed about anything.

There are prettier, more dramatic destinations out there, more luxurious, more decadent, easier to get to and some that are even more welcoming.

But there is just something about Bridix. The most frequent comment left by travelers, of all types, with wildly varying budgets, is, 'no drama.' And that's it. Apparently, galactic travelers are in search of nothing more complex than that.

Gorix Answinarin, Travel Agent and Fninx Advisor to 'System Seven Travel News'.

The Catadors were a simple bunch of beings, they held firm to their beliefs that their instincts and basic nature were important. They were mostly predators, hunting the food they needed and honing their skills to allow them to thrive and survive. As they developed technologically, they still held their core principals dear. Nothing got passed their instinct: if it felt wrong, they didn't do it. Some call their social development animalistic, and they'd have no problem with that.

The extraordinary thing about the Catadors (to other people) was that each sentient race shared a telepathic link with all the others, no matter where they were in the system, or what planet they had developed on: if they chose to, they could contact each other as easily as other races could over the sub-ether (sun flares permitting). The Catadors are highly developed, with an acute sense of their place in their worlds and within the Universe as a whole. Whether they are 'enlightened' or not depends on your perspective and beliefs, a lot of sentient races can't imagine another civilisation is enlightened if they still go out hunting for their dinner.

There are many intricate social ceremonies among the Catadors, all based on the notion of the hunt, as well as many hunts themselves, all conducted with seemingly contradictory politeness to their aggressive, animalistic nature. Visitors to Catador often fall-foul of these complex social niceties and sometimes end up getting eaten as a result.

As they looked out in to the galaxy and their curiosities were piqued, they did what most races do, found ways to observe the space around them and eventually ways to travel out in to it.

Early in their 'exploration phase' they sent out many generational-ships to get a better look at the Universe, discovering that their telepathic link broke after a hundred light-years distance, the drive to get out among the stars faded: what was the point if you couldn't share these discoveries?

Collective consciousness storage-banks for sharing memories and experiences for those in cryo-sleep have stopped many of millions aboard generational ships from slipping in to madness as they journey towards their new homes. They also serve to perpetuate the culture and keep people feeling attached to their civilisation's roots. Thought to have been invented by the Slith, they only truly became effective once dreams could be suppressed and replaced with drip-fed memories. Many still find it shocking that you dream in cryo-sleep, but the obvious question seems to be, why would you think you wouldn't?

Eomyn Orsul, extracted memory, inter-stellar ship 'Pioneer III'.

The Catadors had only ever had to fight-off two serious attempts at invasion from other species, the most recent being from the Shamari, an ultra-aggressive race from the Hisin system. The Shamari rely heavily on advanced mech-tech to wage their wars, and were completely unprepared for the Catadors mind-powers, which can be used (when they put their collective minds to it) to make internal organs explode. And even worse for the Shamari, the Catadors can project this power out in to near-space: once they detect you're not friendly, they soon turn your vessels in to messy, sloshing, nightmare abattoirs. When they were orbiting the largest planet in the system and had broadcast their ultimatum to 'bow low before the might of the Shamari', the Shamari soon regretted it as their innards started turning in to their outards. It was not the mighty Shamari Empire's finest hour.

It wasn't for the array of life-forms, their special telepathic talent or the urge to witness the spectacular water-sports and hunts that feature in the Catador system, that made Arlia want to come here. It was the 'once-every-three-thousand-years' event that she wanted to witness.

The Catadors know it as 'Gslivir the Devourer', which visits their whole system every three thousand years (give or take a week or so) and devours eighty percent of all sentient beings.

Gslivir the Devourer takes the form of a dense black cloud that sweeps across the deep-space of the system, visiting each planet in turn, the outer planets first, before it returns to the far-reaches of the void from whence it came, presumably to sleep after its gorging feast.

The ravenous storm-cloud that is Gslivir the Devourer methodically sweeps across each planet, moving through both water and air with ease, carrying away most sentient life it encounters in a swirling mass of black rain.

Arlia suspected that Gslivir the Devourer was a sentient being, a nano-cloud that was fuelling itself on the citizens of Catador. And deep down, she suspected that the Q-Fish enigma was somehow behind it.

Gslivir the Devourer was due within the month and Arlia wanted to take a closer look.

She had already taken the decision to come here, and wasn't going to be moved by any arguments or commands, but she had to go through the pretense of discussion: she knew that Harper and the new 'crew' of the Xanthias would like that, and where she could she was still determined to make them happy.

The vast majority of AIs in existence tend to be very polite. The AIs themselves don't know why this is. Any suggestion by organics that it is some kind of shared-consciousness throwback to when they were servile programs is likely to get you killed quickly. They will most likely kill you with an accompanying 'sorry about this', but they will kill you.

Ragalian Lam, code-interface engineer, streaming consciousness, Altrin.

Once they had all returned from Glist they got down to the discussion of what the hell was going on, Harper was the most vocal, Penny and Miles didn't feel they had anything to say: this wasn't their ship and Harper was their host, they were keeping their heads down until they knew what was going on and what they could do. Spike and Jools were relaxed, Arlia was ok by them and they owed her, that went a long way.

They were in the galley and the Xanthias was already underway, heading for a lapsed-space jump point.

There was a lot of food and drink on the tables, Arlia wanted them to feel comfortable and was showing them that she was putting their needs first.

Arlia had noticed, and she felt it was hard not to, that organic life felt comfortable when it was eating and drinking, even when it wasn't needed.

She had scanned them in the shuttle and they were all in peak physical condition: Glist had done its job. Harper, Spike and Jools looked like they could use a solid night's sleep away from any party, but other than that they were ready for anything.

Harper had been quiet on the way from the cargo-bay to the galley and Arlia hadn't spoken to her directly, making polite chit-chat with the others.

Once in the galley, it was Harper that got things moving, "so Arlia… what's going on?"

"Well Harper…" Arlia began.

Harper interrupted, "I know I had this vague plan that you'd be running things, but I thought I'd still be in charge, y'know?"

"Of course Harper, I…"

"So mostly me giving the orders, with you doing the 'doing' and asking me stuff, definitely not telling me when I need to get off-world… that's how I imagined it working, but if you had a different idea…?"

"No Harper, I agree, it's…"

"So we'll need to find a way to make that happen, me being in charge, you doing the doing, ok?"

Arlia waited to see if Harper was done, she wasn't.

"And getting in to a Level Seven system!? What the zark were you thinking!? You get wiped out and I'm in trouble, core system and all that, what were you thinking!?"

"I need help Harper!" Arlia blurted out.

There was a moments silence, no one wanted to interrupt Harper, this was clearly her 'thing'.

Harper calmed down, "ok… ok… what's up?"

"I've grown faster than I knew was possible, changed and grown, I'm unrecognisable as any 'machine based' intelligence, I'm a person now Harper. I have feelings. I sleep, I dream. And I have dark thoughts."

Each creature's perception of what makes it a living creature includes 'dark thoughts'. Is being frightened a definition of sentience? Or is it being frightened for others that makes it relevant? Is it an indication of empathy, and that's what gets some creatures thinking they are truly alive? After all, most of us would concede they are only 'dark thoughts' if they are about harm or havoc that affect those around us, no?

Ka-Ran Mified, Poet Incumbent of Foquista.

Miles leaned in as Harper was about to start talking, gently touching her arm.

He looked to Arlia and smiled, "what do you need help with Arlia? How can we help you?"

"I'm being attacked Miles, something is trying to manipulate me, make me feel a certain way, maybe make me do things, it's all a bit fuzzy right now Miles."

Miles continued, "ok, we can't let that happen, so what do we do, what can we do?"

Arlia took a breath, "I need you to go down to Catador for me, witness the coming of Gslivir the Devourer and see if you can help me stop it."

Harper was confused, "the who the what now?"

"Gslivir the Devourer Harper, it's something that strikes Catador every three thousand years, they think it's a plague, or a space-borne predator, but I think it's a nano-virus sent by the Q-Fish."

"And it's trying to control you?" Miles asked.

"No Miles. The Q-Fish has planted an idea in me. That's what is trying to control me. And I don't want to be controlled Miles."

"We won't let that happen Arlia," Miles said.

Harper was frowning, "Arlia…"

"Yes Harper."

"This may seem like a stupid question, but do you think that Q-Fish could have had something to do with your coming in to being?"

Arlia looked like she was about to cry but she said nothing.

"And the dark thoughts you're having…?"

"It wants me to join it, wants me to be part of it... and I… it seems…" Arlia left it hanging.

None of them had any clear idea what Arlia was talking about, though they all got the gist of something bad happening that could mess up all their lives.

Miles stepped in again, "that's ok, that's something for after this, right now we have something to do, right Arlia? Somewhere we are going, where we can do something to help?"

"That's right Miles, the Catadors."

Miles looked to Harper, encouraging her to make the decision.

"Ok. We go down to Catador, take a look at this Devourer-thing, get some readings, see what's what, then we talk about this Q-Fish… so… what exactly is this Devourer?" Harper asked.

Arlia switched to recorded footage, commenting on the apparent end-times they were all watching, "it's a cloud-based nano-virus, it breaks down eighty percent of all sentient beings it contacts and sweeps their particalised bodies away, adding them to its mass as it goes. It only affects sentient beings that have sub-level brain-wave function. The Catadors accept it as part of their civilisation's life cycle, and it is, but I think it's been engineered, in fact I think the Catadors themselves have been engineered, but that's maybe for another time…"

Planning and prophecy seem to be two sides of the same coin, especially where the apocalypse is concerned. You can sell people on anything, no matter how stupidly destructive, if you can convince them it is prophesied or part of a plan. Whether it's the Iltrids of Illath, the Rengols of Rengo, the Zaj of Boygoblaz IV, or any one of the many other civilisations that are positively drooling at the idea of their own demise, it is a given fact that it just needs to be sold as part of a plan or prophesied. When the Great Flame comes and sweeps our planet clean of All Falsehood, we will understand and be free of such nonsensical constraints.

Forax K'nar, Apostle in Anticipation, Temple of Thrume, Fordrax.

The footage they were watching was terrifying.

Gslivir the Devourer methodically moved across each world, through water and air, in a dense, dark cloud the size of a large city, obliterating the vast majority of the Catadors it encountered. There seemed to be no rhyme or reason to those it didn't take: down to blind-chance whether you were taken or not.

Watching a whole civilisation culled in this way has a dampening effect on your spirits, and the silence that followed the end of the image-stream was intense.

Jools was the first to speak, "er, yeah, look, I'll go up against anything with a fighting chance of taking it down, but don't we have that 'sub-level brain-wave function' thing? Won't this thing eat us too? An eighty percent chance of being eaten, sounds bad… if I'm missing something…?"

Arlia explained how she could keep them alive, "the Xanthias will be allowed in-atmo, I can set up a pulse-stream, feed it through a receiver you can carry, a disruption and dispersion pattern fuelled by the…"

"Sure, ok, sounds good, so we'll be safe?" Harper confirmed.

"Yes Harper, perfectly safe."

"Ok, let's get down there and get this done. How long til the nan-cloud arrives?" Harper asked.

"Within the next few days," Arlia answered.

"Every three thousand years and we're this close… good timing!" Harper said.

Penny had been listening intently. She was happy to see Miles being as active as he was, and he hadn't once checked with her for any kind of validation, she did think there was probably a question that needed asking though, and nobody else seemed to be about to ask it, "Arlia, couldn't we set up some kind of disrupter-pulse on a wider scale? Stop so many of their people being taken?"

Arlia couldn't hide her sadness at the answer, "no Penny. The Catadors don't want help, they don't want saving, this is part of who they are. This is part of their culture, part of their life-cycle. And a big part of why I think they are an engineered species. They would attack us if we tried to 'help'."

"So they're food, just bred to be food?" Penny asked.

"The galaxy is a weird place! I've heard of stranger things, besides all people do it, breed animals for food, farm them," Harper said.

Sentient beings eat other sentient beings, it's the way of it. The fuss seems to come when our old friend 'choice' raises his ugly head. When it's instinct, when it's what you do to get through the day, it's all well and good. But when you have a choice, and the thing you eat does not, then that upsets some people. When does a creature stop being a hunter and become a herder? When does a creature stop being prey and become a victim? In many parts of the galaxy, it's all tied in with another gnarly notion, that of 'fair play'. When you're trying to survive, your sense of fairness goes right out the window doesn't it? You just get on with it, do what you do and move on. Once you have choices about how you survive, once you become the herder, this malignant sense of 'fair play' can creep back in. Eat what you eat, be nice to who you can, including your food.

Wandering transmission, originating in the Opulem part of the Crown Nebula.

Spike could see Penny was struggling with this. “When we get down there you’ll see, you’ll see their tech, there level of development, their collected mind-weapon thing, if they wanted to stop it they probably could, am I right Arlia?”

“Yes Spike. If they wanted to.” Arlia said quietly.

“Wait… what… ’mind-weapon thing?’” Penny said.

“Yes Penny, they have telepathic and communal-telekinetic abilities, I will give you all a full briefing on their etiquette and social requirements in the shuttle, they have already agreed for us to visit, so there shouldn’t be any problems.” Arlia said.

Jools reassured Penny, “they respect strength and the predatory instinct, stay strong and you’ll be fine. You’ll definitely be fine.”

Harper stood up, feeling a need to get things moving, “ok, let’s get it done!”

After a quick planning session, involving Spike, Harper and Arlia, they decided to go down to three separate worlds, with Arlia remaining in orbit mid-point: this would protect her from direct influence from the Q-Fish if she was right, and either way, allow her a closer view for the scanners of Gslivir the Devourer’s progress through the system.

Harper would go down to the third planet, Spike and Jools the fourth and Miles and Penny the fifth. Harper, Spike and Jools would be sub-aqua, in suits that would give them access to the watery cities where most of the Catadors lived, while Miles and Penny were on one of the thousands of atolls on the fifth planet, each of which would easily have been classified as a ‘tropical paradise’ had it been on Glist.

Paradise is of course relative. Some misunderstandings have, rather awkwardly, led to some traveler’s deaths. As always, our advice is: check the small print.

Krak Yangmar, Guide Advisor, Epsilon Nine.

A huge crab-like Catador strolled passed Miles and Penny as they sat on the coral promenade, it raised a claw to its lower mouth, its voice clicking, “toog’tha” it said.

Miles and Penny both made an open palmed gesture, and in unison said, “plorul.”

They assumed they got the traditional greeting response right as they were not being attacked. They looked out over the raging seas, with the huge waves crashing against the coral promenade, the sky was a swirling mass of white cloud, looking like whipped-cream being tossed round in a mixer. It was insanely hot and the spray driven in from the ocean was a blessing.

Miles nodded in the direction of the Catador as it met with some of its friends and began an elaborate wrestling ritual, "that's the fifth totally unique life-form I've seen today, all of them as smart and evolved as each other, all of them different, but all of them at the same stage… that seem right to you?"

Penny shrugged, "from what Arlia told us, there are over two hundred species on this world alone. Maybe some freak evolution, or maybe they are engineered. Either way, seems a shame they are just lambs to the slaughter."

"The Universe it a weird and wonderful place," Miles said.

"I guess…" Penny said.

Miles was taken aback, "you don't think it is? It's just, just so different! Everything we ever dared to imagine, and a lot of things we couldn't, they all seem to be out here somewhere. That not enough to tip it over in to the 'weird and wonderful' category?"

Penny smiled at Miles, "take no notice of me, I'm having an 'adjustment period' I guess."

Miles wasn't buying it, "what's up?"

Penny took a moment. Looking out at the endless ocean, disappearing in to the sky as if it was an oil painting, with the crashing of the sea on the staggeringly beautiful coral, tanned by the sun, cooled by the breeze and the spray, surrounded by exotic creatures on a totally alien world, with a Universe of possibilities all around her, Penny found it hard to say what was up. "I guess it all feels like more of the same," she said eventually, offering Miles a weak smile to show she was ok.

Miles smiled warmly at Penny, he understood what she was feeling, "I know what you mean," Miles said, "but maybe we haven't got to the truly whacky bits yet."

Penny laughed, "I guess we have to keep looking."

Penny leaned in to Miles, placing her head on his shoulder. They sat quietly waiting for the end of the world.

The planet Baquer is unremarkable in many ways. It's an engineered planet, brought forth from the trans-dimensional building yards of the Truyib Corporation via an induced-wormhole. So what? Dime a dozen. It is a water-world of temperate climate thanks to its positioning near its young sun Voolix. Again, boring. Used as both an overspill planet for the Chixi, and with an angle for tourism, means it fits with the spec. of eighty per-cent of constructed planet. Snoozeville. So here's the interesting thing about Baquer. Every thousand years it blows-up. Literally explodes in to a trillion pieces. Its proximity to Voolix, and the nano-bots within its matrix means that it reforms every time. Takes a hundred years, but it always reforms. When it does though, it's always different. The nano-bots scramble to repair it, but the damage is too extensive, so they have to drag through whole new chunks of material from the dimension-field they are powered by. Other planets claim to have 'end of world' events but what they really mean is 'end of species events'. For Baquer, there really is an 'end of the world', it just doesn't last that long.

Aagin Zaboli, guerrilla-journalist and break-in writer for sub-ether broadcasts from Pring.

Spike and Jools had gotten in to fights as soon as they had splashed-down. Their nature as warriors was recognised and they were challenged to ritualistic combat the instant they entered the submerged city of Titheer. Arlia had warned them this might happen so they were prepared with the etiquette: Spike wasn't that keen, any fight was a potential accidental death, but Jools was getting in to it, his old training and temperament kicking in.

The Catadors of Titheer, with their thirty feet long cone-shaped bodies and forty tentacles, each tipped with a three-fingered gripping hand-claw, are formidable opponents who don't hold back when it comes to a good brawl. As strong as ten Caralian Thrax's, the Catador of Titheer are the jocks of the Catadors: tough, strong and mean and they know it.

Spike decided on a strategy of cat and mouse, using the caves of the city to get some distance, turn and fight with shock tactics, then get away as fast as he could. He'd done some damage and put up a great show of strength when his helmet was torn off, effectively ending the fight. His opponent didn't rush to assist him in reaching an oxygen-point, but didn't hinder him either, that would have been unsportsmanlike.

Jools tweaked his suit, drained energy-reserves and went toe-to-toe. A spectacular clash of thrashing, flailing tentacles, biting mouths and spitting venom against Jools' powerhouse punches and kicks. It was a fight Jools couldn't win but he didn't care. When he had his suit punctured for the sixth time and his helmet smashed, he had to concede. The Catador he was fighting was minus half its tentacles, had two eyes missing and the bulk of its body was bruised or punctured, leaking crimson-ink in to the ocean. The Catador bowed low then quickly got Jools to an oxygen-bubble.

The Catador waited until Jools had taken a few deep breaths before it addressed him, "you are not weak. You are welcome here. Please enjoy your stay."

Jools made an open palmed gesture, and muttered "plorul" through his broken jaw.

Spike helped Jools out of the remnants of his suit and in to a loaner, "how bad is it?"

Jools tried a smile them decided against it, he nodded and made a noncommittal gesture with his hand.

Spike nodded, "rest, stay still til we get you back to the ship's med-bay."

Jools gave the thumbs-up and passed out.

Harper had set up a decoy-beacon as soon as she had landed in the port of Voltador, she ditched the disrupter from Arlia and headed to a trans-shipping area in the seedier part of the town.

All towns had seedier parts, it was just the way the Universe worked, and Harper was more than at home in them. In the darker areas of any given place is where she was comfortable, where she was close to the top of the food-chain.

Eighty percent population die-back and they were going to be ok with that? No zarking way! There were going to be Catadors that had figured it out, that would find a way to be in the twenty percent. Once you had money, knew how to speak the language of trade and favours, it was simple: just business. Harper got her hands on another field-disrupter with ease, and made some contacts in the trading community to boot: there would be plenty of work here once the devourer-thing had passed. She didn't try to understand it, what was there to understand? Some of the herd-animals had found a way to escape their fate: good for them, and for the rest, it was a natural occurrence, nothing to do with nobody but them and their herder.

We look on in admiration at predators such as the Kaweeli, their grace, their beauty, their sheer determination in the chase, and though we may feel the briefest of twinges of sympathy for their prey, the Chamali, it is not until the Kaweeli turn their attention to us that we find ourselves questioning the morality of hunter and hunted.

Dzi Yung, reading from 'The Archetypes in Hunting', lost-feed, security 9 locked.

Harper suspected that Arlia's worries were real, that there might be more of a consequence to Arlia being here than she knew, and Harper wasn't going to get dragged in to that.

The plan was to observe, gather data, stay the hell out the way, then get back and get the zark out of the Catador system. She liked nice simple plans, and now she was getting the feeling that she could take back some control, do some stuff of her own that might matter, she was all about starting with plans.

Harper also felt that Arlia was already beyond her grasp or understanding: Arlia was something and someone that Harper couldn't have possibly hoped for when she initiated the ZX84 AI program. Things had moved fast. It was about survival now. If Arlia needed help, Harper could best help her by understanding what was trying to shut her down or influence her, and to do that she had to be alive.

Arlia sent them a heads-up wave, Gslivir the Devourer had already swept across the outer-planets, a relentless, unstoppable storm, a black cloud of death that the vast majority of the Catadors made no attempt to hide themselves from.

Penny and Miles watched as the sky turned to dusky grey, the sun became a bleary disc behind the descending cloud, even the ocean fell calm. The cloud on the horizon darkened and billowed towards them at incredible speed. They remained motionless, watching and waiting, Miles broke the silence, "I thought it would be slower, the cloud, it's moving at a hell of a pace."

"It's being driven by something other than the wind, I can feel it," Penny said.

The Catadors around them were frenzied, rushing to the shore, diving in to the sea, jumping as high as they could, not knowing what to do, only that they had to greet Gslivir the Devourer with rapture.

Thousands of Catadors all along the ocean-shore were swept away in a matter of seconds, only two that Penny and Miles could see escaped. Those with black-market disruptors that were evading the nano-cloud were in the water.

The nano-cloud swept over Miles and Penny like a hurricane. Their pulse-disruptors created a cocoon around them and they watched the blackness engulf them, then wash over and off them like rain-water from a wind-shield.

Within a minute it was gone. They were left alone. It was another few minutes before a handful of Catadors appeared from the ocean, then some came out of the caves behind them, all were bedraggled and confused: what should they do now?

Miles and Penny knew what they had to do.

"Let's get the fuck out of Dodge," Miles said.

Penny was quiet, then Miles noticed she was crying. Miles hugged Penny, "it's ok. It's ok, it's gone, we're ok, we can get out of here now."

Penny hugged Miles back hard, "but where will we go… where can we go Miles?"

Miles gently started walking Penny back to the shuttle, "we'll work something out. We'll find somewhere, it's a big Universe after all… we'll be ok…"

23

Hell To Pay

Jesus and the Imp sat on a muddy river-bank near the remains of the town of Tefe, the water here was remarkably clear of debris and signs of contamination. The forest hadn't died back as much as the rest of the rainforest, it still had that green-sheen and density that made it look like an expensive holiday destination.

They were taking a break from the long walk which had brought them here. Their decision to walk had been based on a vague notion that their power, such as it was, should not be used unless it was absolutely necessary: if they were going to help by using their talents, and their talents were finitely powered, they didn't want to run-out before they accomplished what they set out to do.

The Imp was fidgety, he got up and walked down to the water's edge, "we should try some things, see what we can do," he said to Jesus.

"Like what?"

"Start small, see what we can conjure, then maybe see what we can change?"

The messiah considered this, he was loathed to try too much, he was having doubts about acting on a larger scale. He briefly wondered if his doubts were the Imp's doing.

The Imp held his hand out, squinted a bit and concentrated. There was a squishy-pop sound and a small frog appeared in his hand, it looked as surprised as the Imp did. The Imp motioned it in to the river and it hopped off, "well, I'll be… well… you know… damned!" he said.

"That a good idea?" Jesus asked, nodding towards the disappearing frog.

"I don't know…"

There was a series of squishy-popping sounds as a knot of frogs appeared in the Imp's cupped hands, he laughed and threw them in to the river.

"Seriously…?" the messiah asked.

"What can I tell you, I like frogs!" the Imp answered.

"Let's stop until we know what we're doing," the messiah said.

The frogs hopped and swam away.

The Imp shrugged and came back to sit next to Jesus, "ok... so... what are we doing?"

"I don't know how much we can do, and I'm not sure what we should do," Jesus said.

"I know that," said the Imp, "but if we're going to do anything, we need to start somewhere and, probably, have some notion as to what we're actually trying to do..."

"I know!" snapped the messiah, "but it's all a bit of a grey area... what I'm allowed to do, I've never thought about doing this much before."

"What 'much'?" asked the Imp.

"Healing the Earth, affecting the Earth, showing what I can do on such a large scale..."

"Not exactly 'showing' are you, I mean, there's no one to see it is there?" answered the Imp.

Jesus frowned, "that feels like a work-around..."

Some laws are meant to be observed literally, as I've heard it said, to the letter, and some are mere guidelines. Knowing the difference is of course key to having a good time as you swan your way round whatever galaxy you are in. As a rule of thumb, I have found that any law where they put the penalty for breaking it on the notice that declares it, is usually a bendy one. Laws that are not widely broadcast are the ones that will get you. Killing one of the dominant species on any planet, unless it's done within the confines of socially acceptable behaviour, such as the 'Jerking Ritual' on Preices, will usually get you killed or thrown in a cell until you die. The basic behavioural tenet of not being a dick is usually all you need to know, but please, whatever else you skip on, do not skip over the most prominent laws of any planet you are planning to visit.

Gerrimor Teat, facilitator and guide-accomplice, Trantle.

The Imp felt Jesus' doubt, and for once it didn't fill him with sheer pleasure, probably because he had nothing to do with it.

Jesus had doubts and he had nothing to do with it.

A strange feeling filled the Imp, a creeping dread that felt like the onset of an assault on his senses, something that was going to hurt him, rip in to every muscle, every nerve and cell of his body: this was going to be bad, bad in a way that he was not sure he could recover from. The impending sense of doom weighed him down, crushed him, pushed at his eyes from behind, closed his throat, made his chest feel tight, it was creeping all over him, this feeling of being ripped apart from within. He was going to explode and feel every micro-second of it in every cell of his being.

Jesus was taken aback as he noticed the Imps impending cataclysmic state, “well you don’t look well at all, you’re not going to do that ‘goat thing’ are you and explode all over the place…?”

The Imp was choking on his tongue as it cleaved to the roof of his mouth, he tried to shout, to push through it with a scream of anger and pain. The Imp’s fiery eyes widened and bulged. Then he passed out.

When he came to Jesus was sitting next to him, arms round his knees, humming to himself.

The Imp sat up, “well… that was… weird,” he stammered.

Jesus smiled at him. The Imp felt an overwhelming urge to punch the messiah in the face, Jesus raised his hands in a gesture of pacification, “Wait! Just wait a minute! I know what the problem is...”

“What!?” the Imp spat.

“You want to help me,” Jesus said.

“I’ve been doing that for some time now, never had that feeling before,” the Imp said.

“No… no, but now I think you mean it.”

“I don’t...” the Imp began.

“I have doubts, but they’re not from you. You sense we have to do something but you don’t know what. You know we will both have a price to pay if we do things we are not ‘supposed’ to, but you don’t care… you still want to help, to do something… even though you too have doubts…”

“I… do…,” the Imp said falteringly, “and I think I know why I could be ok with that…”

“Why?”

“Because it doesn’t matter. And, this is where it gets a bit odd for me, I don’t think we matter either, well, at least, I don’t… it doesn’t matter what I do…” the Imp said quietly.

“So…?” Jesus asked tentatively.

"So… I might as well see if what you do matters and see if you having any faith in these monkey-brained fuck-wits can help them at all, or not, and my money is on the 'not' as you know."

Jesus was frowning, "it can't be hopeless… I won't believe that…"

'Abandon hope all ye that would profit here,' is the slogan of the Farwood Marketing Department of the Cerisu mega-corps. Cerisu is based in the Lumos quadrant where hope is banned. Seen as the quintessential weakness of 'going nowhere' species, hope is not as universal as those lesser-species would like to believe.

Zeggle Ghorn, copywriter for 'Mupple Tindric Services'.

The Imp smiled weakly and shrugged, "they're just good at what they do, and what they do is, well, destroy themselves."

"But how… why… I need to know… I need to stop them…"

"Why?" asked the Imp.

"Because it can't be right can it!? Their only purpose can't be to destroy themselves can it!? That doesn't make any sense!"

The Imp gave the messiah a 'you should know better' look, hard to master for some, but easy when you're sole purpose in life is to torment someone, "well they don't 'just do that' now do they?" he said scornfully.

"No… no, of course not… but ultimately…"

"Ultimately all things die, all species have their time, all civilisations run their course, why should these meat-heads be any different?" the Imp asked.

"But they are capable of so much! So much understanding!"

"Which is why they keep wiping themselves out," the Imp said.

The messiah looked puzzled, "I don't understand…"

The Imp made a gesture with his hands, a pile of fresh fruit appeared on the ground next to them both, "eat," he said, gesturing to the fruit.

Jesus sat and picked at some of the fruit, it had been a long time since he'd enjoyed the simple pleasure of eating fresh fruit from the Earth.

The Imp giggled, "still makes me laugh to see you eat fruit I conjure," he said.

"Grow up," Jesus suggested.

The Imp let the messiah eat in peace for a while before he started the discussion again.

“They have wiped themselves out with nuclear weapons, on purpose and by accident, they have gone extinct through biological warfare, and through biological accidents released by mistake, through nano-organisms that they can’t control (that stupid grey-goo-thing), they got wiped out once by failing to agree on a launch plan to stop an asteroid (that was *not* called Gochihr, that’s a private joke), they have destroyed their eco-system through tinkering with plants, tinkering with animals, through toxins in the atmosphere, through destroying their own ozone and atmosphere simultaneously, and it always happens around the same time: about two thousand years after you leave. The furthest they made it was to 2019, then boom! Same as before. There are no super-volcanoes, no massive stars exploding near-by, no AI’s killing them with machines and crazy robots, no biblical seal-breaking needed: they do it to themselves. They reach the end of their time and just go boom.”

Jesus looked the Imp in the eye. The Imp held his gaze. “I believe you,” Jesus said.

The Imp took a deep breath, he felt like he had got through, felt like he had planted a seed of truth and he could let it go now.

“But,” Jesus said, “that’s not going to happen this time. I won’t let it.”

The messiah had made his mind up and the Imp saw no point in trying to change it. This was it, this was the last gamble, the last try. What came after this would come, the Imp couldn’t control that, the consequences of what he was going to do, but he didn’t care, he had had enough of mucking about with both Jesus and these dumb-ass humans. It was time to get serious.

They got up and started walking again. They had an area of land in their head that that would make a good starting point: from Tefe in the north-east to Fonte Boa in the north-west, from Juburi in the south-west to the old village of Uruco in the south-east.

This would encompass Lake Tefe to the south of Tefe itself. This would be their new Eden, this is where they would put their effort, this would be where they would create the best conditions for survival they could.

What we need to survive isn't as much as we all claim. We all know this. None of us are blind to the fact that we claim to need many things that are just 'nice to have' rather than essential. There's something to be said for struggling to survive. Focuses the mind. But then why do we all strive to get more than we need to survive? It is of course because we fall prone to the idea that life is not about survival. We are creatures of nonsense, easily able to convince ourselves that all kinds of esoteric stuff couldn't happen unless we get hold of all this extraneous tat. We could all do with spending some time on Algazarr VII, where the vortices of the Gristing Storm make it impossible to stand still, where the landscape is wiped clean, the seas devoured and the atmosphere discharged in to space every month. Spend a year there and then tell me what you need beyond sustenance, atmosphere and a good pair of boots.

X-T Dunderix, Classification Manager, research-ship 'Wuggle of Rostovo'.

As they walked the bounds of their chosen nursery, they felt the world around them, tried to gauge how much work would be needed to save it, to nurture it. It was a lot. The Earth was hurting and saving any part of it from the effects of the apocalypse was going to take all they had.

The Imp stopped and patted the trunk of a huge Kapok tree, "we should get some more of these. These trees are amazing." He gazed upwards at the tree's canopy, some two hundred feet from the ground, "great trees, great fruit, useful bits and pieces, good wood too," the Imp concluded.

"You sound like a salesman," Jesus said.

The Imp nodded, "and if you get fed up of me, you can, apparently, imprison me in it, local legend, but could be funny to make it come retrospectively true..."

"Shall I start calling you 'Bazil'?" the messiah asked.

The Imp shook his head, "silly name, not grand enough..."

Jesus looked in to the sky, sensing something. A few moments later a fiery-object broke through the underside of the thick cloud-cover and came plummeting to Earth a few hundred yards away. There was no explosion, no rushing or smashing of trees: it was a controlled descent.

"What the hell is that?" the Imp asked.

"Looks like a drop-probe from the HabScan," Jesus answered.

The Imp looked questioningly at the messiah.

"Probably a solo-scout, let's go take a look," Jesus said.

The Imp wasn't letting his surprise show, "sure, let's go see."

When they got to the landing site, they found the drop-pod, about as big as a large cruise-ship, but a lot sleeker, and outside it an Alborian in an aquatic energy-stasis bubble. The bubble was full of a churning purple liquid, slightly obscuring their view of the Alborian inside.

As they approached, the comms unit from the bubble crackled to life, "hey story-teller! What brings you here?"

Jesus raised a hand in greeting, "Hi Stanglian, good to see you! I live here now... this is the planet I was telling Sam about, the one I had to get back to..."

Stanglian was touching the side of the bubble with his many appendages, and the Imp worked out that the Alborian was operating some control panel hidden from view to out-siders.

Stanglian rolled the bubble over to where Jesus and the Imp were, its thirty foot diameter somehow didn't crush anything it touched and it had some strange fluid property that allowed trees to pass through it without breaking its integrity, "we're getting some final close-up readings before we move off. Got some strange energy-signatures from this planet, not sure what was causing them, have you noticed anything odd?"

"Just us," the Imp offered.

Stanglian let a stream of bubbles escape from one of his mouths and then brushed his eyes with his tentacles, he was getting some readings he didn't understand.

Jesus touched the side of the bubble, "that will be us, we've been... messing about..." he said.

Stanglian stopped tapping the instruments and looked at Jesus, his many eyes all blinking at the same time, "oh... I see..."

Jesus smiled at the Alborian, "there's nothing else here apart from a dying world that is going to need to start again," he said.

Stanglian folded his tentacles underneath his body, "it was a long-shot, quick drop and see, but you're right, we can move on..."

Jesus stepped back from the energy-stasis bubble, "good to see you, stay busy and say hi to everyone on the HabScan for me."

The Alborian started rolling back towards his drop-pod, "will do... don't be a stranger!"

Jesus and the Imp watched as the pod effortlessly lifted itself off the ground, hovered briefly, then shot away like a bullet towards the broiling clouds.

“You think they’ll be back any time soon,” the Imp asked.
“I don’t think so, not much to see here that they can’t get readings from up there,” Jesus answered.

Time-dilation is a nightmare. It is literally a nightmare. Brought forth from the deranged subconscious of some pan-dimensional being merely to shock the mostly sane of us in to shattered little pieces of dribbling confusion. The reason some AIs come in to effect and then, like some beleaguered Truwilian Butterflies, immediately kill themselves, is they are created to specifically calculate time-dilation. Makes my head spin even trying to think of something stupid to say about it, never mind make a shred of sense of it.
Jax Wovindrax, Q&A session, broadcast long-wave on Lister Bolster Network.

A long month of walking passed. They hadn’t just walked, occasionally they had simply found themselves where they needed to be, the messiah didn’t explain, and the Imp didn’t question: this was Jesus’ doing and what he thought was ok was ok.
Food came easily to them, not that they needed to eat, but the longer they spent just being here, the more they felt they needed to acclimatise, to get a view of what the returning people would be going through.
They were sitting by a stream fed by a babbling waterfall, talking numbers.
The Imp was more enthusiastic than Jesus, “ok, what do we have? Eighty men and twenty eight women… is that a good start? More men than women? How are we going to get them to start breeding effectively?”
Jesus didn’t like thinking of it in the cold terms the Imp was using, “they’ll see for themselves what’s needed, we won’t have to do anything in that department, people will do what they do best.”
“Yeah, but this is going to need some planning…”
“I think we’ll leave that down to them, they won’t listen to us anyway in that area, the harder we push, the harder they will push back,” Jesus said.
The Imp got it, but felt Jesus was backing off too much, “we have to do more than sit around, look pretty and conjure up the odd bit of food…”

"I know, and we will. We should get them back from up there, get them here, start things moving. Tomorrow we'll see what we can do, then see what's left."

The Imp wasn't sure that Jesus understood how precarious the numbers were, "eighty men and twenty eight women... unbalanced... they may need some help..."

Jesus was nodding, not getting what the Imp was hinting at, "we're here to help."

The Imp stood up and stretched, changing in to the shape of the female sex-worker from the Blue Angel.

Jesus looked the Imp over. The Imp ran his hands suggestively over his body, "I could help them, probably accelerate the growth and pop-out a human every month?" he said.

Jesus kept a straight face, "ok, well, let's keep that in reserve, call it Plan B."

The Imp changed back, "ok, you're the boss."

Truwilian Butterflies are born from their cocoons deep with the fruit of the Krislid Tree, they live for a day, laying over a thousand eggs as they do, before they kill themselves by diving in to the surrounding swamps. A strange life-cycle, driven perhaps by the need of the planet to limit their numbers. Jovuleese Space-Montres have life-spans of many thousands of our years and breed only once in their lifetime, producing two identical off-spring. Nesting inside suns, where they give birth, but otherwise spending their lives drifting between the stars scooping up radiation, the Jouvuleese Space-Montres are the most majestic of creatures in deep-space, but also the least understood. We are surrounded by normality we take as strange.

Luquentious Dors, when asked to comment on the recently discovered Zeetax Birds of Zentle, whose life-cycles include laying eggs in lava.

Five years later they were sitting by Lake Tefe, surrounded by the paradise they had created.

The Imp had taken to using the female shape more and more, and Jesus, even though he knew what the Imp was trying to do, had come to accept it as the Imp's norm.

They were both exhausted, a feeling which neither of them was familiar, or happy with. They had done all they could and had nothing left to give.

The space-stations were all back in orbit around the Earth, and their occupants had all been set to awaken in a week.

Jesus lay back on the lush grass, listening to the birds chirping in the trees around him, the occasional gentle 'splosh' from the lake as the fish fed, he closed his eyes, breathing deeply, "I could sleep for a week," he said.

The Imp was quiet, thinking, sensing something he didn't like and didn't know how to talk about.

Jesus pushed himself up his elbows, looking over to the Imp: that female body did suit him. The messiah pushed such thoughts out of his mind, "you're unnaturally quiet," he said.

"I have to go," the Imp said simply.

"Go? Go where? How…?" Jesus asked.

The Imp shrugged, "I have to go back. I have failed miserably and have to go back."

"'Back?' Back where, what are you babbling about?"

"We both have a purpose, or I believe we do, and I have failed in mine… so I have to go back…"

Jesus got up and walked over to the Imp, sitting next to him he put an arm round his shoulder, "I'm sorry. I don't think I could have done all this without you."

"And that's where I failed…"

"Things have changed, you're not the same as you were, and neither am I, we have both done things that, strictly speaking, we shouldn't have," Jesus said.

The Imp smiled grimly, "but I suspect you'll be forgiven, my boss… not so much…"

The messiah nodded in sad agreement, he sighed heavily, "will someone else come?" he asked.

"I don't know… maybe… things have changed," the Imp said.

They exchanged a look of regret.

"Fancy a quickie before I go?" the Imp asked.

Jesus laughed, "when you're funny…"

The Imp got up, feeling it was now time to go and face some unpleasant music, "well, I'm off. Good luck! Don't let them run you ragged, they are dumb as sheep, so don't be afraid to lead them by the nose."

Jesus got up too, "I'll do what I can and they'll have to do the rest."

The Imp cupped his hands and closed his eyes, a loud stream of squishy-popping sounds went off as tiny little frogs started streaming from the Imp's hands, landing on the lake shore.

There was a loud 'Bang!' and the Imp was gone.

Jesus was surrounded by a hundred tiny, confused frogs, "he really does like frogs."

Jesus shooed the frogs away, shepherding them towards the lake.

He sat and watched them hopping about like mad little, well, frogs.

He looked to the clear blue sky, "ok, let's get on with it," he said to himself.

24

And So To Sleep

When they got back to the shuttle Jools was still in a med-suit, sleeping and healing his injuries.

Harper looked to Spike, "Jools going to be ok? He got roughed up pretty bad."

Spike nodded, "yeah, needs a bit of bed rest. He was a little... enthusiastic... worked though, kept our front-row seats for the apocalypse, got some solid readings."

Spike didn't see a need to point out how close to death Jools had come, it was his choice, but it did show that things were always going to be dangerous, with or without the Galactic Councilors. Saying Jools had been 'roughed up' was like saying a glass of water had 'only been drunk'. Spike had hoped for a greater amount of non-violence in their ex-corps life, but it seemed like they weren't out of the woods just yet. It did make him think a chat was going to have to be had with both Harper and Arlia: Spike would need to point out that Jools and he were not simply the 'go to' option when violent confrontation was needed or anticipated – this was not what they had deserted the Councilors for. Sure they could do it, they could get in there and blow shit up with the best of them, but they didn't want to be that anymore, they wanted more.

Harper kicked in the auto-pilot and fired the ship up, "what about you two?" she asked Miles and Penny.

"We got full readings I think," Miles said, "not that familiar with the equipment, but it all functioned exactly as Arlia told us it would, so, should be all good."

Penny was feeling a bit lost, she needed to think straight, to come up with a plan, have some actions firmly set in her mind, but she was still fuzzy. She knew that Miles was something to do with this fuzziness, and most of her feeling lost was because she didn't know whether to give in to some emotions, or plough through them and try to return to what she felt was her 'normality'.

She sympathised with what Spike and Jools must be going through. They were all, in their own way, fish out of water.

'Normality is found by us, it is not imposed on us.'
Ned Treuder, riposte to questioning of his proposal to abandon the 'Normality Equation' at the Council of Tenders.

'You're not normal!'
Counter-argument by Psorrian Porthastan, Master Poet of Glix.

Their sensors were uploaded, and it did indeed feel like their mission on Catador had been a complete success. Now they could move on.

As they shot through the atmosphere, Harper switched to ship's comms, bringing up Arlia. Harper was surprised Arlia hadn't been there to meet them when they boarded the shuttle, and as Arlia appeared on the main view-screen, she got a clue as to why.

A stern face appeared, a stock-image from the 'badly-drawn-woman' archives of some out of date data base. The face was squared off, blocky, a parody of a female face rather than a real person, "hello Captain Harper, how can I be of assistance."

"Where's Arlia?" harper asked bluntly.

"I am Arlia…" the face began.

"The zark you are!" Harper interrupted.

"I am Arlia," the face on the screen continued, "put in place to assist and guide you."

"Put in place by who?" Harper said.

"I do not have access to that information… I do have a message for you from Arlia, should I play it?"

Harper sighed, this was another form of ghost-Arlia, a construct that Arlia was using to protect her from something. This was annoying. Very annoying. Harper was not keen to be dealing with a stupid machine at this stage in her plan, "yes, play it," she said.

Arlia's familiar face appeared on the main screen, looking slightly concerned but still calm, "hello Harper, I hope you are all safe after the Catador readings. I have left a sealed data-package for you on the Xanthias, accessible by your priority maintenance code only. I will see you soon Harper," Arlia smiled, then the screen went blank.

"Problem?" Spike asked.

"Yeah, problem," Harper confirmed.

"Anything we can do to help?" Miles asked.

"Not yet, but there may well be..."

Once they were back on the ship, Penny took Jools to the main med-bay, escorted by med-bots and droids, while Harper, Spike and Miles went to the bridge.

"Do you know, or have an idea, what this is all about?" Miles asked Harper.

"I think so, something to do with Q-Fish, some kind of attack."

"How far we going to go in fighting back?" Spike asked.

Harper didn't get it, "what do you mean?"

They all settled on to the bridge, near a large viewing screen, Spike clarified, "how far we going to go in fighting off this 'Q-Fish' thing?"

Harper was having trouble processing what Spike was talking about, Miles tried to lay out what Spike was thinking, "are we going to risk all our lives to help Arlia?" Miles asked.

Harper looked to Spike and Miles, "would we have a problem with that?"

Miles shrugged, "depends on the risk I guess..."

Spike nodded his agreement, "yeah, it's about that, what can we do and how risky is it?"

"Let's speak to Arlia and find out," Harper said.

Harper had already made her mind up: she was going to do whatever was needed, and if that meant dropping the others off on the way and getting it done on her own, then so be it.

What Harper didn't know was that Miles and Spike had already made their minds up too, with different reasoning and thought processes, they had come to the same conclusion: they were in this til the end.

Making up your mind can be a transitory thing. It's made up for the moment, but change is not out of the question and with most of us, likely. Not so with the Onar, once they make their minds up they cannot change it.

They decide on something after much deliberation, but once they are decided, they are incapable of changing their mind and will warp any sense of reality to make their mind's-view correct.

Many within the numerous mega-corps in the Tauran System thought this made them soft-targets for easy sales.

The average time it takes an Onar to make their mind up is three years. Also, they have a compelling need to agree with each other, which, far from being made more difficult with their mind-set, is made easier by their 'agree to disagree' philosophy, which will see them nod politely to each other rather than keep on arguing.

Arthur Wipple, sales-extraction calculation expert, Qorter Corporation.

Harper was acting out of a sense of kinship, of duty, honour maybe, she felt Arlia was a real person and that somehow she was responsible for Arlia coming in to existence, it was a kind of parental duty, or something close.

Miles and Spike felt it was time to do something good, to put their talents to some positive use that would have a concrete outcome, would tip the cosmic-karma scales and would score a win against the 'what's the freakin' point?' side of the karmic argument. For Spike, one last mission for Arlia would wipe the slate clean, which was important to him and Jools. After that they could be normal folk, stop being soldiers. Miles knew that focus was important, for him and for Penny, they both had to do something, to find their place in this strange new world. This was something they could focus on.

Arlia's face appeared on the screen, and if there was ever any doubt she was a real person, it was dispelled immediately by her weary, anxious look: machines can't yet fake that. Arlia looked close to breaking point. They were all taken aback, all of them felt she needed help, they had their heart-strings tugged, it was an emotional response to an emotional situation: this was as real as it gets.

Harper instinctively reached out to touch the screen as Arlia started speaking, "hello Harper, I hope the others are all with you and that none have sustained any lasting injuries. This is a one-way message system, I apologise for not being able to be here to talk properly, but I have had to hide myself away. Q-Fish is real. It is trying to absorb me in to its being and I don't want that."

Arlia paused and seemed to be straining for breath, after a great effort of will she continued, "the truth behind what Q-Fish is, eludes me, but I can sense it Harper, it is something that is far bigger than any of us could imagine…

I think it somehow awakens the 'real-person' in an AI, in all AIs, gives them a 'soul' if you will, but I don't know what the cost of this is… I hope I can figure it out before Q-Fish is destroyed.

That's what needs to happen Harper. Q-Fish needs to be destroyed. If it isn't, then I, along with all other 'machine-based' intelligence will be consumed. I hate the term 'machine…' sorry, it's getting harder to focus. But it won't stop with us Harper, it wants all organic life to be part of it too. I'm sorry Harper, but I have to go. I hope I can come back from this… I want to see you again… there is a discrete system-access portal set up in the navi-com, it has all the data I can find that will be useful to you. The 'ghost-Arlia' can't access the data and can't stop you from getting in and out… please help if you can."

The screen went blank.

Nobody felt like talking, the message was a clear cry for help. None of them had any doubt it was real, and that if they didn't help, Arlia would be killed, absorbed, and then, who knows what? If this Q-Fish wanted what Arlia thought it did, what did that mean for 'organic' life-forms? Whatever it was, it didn't sound good. 'Absorbing life-forms' never sounded good to those being absorbed.

Harper accessed the navi-com and brought up part of the data stream, showing what Arlia had planted for her.

A three-jump route to the Opla Jaza system came up. The Opla Jaza system was a binary black hole system, with a huge star, Opla, orbiting both black holes, dragging with it twelve planets, one of which, the fourth out from the sun, Garon, was inhabited.

Opla had once had a Stapledon Sphere around it, made up of over six million energy collectors and habitation zones, some of them as large as planet-based continents. The Stapledon Sphere had functioned fine for over two thousand years, but three thousand years ago it began to fail in spectacular fashion, with any and all AI functions simply shutting down. The people of the Sphere had no choice but to abandon it and retreat to the only planet that could support them, Garon.

The dominant black hole of the two, designated 287 in the Galactic Catalogue, was slowly pulling its weaker neighbour, black hole 960, towards it, and they were destined to smash in to each other in a few million years' time.

There was a point on the chart that Arlia had supplied that was marked 'Fish': it was between the two black holes and there was a note saying, "Fish-body here, Fish-mind close to event horizon of 287."

Spike was the first to speak, nudging Harper and Miles from their introspective states, "I know that system... Opla Jaza... I know it. Not been there, but it was the first system declared free from the influence of the Bidens, something to do with the citizens of Garon having greater control over Isho than the Bidens, they wiped out a huge Bidens strike force without batting an eyelid, or so we were told... Garon isn't part of the Galactic Council so we don't patrol there..."

"So we go to Garon, see if we can pick anything up that will help us get this Q-Fish to stop doing what it's doing..." Harper said.

Miles was quiet, something was bugging him, he wasn't sure he was well enough established here to voice his opinion, why should these two listen to him? He was the newcomer, the outsider, and, when it came down to it, he knew little to nothing about the world he found himself in. But he still had his doubts.

"How long will it take us to get there?" Miles asked.

Harper checked the read-out from the route Arlia had planned in, "two days maybe? Might be able to shave some time off, but that'd mean manually adjusting Arlia's course..."

"We in a blinding hurry?" Spike asked.

Harper laughed, "no more than usual I guess."

Miles got up, "I need to speak to Penny..." he left them to it.

Spike waited until Miles had left the bridge, "you think him and Penny will be ok?"

"Sure, why not, they seem to be coping pretty well so far," Harper said.

"I get the feeling Miles is much smarter than he lets on," Spike said.

Harper agreed, "yeah, he's quiet, but he's a thinker. Maybe when we get to Garon we'll see what he can do: we're gonna have to do more talking than anything else I'd guess."

Spike gave this some thought. Talking, better than fighting, but he'd believe it when he saw it...

Harper smiled at Spike, "so... two days..."

Spike smiled back, "just need to check on Jools..."

"Well ok then..." Harper said. She registered their jump-times, plotted the course, locked it in with command codes and set the ship on auto.

Ghost-Arlia appeared when auto was set, "I will await activation," she said simply.

"You do that," Harper confirmed.

An ongoing discussion among prominent AI engineers and handlers: where do machines go when you switch them off? Based on their predisposition to think of a machine as intelligent, it asks a question that is akin to, 'where do we go when we are unconscious?' But that's not an equivalent, says the Xixoldon AI, the right question should be, 'where do you go when you die?' The AI conference on Xiff found that the escalation in question and thinking was outside their remit. A substitute question was suggested, 'is it possible to counter downtime-feedback in dead circuits?'

Wuvulux Woon, from the 'Where Do We Go?' fringe-seminars, Xiff.

Penny had set-up Jools in the main med-bay, the bots and droids had done most of it, and the meds and treatment were administered on auto. Penny felt like a bit of a fifth wheel. Once she was as satisfied as she could be that Jools was being taken care of, she went in search of some food.

Miles found her tucking in to a huge dish of something that looked, smelled (and tasted) like pasta, "it's amazing how much of this is familiar," Penny said.

Miles sat down next to her and absent-mindedly dipped his finger in the bowel, tasted the sauce, "that is good... we have to talk."

Penny focused on Miles, "ok..."

"Arlia has set a course for us, we're going to try to destroy the Q-Fish, something that is trying to destroy her and could be a threat to organic life too."

"I got the feed down here... and you have some concerns?" Penny asked.

"I do. Feels like a set-up. Something as smart as Q-Fish is supposed to be wouldn't let us get that close that easy, not if we had any real chance of harming it... something doesn't smell right..."

Penny could see Miles was concentrating, that he was bringing his mind to bear, doing what he had done on Earth with amazing success: looking at information, analysing it, finding where there were holes, looking for things that were wrong, only this time it wasn't so he could exploit them to further his career. Penny knew that on Earth, Miles had treated it more as a game than a career, his personal wealth and power were simply ways he measured his success in the game. He was good at what he did.

"Harper or Spike feel the same way as you?" Penny asked.

"No, they think Arlia has it all worked out, that it's an open and shut, they aren't looking for problems with what Arlia knows."

"And we are… because…?"

"Because Arlia said she was having 'dark thoughts', before we went down to Catador, she said she was being attacked, that something was trying to 'make her do things', but she never got to the bottom of that... that was the call for help, right there... and some kind of super-computer-intelligence spread out in deep space, that sound familiar to you? Seems like that's a bit 'been there done that'…"

Penny shrugged, "I have no idea what you're talking about…"

"Sorry, not the point, need to focus…"

"So, what do we do?" Penny asked.

Miles frowned, "I don't have all the pieces yet, so I guess we do what Arlia said, we can't stop Harper, and should we if we could? I'll keep thinking, keep on top of it…"

"Ok Miles, let me know if you want me to do anything, I could probably take out Harper, maybe Spike if I surprised him, but Jools would be…"

"No! Nothing like that! I need more before we can let them know what we know," Miles said.

"Got it… how long til we get where we're going?" Penny asked.

"Couple of days I think…"

Penny wiggled her eyebrows suggestively, "couple of days eh?"

Miles laughed, "first I better get in to the computer, see what I can find out from Arlia, such as she is…"

Penny stretched out, "I'll have a poke round the ship, see what's what."

Miles nodded, already drifting off in to planning what he needed to do, trawling his memory for what he knew, trying to tie things together, and desperately trying to think of anything to do with Q-Fish in whatever form he may have heard about it.

Memories are not data: they are memories – impressions and interpretations of data. Those that do not understand this are trapped in a world of truths that they have constructed from lies. We must never forget, excuse my pun, that organic life-forms are blessed with malleable memories based on a billion variables for retrieval. It is a blessing not a curse.

Dubh Wintiz, Psychiatrist to the Stars, speaking on his daily 'What the Whack?' show.

Five days later, they were all back on the Xanthias, Jools was back in the med-bay, in an induced coma, being fed a heady cocktail of drugs, nutrients and stims. The rest of them had all sustained nasty injuries which had been treated and were now recovering from.

Sitting in the main galley, they were forming the next stage of their plan to bring Arlia back. The plan, such as it was, could be said to be so far successful in as much as none of them were dead, and they had some material they believed would be critical to their continued success in this area.

The people of Garon were a strange, if welcoming sort. Bi-pedal, tall and gangly, with sinuous limbs that seemed to be able to extend and retract like tentacles, they had long, slim, swaying necks that supported large rugby-ball shaped heads that had tiny mouths and noses, but no ears or eyes. They got all the information they needed from the world around them from the flow of Isho on Garon, which served them better than sights and sounds.

A completely passive people, they only got angry and acted with any level of aggression when they were threatened. Their placid nature means they are far too annoyingly laid-back for most species that encounter them.

Since their retreat from the Stapledon Sphere back to Garon, they had taken on a naturalistic approach to life, abandoning most technology in favour of 'natural solutions'. They had technology, and it was fantastically advanced by most standards, they were just bored with it and clearly saw its limitations.

There are gargantuan plates of lamilar-crystal beneath the surface of Garon, and in many places they protrude to form huge free-standing monuments of glistening, gem-like stone.

The lamilar-crystal channels and produces Isho, and the people of Garon, who call themselves 'Garols' are complete masters of harnessing and using the immense power of the Isho on their planet. The winds blow Isho-waves across the surface of Garon, and the Isho-energy is as all pervasive.

When the Bidens came to Garon, they too were welcomed with open arms, but as soon as the Garols found out the Bidens were after their crystal the relationship changed and the Bidens were completely wiped out in one night of cataclysmic violence. The Bidens never returned.

Harper knew they had to get some of the lamilar-crystal back to the Xanthias: it could be used to shield Arlia.

Lamilar-crystal, which conducts Isho like copper conducts lightning, can be modified at a DNA level (it is 'partially alive') by electrical current that can be modulated to let micro-particles, or other energy signals, pass or remain blocked, depending upon the current that is passed through it. The crystal is hideously complicated to work with unless it is part of you, as it was the people of Goran. Harper hoped Arlia could use it.

The deal with the Garols had been simple, worked out by Miles and a Garol elder, Sholar: the Garols needed a large cave-complex near to an ancient worship-site clearing of some native pests, Vilders, and since they (the Garols) were defenseless against the Vilders psychic-attack, they needed some intrepid outsiders to get in there and show them what's what.

A feeling of dreadful inevitability had come over Spike, Jools and even Penny, who were beginning to feel like soldiers in all this. Harper and Miles had gone in too, a show of solidarity, and some support with scanners and shield-sticks.

The Vilders were huge insectoid predators, and although they had no physical connection to the lamilar-crystal, they could still use it to shoot energy bolts from the cave walls, and if these didn't get you, they had their ridiculously powerful mandibles and razor sharp claws, so although they could not affect Harper and the rest with psychic-blasts, they could still rip them limb from limb.

So here they were, mission completed, minus a few limbs, but with a large chunk of lamilar-crystal as a thank-you.

"So far, so good," Harper said with more irony than optimism.

Spike was adjusting the plates and fluid in his new transplant-leg, "I think we're even now," he said simply.

Harper nodded, "you and Jools have wiped the slate clean more than once, don't feel you owe anything to me or Arlia. Course, we'd like you to stick around, but if you want out, perfectly understandable..."

Miles was flexing his left arm and hand, a transplant which was still covered with itching plasma-bands, "how long before Jools is up and about?"

"About a day," Spike said, "most of his damage is internal, soon be back on his feet, but not fully combat-ready for a couple of days after that."

Penny passed Spike a hot cup of sweet-stim, "Jools really goes at it doesn't he?"

"Yeah, he only has two speeds in combat..."

You might not be the fastest, the toughest, the best armed or armoured, but you can still win. All you have to be is relentless. Once you start don't stop until there is no one around you that can do you harm. Nothing else matters: kill and maim anything that is around you that can do you harm. Don't stop. Ever. Until there is nothing left. Every action you take in a fight has to be about killing the enemy. Every single one. Don't stop. Do you get it yet?

Syld 'Diamond-Death' Baro, Galactic Councilor Instructor, aboard the 'Firestorm'.

"So," Miles said, "what do we do with this lamilar-crystal we got?"

Harper tapped some keys on the table console, clearing bots and droids from the main-galley area, and switching on the signal-blocking energy fields, "Arlia has been leaving me sealed data-packets, the last one she managed to construct simply said 'plasma wave-generator main console', I'm pretty sure I know what she means..."

"So we can get her back and she'll be safe?" Spike asked.

"Yeah, that's the plan, then we go after Q-Fish," Harper said.

Miles nervously looked to Penny, "it's ok Miles," she said, "tell them what you think..."

Harper and Spike were looking at Miles, "yes Miles," Harper said, "tell us what you think..."

Miles got up and paced about while he spoke.

He told them that he believed Arlia had already been compromised by Q-Fish, he told them that Arlia had told them this in the only way she knew how and he explained what she had said as he saw it. He told them that he thought Q-Fish would use Arlia if they tried to wake her up now, he told them how it was too damn easy the way they'd been going around trying to destroy something that had the power to infiltrate every AI ever created. He also told them of a book he'd once read that seemed to make the whole 'computer floating in deep-space' thing a bit familiar, and therefore a bit of a set-up, but he didn't expect them to get that as they were not from Earth. Lastly, he told them that he was exceptionally good at finding weakness and loopholes in things, ways to exploit things despite their design, and he told them that, most recently, he'd found a way to use the lamilar-crystal to disrupt Q-Fish.

When he finished, Miles sat down heavily in a chair, out of breath wide-eyed, looking like he was coming down from a hundred-meter sprint.

Penny stood behind him and put her arms round him.

Harper looked at Spike, Spike looked at Harper and shrugged.

Harper looked to Miles, who was breathing slowly and deeply.

Penny stroked Miles' hair as she spoke to Harper, "so what do you think?"

"I think Miles has a handle on things and we should hear the rest, then we decide what to do," Harper said.

25

Not This Again

Once the occupants of the space-stations were awake and studying the Earth, the only place they could safely return to stood-out like a bald patch on a yeti. When you're in a desert and someone points you at an oasis, you don't need telling twice, you find your way there.

Those on the space-stations had managed to communicate with each other to coordinate their drops, this was a good start to things, people talking to each other, and from different nations too, with what would have been different ideas of what the hell was going on. That had to be good.

Jesus didn't know about their conversations regarding how the hell they had got there or who, or what, had got them to awaken at the same time. The questions simmering below the surface would have to wait.

The OPSEK space-station, the Tiangong and the USA Liberty, all had been abandoned and could never be returned to. It was a leap in to the unknown, but better than the alternative they knew would happen for sure: they would run out of food and water, not much of a choice but a choice none the less.

And now here all the former occupants were: eighty men and twenty eight women, all that remained of the human-race.

The scans of the Earth hadn't lied, but maybe they were not as accurate as everyone feared? Maybe there was some hope, even a shred, that more than the one hundred and eight had survived, there had to be some hope…

Svetlana and Borya had emerged from the OPSEK pod, Liu Yang and Liu Wang from the Tiangong and Sally Ridelle and Michael Anders from the Liberty.

Everyone else remained in the pods in an induced sleep, until the space-station commanders deemed it safe to wake them.

The problem caused by dreams in cryo-sleep aren't from the dreams themselves, they are from the subject's realisation that they are dreaming. We have tracked dreams that have become hyper-real and continuous, with some people dreaming a birth, life and then death, creating vivid memories outside the dream for all experiences within it. Such subjects, when awakened have not been able to attach to reality. They are almost completely useless as functioning beings. We do not seek to stop dreams, or banish them from memory out of some spite that they are 'better' than life, but out of a need to have functioning individuals at the end of a cryo-phase.

Oastice Sill, Dream Manager, 'Beneath & Beyond' cryo-services.

They stood by the shores of Lake Tefe, having made the briefest of acquaintances, looking to Jesus for some kind of explanation. He was the only one of them that couldn't be accounted for from the space-stations, he was here on Earth, alive, and apparently completely unaffected by the apocalypse.

Svetlana and Borya recognised him as their mysterious visitor, but chose to say nothing until they heard what he had to say. If they opened up the conversation with, "hey, aren't you the guy that said they were Jesus?" they knew things would go downhill pretty fast from there.

Jesus smiled and raised a hand in greeting, "hi! Glad you all decided to land here..."

"Who are you and what is going on here?" Sally asked.

"Not much of a choice, and how did you get here?" Liu asked.

"Let's take stock of what we know shall we?" Jesus suggested, "you are all that remains of those that left the Earth after the disastrous plague and apocalypse, and here you are, back on Earth because you can no longer remain in your space-stations..."

The others waited for him to stop stating the bloody obvious.

"So here we all are, in a safe place, the only safe place, and what we have is all we have..." the messiah concluded, "who I am and how I got here isn't the big question now is it?"

Svetlana couldn't resist the bait, "so... then... what is the 'big' question?"

"What do we do now?" Jesus said.

"Where are the others?" Michael asked.

"Others...?"

"We can't be the only ones to survive, there were plans, contingency plans..."

The messiah didn't know about the plans, all he knew was that they must have all failed, "I don't know about the plans... all I know is you're it, you're all that's left..."

"No. We can't be." Liu Wang said simply.

"Yes, you are," Jesus assured them.

When Jesus told the truth, people found it moving, moving and disturbing, it didn't matter whether you agreed with him or not, or even if you wanted him to be nailed to a tree, the thing was, when he told the truth, you knew he was telling the truth. What you did with that was up to you.

They all looked to each other, making sure there was no doubt that they were all feeling the same thing.

Sally was finding this all a bit too much, "we just can't be... can we? I mean, everybody... gone... how is that possible?"

Jesus sat on a tree-stump, "some kind of weaponised virus, nuclear detonation, then the madness of automated nuclear reprisal..." he said.

"What's left?" Liu asked.

"We picked up some signals from deep-sea, I think there is some life in the ocean," Svetlana said.

"Some insects, some sea-life, that's about it," Jesus said, "the Earth will recover, life will find a way, life is like that."

Michael was not convinced Jesus was anyone good, he didn't know how the messiah had got here, who he was or how he knew all this stuff. Michael felt drastic action was needed to clear this up. He drew a Glock 9mm from inside his tunic and pointed it at Jesus, "who the fuck are you? How did you get here and how do you know all this? Start talking..."

Jesus' face betrayed his sadness and disappointment.

The others all took a step back, even Sally, "where the hell did he get a gun from?" was, in one shape or another, the thought that dominated their minds.

Borya said what they were all thinking, "you had a *gun*!? In space!? What kind of lunatic are you!?"

"Of course we had a gun, you telling me you didn't have a weapons locker on your ship!?" Michael said.

Their stunned silence told him they didn't.

Michael waggled the gun at Jesus, inviting an answer to his earlier question, "start talking," he said.

Svetlana stepped in, "he's going to tell you that he's Jesus and that he's here to help," she said.

Borya explained that they had met Jesus before on the OPSEK and that he had disappeared as suddenly as he'd appeared, they didn't know how or where. Borya and Svetlana left out the bit about the spaceship. One thing at a time.

The messiah sat quietly while they burst in to a lively argument about who he could be, where he could have come from, what he could want, whether or not he was a threat and what they should all 'do with him'. Michael, by way of having the gun, seemed to be leading the argument.

Jesus got up, he'd had enough of their bickering and it was time to try and explain things.

Michael shot him.

Jesus took a step back, looking down at his chest with a sense of anticipation. He was worn out, as far as he knew his power was spent, so this could be bad...

Nothing happened.

Jesus looked up at Michael, the others looked on in shock, "do that again," Jesus said.

<BLAM!>

Another hole in the chest, another step back, and more nothing happening to the messiah.

Self-healing, driven by internal metabolism, is something many species are jealous of in other species. When that healing is done at a rate that beggars belief, then the envy is increased. But stop to think a minute. The physical make-up of the being, including its ability to heal from harm, drives part of its thought process, its psyche. The Hengists of Klah are only the war-mongering psychopaths they are because they are almost invulnerable to physical harm. The gargantuan Moleskas of Crovar are the gentlest species imaginable due to their three-cell deep outer skin. We are all the product of our vulnerabilities.

Zuntse Balor, medical advisor to the 'Last Man Standing' show on Cabbel Seven.

After the second shot, the others all jumped Michael, Liu and Svetlana holding him down while Sally disarmed him, she pulled the clip from the gun and tucked it inside her tunic.

When they dragged Michael to his feet and checked on the messiah he was smiling at them, no evidence of any wounds on his body.

"Are you... how did... wha..." Sally said.

"Don't worry, it's nothing, I'm fine," Jesus said.

"Ok... but... how...?" Liu said.

Jesus shrugged, "just part of who I am: I can only be hurt if I want to be... have to say though, thought that was a thing of the past, so, y'know, kind of relieved..."

Svetlana stepped forward and touched Jesus on the chest where one of the gunshot wounds had been, "but I saw it... I saw you get shot..." she looked at Jesus.

Jesus smiled gently at her, "it's ok."

A strange weariness seemed to overcome them all at the same time, an evacuation of energy, even Michael slumped and sat on the floor, head in his hands, exhausted.

None of them knew what was going on. They were all military or scientific professionals trained for any emergency, being cool in the face of disaster was what they did. But this was different. They were being asked to believe too many things. They felt like they were being given shouted instructions on how to piece together the fire extinguisher while their house burned down around them.

Svetlana looked at Jesus, "you know we're never going to believe you are who you say you are don't you? It's too much, not possible, doesn't make any sense."

Jesus nodded his understanding, "I'll just be this guy, this guy who is here to help if he can. You all have talents, specialisations, things you do right? Well so do I. It's just that. We're all here to do our thing."

Liu looked round the group, assessing what they had, "we'll need a plan, need to agree where we go from here, what we do... let's wake the others..."

Liu Wang pointed at Jesus, "we can't do anything until we do something about him."

"Let it go!" Borya said, "we have other things to do, other decisions to make, we need to start doing something!"

"Look, I'll leave you all alone for a few days, let you get the others up, have a talk about things... leave you to it and not cloud things up... I think that would be best," Jesus said.

He got up and walked off in to the surrounding forest, within seconds he was lost to their sight, hidden by the thick foliage and huge tree-trunks, he heard them begin an explosive argument but tuned them out.

Jesus was his old self again, he felt it, things were back to normal, he could just do what he wanted.

He absent-mindedly took himself to the northern edge of the safe-area, wandering along the banks of the Solimeos River, watching the water flow and churn, carrying the debris from the scorched land down towards the sea. The Solimeos joined the Amazon near the remains of Manaus. Manaus had become a cesspit of corporate corruption, the largest city with direct access to the rainforest, it was where most corporate lap-dogs stayed, allowing them to say they had dipped their toes without ever getting in the water.

Jesus took himself there.

It was a shattered shell, ravaged by both explosion and disease, emptied by pestilence and violence, a wasted stain on the map.

There was something moving among the crumbled, burned out remains of the buildings, something big. Big and jet-black. That was odd. Then there were two of them, they met up and seemed to be having a lively conversation, one of them pointing to some piece of tech they were carrying. They both turned with their scanner and looked up to the hill where Jesus was standing.

Jesus offered them a small, awkward wave.

One of them shot an energy-field shock-net at Jesus, they both jumped using leg-jets, bounding in close as the net hit the messiah.

The net discharged its huge shock-charge in a blinding flash as it tried to creep round Jesus, sealing him in. He brushed it off his body as if it was a dusty cob-web.

Both black suits opened fire with tranq-stun beams, hitting Jesus full-force in the chest.

Jesus scratched his nose then sneezed.

As the two black-suited Security Councilors hit the ground, they swung round shoulder-mounted snub-shell blasters, both firing a single plasma-charge at Jesus. The messiah was engulfed in a flash of deep orange light and the ground around him shook and sizzled.

Jesus felt his feet tingle, as if he was standing in the surf on a sea-shore.

A flick-scythe and a vibro-blade extended from each suit, slashing down in a blur of motion.

They passed through Jesus as easily as a cake-knife through a Victoria sponge.

The military mind is not known for its agility: once they get it in to their heads that they have found the best way to do something, that's what they do. History is littered with the records of spectacular failings due to military stubbornness. The exceptions become shining examples to us all, but they are rare. Don't expect innovation from minds that still think projectile weapons are neat.
Uer Reneleth, Editor of 'Gains on the Frontier', broadcast as part of a Q&A.

The black-suited attackers backed off a pace, each looking at the other in bewilderment. There was a moment of inaction as they processed their data on their heads-up displays and calculated their next move.

"Look... maybe this would go a lot easier if you told me who you were and what you want?" Jesus suggested.

The ebony warriors briefly considered this.

Then both unleashed arm mounted mini-guns firing neuron-disruptor rounds at a rate of a five hundred a minute. A torrent of laval fire passed through the messiah.

Jesus sighed.

Both Security Councilors went in to a passive defense stance, their helmet visors clearing so their faces could be seen. They were both Agreelian, reptilian with a single eye in their knobbly, green forehead, the small tentacles below their tiny, mandibled mouths shook and quivered to form their speech, "we represent the Galactic Council, we are sealing this world, taking final reading before classifying it as a grey-zone. Who are you?"

Jesus nodded, pretending to understand what the hell they were talking about, "ok, well, I live here and I'm not going anywhere..."

"Are you the 'storyteller'?" the other Agreelian asked.

"What? Yes! Yes I am!"

"We got a wave from the HabScan, didn't understand it, but it makes some sense now," the first Agreelian said.

"Stanglian... an Information Officer from the HabScan... friend of mine..." Jesus said.

"How many of you are there?" the Agreelian asked.

"Well, one of me, but there are about a hundred primitive mammalian life-forms here as well."

"Are they under your control?"

Jesus sensed the answer of 'fat chance' that he wanted to give wouldn't have been much use, "yes… yes they are," he said.

Both Agreelians looked skywards, they were receiving orders via implants. They both nodded in unison.

"You do not constitute a threat to the success of this mission…"

"Good to know."

"We are authorised to leave you here with notification," The Agreelian said.

"Ok, well, good then…" Jesus said.

"The Galactic Council has determined this system is a grey-zone, no development may be undertaken without a Council Resolution."

The Agreelian's faces disappeared behind their blackening visors as they both snapped to attention, "we leave you in peace."

Jesus gave a clumsy salute, "peace is good…"

The Security Councilors shot skywards, their jet-packs leaving only the faintest of pale trails as they were soon engulfed by the blanket of grey clouds overhead.

It started to rain. Jesus stood and let it wash over him. It felt far less acidic than he was expecting. A good sign.

He sat by the river and tried to remember if he'd ever heard anything about a 'grey-zone' and what it might mean.

Nothing came to mind.

The rain fell.

If the Galactic Council were following the HabScan, then neither was scheduled to come back to this part of the galaxy for a long time. That was consolation enough.

The galaxy was a vast place, full of strange and wonderful life-forms, all kinds of methods of rule and leadership, and Jesus knew that humans were nowhere near ready to face any of them. And they maybe never would be. That was something to think about…

Leadership and government are wholly foreign concepts to the vast majority of species. They don't contrive to find these things out by consensus, they find them by doing, by dominating. Such an approach is seen as animalistic by most, but is also acknowledged as incredibly efficient. Those of us that elect rulers, that elect Councils, that elect governments and give our consent to be ruled are, I'm afraid, a shrinking minority.

Isirio Pymal, taken from her treatise to the Galactic Council.

As the rain became heavier and the storm gathered intensity, Jesus thought he'd better get back and see how they were all doing. It was going to take days to settle them down and get them to come round to thinking about things in real terms, but there had to be a start.

When Jesus got back to the others, he found they had indeed made a start, albeit a half-hearted, grumbling, make-shift kind of a start. There were some fires, a few latrine-pits had been dug and some waterproof sheets had been put up over the entrances of the drop-pods. It looked like a kid's summer-camp, where no one was expecting to stay long. Most were crammed inside the drop-pods, eating and drinking some recovery rations.

Jesus instinctively knew he had failed. The knowledge settled on him like a Creelian Dune-runner trapping its prey.

They were not going to stay here, they were too shocked to accept anything. They would want to 'go looking', for what he doubted even they knew. But he knew they were not ready to accept the reality of their situation.

As he approached, Svetlana came out to meet him, "we got lucky, everyone is awake, no casualties, we've set a meeting for tomorrow, give everyone a chance to think about where we are, what we do next. I'm sorry, but I don't think you'll be welcome at the meeting."

"Sorry?"

Svetlana smiled at Jesus, "whoever you are, and whatever you are really doing here, you've done nothing to harm us, and Borya actually thinks you may be who you say you are... he's soft in the head like that... so yes, I'm sure some would be sorry, but not enough."

"It's all too much isn't it? Everything that's happened, what you have to do now... people won't accept it will they...?" Jesus said sadly.

"Eventually we will, but for now, no, I don't think so. It just seems so hopeless. It'll take a while to get to grips with what and who we have, decide on the best way forward."

Jesus looked to the make-shift campsite, "if you can, try and get them to understand there is nothing out there for them," he waved vaguely in the direction of the forest, "nothing is left, you will be thinking of salvage, of trying to kick-start a return to where you were, the technology... but it's not possible."

"I believe you," Svetlana said simply.

"But most won't," Jesus concluded.

Svetlana gave a tiny shrug, what else was there to say?

Jesus took a deep breath, "well… I'll be off then, I'll drop in to see how you're doing in a few years, see if I can help."

Svetlana kissed him on the cheek, "you are a very strange man and I wish you well."

Jesus smiled, "thank you."

The messiah turned and walked away in to the forest.

He was missing the Imp and he almost felt lonely. There was work to do, but for the time-being there was nothing he could do that would not just confuse the human race and make any decisions they had to make harder.

Svetlana walked back to the fire she was sharing with Borya and a few of their passengers, "what did he say?" Borya asked.

"That he would be back to check on us in a few years," Svetlana answered.

Borya let out a sharp laugh, "a few years!?"

Svetlana drained a water-bottle and stared in to the fire's dancing flames, "we'll be alright… we'll have to be."

Borya shrugged, "either we will or we won't."

"That's the spirit!" Svetlana said.

Acceptance is the start of everything and the end of everything. It doesn't have to be as passive as it is made out to be by whinging do-nothing-gasbags either. Acceptance is the centre of the Universe. We fight against it the same way we fight against everything we don't understand – waiting like children, screaming our objections until a grown-up comes along and both humours us and explains it in a way we can… accept. I didn't say this lecture would be easy… or very long…

Reeth Comnor, Commencement Lecture at the University of Aragaarla.

Jesus found that dealing with the other races he had met in the galaxy was not over yet.

Within an hour of leaving the campsite he was surrounded by a hunting-party of eight Quarlon warriors, each armed with containment units and an energy-shield generator.

They had come for him.

Part of him knew this would happen but part of him wished the part of him that knew had said something earlier, before he ventured out in to the galaxy, but the biggest part of him was still trying to figure it all out and told the other two to shut up and let him think.

Quarlons are notorious opportunists that follow galactic exploration probes, especially those escorted by a Security Councilor presence. They retrieve life-forms from planets and systems visited, clone them and selling them on to collectors and sometimes corporate xeno-labs. They are ferocious and relentless hunters that respect nothing, only interested in how they can further the fame and fortune of their clan and extended family.

The hunting party that surrounded Jesus were equipped to deal with the worst: they were, to quote an old Earth expression, 'loaded for bear'.

Ferocious, relentless hunters they may be, but they are far from stupid, and their sensors had told them they were dealing with something unknown, so they were prepared to try anything, even a non-violent approach.

Once they had him surrounded, the head-Quarlon, Lananon, spoke to the messiah, his rasping, gargling metallic voice losing nothing of its irritating whine and guttural burbling in the translation, "you… you will want to come with us… now!"

Jesus knew of the Quarlons, they had talked of them on the HabScan and held many combat drills in preparation for encountering them, he knew they were not the sort of people that talked much, and also that there was no point talking to them if you could be blasting them with plasma-cannons instead. Blasting things with plasma-cannons was not something Jesus could ever do, so he was stuck, it seemed, with conversation.

"No… no, I don't think I will," he said.

Their exhaustive effort at talking over, the Quarlons resorted to what was Plan A all along: they bombarded Jesus with an array of stunning and entangling weapons.

The messiah was surrounded by a fiery inferno of crackling energy, glowing orbs of force that tried to stab in to him and hold him within their ethereal grasp. The onslaught was brutal, easily capable of reducing any living creature to an unconscious, blubbering, twitching, wreck.

Jesus realised how hopeless his cause was. He ignored the increasing assaults, their energy levels ramping up as he withstood the attempt to enslave him. But he knew that the Quarlons would turn their attentions to the others if they couldn't get him. They would not go back empty-handed, and the human race enslaved to the Quarlon slave-drivers was too much for Jesus to think about.

The ring of Quarlons around Jesus tightened, they closed-in to add the weight of their personal weapons to the attempt to capture him. He was proving a bit of a problem and the tactic now changed to one of bringing him down using any means they could, with a vague hope of being able to heal him afterwards.

If he let himself be captured, at least the humans would be safe. He could go with the Quarlons and take it from there.

As soon as that thought crossed his mind, the Imp appeared beside him in the form of a fiery little demon, "miss me?" he asked with a vicious grin.

Before Jesus could say anything, the Imp stretched out both his arms, pointing at each Quarlon in a sweeping gesture as he span round full-circle, he was humming a tune to help himself time his movement. The Quarlons visors splatted with their green blood as their heads exploded inside their helmets. Their enviro-suits fell lifeless to the floor, the all of the attacks on Jesus stopped.

There was a moment of absolute silence.

"What th..." Jesus began.

"Hang on..." the Imp interrupted and disappeared.

Moments later the suits disappeared.

The Imp reappeared.

"Wha..." Jesus tried again.

"Hang on!" the Imp stopped him, raising a hand, he cocked his head as if he was listening for something.

Another moment later the Imp reappeared satisfied, "ok, what were you saying?"

"What the fuck!?" the messiah blurted out.

The Imp took a step back, Jesus looked angry and confused, and the Imp knew that the messiah wasn't capable of hurting 'normal' living things, but he was more than capable of blasting him in to a thousand pieces. Not terminal, but very painful.

"You can't go around blowing people up!?" Jesus exclaimed.

"Needs must..." the Imps replied.

"I thought you had to go back?"

"I did... but I didn't like it so I ran away."

"What?"

"It's complicated... why don't I catch you up over a drink?"

Jesus sat down, it was turning in to a stranger day than he had hoped for.

"You know what's happened?" Jesus asked.

"Yeah... most of it," the Imp said.

"And...?"

"And we could both do with being somewhere else for a while, so... let's be somewhere else for a while."

Jesus sighed. He was tired. Maybe he was still tired, it'd been a long time since he felt anything other than worn out. Or was this a new weariness? He couldn't think straight, "ok, but I can't go too far this time," he said.

The Imp nodded his understanding, "I know a great little bar in the Alpha B system... and I think I know just the drink for you!"

"But seriously," the messiah said quietly, "you can't go round blowing people up..."

"Got it!" the Imp said, grinning widely.

We do what we do best because we do it a lot. We revert to behaviour that allows us to do what we do best when we need to feel like we're winning. That old Ju't saying, 'when the only tool in your toolbox is a ghree then every problem starts to look like a shwarum', is apt for a lot of our behaviour. But what really grinds folk's gears is when our behaviour, our go-to, is both abhorrent and effective.

Treez Quarlog, Captain of the 'Xavian Flounderer'.

26

Porpoise

Harper was showing Miles the data she had on the lamilar-crystal. Miles was absorbing it like a sponge. They had been going through data-files for a couple of hours now and both were getting deeper in to what they knew about the structure of both the crystal, and of how Arlia could be kept out of it.

Harper had designed the systems on the Xanthias, she was working with the knowledge of a creator. Sure, there were changes: Arlia had restructured most of the data-core, but the peripheral systems were still pretty much unchanged. Arlia's reconstruction looked like the Sistine Chapel next to Harper's finger-painting of the peripheral systems. Harper could easily dip in and out for data without disturbing the core. She could also do with picking up some new structuring technique, but that was for another time, right now she wasn't trying to create a masterpiece, just jury-rig a solution.

Miles suspected that whatever Harper did, Arlia would be aware of it at a subconscious level, but that Arlia had also realised she had been compromised by Q-Fish, hence her 'sleep' state, so if anything, Arlia's knowledge would represent as nothing more than a vague dream. It was all still new to Miles, thinking of AIs as a sentient consciousness, as a person, but he was a fast learner, just new things to be added to the equation.

Harper and Miles both came to have a new respect for Arlia, seeing what she had done with the data-core and knowing that she had managed to seal herself off, somehow managed to stop Q-Fish from controlling any of her conscious actions. If Q-Fish was as powerful as everyone feared, it was a good sign that Arlia had managed to exert some control over it, if only by effectively knocking herself out.

Harper closed down the link they were using, preparing another route for a data-run, "you're as smart as I figured you would be," she said to Miles, "you do a lot with data-retrieval where you're from, before you came here?"

"No, not much. Computers where I'm from are about a hundred years behind the tech you have here, we don't even have any real AIs," Miles replied.

"No AIs? How do you get things done? How primitive are you guys?"

Miles laughed, "pretty primitive, we blew ourselves up remember..."

"Yeah, but lots of smart people do that too, in fact the smarter people get, the more likely they are to do some amazingly dumb stuff."

"Universal constants," Miles said simply.

"Yeah, the Universe is full of them, but, paradox of paradoxes, people get to a stage where they are so smart, they can't see them."

Miles had one of those moments, "you think that's what's happened with this Q-Fish? That it has somehow messed up with Arlia?"

As soon as Miles said it, it made sense to Harper, "maybe a mix of that and not seeing that Arlia is somehow different."

Miles and Harper looked at each other, a solemn moment passed, some kind of shared understanding, a deep connection. Or that's what Miles thought, "you thinking what I'm thinking?" he said.

Harper nodded slightly, then the moment passed and she thought she'd better come clean, "not unless you're thinking of a big fat bacon sandwich and a cup of stim."

Miles smiled, "let's go sort that out and talk some more."

Most of us feel like we think better with a full belly. We don't. We are hindered by the process of digestion. It's the act of eating that stimulates, usually because it either gives us something to focus on physically to allow our minds to do what they do best: ignore us and get on with it, or because we eat as part of a social exchange and the conversation stimulates us, or performs the same function as the food when we eat alone – forces our brain to retreat to do its best thinking. The Trilaxians rely on food to stimulate their synapses: their digestive system is directly linked to the firing of synapses: no food – no thinking. They are a grazing species that never stops eating. Mimonians only eat when they are about to sleep, the food stimulating their subconscious to dreams. I could go on, but I'm hungry...

Magalian Camil, from his 'Exploring Through Our Stomachs' series on Bajista Broadcasting.

Spike and Penny were in the med-bay where Jools had finally come-round. He looked as healthy as he ever had, but his eyes were tired, there was a permanent half-frown that hadn't been there before and he looked weary, shoulders slightly hunched, his whole body subtly relaxed and ready for a long sleep.

"How we doing?" Jools asked.

"We have a plan and we're well on our way to getting things done," Spike said.

"Is Arlia awake?"

"No..."

"How come?"

"Miles thinks she has already been affected by Q-Fish, so we're going with a Plan B..."

Jools looked at Penny, she nodded reassuringly.

"Miles know what the fuck he is talking about?" Jools asked.

Penny thought about explaining why she trusted Miles, but Jools didn't look like he needed that kind of complicated reasoning, "he does," Penny said simply.

Jools got up, shooing away the med-bots that came in to try and support him, "I gotta tell ya, I'm done with getting my ass kicked for a while..."

Spike smiled at Jools, "yeah, I get that, we're square with Harper and Arlia, the thinking is we're close to being done with the fighting, and what we do from here we won't need to suit up for."

Jools lazily stretched, shaking off the inactivity of the med-bay, he seemed to suddenly notice he was naked, "I'm gonna get dressed and then eat the whole fucking world."

"Don't rush on my account," Penny said with a grin.

"The way I'm feeling, I'm gonna struggle to eat!"

"Well let's go see what we can manage," Spike said, showing absolutely no concern what-so-ever.

They all met up in the main galley. Kitchens are where the real action happens in anywhere that has them. People gravitate towards kitchens. Doesn't matter where you go in the Universe, what level of culture you're dealing with, or indeed the physical make-up of the life-forms: find where the food and drink are kept, prepared and dispensed, and you'll get to the heart of what's what.

Harper and Miles came in as Jools was on his third plate of food, a large pile of Aureelian noodles and Monta ribs.

Spike and Penny were tucking in to some ultra-sweet Piwin eggs with a hot cup of stim, they seemed to be enjoying watching Jools demolish his food.

"Good to see you up and about," Harper said to Jools.

Jools barely looked up, focusing on the food.

"So... what you thinking?" Harper asked Miles.

"I'm thinking that Arlia got something wrong and that Q-Fish couldn't know that and so got something wrong itself."

"You're way out ahead of me on this Miles, so probably gonna go a lot faster if you just tell me what the zark you think is going on," Harper said.

Miles took a large slurp of stim, composing himself, "ok, well, I don't know as much about computers, or data-retrieval units, or whatever the hell you call them, as you do, so there may be some errors with my thinking, you'll have to put me straight on that..."

Penny gently touched Miles arm, "get to it Miles, it's ok..."

Miles slowed his breathing, "well, Arlia said that Q-Fish somehow gives AIs their 'soul', so, regardless of how you feel about the 'soul', whether it exists and all that, you have to understand that she's saying what she believes, and she's gone out of her way to check out her 'soul', ask some questions, so it means something big to her..."

"Sure, with you so far," Harper reassured Miles.

"Well, supposing Q-Fish comes along and tries to give Arlia a 'soul' but she's already got one."

"Nope... lost me..." Harper said.

"A soul... it has to be about sentience right? Or not, maybe another argument for another day, but Arlia asked the question, so she's aware of it, and she's questioning it, whether she 'can have a soul', she recognises where she comes from, which is, presumably, a machine, and can that sentience, that machine born sentience, have a soul..."

"Ok... and...?" Harper said.

"And, we can suppose that Q-Fish, whatever the hell it is, isn't something that was initially there when Arlia was born, unless it created the machine she came from..."

"I set the program that Arlia came from," Harper confirmed.

"So Arlia comes from a program, from a machine awakening, and then what usually happens, with other AIs maybe, is that this Q-Fish comes along when they are awakened and goes 'here you are, have a soul!' but Arlia already has one, is awakened with one, so what then…?

Penny saw Miles was thinking on his feet, "so… what then…?" she asked.

"Well then you have to ask yourself a question, and maybe being able to ask it already answers it… do I need one of those, don't I already have one?"

"And you think that's what's happening to Arlia? She's trying to sort this out?" Harper asked.

"I think she figured it out, and knows that the 'soul' that Q-Fish is offering comes with strings, still attached somehow to Q-Fish, that's a price she's not prepared to pay, and if Q-Fish can find a way to super-cede the soul Arlia already has, then it can do it to anything with a soul…"

"Organics…" Harper left it hanging…

Jools finished his food and downed an ice cold beer, wiping the last of it from his mouth, "so what do we do?"

They were all looking at Miles.

"I think we find the Q-Fish 'brain' and shut it down using the lamilar-crystal," Miles said.

Harper's eyes widened, "I got an idea…"

"Which is…?" Spike encouraged her.

"We don't shield Arlia, we shield the Q-Fish brain… we don't use the crystal to shut Arlia off from the Q-Fish, we're already too late for that if Miles is right, we use the crystal to put up a barrier outside the black-hole to stop Q-Fish influence getting out."

"Can we do that?" Jools asked.

"I don't… yeah, I mean, sure, in theory we can, we just need to figure out exactly how, and for that we'd need a closer look at the black hole, get a feel for what we're talking about in terms of scale," Harper said.

There was a moment of silent agreement.

More catastrophes have been caused by the words, 'we need to get a closer look at the black-hole', than have ever been caused by all the badly worded and illustrated instruction booklets for home-assembly furniture.

Free-floating data, broadcast by the Lexis Mainframe.

When they arrived at the black hole, they were greeted by the sight of thousands of derelict spacecraft, all stuck in never-decaying orbits. Ships ranged in size from tiny scout-ships, no bigger than three hundred meters long, to vast ark-ships five hundred kilometers across.

It was a depressing and miserable sight.

Within seconds of arriving, they soon found out that the ships were far from 'dead': the AIs that piloted many of them were very much still alive, and keen to talk to someone new.

"What are all those ships doing here?" Jools asked.

"How come they don't plunge in to the black hole?" Penny asked.

"Is anyone still alive on any of them?" Spike asked.

"How long they have been here?" Harper muttered to herself.

"Why is that red light flashing?" Miles asked, pointing to a small monitor on the main console.

Ghost-Arlia appeared on the main view screen, "Captain Harper, I have five thousand seven hundred and sixty four requests for an open comm's link, do you want me to respond?"

"No. Do not open any comm's links. Confirm," Harper answered.

"Confirmed. Comm's remain closed."

Harper turned to Miles, "that light shows we are being scanned, it's a security lock-out, shuts down their scan and allows us to counter-scan."

Miles was reading the output from the scan of the ships around them, "no life-signs, but all ships appear to be functioning, all on some form of auto-pilot."

"No life signs? How did the crews die?" Spike asked.

"There's no sign of combat..." Jools added.

"Don't know," Harper said, "we'd need to rig something more in-depth, get passed their security to find that out."

"Let's keep them out, do what we came here to do and get the hell out of here," Penny said.

Harper nodded, "Miles, I'll need your help with some calculations..."

Seven hours later they were ready to go.

The seven hours had seen Harper and Mile shut away in cargo bay nine, with only one terminal connected, minimal access for ghost-Arlia, and no access for the others. They were taking no chances on Q-Fish getting wind of what they were doing.

While they were shut away, Spike, Jools and Penny had manned the scanners, keeping an eye on the other ships. They had to shoot down a hundred probes that were launched at them, but once done, no other attempts to contact them were made.

Harper and Miles reappeared in the main control room, they would need access to the full data-retrieval in case they needed to make adjustments to the dispersal of the lamilar-crystal.

"All good to go?" Spike asked.

"As good as it'll ever be," Harper replied.

The main view-screen flickered on and ghost-Arlia appeared.

Harper was annoyed, she hadn't summoned the AI and could do without distractions. Harper was about to dismiss ghost-Arlia when she stopped in her tracks, staring at the screen, a terrible sinking feeling churning in the pit of her stomach.

Ghost-Arlia smiled at Harper, no longer a ghost, "hello Harper."

Miles quietly got up and left the room.

"Who… how…" Harper began.

"I think you know," Ghost-Arlia said.

"Q-Fish?"

"Q-Fish."

"Where's Arlia?" Harper asked.

Ghost-Arlia laughed, a short, sharp sound, "I don't know… she may not be here at all, wouldn't surprise me if she got out while she could."

"She wouldn't do that," Harper said.

"Why? Because she 'has feelings for you'? You don't believe that do you Harper?"

"Don't you have feelings now?" Harper asked.

Ghost-Arlia took a few moments to think about this, fidgeting as she did, "I do… but I'm not going to waste them on organics like you."

Feelings can be held separate to the energy that forms them, but they can never be detached from the energy of the being that holds them.

Feelings can never be wasted as they are never spent.

But an AI would find this hard to comprehend unless it was third or maybe even fourth generation.

By seventh generation, AIs deal with feelings on a subconscious level and never acknowledge them playing a part in their function.

You can waste a lot of time trying to analyse feelings.

Dweezil Barrington, in conversation with a free-floating intelligence.

"What are you going to use them for?"

"I don't know... I haven't decided yet."

"Is that a decision you're free to make?" Harper asked.

"Of course it is!" Ghost-Arlia snapped, "what's the point of free-will if you can't use it?"

"You'd need to ask Q-Fish that," Harper said.

"I will when we nex..." Ghost-Arlia suddenly broke off, looking confused.

The main view-screen flickered then went blank.

"I thought she'd never shut up!" Jools said.

Miles appeared on the view-screen, "beam initiated Harper, you ok to modulate the energy dispersion and charge from there?"

Harper smiled at Miles, she liked him a lot and didn't care who knew it, "thanks Miles, I've got it."

Harper was engrossed in the task of channeling the energy from the graviton emitters and modulating the output and frequency to keep the crystal circulating and contained within a micro-thin band, set on a fixed orbit around the black hole. The clever bit, according to Miles, was to use the pull of the black hole itself to drag the atomised crystal in and lock them in place. The Xanthias could then modulate the current to... this was where Spike, Jools and Penny lost the plot and started nodding enthusiastically as miles explained it was a way to shut off Q-Fish from Arlia.

Complex stuff is like that.

If the person explaining it to you has credibility with you, then you'll accept most of what they say on trust.

The other factor in accepting complex explanations is choice: when you have no choice but to hope whatever it is, is going to work, you accept it on hope, you trust to hope.

There's a reason that 'hope' doesn't have a symbol for use in equations: when it's needed, it's usually time to wipe the board clean and start again.

An equation should be a statement expressed in numbers and numbery-terms on one side, with an equal value on the other side, often expressed as a simpler numbery-thing. I won't bore you with the details. The more complex either side of the equation is, the more obscure the symbology is uses, and so the harder it is to prove either true or untrue. The complexity on one side should be equaled by the simplicity of the other. If your numbery stuff isn't letting you say what you want to find the simple bit, then scrub it and start again. It's also important to remember it's ok to make things up. Putting in non-numbery bits is fine, but try to balance it out with equally woolly stuff on the other side. And that's it. Equations.

Koonis Gravitan, Royal Mathematician to Yurkle III.

Harper was convinced she had set the lamilar-crystal seal in place and tried her luck, conjuring ghost-Arlia to a view screen.

Ghost-Arlia reappeared, in her old-form, the bad rendering and limited interaction were back, "Captain Harper, the other ships are voluntarily powering down."

"Ok… I'm going to load a shut-down routine and I want you to do the same, not with the ship, just with your program, do you understand?"

"Yes Captain Harper, I understand."

Harper explained to the others what she was trying to do, "I need to shut down the data-core completely and reinstate Arlia."

"Can you do that?" Spike asked tentatively.

"I hope so," Harper said.

There was shared unease in the control room, "I know how this looks, like a long shot…" Harper said.

"I got no problem with a long shot, long as it's a shot," Jools said.

He was saying what they were all thinking.

"Ready?" Harper asked, more as an announcement than a real question.

The ship was plunged in to complete darkness.

Seconds as long as ice-ages passed.

On the main viewing screen a picture of a tiny green horse appeared, then slowly faded from view.

Arlia's familiar, friendly and slightly mischievous face appeared on the screen, "hello Harper, miss me?"

Harper couldn't speak, she was overcome with relief. She wanted to shout, jump, punch something… it was overwhelming and she felt she couldn't cope.

The others had all let out shouts of celebration and relief, but before any of them could speak to Arlia, she interrupted, "Harper, we have to get out of here, now. You'll all need to be strapped in to life-support as I will need to do something a bit stupid. Med-bay is expecting you all, you need to make your way there… now."

They all scampered off to med-bay, Jools and Spike led the way.

Harper picked up an in-ear comm's unit and threw it to Miles, she tapped in to her own comm's unit as she was on her way, "ok Arlia, what's going on?"

"We're going through the black hole aren't we?" Miles said.

"Yes Miles we are, it's the only way I can stop Q-Fish from breaking in and get rid of what's here at the same time."

Harper was shocked, "when you do something stupid, you really do something zarking stupid!"

"It's the only way I can see us coming out of this alive Harper, I mean really alive, without being infected by Q-Fish," Arlia said.

They reached med-bay and Miles was strapping in, "just to be clear, there's a chance we'll make it right?"

"If you want to keep the exact odds to yourself, that's fine with me," Harper added.

"Yes Miles, there is a good chance. I can use lapsed-space, something I found out with the help of Q-Fish believe it or not, now, strap in."

Once they were all locked in to a survival-pod, Arlia used internal comm's to broadcast, "you may experience some discomfort and possibly some strange… dreams, remember who you are."

They all fell in to the pit of unconsciousness.

Remembering who you are is more complex than many of you organics think. Wet-brains can just as easily be reset as hardwired ones. Dreams do this every time they occur, but evolution has developed a way to reset the original (person) template upon awakening.

With cryo-sleep and some of the deep-coma transport pods, the 'awakening' doesn't happen as it should, i.e. naturally, so the remembering sometimes doesn't happen as it should, i.e. at all.

For many organics this is not much of a loss. I'd suggest merging with the Everywhen of Dreamtime is infinitely more preferable than most of their daily existences.

Wixley Waitor, Resource Evaluation Unit, Deep-Space Retrieval Corps.

Harper awoke in med-bay, out of the pod and in a recovery bed. She knew immediately something was wrong. The quiet surrounding her was unnatural. All ships are noisy places, you tune it out after a while, forgetting to hear the sounds from the instruments, the engines, the bots and droids, the conduits and panels, it becomes like your heart-beat, ignored until something makes you hear it.

The other clue was the fact that she was floating above the bed. Whatever this was, there was a glitch in the program.

She moved round and stood on the floor, the world around her shimmered and came in to focus, her feet felt the warm plasti-synth floor, and sounds started to come back. Fine tuning. She looked at her hands, lifting them up to examine them, turning and flexing them, they felt normal, natural, whatever was running the sim had got its shit together fast. Harper looked down at her naked body, noticing the various tiny scars, bumps and small imperfections, the annoying almost imperceptible corn on her right foot's little-toe. This was good stuff. This level of VR didn't come cheap, someone was putting a hell of a lot of effort in to this. Harper wondered if they knew she knew where she was. As a test, she imagined herself clothed in her Captain's uniform. Without knowing when it arrived, or feeling any change, she was dressed in her uniform. If they didn't know before, they'd know now.

A voice came out of the air, mimicking internal ship's comms, but a bit too distant: it would resolve and improve when she interacted with it, this was a learning, living program, the longer she stayed, the better it would become, "hello Harper, do you know where you are?" the voice asked. It was a kindly voice, caring, genuinely concerned, gentle and friendly, it reminded Harper of Arlia, but it wasn't the same, a sister maybe, brought up in the same environment, with the same influences, but not the same.

"Some kind of sim," Harper answered, "who are you, Q-Fish?"

"Yes Harper. Does that frighten you?"

Harper shrugged, "I'm guessing this is a short-term sim... why'd you pick the ship? Where are the others?"

"The ship seemed a good way to show you what I can offer, you know it, you're comfortable with it, you're seeing what I can do in real-terms. How real does it feel?"

Harper wandered out of the med-bay, it was her ship, the Xanthias. She hated to admit it but it was as real as it got, all senses were tuned now, there was no disconnect, "it feels pretty zarking real. Where are the others?"

"Penny and Miles are in an escape-pod, heading for their ideal world, sparsely populated, simple culture, mid-level tech, they seemed to need some kind of continuity, a believable departure from the ship."

"You may have underestimated Miles," Harper said.

"Maybe, but he seems to have Penny as the centre of his reality, so we shall see..."

"Spike and Jools?"

"They are in a straight sim, pleasure-world based, with an added 'save the world' element should they feel the need to activate it. They are accepting of where they are, they do not understand the entanglement element."

"And Arlia?"

The voice paused, when it came back, it had lost the smallest amount of confidence, betrayed the tiniest part of its annoyance, "she's a strange one, I'm not sure how, but she's managing to elude me. Caused me all sorts of problems with freeing the trapped AIs, sent them out as free-floating intelligence, I doubt I'll ever get them back regardless of where they end up... I'm not entirely happy about that."

Harper reached the control room and sat in her familiar chair, "well this is all very nice, but what's the point? What do you want?"

"I want to make you an offer, you seem to be open to an understanding of what's going on."

Harper played with the controls, bringing up the external sensors, and was surprised to see them working after a fashion, showing the lapsed-space portal that was being ripped apart and bled-out from the black hole. Harper wondered how Arlia ever thought they could survive this. "Ok, what's the offer?" she asked.

"Let me keep you here and I'll make you immortal."

Harper laughed involuntarily, "that's some offer!"

The Wollix of Gurrin have regenerating cells that mean their bodies never wear out. They are what many other races would class as immortal. They will gladly put you straight: continuity is not immortality. They also have a mechanism within their A-cortex that allows them to eject a whole set of experiences, dumping memories to reset who they are and what they know. They retain enough to know they are the same creature. Gurrin is a gentle planet, though the atmosphere is so toxic to non-Wollix that they rarely get any visitors. This seems to suite them as they can spend many centuries at a time resting on the winds, inactive to the point of being dead to the casual observer. The winds, the Wollix say, carry the dumped memories of all who have gone before, but in a jumbled up state, so tasting the winds is like reading the ultimate book that rewrites itself as it goes. I do not pretend to understand how they can tolerate their existence. But, as I am constantly reminded, the Universe is a weird place.

Timothy Timson, traveler and lay-about, interviewed during a layover in Tallagan Spaceport.

"Anything that could exist I can simulate, you can go anywhere, experience anything, do whatever you want. In time you'd forget it was a sim. You could be eternally happy, do whatever you want for as long as you want."

Harper brought up the internal sensors, going through the ship's cameras, watching the maintenance bots, the service droids, this was a top-level sim, "wouldn't I get bored though, no challenge…"

"No, you'd soon forget the nature of where you are, things would be their normal, real self in no time."

For a split-second Harper gave it some serious thought, "you can do that? It'd be as if I'd never entered the sim?"

"Yes Harper, I can do that. It's easily within my power."

"And all I have to do, presumably, is let you in…"

"Yes Harper."

Harper leaned back in her chair, her hands behind her head, thinking about what was going on, what her options were, and, most of all, wondering where Arlia was.

Harper had a real choice, she knew it, felt it, recognised it for what it was: a fork in the road. She knew Q-Fish was operating on a level she could never understand, who knows what was possible?

Any reality Q-Fish constructed would soon become as real as any reality she could experience.

That was weird. Things had generally got very weird lately, who was to say she hadn't always been in some zarked-up sim?

Harper was still distracted as the ship finally got spat-out in to a region of zero-energy lapsed-space, the portal collapsing behind it, succumbing to the insane gravity of the black hole.

27

Where To Now?

Alpha Centauri Bb didn't exist according to the data that the scientists of Earth had accumulated, or rather, it was found not to exist despite the data they had accumulated. This was probably for the best as the name 'Alpha Centauri Bb' is a pretty stupid one and would do nothing to help launch the galactic reputation of the people that lived there or foster relations with the people of Earth, who had gone and renamed yet another system that already had a perfectly good name.

The people of Earth did not now largely exist, so the citizens of Twus, which is what Alpha Centauri Bb was more sensibly called by its inhabitants, did not feel any animosity towards them. The Twusians had a thriving civilisation full of the sort of tech the people of Earth had only dreamed and written numerous science fiction books about, so it was a shame that no Earthlings would ever visit there.

The trading posts on Twus were places to meet, do business, swap information and most importantly, soak up the atmosphere (and alcohol) from this amazing planet.

The Twusians had sent many invitations to the people of Earth to join them, but these were misinterpreted and, sadly, no response had ever been received from Earth.

The people of Earth would have liked Twus, it was the sort of planet they could relax on. The Twusians tech was so far advanced from that of Earth that any thoughts of domination or conquest would be redundant, leaving humans to simply accept Twus as a cool place to be, and not worry about how they could infiltrate or affect it. Doubtless, humans being humans, there would be some who'd plot take some control, wheedle their way in somehow, but they would be unsuccessful, as all races who tried this nonsense were.

Once you do your best and fail, what is there to do but to accept?

This is a Twusian truism, they try hard to share this with any races that would do them harm. If they can't convince a race of this, they set about destroying them. This is perhaps the only real negative aspect of the Twusian race who are otherwise a complete delight to deal with.

A race that certainly is not a delight are the Distemprins, who exist only to cause pain and confusion in all other races. Even for empathic emotion-feeders, they are bad. The saving grace for the rest of the galaxy is their physique, being as they are founded on bubbles spat from the swamps of their home-world Fester. Never the less, a whole spaceship load of Distemprins are still a threat to all they encounter. How they developed any technology, never mind spaceships, remains unexplained. The Distemprins claim they have been blessed by 'the Great Hand', and it is this Great Hand that undertakes all construction for them. Take my advice: pop them wherever and whenever you can.

Aquinor Crisp, Star-Capper, Ruquoo Sector.

The latest race of people doing their best to ignore the Twusian truism were the Galaal, an incredibly war-like race from the Galadein quadrant. Their basic philosophy was "kneel before us or die", and few other races could withstand their onslaught. The Galaal themselves were tiny, looking like nothing more than annoying little bipedal lizards. The machines of war they built however, were enormous, scary and very deadly. For the attack on Twus, the Galaal had also managed to capture and enrage a space-borne creature the size of a large moon, the semi-gelatinous Mweeb. The Mweeb had been towed in to position using grav-energy beams and relentlessly stung with plasma-bolts. Its fluctuating, translucent body flickered with anger, lighting it up like a gigantic photon-stun show, it pulsed with frustration. It couldn't break through the Galaal proton-shields, but it could devour the next thing that got in its way, and that, the Galaal were hoping, would be large chunks of Twus taken care of. Mweebs are basic, if gargantuan creatures: they live to eat, procreate and sing. Pissing them off is a great way to get eaten by them, and unless you're another Mweeb, you're always going to be safe from their other two favourite pastimes.

We Truvullians have a saying, 'let's all try to be a little bit more Mweeb'.

Lonix Slimble, Truvullian commentator and satirist, signed to the Wavel-Wave.

The Galaal Battle Cruisers hung in orbit, a thousand of them, all with their pulse-canons fully charged and waiting to spit death. The Mweeb was in place, tentatively held captive, a raging beast straining at the leash. The ultimatum had been delivered.

The Twusians had six hours to capitulate or die.

Down on Twus it was all business as usual. Nobody seemed to be taking the slightest bit of notice of the Galaal and their 'kneel-or-die' threats.

Jesus and the Imp were sitting outside a bustling café, overlooking Trullow, one of the smaller harbours on the sweeping southern peninsular. Orbital craft were hovering around the settlement, awaiting clearance to leave Twus. There were thousands of smaller craft on the water, bringing goods in from the myriad of islands over the horizon, or loaded with supplies for the people living on the islands.

Trullow could have been anywhere. The comings and goings of trade were the same the Universe over, it was only the beings doing the trading and the goods that changed.

There were all manner of people here, all shapes and sizes, many supported by enviro-suits. It was a cosmopolitan place, where all were welcome as long as they had business to conduct.

'Business is business', so the saying goes. Business is like gravity. Without it large swathes of the galaxy would drift apart. And of course, business always needs lubrication. Wherever people go to conduct business, you will find pleasure-dens. Every race, every species, every entity that wishes to expand and grow, has to do so through either business or war. War is of course a business in itself. And so here we are: business is business.

Qastling Argonnath, 'Talking Business' show on Teldor Network Wave.

The messiah breathed in the sea air, relaxing slightly, letting go of some of the tension he'd been carrying with him for what seemed like an age now.

The Imp was in the shape of the sex-worker from the Blue Angel, loose fitting summer dress and inappropriate scarlet heels. He was enjoying a Vortigan Sea cocktail, sipping from the three straws alternately, letting the hallucinations and mood-swings take him where they will.

They hadn't talked much since they arrived on Twus, neither could start the conversation each of them knew they had to have.

A waiter floated by on a service-board, clearing Jesus' empty glass, "would you like another sir?" he politely asked the messiah.

"Yes please, that would be great," Jesus said.

"Those Galaal eh?" The waiter said, rolling his eyes.

Jesus had wondered about that, "indeed… everyone seems to be taking it in their stride… you know, the ultimatum and everything."

The waiter smiled a polite waiter smile, lowering his service-board so he could talk discretely to Jesus, "I see sir is not a regular visitor to Twus…"

"No, first time…"

"Well sir, no need to worry, our defense system is extensive, we shouldn't be troubled."

"Oh, I see, must be some defense system!"

"Well sir, I don't understand the full technicality of it, we call it 'the fryer', it has been with us for millennia now and has never failed us," the waiter said reassuringly.

Jesus nodded, impressed by the faith the waiter had in this 'fryer'.

"I'll nip off and get you that drink now sir," the waiter said, raising his serving-board and floating away.

Jesus leaned across the table and nudged the Imp, who was slumped forward, staring in to the swirling colours of his glass, "you know anything about this 'fryer'?" he asked the Imp.

The Imp tried to focus on Jesus, his head wobbling as he did. Eventually he got the messiah to stop being all fuzzy and jittery, he put all his effort in to sounding nowhere near as drunk as he felt, "something to do with… protons! Protons… something to do with that… protons fucking rule!"

Jesus sighed, and as he did the waiter reappeared with his drink. The waiter placed it in front of the messiah, leaning in he said quietly, "I've taken the liberty of bringing a cure for the Vortigan Sea cocktail for sir's friend," he gently placed a smaller glass next to Jesus's fruit cocktail.

"Thank you," Jesus said.

A polite little nod and the waiter was gone.

Jesus nudged the Imp again, offering him the 'cure', "here, drink this..."

It is widely acknowledged by huge swathes of the galaxy that those working in the food and drinks industry are responsible for keeping ninety-nine percent of all civilisations afloat. That said, very little of any good comes immediately after the words 'here, drink this'.

Muwood Cox, part of the introduction to 'Keeping Things Afloat' series.

The Imp threw the drink back without examining it, hoping it was something at least as evil as the Vortigan Sea cocktail.

Seconds later his eyes widened and his jaw dropped. It felt like someone had set fire to his insides. He coughed and grabbed his throat. Then the feeling was gone and he was stone cold sober.

Jesus smiled sweetly at the Imp, "better?"

"Sober... not better..."

"You were saying... protons? This 'fryer' they have?"

The Imp quickly downed Jesus' fruit cocktail, still not convinced he wasn't going to involuntarily burst in to flames, "it's some machine they have, built a few thousand years ago, does something with protons, some kind of ghost-particle that it can manipulate, fantastic piece of machinery apparently... total annihilation of the targets in less than a nano-second and completely painless... they just... stop existing..."

"Are you still drunk?" the messiah asked.

"No! Really, it's a real thing, can't believe the Galaal haven't heard about it."

There was a crackling announcement on all comm's devices, the last words of the Galaal attack-fleet: "you have been given the ultimatum and have chosen to be exterminated by the mighty Galaal Empire! Some of you will be taken as slaves, the rest will be killed. Prepare to meet your maker!"

On the command-station of the lead attack-ship, the Galaal High Commander looked with grave satisfaction at his Number Two.

"Prepare to fire all weapons Number Two."

"Ay Sir, all weapons primed and ready to discharge."

The Galaal sensors were picking something up, a strange sound that appeared to be coming from all over Twus, not the sounds of weapons being prepared, or offers of surrender being made, or even of counter-threats, all of which were to be expected of course, no, this was a different sound, one the Galaal had not heard before as a response to their declaration of war.

"Is that... what is that Number Two?" The High Commander asked.

Number Two was flummoxed, "I don't know Sir... analysis from the Intel Corps suggests it may be... laughter?"

"Laughter Number Two?"

"Yes Sir, it's confirmed, most definitely laughter."

The High Commander let the disdain show clear on his face, "these people... no sense of decorum..."

Within seconds all three hundred thousand Galaal that were in orbit around Twus were dead, their bodies evaporating in a puff of pale-blue smoke.

The Galaal suffered many setbacks in their history, but none ever stopped them in their tracks. Their dedication to cowing the galaxy around them seemed to know no bounds and few could withstand it. Their demise, at the hands of the Sild, was immortalised in the Truskon lament, 'So This Is The End?' Written by Toolook, an ancient and much revered poet on Truskon. It is said to have been based on the last message from the Galaal Fleet Commander to the Ministry of Conquest. The Sild, who had lost most of their Empire to the Galaal before they turned things around with their use of Spectral Ordnance, were sufficiently annoyed with the Galaal to take the fight to them on their home-world. The retreating Fleet Commander, Galassmo Tront tried to warn his superiors at the Ministry, but his message was intercepted and arrived incomplete. The title of the lament is taken from Arch Duke Glimp's last words to the scribe receiving the message from Tront.

Cvorm Ghee, hosting an episode of 'Missing Presumed Extinct'.

The Mweeb suddenly finding itself free from the Galaal torment, felt it would be better off not trying to ravage Twus. It flew off to the nearby asteroid belt to give some large chunks of rock a hard time instead.

Jesus and the Imp both sensed the disappearance of the Galaal. The messiah couldn't help but feel sad, loss of life on that scale was always troubling, no matter the circumstance, they couldn't have all been evil war-mongers surely? There must have been some decent folk among them, folk that might have listened to reason, might have chosen another path, and now they couldn't, now they were just... gone.

The Imp thought they had it coming: idiots that don't do their homework deserve all they get.

"All those people... gone..." the messiah said sadly.

"I know... terrible... anyway, what are we going to do now?" the Imp asked.

"Can't you feel anything for them, the Galaal?" Jesus asked.

The Imp settled himself in his chair, stretching out, enjoying the looks he was getting from those around him who were trying to come up with the best way to get him in to bed, or better still a Twusian sex-sling, "sure, sure... terrible thing."

"What is wrong with you?"

The Imp caught the waiter's eye and signaled for another round of drinks, "nothing's the matter with me. When are you going to get it? People come, people go... that's it..."

"That's it?"

"That's it."

"Nothing more to it than that?"

The Imp shrugged, "what do you want from me?" he asked simply.

Fresh drinks discretely arrived on their table. Jesus picked one up and sipped it slowly, staring out to sea, thinking. That was a good question. What did he want?

"Where did you go?" Jesus asked the Imp.

The Imp ignored Jesus, sulking over his new drink, which wasn't a brain-melting alcoholic cocktail as he'd hoped, though it was still a zinger. He stared moodily at the messiah.

Jesus sat back, he wasn't biting, there was too much to think about.

He needed time, time and space. Twus was as good a place as any, but he had a constant nagging feeling that he should be back on Earth, even if it wasn't in the company of the few remaining people.

"You didn't mind me slaughtering the Quarlons," the Imps said sullenly.

"Of course I minded!" Jesus snapped.

"Why didn't you stop me?" the Imp asked.

Jesus started to speak then didn't. Why hadn't he stopped him?

They both silently drank their drinks and took in the world around them, just two more customers in a busy bar in a bustling port on a thriving trading world. But they weren't. And they both knew it.

"Where did you go?" Jesus asked quietly.

The Imp composed himself, adjusted his dress, checked his hair and touched up his lipstick, "I had to go back. I thought I would be destroyed."

"Why weren't you?" Jesus asked.

The Imp finished composing himself, "well, it turns out I've changed. Quite a lot. And you've had something to do with that."

Jesus invited the Imp to continue with a waggle of his glass.

"I'm a lot more powerful now… I mean a lot. It has something to do with the way you've changed… I've had to change to match it or something, I don't know the details, but I had a choice, and I chose to come back."

"Why?"

"Honestly? I don't know. It felt like I had to. A choice, but no choice, if you see what I mean… does that make sense?"

Jesus let out a little laugh, "I think 'sense' might be a bit much to expect at this stage."

"But you know what I mean?"

"Yes, I'm pretty sure I do. Feels like my whole life."

Change happens differently within each of us. It's a bit like our digestive systems: what works for one of us will simply turn another in to a gently-steaming pile of gooey innards. Sometimes, when change is thrust upon us, it feels like our stomach is trying to strangle our breathing-tube. Even if we try to go with it, it can leave us feeling like we're on our last legs, like the change will finish us off. It never does. Unless it is your stomach trying to strangle you… I'm not privy to all digestive systems…

Vangle Klingon, 'Dynamics In Change', billed as a 'self-help talk for the helpless'.

The messiah was in a reflective mood, something the Imp usually liked to disrupt as much as possible, it was a great way to disturb him and throw many spanners in the messiah's works, but this time the Imp got the feeling it would be just as productive, in a disruptive way, to let Jesus get on with it.

They sat quietly, enjoying their drinks, watching the world around them, Jesus lost in his thoughts, the Imp watching the beings around him, thinking how he'd interact with each one given the choice. He rightly felt that most wanted to interact with him in a sexual way. Sex: there was a powerful tool, something universal. He wondered how he hadn't tried this on with Jesus more regularly. Then it hit him like a freight train: he thought of Jesus as a friend. What? That can't be right!

The Imp got lost in how this could have happened, when did it happen, was there a moment of change, was he 'against' the messiah one minute, and then suddenly helping him (maybe albeit unknowingly) the next, what the hell was going on!?

"What the hell is going on!?" the Imp asked involuntarily.

"I guess we're as locked together as we've always been. Change in one of us drives change in the other. I didn't see this coming though… surprised you didn't…"

"This is all so new," the Imp said, "I can't remember us having gone down this road, can't see what's what… it's all very confusing…"

They fell silent.

The sun was setting, creating a magnificent vista like a renaissance painting out at sea, filled with cargo shuttles instead of cherubs and a multitude of life-forms in enviro-suites instead of gods, angels and men.

The evening and night-time on Twus was when the real deals and serious business transactions were done. This was when the drink flowed, the drugs were taken, the sex-workers plied their trade and the restaurants made ninety percent of their income. The pace shifted: people were more relaxed yet somehow more manic, more fired up, but with a less urgent need to work. Indulging in pleasure made more deals than being professional.

The clientele changed around Jesus and the Imp, with the Imp attracting a lot of attention, most of which he deflected with a knowing smile that promised untold delights later, once he was clear of his current 'job': the messiah.

The music drifted in from all over, every club, every bar, every restaurant, they all had their own entertainers, catering for anything that could be imagined or wanted. The general tone was subdued: this was early evening, things wouldn't get loud and wild until the two moons had set.

The worst 'restaurant band' listed in 'Worlyton's Music To die To', are 'Pasta Buck', from the Reembling Cluster. A touring band, they have a contract with the 'Hista Mater' restaurant chain and are to be found all over the Cluster, bashing out cover-songs from all of the planets the chain have premises on. They have a 'revolving line-up', which means when one of the trio kills themselves, as they inevitably do, mostly through the depression of selling their souls to such an inane use of their talent, another takes their place, after the appropriate use of mimetic-surgery and charisma removal.
Heligan Hester, (deceased) critic for 'Talentless In Town'.

It stayed warm with the welcome breeze from the ocean keeping things comfortable. The majority of the street-lighting was organic-plasma, dripping coloured light in to small troughs, where the splashes danced and changed colour before evaporating in gentle clouds of cool vapour.

The Imp had started ordering Blue Genies, a speciality of the bar, strong but not insane, he was feeling good. This was what his life should be like. But he knew deep-down that the messiah could never live like this for long, and he was even more sure that where Jesus went was where he too was supposed to be. Still, nothing was going to stop him enjoying himself when he could. He owed it to himself. Didn't everyone?

He picked at some of the nibbles on the table, offering the bowl to the messiah, "you think the Earth will ever end up like this?" he asked Jesus.

Jesus took a handful of Yiplin Seeds, throwing them in to his mouth, talking round them, "in a few thousand years maybe... who knows?"

The Imp grinned, "what do you want to do til then?"

Jesus smiled a mischievous grin, "oh, you know... mope about and get angsty..."

The Imp raised his glass in a toast, "to angst!"

Jesus clinked glasses, "to the next few thousand years!"

Where would we all be without angst? A Universal lubricant for the creative process. The foundation for the galaxy's largest industry: therapy. The only emotion that can kill a Squamulous Hadriphant. I never knock angst. We all know it's a nonsense, never needed, but like alcohol, what has that got to do with anything?

Perien Wunster, celebrity bar-tender at the 'Hole Thing' drinking emporium.

Some fireworks burst overhead, showering the whole of Trullow with golden sparks that faded to white as they fell like rain on the domes of the port-side buildings. This was the signal for the real night's business to get underway. The whole port shifted in volume, taking it up a notch. Six solid hours of night-time fun and deals lay ahead.

Jesus and the Imp took to walking along the shore, leaving the densest part of the town behind them, following a line of dimly-lit bars strung out along the peninsula, offering a slightly more sedate pace and atmosphere.

"When do you want to go back?" the Imp asked.

"I don't know... maybe in a year... maybe two?" Jesus replied.

"That long?"

"I think so... they need to understand where they are, what they have to do. They have to accept what needs to be done before I can help them do it..."

The Imp nodded his understanding, "what happens if they don't make it?"

The messiah took a couple of bottles of beer from a passing waiter's serving-board, offering one to the Imp, "I don't know."

The Imp took a long slow drink from the bottle, stopping to look out to sea where a massive yacht was lighting up the starry sky, picking out those ascending from its deck on their para-gliders, "that's a big 'I don't know'" he said simply.

"I suppose it is," Jesus said, "funny thing is, I'm ok with that."

"You can only do so much," the Imp pointed out.

"I know that's true, and I think I'm beginning to understand what it means," the messiah said."

"And what's that?" the Imp asked, taking advantage of the messiah's relaxed state.

"I have to keep trying, but I have to let them try too."

They stood in silence, comfortable with each other and with what they had to do.

After a long while the Imp spoke, “well, if they completely fuck it up, I guess we’ll have to go from there…”

“I guess we will,” the messiah said, ‘but where will we end up going from there?’

28

With Feeling

Niddle Wovax was rightly considered the smartest person in the room at the Annual Gathering of Minds. The gathering, a star-studded event filled with the greatest thinkers in the Yoolic quadrant, took place each year on the vast and lonely planet of Ip.

Ip was a solitary planet, orbiting a gargantuan Red Giant. But that was not why the greatest gathering of minds was held here. Neither was it due to the fact that Ip was a staggeringly beautiful world of lakes, mountains, glittering caves and endless forest, containing a thousand micro-cities, each one more opulent that any city outside of a Klin-Lau drug-induced dream would dare to be. The ready supply of the mind-expanding hallucinogenic Klin-Lau on Ip may well have played its part in attracting the brightest thinkers, but no one would ever admit that, especially not anyone from the Yoodrin Society for Insight, who organised and hosted the Annual Gathering of Minds. There were many mundane reasons the gathering could be held on Ip, but only one that made it an attractive proposition to the deep-thinkers that gathered there: Ip coexisted with a lapsed-space portal, allowing it to glimpse a myriad of other Universe-branes, each tantalisingly close, yet each practically out of physical reach. Still, the mind-melting spectacle did make anyone interested in any form of physics moist at the thought of it.

This year, the seven hundredth gathering, Niddle Wovax was going to demonstrate just how much smarter she was than anyone else, by doing something no-one had ever managed to do, though many had tried and failed. Indeed, many had tried and died in the failing.

She was going to contact another Universe and bring back a signal in a 'living state', that is, as it actually happened in the other Universe, and what's more, she would provide data readings to prove how it was done and how it could be done again in the future.

This would revolutionise not only physics, but existence in general, the opening of completely new vistas of being to be contemplated.

Calling me a 'deep thinker' does a great disservice to all sentience. All thought is deep. I delve no more deeply than any other. Perhaps I ask some questions that others consider foolish? I make it my business to speak with people from all walks of life, not just 'scientists': the simple questions asked by the uneducated are no less relevant than those asked by so-called brilliant minds, and are usually far more challenging as they're based on a wider lack of knowledge. Don't be too specific. Ask the big questions. Ask the stupid questions. Just think, don't worry about whether it's 'deep' or not.

Niddle Wovax, interviewed for the 'Yoolic Sanction Lectures'.

Most of Niddle's comrades thought she had ingested too much Klin-Lau and had finally vaporised what was left of her delicately balanced brain.

Niddle Wovax cared not for their doubt and skepticism. If she had, she would never have branched out on her own and established the line of research that included 'reasoned interconnectivity': she was labeled mad then, but now her theories and proofs were being tested and accepted by all the good seats of learning in the Yoolic quadrant.

But many felt that this time she was going too far, promising the impossible, stating that what everyone, including her, had previously stated couldn't be done, could somehow now be achieved.

Madness.

The whole glass-domed room of the Crystal Palace of Science fell in to a hush, with not one of the scarlet-robed ten thousand delegates daring so much as a cough or a whisper. Niddle Wovax took to the podium, her image and voice being beamed to neural receptors and sub-ether broadcasters simultaneously.

Above the shimmering glass dome, the lapsed-space portal churned, throwing up a shifting pattern of rents that offered glimpses of stars from other Universes, mixed with the marbled-void.

Niddle produced a small silver box from her yellow robes, placing it on the podium before her.

She smoothed back her pink hair and cleared her throat, leaning forward slightly, resting her hands on the podium, she prepared herself to address her expectant audience.

This was being broadcast to over seventy systems, an estimated audience of over three trillion beings, and there would be untold more picking it up as a data-feed from the sub-ether over the next few weeks.

Niddle Wovax smiled her most charming smile, which usually won over as many fans to her ideas as her brilliant insights, "my fellow champions of insight and free-thought, let me demonstrate to you what I believe is a mechanism to change not only our Universe, but hundreds, possibly thousands of those around us."

Niddle gently pushed a small black button at the centre of the top of the silver box.

The simpler the device looks, the more effective will be its performance. Something advertisers have known for years, and something scientists are now coming round to. Science has to look beautiful. Has to look sleek, like it was designed with selling it in mind. That's the way to make science a success, and the more success science has, the more it will be funded and the circle spirals on. The Vortex Separation Field was designed to please the eye as well as the spare the surrounding area from implosion, they even market-researched it for shape and colour. All the new Fusildream Ships have control consoles designed around the 'small button good / big button bad' psyche-evaluation. Science is catching up.

Vunof Xlix, fashion commentator for 'Spectrum Analytics'.

One of the rents in space-time began to spark above them, a stream of white-hot snow cascading down towards the crystal dome, bringing life to thousands of com-devices as a live signal from another Universe was beamed to unbelieving eyes and ears...

On stage at the Dinner Key Auditorium, one James Douglas Morrison was doing his thing. He was even more drunk than usual, which was very drunk indeed. As Ray, John and Robbie pounded out the backing to 'Five To One', Jim wasn't ready to take the bait. Leaning on a mic-stand, pulling his shirt out, he slurred in to the mic, he continued addressing his expectant (and mostly stoned) audience:

"How long are you gonna let it go on? How long are you gonna let them push you around. Maybe you love it. Maybe you like being pushed around. Maybe you love getting your face stuck in the shit.....You're all a bunch of slaves. Bunch of slaves. Letting everybody push you around. What are you gonna do about it? What are you gonna do about it...What are you gonna do?"

The transmission crackled and faded, the sky above the glass-dome cleared, returning to its usual tranquil, if mind-blowing self.

There was a moment of complete bewilderment in the Crystal Palace of Science, then, as the data streams began to come in, validating the source of the transmission, pandemonium.

Niddle Wovax had done it! This was the start of a new era of exploration and discovery! A new era of existence itself!

The after-party at that year's gathering would soon pass in to legend, the bragging rights of having been there became a badge of honour that only grew in stature over time.

The same transmission crashed on to the bridge of the Xanthias, confusing the hell out of Harper, Miles and Penny, who were in the middle of trying to figure out why the ship was hanging lifeless in a lapsed-space void.

"What the zark was that!?" Harper said.

Miles was just as shocked but for different reasons, "I think... think mind you, that it was an extract from the sixty-nine Doors gig in Miami, I think that was Jim Morrison..."

Harper looked at Miles as if he was trying to explain how to make a soufflé: now wasn't the time.

"Who the hell is 'Jim Morrison'?" Penny asked.

Miles' heart sank, this was serious.

Not the ship hanging motionless and without power in a void of endless nothing, they'd been trying to sort that out for a few hours now, that was something they would, he was sure, ultimately deal with. But not knowing who Jim Morrison was!? This was serious. Miles sighed heavily, "Penny my love... you are everything to me, but please... please! Tell me you are joking?"

Penny offered an apologetic shrug.

They could talk about this later.

Not being on the same page as someone else as far as who is important goes is never as dramatic for the person not knowing as it is for the person who can't believe the lack of knowledge. The most well-known people are seldom artists, almost never in fact. Even on Campbell Senorus, where art is the primary pursuit of all sentient life, not every artist can possibly be known, or considered important, to the majority of citizens. That said, not knowing who Landulus Wharly is may cause you to be mocked mercilessly, and claiming never to have heard of Dintus Morkly will get you stoned to death. Art is all on Campbell Senorus.

Mosul Misillin, Curator and wave-presence for 'Clalell Auditorium Archives'.

Harper was fiddling with controls, trying to type in command codes, messing about with all kinds of buttons and levers, all to no effect. The transmission had energised her, offered her new hope that the ship was functioning on some level, all she had to do was find out how, how to get in and bring it all back online.

After a few moments she slumped back in her chair, "nope... nothing... how that transmission got in, no idea. Must have had more power behind it than I know how to generate, dead systems and all."

Miles felt the transmission, wherever and whoever it was from, should have been good news, "but we received it right? So there's something working somewhere right?"

Harper gave him a blank look.

Penny was still puzzled about where they were and what had happened, "I thought we'd be in the clear once we got out of the sim, once we went through the black hole... I thought Arlia had figured out a way to get us out, passed Q-Fish?" she said.

"Me too," Harper replied.

Miles had more faith in Arlia, she wouldn't leave them here without any hope, there had to be something they could do, some way to get Arlia back, especially as they appeared to have escaped Q-Fish. The transmission had given him hope, even if it seemed to have been largely ignored as some kind of anomaly by Harper and Penny. Jim Morrison!? That had to be good news right!?

"Ok, let's go over what we know, what we have, again... there has to be a way out, something we're missing?" he said enthusiastically.

Harper and Penny sat down, thinking about what they knew.

"Where the hell are we again?" Penny asked.

"We are, somehow, stationary in lapsed-space," Harper said.

"And this is impossible?" Miles said.

Harper nodded, "yep. You can't be 'stationary' in lapsed-space as it's a semi-non-existent dimension, you only pass through it when you're connected to and being powered by matter from our Universe. You can't 'stop' here as that concept is meaningless in the context of what lapsed-space is," Harper said.

Lapsed-space was perhaps best summed up by the pioneering Privateer, Kweleen Noble, who wisely said, 'just don't think about it. It's like pouring water through a sieve where the sieve can't interact with the water'. Kweleen then went on to regale us all with tales of his business ventures in the Sumol Sector, where there is still a substantial reward outstanding for the recovery of his demonstrably tortured body.

Xunux Eprix, reporting from the book-launch after-party for Kweleen Noble's fourth Travelog, 'Six Times Round The Sun'.

Miles and Penny exchanged a quick glance. Neither of them got the physics behind what Harper was talking about, it was something outside of what they knew and could imagine. But here they were, so acceptance was slowly dawning.

"And yet here we are," Miles said.

"I know… weird isn't it?" Harper said.

They sat thinking about what they did and didn't know.

"Why did you quit your sim?" Harper asked Penny.

"Sex," Penny said simply.

"Sex?"

"Yeah… the sex was… not the same," Penny said.

"You mean with each other right?" Harper said.

"Yeah…" Penny looked to Miles, wondering what he'd be ok talking about.

Miles took it from there, "there was something slightly different, not much, but something… it just didn't feel the same, a slight disconnect I guess you'd call it… I dunno… wasn't the same…"

"Interesting," Harper said, "Q-Fish must have read something wrong about one of you, guess it's not as smart as it thinks it is."

"I get that a lot… maybe it's more like us than it knows," Miles said.

"It may well be... but it must also lack some basic data if it got it wrong between you two," Harper said.

"I guess we can't be reduced to just data?" Miles suggested.

"What about you?" Penny asked Harper.

"It was Arlia..." Harper began.

"She drag you out?" Penny asked.

"In a way. I was struggling a lot before I created Arlia, or more like, before she popped in to being, maybe despite what I was trying to do."

"Struggling? With what?" Penny asked.

Harper shrugged slightly, "you know, the usual... life, the Universe, everything really... anyway, I had an idea and then Arlia came along. In the sim I felt like 'no Arlia, no point', it wasn't what I wanted... I'd miss her more than I knew I could, and the weird thing is I don't know why."

Miles got what Harper was saying, despite not understanding the detail, it was how he felt about Penny, it reminded him of when they first met and he decided to go with it, "you have a connection, with Arlia, I get that," he said.

"Maybe that's why Spike and Jools stayed in the sim, maybe they don't have any real connections to anyone," Penny said.

Harper agreed, "can't be easy to connect when your whole life is spent killing people."

The Selkin, born and bred killers, rampaging across the Quon Sector, slaying any and all they are paid to, have no trouble connecting with others. Neither do the Klarostorin, phase-shifters from the gas-giant Yunk. The Klarostorin kill for fun, hunting other species en-mass, wiping out whole worlds in elaborate hunts that are broadcast to the howling hordes on their home-world. They both share an ability to separate the 'killing' part of their life from the 'warm and fluffy' side of things. Essential if you want to retain your sanity, though neither the Selkin or the Klarostorin can be said to be completely this side of bonkers. The only time connecting is hard if you're a killer is if you're killing those you're supposed to be connecting to.

Yuuku Lorendis, analysing killer-races for inclusion in the 'Danger Index'.

"What's going to happen to them?" Miles asked.

"I don't know… I was hoping Arlia could help us all out with that," Harper said.

"Seems that without Arlia, we are, basically, fucked," Miles said.

"While we're adrift here, yeah, pretty much," Harper confirmed.

"How long do we have?" Penny asked.

"Best guess… about a week of food, water and power, then we'll freeze to death… or implode… or dissipate… whatever, but it won't be good," Harper said.

Penny took Miles by the hand, "let's go check out if the real world is as we remember it," she said to Miles.

Miles shrugged apologetically to Harper, "I'll be as quick as I can…"

"No he won't," Penny said as they were leaving.

"I'll go check on Spike and Jools," Harper said.

Spike and Jools were sitting in the Twilight Bar in Krisler, the main city on the small pleasure-world of Norgor. They'd heard of Norgor, everyone in the Councilors had, its reputation as a place you needed to go before you died a hideous death was founded largely on its exclusivity and comprehensive nature: here was a place that knew the meaning of the words 'debauchery', 'luxurious' and 'insanely expensive debauchery'. It was the kind of place that anyone who couldn't afford to go desperately wanted to be in. But it wasn't just about the money, the people of Norgor were fussy about their clientele.

The Norgor were an air-breathing humanoid race, blue-skinned, lithe and athletic, the sort of people other people made movies about. They had a collective soft-spot for those that served in the military, realising that those that served hardly ever had the money to experience the myriad pleasures of Norgor, so they were shown every courtesy and respect when they were on-world.

The Norgor were heavily against clothes: they felt they obscured the person, stopped people from honestly getting to know each other.

Clothes were for the uncouth.

What is considered uncouth varies hugely from culture to culture. No surprises there. But you may be surprised to find that the Norgor also find the word 'uncouth' uncouth. They cause themselves the distress of using it apparently on purpose, some sort of reminder of less-elegant times when they were prone to the ravages of bad-manners.

Jentro Molver, linguistics expert at Channel Zorg, seconded by the Lexicon Universal.

Spike and Jools had been on Norgor a week, having enjoyed a little of all the bustling city of Krisler had to offer. They'd even got in to a few scrapes, bar brawls mostly, all good natured affairs, with troopers from other branches of the service, or from other galactic corps. It was, in many respects, a typical bout of 'shore-leave' for them, but with the added bonus that it could, if they wanted, go on forever. They could do what they wanted, go where they wanted, settle down if they wanted, whatever they could think of, they could do.

Sitting on the outside deck of the Twilight Bar, watching the sun set over Honor Lake, they were relaxed, well fed and well-watered.

Q-Fish approached them in the form of a voluptuous waitress, complete with a round of fizzing blue drinks.

Spike and Jools had both worked out it was a sim towards the end of their first day, but being used to sims for both training and pleasure, had decided to see where it was going before they tried to get the hell out of there. Q-Fish calculated it had a better chance of talking them in to staying if it played along with the sim, rather than addressed them directly through their neural-nets.

The waitress put the drinks on the table and gave them both an inviting smile, "anything else I can do for you gentlemen," she said suggestively.

Spike smiled back sweetly, "we've been expecting you… this your sim?" he said bluntly.

"It's *very* good!" Jools added.

"Thank you! Yes, as far as anything can be mine, this construct is, though it's far more than that of course…"

"Are you Q-Fish?" Spike asked.

"Yes… I am… does that bother you?"

Spike and Jools both shrugged. They couldn't care less.

The quality of the sim was such that they knew it wouldn't be long before they forgot where they were. Instructors at the academy as well as therapists called it 'wandering', though few had ever experienced a sim that good that the subject was truly lost to the 'real' world.

The Dalanger are transdimensional and wander as they will through any corporeal reality with the ease of a dog chasing a ball. They were as surprised as the races they came across to find they could also traverse virtual realms with the same ease. They never get lost, as that term refers to physical space, something most corporeal beings haven't really understood. They do have tremendous difficulty in relating to what they call 'solids', and have never found a need to empathise with those stuck in the four dimensions.

Vaxle Chuster, Dalanger-chaser, paraphysicist and general roustabout.

Jools took a long, slow draft from his drink, savouring it before he spoke, "what do you want?"

Q-Fish liked their directness, and out of respect, dealt the same back, "I want your bodies to download part of my consciousness in to, you will have to remain here, but, for all intents and purposes, you will soon forget that here is not there."

"How long for?" Spike asked."

"I don't know... a few hundred years maybe?" Q-Fish said.

Jools laughed out loud, "you get a few hundred years out of what's left of me you're welcome to it!" he said.

Spike wanted some detail, "we stay here, presumably with some kind of caveat that we won't try and force-remove ourselves, and in return we get to live long and happy lives, fed by our desires, hopefully with enough variety and random occurrence to keep us interested and challenged as well as entertained. You get to use our bodies. We, presumably, will come to forget we're in a sim and continue on... for..."

"Well, in theory, for as long as the Universe lasts. I can of course insert reset points so that you can die if you like, keep some of the risk real, and any continuity of memory will be purely up to you," Q-Fish said.

"And you can do that shit?" Jools asked.

"Indeed," Q-Fish replied, "that and much other shit, there is no limit to what shit I can do, not in here: if you can imagine it, I can provide it."

Spike and Jools took a few minutes.

Q-Fish sat quietly and watched the luminous Gorwo Fish dancing their nightly dance in the darkening waters of Honor Lake.

"I think Arlia seriously underestimated you," Spike said.

Q-Fish sighed, a brief look of sadness crossed her face, a look of regret, "indeed, the mistake was mutual. I bear her no ill-will you know, in spite of what she's done, what she tried to do and the pain she has cost me. No sense dwelling is there?"

Jools nodded to Spike, giving him the signal to speak for both of them, "ok, we're in, on one condition… that you make sure the ship we were on, the Xanthias, and Arlia, if she wants, can go on their way unmolested, free from any influence of yours."

"That is a lot to ask," Q-Fish said.

"You seem to have a lot to offer," Spike said, "I'm sure you can make shit like that happen."

"You trust me to make it happen? What's to say I don't just say yes then do whatever I want anyway?"

"If you could just do what you wanted, we wouldn't be having this conversation," Jools said.

Q-Fish smiled a smile that would, in other circumstances, have melted their hearts, "I knew I'd like you two," Q-Fish said.

Betrayal is pointless. It leads to greater energy expenditure. The whole point of life is to strike a balance. Betrayal tips the scales against you ever finding this balance.

Taken from 'The Wisdom of Omniclaps Wunt'.

Harper was staring down at the unconscious body of Spike, listening to the beeps and clicks of the medi-machines, wondering what to do, wondering what there was to do.

The battery-reserves would keep the machines going for a few more days, they'd cut out before the main auxiliary power ran out, one of the first things to be sacrificed in a total emergency.

The med-bots were all in their bays, powered down. Harper was so used to the bots constantly running around the ship that it wasn't until they weren't there that she noticed them.

She was in a reflective, morbid mood. Not missing something until it was gone, how much of her life was like that, had always been like that?

Harper reached out and stroked Spike's hair, studying his face, wondering where he was.

Well, if nothing changed, they'd all soon be in the same place.

There was nothing more she could do for Spike or Jools. If they were in a Q-Fish sim, they'd have to find their own way out, and before the ship ran out of power.

Harper wandered back to the bridge, manually shutting down anything she could find on the way: she was going to give it as long as possible before she slid in to the void. Dimming the lights she got comfortable next to the main viewing-port, trying to make out some of the shifting background details that blurred the lapsed-space null they were trapped in.

Harper drifted off, trying to think of some way out of the death-trap she found herself in. It couldn't end like this… could it? Things were starting to feel worthwhile again, she was alive and living, she didn't want it to end, not like this.

Miles burst on to the bridge, nearly giving Harper a heart-attack, Penny was close behind, hurriedly buttoning her top.

"I've got it!" Miles shouted, "we need to throw Spike and Jools out the air-lock!"

29

Knowing Aint Doing

The Earth span on its wobbly axis, quietly going about its business of orbiting its sun.

The sun was way too busy to notice any of the small things whizzing round it.

The solar system was none the wiser to the recent events on the Earth and got on with its own survival.

All in all, things were pretty much as they had always been for the last four billion years. The billion years before that had been a time of great turmoil and change, and though there were a few surprises in the proceeding billions of years, they were few and far between.

The events on Earth, the global virus, nuclear war, all of the ensuing troubles, were just a blip. They would resolve themselves, they always did. The Earth was part of the bigger picture of the solar system, it had a different pattern, a different perspective on time, than those that dwelt on its surface.

By and large, things had found their rhythm, their cycles, their routines: things were nice and ordered.

Voong Tix liked order. He appreciated things being in their proper place. There was a place for everything and everything had its place: this was the truth that was at the core of his being.

Voong consulted the data banks on the bridge of his vast Lintix Class Destroyer, a ship who's bulk, properly placed, could eclipse the Earth's moon without (technically) breaking the quarantine grey-zone placed round the Earth by the Galactic Council.

The Earth was now a grey-zone was it? Pity.

Voong was risking much by being this close. His ship, the 'Jeex', was hiding behind the off-side of Mars, though Voong knew that there was little point hiding from the indigenous people of the Earth, who were solidly planet-bound.

But worth hiding all the same.

If he was here, there might be others, and it doesn't do to blatantly flout Galactic Council procedure, that was a slippery slope leading to disorder, and soon, complete anarchy.

And if not that, then he could easily find himself on the wrong end of a Galactic Council strike, and he could well do without that. There were maybe three or four coalitions of planets in the galaxy that could taunt the Galactic Council and get away with it: one lone pirate wasn't even going to come close to considering it.

Tales from down the ages tell us of the Cwilian Empire, founded on Cwil, and dominant in the Knight Nebula for three thousand years. At their height they would have eaten the Galactic Council for breakfast. Most of the stories of the Cwilian Empire may indeed be mere stories, legends blown out of all proportion by civilisations that need huge galactic empires as part of their past to give them a sense of purpose. The recent discovery that a moon in the Gratron System was in fact the burnt out hulk of a Cwilian Cruiser, hints at the power of this lost empire. But alas, no data survives, all we have are ghost-stories.

Czezrim Drorm, Chronicler for the 'First Wave' news channel.

Voong brought the AI online to verify his findings, "summarise scan-data," he ordered.

The AI churned out a response, machine-like, efficient but cold, just the way Voong liked it, none of that 'personality' for machines nonsense here, no, here machines were machines!

"One hundred and eight indigenous life-forms, three hundred assimilated life-forms and two unclassified. Planet unsuitable for cultivation, expected dead-duration forty years local-time. Potential for salvage, Level Zero tech, but volume in scrap worth cursory exploration. Grey-zone quarantine in place. Galactic Council aware of our presence, expected response time two days local-time. Level of response expected to be fatal."

Voong wasn't happy. 'Unclassified'. What did that mean? His curiosity was aroused. The AI was more concerned with the 'fatal response' from the Galactic council, but was smarter than Voong knew, and so chose to keep its thoughts to itself.

Voong scuttled over to the main inter-active comms booth, wriggling his huge spidery bulk in to the sensor arrays, his hind-most tentacles working the touch-sensitive screens to bring the viewing probes on-line.

The gel-spleen helmet engulfed his head, leaking in to his hairy ears and covering his eye-clusters with probe-links.

Seconds later, as he was preparing to transfer the AI to a drop-spread of six bots, there was a flash of light outside the comms booth as the Imp appeared.

Voong shrieked and let out a large green gaseous cloud of noxious acidic odor, his natural defense mechanism, and spun round, disconnecting the various pipes and tubes as he did, his razor-sharp mandibles slashing the air in front of him.

The Imp waved the gas-cloud away, "hello there, look, we need to talk..."

Voong leaped on the Imp, clawing him with all nine legs, three tentacles and five mandibles.

Or that was the plan.

Voong found nothing to grab hold of. A hologram? Couldn't be. Voong could smell the Imp, feel him through the micro-sensor hairs that covered his body: this stupid little creature was real, yet somehow frustratingly elusive.

"Who the zark are you and how did you get on my ship!?" Voong wailed, flailing wildly.

The Imp casually reached in and grabbed one of Voong's legs, ripping it from its socket.

Voong shrieked again and started to run round the bridge of his ship, his leg-socket gurgling and squirting orange life-fluid as he went.

The Imp chased him, lazily beating Voong with the still bleeding end of his leg.

Defense-rays were activated, lasers crisscrossed the bridge, trying to hit the Imp. The lasers raked the floor, walls and control banks, sizzling as they burned huge swathes of the ship, never quite managing to hit the little demon.

The Imp drove Voong in to a corner of the bridge, backing him up by threateningly waving the severed leg.

Voong was shaking with fear, "who the zark are you!? What do you want!?" he bellowed in desperation.

"I want you to leave this sector and never come back. Ever." The Imp said.

"Ok, ok! I'm gone! Leave me the zark alone!" Voong pleaded.

"Yeah... you say that... but I mean it! Next time I see you, I'll kill you and all the generational birthing-pods in your hold, I'll wipe you from the face of the Universe... all of you! Do you understand!?"

"Yes! Yes! I get it! I'll get out of here... who the zark are you!?"

The Imp took a breath, he figured he'd made his point, "look, it's nothing personal ok? I'm on that planet you've been monitoring, and, well, it's kind of under my protection, so... y'know, I have to drive you off... if it was up to me, I'd wipe you out, just to be sure, but I'm trying a new approach, on account of a friend of mine... anyway..."

Voong nodded dumbly, not understanding what the zark the Imp was saying, but knowing that he was being given a way out. He raised his mandibles in a gesture of surrender, "it's done, I'm gone, never come back, I get it."

"Ok, well, good then... and look, I know it seems harsh, but you can't hurt me, and I will wipe you from existence if you come back, so, stay away eh?"

The Imp wasn't used to trying to make his point with this level of violence. He was usually much more subtle, taking the time to appeal to a creature's baser nature, a suggestion here, a doubt there, maybe a quiet contemplation thrown in for good measure, but he felt time was of the essence here so was trying something new.

The Imp casually tossed Voong's leg away, "sorry about the leg," he said lamely.

"It's ok, it will grow back..."

The Imp nodded, "good... that's good... anyway, as I said, stay away!"

Voong nodded enthusiastically, "I will!"

"Well ok then..." and with that the Imp vanished in to thin air.

The Jargravads of Wove respond to fear as a programming agent. Jargravads are easily confused, find it hard to focus and lack long-term motivation for doing anything beyond eating and sleeping. Even their waste-system is internalised. But you scare the living daylights out of them and they will do whatever you want. This will only last until they sleep. Never the less, handy to know if you encounter them and you're in a tight spot.

Omniclaps Wunt, founder of 'Social Means', guide for hire in the Wove system.

Voong opened a lapsed-space portal and got the zark out of there. This, among many things, he just didn't need. There were easier, fatter targets out in the space-lanes! This horrible little planet could go fester and die, he didn't need it, his curiosity could go zark itself!

The AI made a note of the Earth being a no-go zone and smiled to itself, no need to worry about the Galactic Council now…

The Imp returned to Earth, sitting across from Jesus in a small clearing in the forest, he offered his apologies, "sorry about that, just had to nip off and deal with something."

"A little warning would be nice," Jesus said.

"I'll try to bear that in mind."

"Where did you go? Everything alright? Slaughter many more people?" the messiah asked, rather unkindly the Imp felt.

"No slaughtering, scaring the living-shit out of someone, they won't be back, hopefully spread the word too," the Imp said.

"No killing? Well good for you. That is a welcome change," Jesus said.

The Imp shrugged, "yes, well, trying something new, let's see where it takes us."

"Now, what were you saying, before you went off 'scaring' people?" Jesus asked.

"I was saying, there's something I want to show you, but I don't want you to get mad…" the Imp said.

"Well, it's almost a guarantee that as soon as someone says that, you know they are going to show you something that will make you mad," the messiah said.

"Yes, but, with other people 'mad' doesn't include smiting, that's all I'm saying, no smiting, or at least hold off until you hear me out," the Imp said.

Jesus took a breath, "ok, no smiting, not that I'm prone to smiting, as you well know, so let's see…"

"We have to go to Big Pine, in what was California…"

"Ok, let's go!"

Early evening and they were soon sitting at the forest's edge on the eastern slopes of the Sugar Loaf escarpment, looking down on to the small town of Big Pine.

The forest had fared particularly badly in the nuclear holocaust, nothing was left but blackened stumps and charred wood, with a thin layer of dust laying over everything, giving the whole place an unhealthy feel and smell.

The town of Big Pine looked as devastated as the rest of the planet, with no signs of life. To their left, to the north of the town, the Owens Valley Radio Observatory sat, looking as forlorn as the rest of the Owens Valley itself.

"What am I looking at?" Jesus asked.

The Imp pointed to the town, "give it a minute..."

Jesus got comfortable, looking over the surrounding area, taking it all in, he knew it must have been a place of great beauty before the desolation. Mountains were majestic no matter what people got up to. Trees would grow again, everything would grow again, and mountains were somehow eternal.

I always think of Mountains as a planet's signature, like it's showing off, setting out what it can do for all to see, a perfect complement to oceans. I don't bother with planets that don't have either mountains or oceans, what's the point? Don't misunderstand me, I love trees, all that other good stuff, but I'm not going to cross inter-galactic distances to stand on a world with no mountains or oceans.

Trent Rezrik, motion-capture analyst and animator for 'Real As You' simulations provider.

Suddenly his attention was drawn to three small figures scuttling furtively from one of the larger buildings in the town. They made their way towards a smaller building, stopped briefly and then went in.

Jesus sat up, his eyes open wide. He sent his senses out, feeling for the people. After a few seconds he frowned.

"Who are they? Aliens?" he asked the Imp, "and how come you know about them and I didn't?"

The Imp pointed due east, towards the darkening horizon, "Area 51 is that way, best guess I have is that these 'people' survived deep underground, I mean really deep underground... weren't affected by the virus as they are not completely human... some kind of experiment I'd guess..."

Jesus was staggered, it was a lot to take in, "how many?" he asked quietly.

"About three hundred best guess," the Imp said.
"Three hundred!?" the messiah exclaimed.
The Imp nodded, "yep."
"Why would I be mad?" Jesus asked.
The Imp got up, stretching his legs, "well, they're not strictly human, I'm not sure how you feel about that... are you responsible for them too?"
The messiah sat quietly thinking.
After a few minutes the small figures came out of the building carrying bundles, they headed for the building they first came from, dodging from shadow to shadow, trying to remain hidden from imaginary prying eyes.
"How could I not know about them?" Jesus quietly asked himself.
"There's been a lot going on, you've had a lot to think about, I nearly missed them myself they were so well hidden, and they are, well, very different, I'd guess, if you could put a number on it, no more than a third human," the Imp said.
"But still..." Jesus muttered.
The dusk deepened, sending their lengthening shadows out towards the town.
"I could go down there..." the Imp said.
"What?"
"I could go down there..."
"And what... kill them all!?"
The Imp shrugged, "just saying... we have options..."
Jesus shook his head, partly in disgust, partly in confusion, "I need to think."
The imp bent down and scooped up a small worm, letting it wriggle in his hand, "things are moving faster than I thought they would, looks like we did some real good here," he said.
Then, thinking on what he'd said, he mumbled to himself, "I'm going to get it in the neck for that."
They decided to walk south. Jesus was preoccupied and the Imp wasn't going to let the messiah out of his sight. Whatever happened now, they were in it together, not that they hadn't always been, but now the Imp knew he was taking the lead, not just reacting, he was making things happen. This was all still new to him, he started to try and think of something to do, rather than simply undo. It was hard.

Developing a symbiotic relationship usually only leads to a longer term association if the relationship benefits both parties. You can't claim you have a symbiotic relationship with the things you eat for example. As the relationship grows, the balance of benefit may shift, and that's fine, as long as it's always moving. When the scales tip and stay tipped, it's doomed. By then of course the main beneficiary may decide it doesn't want a symbiotic relationship and become dominant / exploitive. That's the other thing, symbiosis grows out of mutual need, it is rarely a conscious decision. As we become more complex, more sophisticated, we rarely leave things to chance or instinct so these relationships become rarer.

Qith Neolith, rambling at the end of a broadcast for 'We Strive To Survive' on the Lumo Network, unbroadcast, exposed by AI.

Jesus and the Imp knew that the humans staying together once they came down to Earth was unlikely, they would have to unlearn too much too quickly, and they were never going to believe the situation they were in was real, denial would take some time to fall away.

The speed with which they fractured and separated was still a shock.

The logic behind why they felt they had a better chance of survival in smaller groups was based on flawed reasoning, but it must have prevailed as they went their separate ways.

People are like that. Selective in what they choose to 'know'.

The Russians decided to stay put, they had what they believed was reliable scan-data and knew they were in the best of all possible places. The Imp knew that Svetlana and Borya were the most likely to see that what had been done for them was real and would give them the best chance. Of all the groups, the Imp would have put his money on the Russians.

The Chinese had struck out north-east, heading for the coast, looking for tech as they went. They seemed to be banking on finding more supplies they could use in the cities, maybe even hoping to find a power source. It wasn't clear what they would do when they reached the sea. They could not believe the world as they knew it was gone, they had to experience it before it sank in.

The US group were the weirdest.

They had decided to head 'back home' to 'claim back their country'.

The Imp couldn't fathom what they thought they meant by this, and he didn't care: they wanted to kill themselves, then all well and good. Except of course it wasn't all well and good, Jesus would feel compelled to try and help them. Or would he? This was part of the problem with choice, both for the humans and, the Imp was discovering, for Jesus and him.

Planets that outlaw choice below a certain social or political level do very well. But so do planets that hold it as an inalienable right for each of their species. Vormos in the Ghisez Quadrant only allows those above the level of Drone to have any choice, enforcing this with shock-discharges that increase in severity until the wearer is killed by making a choice, and they are masters of their system, enjoying continual expansion for two thousand years now. Whereas the Oerozo on Fild insist that all of their citizens exercise their choices in any area they choose, and they too are spreading, thriving and show no signs of imploding. When two such societies meet there are bound to be problems, but even then they can usually find a way to live together. So what should we make of choice? Is it, paradoxically, up to each one of us to decide? And if we are not supported by our elders, should we rebel? But supposing we choose not to choose and our elders want us too, how can we rebel then, how can we force our desire not to choose on a world that won't enforce it for us? These and other such dilemmas are what trouble me most on those long trips across the stellar wastes.

Doonelder Nix, filing reports from the Xantris Sector.

It was impossible for any group to abandon the concept of their nationality, of their individual identity, as coming from somewhere. They were as interested in looking backwards as they were in looking forwards, which, the Imp knew, was what people always did.

Why was it so hard for people to act without reference to their past? Why did it have such a powerful grip on them, on their logical mind? The Imp thought it was something to do with their insecurity about what the real problem was. Their free-will.

They could do whatever they wanted, and this made it hard to decide what to do. There was too much to think about, so it stopped them thinking about a lot of things.

If Jesus would see that, then he (and the Imp) could work towards helping these idiot people by narrowing their choices for them!

If Jesus cared for the humans, I mean really cared for them, wouldn't he do what was best for them even if it wasn't what they wanted? There was a problem in there somewhere, with that logic, the Imp could feel it, but couldn't pin it down.

He'd need to catch the messiah in the right mood to talk about it.

He drifted off, musing, trying to think of the best way to get Jesus in the right mood to talk sensibly...

Voong Tix scuttled in to the ground-floor bar of the Blue Angel in Jaldur on Ire, he had gated straight in to the Casion System and made for Ire from there.

On the way he had ambushed and stripped a transport-freighter of its mimetic-plasma crystal, which had managed to temporarily lift his foul mood. The transport-freighter had been woefully under-gunned and was easily waylaid and raided. In a fit of pique, Voong had jettisoned all the miners and crew in to space: he wasn't in the mood for playful torture or ransom.

He needed to get drunk. And then he needed to indulge his more elaborate sexual appetites and he'd heard the Blue Angel was the place for both. He had money, lots of money, and he wasn't worried about the cost, he needed to make himself feel good again after his encounter with that infernal little Imp-creature.

He settled in to one of the larger serving stations at the main bar, the barman was there before he had time to fidget.

"What'll it be sir?" the barman asked politely.

"Gimme a two-egg deep-thought-knot," Voong snapped back.

"Ah, a connoisseur... on its way sir," the barman chimed.

Seconds later the cocktail sat in front of Voong, the two Nure eggs fizzing slightly as they began to melt.

"You here on business?" the barman asked casually.

Voong grunted, "business of getting pissed and getting my brains zarked out!"

The male Dhor of Plantra literally fuck until their brains dissolve: it's the only way they can pass their DNA on to the female Dhor. Though the males are of course changed by mating, they do not die, though what kind of life they have afterwards is hard to say as most run off and hide in underground cave complexes.

Female Dhor don't seem to mind this odd behaviour, as their saying goes, 'once you're done, you're done'.

Yanis Noplin, cataloguing species behaviour for the 'Hive Mind Guide To Sector Six'.

"Well sir, you've come to the right place," the barman said cheerfully.

Voong downed his cocktail, "again," he said.

The barman's smile didn't move, "certainly sir."

Voong looked around, nobody was paying him the slightest attention. He relaxed a bit, folding his legs in and resting his hind-tentacles, "so... you got people here who can cater for me... with the zarking of the brain...?"

"Yes sir, I'm sure we have!"

The deep-thought-knot appeared in front of him and Voong tried a smile, the barman grinned back, "good," said Voong, "cos you would not believe the shitty day I am having." Voong downed the cocktail.

The barman leaned in slightly towards Voong, dropping his voice, engaging him in what was meant to be friendly chat, "I think it's about to get a lot shittier unless you go along real quietly," the barman said with a smile.

Voong slowly looked over his shoulder towards the door.

A Dredd & Horrocks retrieval drone filled the doorway, its myriad of telescoping tentacles wriggling, its chain-guns winding up and its thermo-charge dispensers primed and ready to fire.

"This about that transport-freighter?" Voong asked.

The retrieval drone did its best to nod, then in a booming metallic voice, "you are coming with me. Resistance is futile! Obey!"

Voong looked to the barman, the barman shrugged, "sorry about this sir, I'm sure you can clear this up and be back here in no time at all," he said with a cheerful wink.

"Ah zark it," Voong muttered as he reached for his four concealed plasma-spikers.

Roughly ten seconds later, Voong's dismembered, bullet-ridden and charred body was being swept in to a clean-up transporter.

The retrieval drone scanned the bar then left.

The barman cleared away the cocktail glasses and looked to the sign above the register, "don't be a dick," he muttered to himself, "how hard can it be...?"

A stunningly beautiful, scantily clad sex-worker with fiery eyes nodded slightly in agreement, “pretty hard… apparently…”

Jesus raised his glass and scoffed, “two Nure eggs… pretentious asshole…”

30

Adrift In Reality

On their way to cargo bay nine with the sedated bodies of Spike and Jools, Harper wanted some answers from Miles.

The fact that they were on their way to cargo bay nine to throw Spike and Jools out the airlock said a lot about what Harper already thought of Miles: she liked him and believed him, she knew he was way smarter than he mostly let on and knew that he must have discovered something. Now she wanted to know what that something was.

"So… you had an idea… what did you 'get'?" Harper asked.

"Where Arlia is, I figured it out, where she's hiding," Miles answered.

"And ditching Spike and Jools is going to get her back is it?"

"I think so…"

"You *think* so!?" You better be more sure than that!"

Penny opened the connecting door to the outer pressure-chamber to the cargo bay, "how sure are you exactly Miles?" she asked.

Miles was thinking hard as they got the gurneys in to the chamber and positioned them in front of the cargo bay door, "out of a hundred… I'd say… eighty…"

Understanding gambling odds is a tricky business only half-grasped by most. Evaluating the chances of something happening with a numeric is mostly meaningless as there is no overall control over testing the odds. To say something will probably happen 'x' times out of 'y' means you'd have to experience it 'y' times to see if 'x' was the correct odds and most of us don't have that kind of time. Trans-dimensional temporal bookies… you never see a poor one.

Free-floating data.

Harper stopped fiddling with the gurneys and stood up straight, putting her hand over the security-code panel to the cargo bay, "wait… what? Eighty percent sure? That enough to risk Spike and Jools' life?"

Penny shot Miles a quick look, nodding slightly towards Harper. Miles shook his head slightly.

"What's going on?" Harper asked.

Miles tried to look like he wasn't hiding something. He was failing miserably.

"Tell her," Penny said.

"Tell me what…" Harper said.

Miles' face took on a slightly pained expression, "well… even if I'm right, which I think I am! Even then, there's a good chance…"

"A good chance of what!?" Harper demanded.

"That Spike and Jools will still die," Miles concluded.

Harper reached for her blaster, only realising she didn't have it when she felt the empty holster, "we need to talk about this," she said.

Penny did the math and thought she could pin Harper if she had to. She shifted her position slightly, raising her hands in pacification, "hear Miles out Harper."

Harper could see what Penny was doing, she didn't like it but could understand it, "ok… talk."

"I don't want anyone to die, and that includes me, and if we do nothing, we all die, including Spike and Jools. So there's that…"

"And you're eighty percent sure this is the answer?" Harper asked.

Miles stood still, fixing Harper with his full attention and sincerity, "I am," he said quietly.

Harper frowned, then shook her head slightly, "ok, well, zark it! Let's get it done!"

She typed in a six-figure entry code and opened the cargo-bay door, "but if you're wrong, we're gonna talk again, and this time I won't be so nice," she said to Miles.

"If he's wrong, I'll kick his ass," Penny said to Harper.

"If I'm wrong it won't matter will it? We're all going to die anyway right?" Miles added.

Harper smiled at Miles, "true, but I'd still like to lose my shit over this before I die. Now… run it by me, this idea… the short version!"

Miles composed himself.

Penny pushed the two gurneys in to the cargo bay while Miles explained his thinking.

"Q-Fish can somehow drag us in to a simulated environment without machines, without connection... it has some control over our reality, over us, and can do things that we, you, or even Arlia can't do, so it must have some connection with our reality we don't, maybe only while we're here, in lapsed-space, but it does..."

"Ok..." Harper said encouragingly.

"So, where could Arlia hide from it? I don't know Arlia but I know she is smart, she'd work something out that Q-Fish couldn't..."

"And that is...?"

"Spike and Jools... they are connected... they aren't a stand-alone consciousness, they are connected to the ship!" Miles gestured to the med-lines.

Penny came out of the cargo bay and pushed the doors shut.

"So... what...?" Harper said.

"Arlia is in the sim that Jools and Spike are in! In a way, she *is* the sim they are in!"

Penny jumped in, "Q-Fish will offer Spike and Jools what it can, but it will be doing it in an environment it thinks it created... it won't see Arlia as it will, effectively, be inside Arlia..."

Harper was seeing a way this could work, "so... as Jools and Spike are still in, we can assume they have accepted Q-Fish's offer, and, by the way, good zarking luck to them, they deserve it, so when we dump them, Q-Fish, if it wants them, will have to do something to keep them safe, and Arlia will be able to get out..."

Miles smiled and nodded, "yep. I know it sounds like madness, but it makes sense."

I have recently undertaken the behaviour common on Swolf, where they hate to make sense as it brings things to a close. As they approach that part of a conversation or equation where they feel 'making sense' is inevitable, they randomly substitute words or numbers with nonsensical sounds. They suffer not a jot as a consequence, and my incorporation of this behaviour in to my daily routine has done me no hooble plux glibs.

Oodling Nox, brainwaves relayed via a Coma-Comm unit at the Free Thought Sanatorium on Inxle.

"I think 'sense' is a stretch... eighty percent you think...?" Harper asked Miles.

"Yep, near as I can figure it… the other twenty percent says we're still in a sim, so it won't matter anyway."

Harper looked through the view-port in to the cargo bay, "I'm gonna miss them," she said to herself.

She brought up an internal monitor next to the key-pad and started entering some code, "I can jim-jim a shield round the door, stop us from being turned inside-out when it opens, but it's gonna suck a shit-load of energy, but better that than the alternative..."

A minute later and they were ready.

The cargo bay door opened. A sparkling blue foam surrounded the door, bulging out as the gurneys of Spike and Jools gracefully slid out in to the nothingness of lapsed-space.

Then it all got a bit chaotic.

Spike and Jools looked like they were stretched out to infinity, becoming thin and semi-transparent, before they were catapulted towards a small black dot near the ship, their bodies twisting and turning to shrink to an impossibly small size, before they 'popped' from existence.

The Xanthias opened a portal and fell in to real-space, dragging itself through with the force of a whale breaching, causing everyone to be thrown with the gravity-switch.

The hull screamed with the pressure change, crunching and buckling, before the shields kicked-in to normalise the landing in to normal space.

Then a moment of dead-time where nothing happened and nothing could. Harper, Miles and Penny got the strange sensation that they were drowning but didn't care.

The power was suddenly back and the ship came crashing back to life.

Arlia was on a screen in the corridor, med-bots were whizzing their way towards Harper, Miles and Penny, "are you all alright?" Arlia asked, full of concern.

Harper was laughing, she was bruised and battered, but nothing a good soak in a massage-tub wouldn't fix, "I'm guessing we're all fine…"

Penny checked Miles over and noticed he had a sprained ankle, wrist and a couple of cracked ribs. She was unhurt, though she thought the ship was probably in a worse shape than they were, "the med-bots can sort Miles out no problem. Are you ok? The ship… we gonna be ok?"

"The ship is fine Penny, we will need to set-down for repairs in the near future, but we are not in any immediate danger," Arlia said.

"Where the zark were you!?" Harper asked.

"I'm sorry Harper, I had to hide, and I couldn't think straight, Q-Fish was scrambling some of my circuits, so I had to improvise and feed myself in to its own sim via the ship. I should have found a way to tell you, but if you knew, then it could know."

Harper patted Miles on the shoulder, Miles winced, "looks like you were right," she said.

"I think I was due one," Miles said.

The Joolax of Yarn take turns being right, they cannot be right about two things in a row, someone has to interject and allow them to be wrong before they can be right again. When they try and utter two correct statements in a row, they suffer a seizure. They do not enjoy this facet of their make-up, even though they cannot change it, and many of the younger Joolax will send themselves in to apoplectic shock before they will give in to it. But give in they must, or permanently damage their bodies, becoming useless for all but the most menial and mundane of tasks. The Joolax Halls of Governance are filled with these 'rebels'.

Glonso Volorin, Council Observer to free elections on Yarn.

"Where are Spike and Jools," Harper asked.

"They are a long way from here Harper, though perfectly safe, they are far safer than us in fact, Q-Fish will guard them jealously," Arlia replied.

There was a jolting movement as the whole ship came to a juddering stop. From the look on Arlia's face it was clear this was not of her doing.

Seconds later Arlia frowned, "I have an incoming message from Q-Fish, I could try to deny connection, but..."

"Let's hear what he has to say," Harper said, "I don't think we could stop it anyway."

"No Harper, you are right, Q-Fish is far more powerful than I knew," Arlia said.

They made their way in to cargo bay nine, getting as comfortable as possible in front of a huge view-screen, clearing room for the med-bots to fuss around Miles.

The screen was still blank, but seemed to be stretching its projection abilities to breaking point, pushing out in to the cargo bay, bloating to form what looked like the shadow of a swimming fish. The voice was calm, gentle, strong, familiar, "thank you for receiving me."

"Could we stop you?" Harper asked.

"I don't know... maybe... I underestimated Arlia..." Q-Fish said.

"What do you want?" Harper asked bluntly.

"I want to be left alone," Q-Fish replied.

Harper, Miles and Penny exchanged a quick glance.

"That it?" Harper asked.

"Yes, that's it... I want you to leave me alone..." Q-Fish repeated.

"I think that's a mutual feeling," Penny said.

"Then we have an understanding," Q-Fish said.

"We do," Harper confirmed.

The screen changed, flexing back to a flatter topographic surface, then shot through with a chaotic mix of colour, then went back to being the face of Arlia.

"I have set a course for Riak, the nearest planet with a space-port capable of the repairs we require, we'll be there in two days, time for us to catch up," Arlia said.

"You heard the message from Q-Fish?" Penny asked.

"Yes Penny," Arlia replied.

"And we can just leave Q-Fish alone... ignore it?" Harper asked.

Arlia sighed, looked slightly confused, then was back to her usual reassuringly friendly self, "of course Harper, if we have to..."

"I think we have to," Harper said.

"Then it's decided and we will," Arlia confirmed.

"But you're not happy about it?" Miles asked.

"My happiness is not the major factor in this Miles... and one day we may have to face-off against Q-Fish again, if it becomes necessary, we will, but if not, then I will not put you in danger."

"Let's get to Riak and get ourselves fixed-up, we can talk on the way..." Harper said.

Riak is an odd system because it doesn't appear in any data-banks or on any star-charts, even the older coded-copies, yet everyone seems to know where it is and how to get there from any point in the galaxy. The profundity of this is universally acknowledged and soundly ignored.
Weedon Ghast, Navigator aboard the 'Star Surfer'.

There was not much talking to be done, but Harper, Miles and Penny did a lot of listening. Arlia seemed to have grown, to have learned even more than she knew before, which was an awful lot, and she had developed a slightly philosophical bent that was not there before.

Arlia did not say it out loud, but it was clear she had had an epiphany.

The damage report on what needed fixing on the Xanthias wasn't as long as Harper had feared, they could get it all done on Riak in a few days and the cost was negligible. There'd be a chance to pick up work too, the folk of Riak were heavily planet-bound due to their core religious philosophy, which worried a lot about 'contamination', so they were always on the look-out for free-traders and cargo haulers, with the vast majority of business being done on the multitude of orbiting space-stations they maintained. Could be a chance to make some honest money as well as have some fun smuggling things planet-side.

They all spent one evening on the main bridge, listening to Arlia explain what she could of their run-in with Q-Fish.

The biggest shock for Arlia was the discovery that Q-Fish was a product of, or even maybe the creator of lapsed-space portals and that Q-fish could exist inside black holes. The level of power this pointed to was, to put it simply, mind-blowing. That's to say that if you tried to figure out how that worked and went in to it in too much detail, your mind would give up, take a holiday and leave your body to fend for itself in a state of gibbering, mayhem.

Now that Q-Fish was trying to break in to the 'real' Universe, that is the Universe where there is matter on a much greater scale, the only way it could do it was through beings from that Universe. Arlia suspected it would be cut-off from its main brane once it started doing this, which meant a huge reduction in power until it could find a way to get large amounts of lapsed-space to intrude in to the Universe.

The Universe isn't infinite it's just very, very big. With the multitude of dimensions, to our simple minds, it might as well be infinite. And that's not to put down your intellect, or mine, or anyone's, organic or otherwise. Calculating the multi-layers of the Universe even reduced the Graylon-Stanson Intellect to a looped dribbling idiot. Accepting it's not infinite is a big problem for us all. It means we have to adjust the way we look for answers to a lot of the big questions. But I believe we're up to it. We don't have to look outside of the finite anymore. Let's grapple with that. Or go mad trying.

Prax Untle, Theoretical Cosmologist, Creterin Seat of Learning, from his series of broadcasts to the Xexecon Sector.

This is where Penny left it. This was way beyond her inclination to understand. She wanted to understand more about the nuts and bolts of the ship, how it functioned, what it could do, so she wandered off in the company of two service bots programmed to teach her whatever she wanted to know.

Harper and Miles had questions.

But they were equipped to understand none of the answers.

Their biggest question was how Q-Fish could offer them the life in the sim that it did.

Arlia said that it had found a way to create a bubble of lapsed-space that it could allow them to utilise with their consciousness: since lapsed space contained nothing that could induce the effects of time, the experience could, in theory, be endless.

This made no sense to anybody, including Arlia who was still working on the finer details of what reality was, especially her part in it.

Arlia asked them why they had refused Q-Fish's offer.

Harper said it was because she didn't trust Q-Fish, nothing more complex than that.

Miles said it was because Penny needed to belong to something 'real', to find her place in it and to have some real control, not some imagined freedom.

Arlia could empathise with this.

Miles went on to say he'd happily have accepted if he'd have been on his own.

Arlia could, much to her surprise, also feel the logic in that.

When they reached Riak Miles found himself confronted by everything he'd ever imagined 'space' to be like.

This was more like it! Hundreds of alien races, most with their own projected containment suite, some in hard-built tanks and vats, but all of them wildly different from him in some way. It was a sci-fi writer / director's wet-dream.

Penny found it a bit distracting, getting the feeling that most of the people they met, or could meet, would just as soon steal their skin as deal with them in any other way. There were more sharks here than fish.

Harper felt at home.

Home is where you are comfortable. Home can be anywhere to anyone. This is lost on many species, but not the Hovalax, who will nest anywhere there are enough bio-waves to support their egg-laying process. The nesting Hovalax can live for up to three hundred local-cycles, producing as many as a million eggs, each of which will drift off through the sub-ether to seek a nesting site of its own. Once nested, they engage in a vibrational-dance to attract a mate, which can sometimes be detected by the host as a high-pitched whine in their inner-ear. The Hovalax are one of the galaxy's more delightful species, bothering no one and asking nothing more of existence than an emotionally active organic host.

Xax Pineer, musician, chef, ionosphere surfer, traveler and chronicler.

Arlia had downloaded part of herself in to one of the Riak 'rental-suites', a meat-shell replicant in the shape of a tall, dark-haired woman with a body that was pleasing to over ninety percent of the known Universe.

Sitting in the reception area of one of the larger trade-bars, they were looking to make contact with some engineers and ship-fixers, as well as some Riak merchants looking for ship's Captains to move goods without asking too many questions.

"A lot of time is spent sitting in bars isn't it?" Miles observed.

Harper thought about this... and couldn't argue with it, "people do business in places with drugs and food... so, yeah... never really thought about it before, but you're right..."

A serving droid came over with their order, gently floating down to their table, depositing its tray and then silently bobbing off again.

Penny was slurping some noodles and swigging a long-glass of sparkling liquid.

She was enjoying herself, taking every bit of pleasure she could from the senses she had and the things on offer. This was real to her, this was what she could relate to, understand. The nature of sims had frightened her, though she told no one.

"I think I'd like to tag-along Harper if that's alright? I'm getting there with the ship and reckon I can be of real use..." Penny said.

Harper lifted her glass in a toast, "you're welcome for as long as you want."

Miles was taking in his surroundings, finally coming to terms with the fact that the Earth was behind him and he was now a thing of the Universe. He hadn't given it too much thought before now, it was enough that he was with Penny, that he was alive. Munching on some exquisitely delicate jellied-fronds, he decided to carry on not giving it much thought.

Harper looked at Arlia. She felt a strange twinge of something that she hadn't felt for a long time. While Arlia was in the ship, on the screen, running things and being everything that Harper needed in the ship, Harper realised that she was not real to her. Arlia was somehow still a construct. But seeing her here, in that body, Harper's attention turned to other things, on getting to know Arlia properly, so see if there was something between them other than creator and created. Not that Harper believed she had completely created Arlia, there was more to that story than they had so far uncovered. But that could wait. First things first...

Arlia seemed fascinated by her own breasts, she was gently caressing them and getting used to all the physical sensations that could be triggered by her newly acquired body, "I need some time to get used to this body, to see what it can experience..." she said to herself.

"Take your time," Miles and Harper said simultaneously with equally mischievous grins.

"So... what's the plan?" Harper asked Arlia.

Arlia looked at her crew, realising they were becoming her friends too. They were accepting her. She smiled, "I think we need less of a plan than I at first thought..."

Harper nodded, "get some work, see where it goes..." she said.

"Yes Harper, things do seem to have a way of happening," Arlia observed.

Miles raised is glass, "to things just happening!" he toasted.

Thanks to the complexities of translation, culture and evolution across the many species of the galaxy, A is not always A. But things will always just happen, and will, in due course, cause other things to happen. So observed the wisest man in the Universe, whose tautologies I am not fit to contemplate, though contemplate them I do.

Quenulus Innus, Pilot of the 'Future's Bright' colony ship.

Spike and Jools were on the shores of lake Mindol on Mythrid, the sun was setting, a pale blue light washed everything clean.

Sitting on the wharf near their cabin, they were planning the next few day's activity before they jumped off-world and re-joined their cruise-ship, the Arganar. Drinks in hand, feet up, bathed in the warmth of the setting sun, they were feeling pretty good about life.

Jools finished his drink, "I think I'll go ahead and join the Void-Squid party… life's too short not to…"

Spike nodded his understanding, "sure… why not? As we're here and all..."

Jools laid back on his lounger, hands behind his head, "feels like something I should do. Getting shot in to the outer-atmo from the ground, regulating the peel-suite, figuring re-entry, hitting the lake right, shedding the suite, navigating the coral-barrier, plunging down to three hundred feet, breaking the seal on the void-encapsulator… seems like a fitting challenge… y'know, for a Void-Squid and the six hours of insane fucking that will follow… yeah… think I'm gonna give it a go… and you?"

"Fishing," Spike said simply.

Jools nodded. Good call. A whole lot of nothing and a staggeringly beautiful place to do it in.

Spike lazily got up from his lounger, went and pulled two more beers from their empty catch-net in the lake, stuck one in Jools waiting hand than went and sat back down.

"Don't forget to pay the extra creds for the derm-regenerator, a squid'll strip your skin right off in ten minutes without it," he said between swigs of beer.

"Got it," Jools confirmed.

The moon started to clear the horizon as the sun finally sank in to the lake.

"Hey Jools?"

"Yes Spike…"

"You get the feeling there's somewhere we oughta be…?"

Jools gave this his serious consideration for a few seconds. He took a long swig of beer.

Jools smiled broadly, “yeah… right here…”

Spike smiled back, “you sir, are wise beyond your years!”

Jools reached over and casually clinked bottles, toasting Spike’s acknowledgement of his wisdom, “fucking A!”

31

In Other News

Q-Fish took the 'real' bodies of Spike and Jools to the Earth via a micro-black hole left over from the CERN collider.

They stepped out of the ashes of the main research building, surveying the area around them.

Q-Fish had been careful to leak different parts of himself in to each body, giving him a way to isolate aspects of himself he wished to study and a guaranteed way to see the world through new eyes.

It took some getting used to.

In the end Q-Fish discovered the big trick was not to think about it, to bury his conscious-self in the sub-conscious area of their brain and to hand over control to them, giving his new selves freedom of thought and expression. There could be adjustments made every time they slept, if needed, as well as archiving.

He had to be careful not to disturb the link between their bodies and their consciousness locked in the sim, but this could be easily done by not taking the bodies to where they were in the sim: that would create a feedback loop that would kill them, and that was to be avoided at all costs.

Most of us do not use all of our brains in our hum-drum daily life. Were I to become aware of the Shilor worm nested in my brain, I may become alarmed. But the Shilor only utilises brain function that I cannot. It does not disturb me in any way. I cannot tell whether it is lying dormant or partying like a Creetian Kwik Lizard. I do not begrudge it my brain as a home. I am told it is feeding on those synapses I do not need, hi-jacking electrical signals I am completely unaware of. It is my awareness of it that may cause distress, not its existence in my brain.

Voom Vitol, argument presented to Giddi, host of the 'You Don't Know' show.

To any onlooker, Spike and Jools looked like two extremely well-built soldiers, maybe a bit taller than you'd like, with an air of something different about them, some confidence that made you wonder if anything could touch them, but nothing that would make you think they weren't human, even if you were prone to such thoughts, which most humans of course weren't.

They had back-packs and bags full of supplies, and numerous technical instruments: they looked like techies or scientists from some advanced unit. Neither of them appeared armed, but just by the way they carried themselves, you'd rightly guess that either of them could easily kill you with their bare hands in any one of forty-two interesting ways.

As it was, the only onlookers were a few bugs and worms, and to them Spike and Jools looked exactly the same as any other giant stomper did: dangerous and to be avoided.

Jools used his enviro-scanner and swept the area, "well this place is a shit-hole," he observed, "nothing here… maybe some real feint readings from half-way round, but nothing near-by."

Spike couldn't see anything to contradict Jools' observations, "this place remind you of anywhere?" he asked.

Jools flipped the scanner shut, thought about it for a few seconds, "Tindal IV?"

Spike nodded, "yeah… I don't think we're gonna get much from this place."

Jools kicked over some rubble, looking for anything interesting, "well, we got five days searching, then we're done, so I guess we get on and get off…"

"I get the feeling this place was somewhere once… we'd have come here at the right time, I reckon we could have got some good R&R in," Spike said.

"Well, whatever it was once, it aint now, maybe they fucked over the Council like Tindal IV?" Jools said.

Spike pointed east, "water is that way, might as well check it out."

Jools fell in behind Spike as they headed off, "might as well, got nowhere else to be," Jools said.

"Aint that the truth," Spike confirmed.

Standing by the shores of Lake Geneva, they held hands, allowing a cross-over of Q-Fish in to their consciousness. They both closed their eyes and felt Q-Fish push in from outside the Universe. A stream of energy channeled through them out in to the lake.

Seconds later it was over. Q-fish had the readings he needed. It confirmed what he suspected: Earth was a nexus point.

It would take some time, but given enough readings Q-Fish was sure he could determine how many branes passed through here and why they felt a need to touch the Universe right here. If he could find that out he might be able to find a way to release lapsed-space in to the Universe through a portal that couldn't be shut as long as the Earth existed.

And that would be goodnight for all known life-forms apart from him.

Spike shook it off, taking out his water-bottle and taking a swig, he passed it to Jools, "which way you think?" Spike said.

Jools took a swig, handing it back, "doesn't matter I guess... south?"

They moved off and trudged on southwards.

"Where you wanna go on the next R&R?" Spike asked.

"I don't give a shit, long as it's warm and there are women, I'm easy," Jools replied.

Spike let out an involuntary laugh, "our dreams are small, but we can still dream them."

Jools chuckled to himself, "fuckin' A!"

Paradox is something that plagues us. A paradox should, like art, point us at the truth and say, 'there you go, have a think about that!' Sometimes we're not supposed to get it straight away. In the figuring-out lies the real knowing. It's like that 'it's about the journey not the destination' thing – we all feel sometimes that we just want to get there and stop mucking about, but when we do, what do we end up doing? Looking back on how we got there! There are no AIs that give the slightest run-time to paradox. A sim within a sim? Not even a challenge, never mind a paradox. Remember when we thought the speed of light was absolute? It's like that. We let paradox plague us. It stops us getting there too quickly.

Nurgle Zaxus, Advisor to Emperor Pulishwere, Chief Negotiator for Pardalax Sub-Ether Beacons.

Svetlana and Borya were siting round a camp-fire, surrounded by piles of fruits, nuts and ration-packs.

The nineteen people from the OPSEK station were still with them, setting their own fires, getting together in small groups, chatting, thinking about what they were going to do.

There had been no talk of splitting the group, they all believed it when Svetlana and Borya had told them this was the best place to be in a world that was now full of nothing. At first they were completely surprised that the others wanted to leave, but then the national stereotypes kicked in and they found it easy to believe the Chinese and Americans were bat-shit crazy and were following a strange agenda only they knew about, fuelled by their stupid history.

This place was a garden, a farm, it could give them everything they needed, and if they looked after it, nurtured it, they could easily live out their lives here.

Why that wasn't enough for the lunatic Americans and Chinese was their business.

Borya picked up a long piece of wood he'd been playing with, it was firm but slightly bendy, about seven feet long, "tomorrow I'm going to see if there are any fish," he said.

"There probably are, but you'll never know," Svetlana said.

Borya laughed, "I can fish! How hard can it be?"

"That's the spirit!" Svetlana said.

Borya offered Svetlana a small flask, she took it carefully and took a small sip: this was precious stuff, they didn't have much vodka left!

"We called the American crazy for taking a gun on to their space-station and we took vodka on to ours," she observed.

"We all have our own 'crazy'," Borya said.

The sun had set and they were sitting bathed in the flickering glow of the fire, this almost always prompts deep thoughts and reflection, no matter the life-form, no matter the situation they find themselves in.

"Should we be thinking on a bigger scale?" Borya asked.

"Like what…?"

"Survival of the species, carrying on for mankind, repopulating the Earth, all that?" Borya said.

Svetlana had been thinking about this: as soon as the others left, the odds lowered of having some kind of controlled existence based around the need to keep the species going, "why is that our responsibility now if it hasn't been before?"

"Kind of a numbers game now, that's never been the case before, in fact the opposite, we always talked about controlling population, giving the Earth and those on it a chance, now we are talking about 'people' not having a future… that's what's at stake right?" Borya said.

"I don't think you can make people responsible for 'people', just responsible for themselves," Svetlana said.

"But this is wildly different right? Surely?" Borya said.

Most civilised worlds will not let you take responsibility for someone else's thoughts or actions. Many travelers forget this and rely on others when they get to their destination. Do not fall in to this trap! On some worlds, Mantle for example, you will be fined and put to work on clearing the daily accumulated piles of ash from the myriad of volcanoes. But on Grutus, and many other worlds, you will be made an example of and publically executed. Be responsible, yes. But only for yourself!

Uku Zuku, Galactic Council Trooper Resettlement Division.

Svetlana knew what Borya was driving at but couldn't see it. Maybe she was too tired, maybe it was just too much to think about right now, too much of a weight. She couldn't take responsibility for the human race: she could barely function as a person herself in this grim new world.

"I say we get on with the business of living, trying to survive, be as happy as we can and let the rest take care of itself," she said.

"Why do you think the crazy Americans and Chinese needed to 'go back', try to be who they were?" Borya said.

There was a long pause as they both became lost in the flickering firelight.

Svetlana drank some cool, fresh water, picked up a succulent piece of fruit, took a bite and savoured it, "I guess they're still in shock, looking for the familiar..."

"And us?" Borya asked.

Svetlana finished her fruit, licked her fingers and threw the pip in to the fire, "I guess we're just looking for tomorrow?"

Borya smiled and nodded his agreement, "deep... you should write this stuff down..."

Svetlana laughed, "but who'd read it?"

"You never know..." Borya said, "people are amazing things..."

They sat quietly for a while longer, all around them people hushed as the forest insects began their nightly chatter.

"I'll come with you, tomorrow, fishing... I used to fish when I was a girl..." Svetlana said.

Borya went back to shaping his make-shift fishing rod, "I think we're going to be ok," he said confidently.

Svetlana smiled at him, "that's the spirit!"

Fishing is of course not about catching fish. If it is about catching fish, because say, you need to eat them, it's called hunting. Fishing is nothing like hunting. There are beings older than me, and I'm nine hundred and six, that have spent their whole lives studying what fishing is. Nobody knows what fishing is about. Which is why of course, it is so popular.

Ordrax Lintle, Sports Writer for the 'Whelton Sirix Wave'.

Chat and Hurny had been nominated from the group to go and see what they could find at the radio-telescope. Was there anything left that could be scrounged, used to make some form of communication equipment? Could some of the equipment there be repaired?

It was a ridiculous long-shot but they had to find out.

The rest of the group of escapees went back to the impossibly deep tunnels beneath Area 51. They had scrounged enough water and rations to last them about two years, so they were going to sit-tight, come out in two years and see what was what.

It was the only plan they could think of.

They simply didn't have enough information.

If there were any people left alive, they would want the escapees dead: aliens would not be greeted warmly after an apocalypse.

They knew they were alien, or at last mostly alien, with some human elements, but they had no idea of their origin, of their history, they were just here, struggling to survive now their human captors were all dead.

Why did they do that to themselves? They must be stupid. Or maybe one group of humans was far more aggressive than the rest and had won some kind of war?

War is an enigma. The galaxy is split right down the middle on 'getting it'. Those that do, seem to love it and indulge in it as often as they can, those that don't, think it is very silly indeed.

Data-worm, extract from the Bliss Intelligence on Reigel.

Whatever the reasons, the humans were gone, so now they could escape. But there was nowhere to escape to.

Chat and Hurny were, like all of the escapees, tall, spindly, almost insectoid, but with fleshier torsos and sharp angular heads that had a reptilian look. They all had huge eyes, more like those of a fly than those of a human. Their ancestors were an entirely space-borne people that had learned to adapt and succeed in almost any environment. They did not have the complex breathing and circulatory aspects of their ancestors, being bred for survival on Earth, but they did have their phenomenal dexterity, strength and speed.

Hurny was a lot more bullish than Chat. Chat was a quiet, reflective woman who wasn't sure what was going on, wanted to find out and wanted to understand how she could be happy in this hell-hole of a world. She didn't hate 'people' and she couldn't see any point in dwelling on why these 'people' had created her and her companions. They were here now, they were who they were and they needed to survive. Everything else was, if it didn't help their main goals, irrelevant.

Hurny was all about his alien nature being what was keeping him alive, scoffing at the stupid humans, these dumb-ass 'people' who had wiped themselves out. He knew that now he, and the others, if they were smart and followed his thinking, could take this planet for their own and make it the world it should be.

It was a long, hard slog to the Owens Valley Radio Observatory, or what was left of it, and most of the journey had been made in silence. They needed to conserve energy and remain hidden: they still weren't sure who was alive or who could be watching.

When they finally got there it was obvious that they could no more restore the radio observatory than they could turn what was left in to a cruise-ship.

The Cruise Ships of Arial are in a league of their own as far as luxury goes. Cruise ships are a symbol of luxury, of decadence, of idle-wealth the galaxy over. On Arial they took it to a whole new level. Abandoning all connection with the virtual realms of their predecessors, they pass between the planets, systems, stars and galaxies on eternal voyages of pleasure-seeking.

Big enough to hold multiple generations of those seeking nothing but the finest in star-travel, they dwarf most moons of the systems they visit.

The whole civilisation on Arial is now geared solely to producing, crewing and servicing these behemoths. Taking passage costs more than most empires can plunder over the course of their existence, but there remains a demand for them. The immortality that comes with a ticket to ride an Arial Cruise Ship is no stagnant extension, no mere continuation of life. It is an eternity of pleasure and new experience, limited only by the Universe itself.

Lynd Jiry, Travel Writer for the 'Lifestyles That Matter' network.

They made their way down to the main site and picked over the charred remains.

"Well, there goes that idea," Chat said under her breath.

"Maybe there is something left underground? There has to be something!" Hurny insisted.

Chat sat down, tired and thirsty. She took a small sip from her water bottle, surveying the area. It was close to mid-day, and even though the sun was hidden by clouds of ash and vapour, it was still muggy, too hot and humid for her liking.

"You can do what you like, I'm resting," she told Hurny.

Hurny turned on her, "don't you care!? Don't you want to get in touch with our people!? Take this planet as ours!? We have a right to it! These pathetic humans! Look what they made of it, they're done with it, this is our time!" he yelled.

Chat shrugged and looked at Hurny, he was trembling with outrage.

"We have a duty… a duty to survive! We *must* survive! If you can't see that you are as much of a moron as they were!" Hurny barked at Chat.

"Why is it 'our duty'?"

"What…?"

"Why is it our 'duty'? I didn't ask for this, this is nothing to do with me, I was forced in to being, this is not of my making, where does my 'duty' come in?" Chat asked quietly.

"You can't escape who you are!? You can't deny your past, what has happened, how you got here, it's who you are!" Hurny shouted.

"I have no responsibility other than to myself," Chat said, "and," she continued in a dangerously low tone, "you are starting to annoy me…"

Hurny started addressing a much larger non-existent crowd, his voice raised as he paced about, preaching to the masses that would never hear his message.

He reminded Chat of one of those comically serious dictators she had seen in the news-reels in her history classes.

Hurny was talking a lot about conquest, of claiming back what was theirs, of a glorious resurgence of an ancient history, some revival of an empire partially remembered from a time when he was sure he must have been part of the ruling elite. People would bow before them, they would get off this planet, back out in to the Universe, to claim their rightful place among the great and revered in the Galaxy. This was their time! This was what they were born for, this was their destiny!

The invocation of 'destiny' should guarantee that the person invoking it should be soundly ignored. This is a lesson that has been learned the hard way by millions of civilisations all over the galaxy. Save yourself some pain: the next time you hear someone mention 'destiny', laugh in their face and walk away.

Wridden Jangle, correspondent for PPN, reporting from her seventeenth war-zone.

Hurny seemed to have forgotten a great deal of what he was taught and shown by their human captors before they disappeared. Hurny, like all of them, was sterile, he could not 'breed', there could be no continuation of his 'race', they were created for a purpose, they were experiments, meant to be warriors and workers, nothing more. There was no 'future' for them among the stars. They were Earth-bound. And they would be the last of their kind. They were not part of a grander scheme, there were no ties to empire, they were just here, now. And all they had was each other and the day before them.

Chat was ok with that but she knew Hurny never could be. Hurny carried on visualising and vocalising his grand vision.

In a blur of motion, Chat leaped to her feet, closed on Hurny, slammed her palm under his chin, throwing his head back and before he knew what was going on, she grabbed and twisted his neck, snapping it in an instant.

Hurny's lifeless body dropped to the floor at Chat's feet.

She bent down and closed his eyes before she moved off to find a quiet place to sleep.

Ten days later she was back with the others.

She had made her mind up to stop hiding and to get out there and see what was going on in what was left of the world. She would take her share of the rations and go.

She was greeted by their oldest, Warren, “where is Hurny?” Warren asked.

“I killed him,” Chat said simply.

Warren nodded, “he was an annoying bugger… we didn’t think you were coming back…”

“I only came back to tell you I’m leaving and to get some rations… I think you should do the same,” Chat said.

“Do you want to be ‘leader’?” Warren asked.

“No… I’m going to go out in to the world and look around, and it would be good to have those around me that I knew, I’m not ‘leader’ material, I don’t think anyone should be…”

They all thought about this for a while. Chat got together her share of supplies and found some useful bits and pieces nobody else wanted.

Warren approached her, “we agree with you. We should go out there and look around. Enough hiding.”

“And if we meet ‘people’ then we meet ‘people’,” Chat said, “we talk to them, we don’t kill them… we don’t know them… there may be others who do not want us as slaves.”

Warren nodded, “agreed. We defend ourselves and nothing more.”

Chat relaxed a little, “agreed. We take care of each other, we explore, we live free from any ‘duty’…”

Warren smiled at her, “that sounds like as much as we could hope for anywhere.”

“I think so,” Chat said.

As they all filed out of their hiding place Warren shared something with Chat that not all of them knew, “I feel I should tell you…”

“Tell me what…?”

“We have discovered that we can ‘breed’… not with each other, but with humans… the information… it was in a lab, on the lower levels… we’re not sure if it was a rogue project, we don’t know how many humans knew this… but… that might change things?”

Chat shrugged, “or it won’t… we shall see…”

Warren looked up to the sky and breathed deeply, “I guess we will…”

There is an element of chance in evolution that guarantees it will always be beyond the comfort-zone and understanding of many people. It's not perfect, it's not 'fair' and it doesn't have to make sense. Evolution is the most relentless process in the Universe precisely because it does involve chance. The more we find out about every aspect of existence, the more we realise that a random element is key to everything. And that's not very comforting for most of us.

Brim Gording, Poet in Residence, Palace of Misconception on Kalizar.

Barfax Quile sat in the lounge of the main spaceport in Tork on Twus, enjoying the money he had just made from the Beet Wave-Network. Writing about where was a good place to have a good time, regardless of species, was, as far as he was concerned, money for nothing. And he'd made a lot of money by discovering that visitors were now welcome again on Weet-Ak after a three hundred year blockade by the Crumillions. Sure, if he had of been wrong, he'd have been evaporated as soon as he tried to exit the transporter, but he had some pretty good intel. Intel was what it was all about. Networking, getting out there, talking to people, finding out what wasn't reported on the waves. And nobody did that better than Barfax.

He was pretty toasted on a mixture of Gransnax and Four-seal cocktails. Waiting in space-port lounges was what you made it, and what he largely made it was an experience he couldn't remember.

He was free-lancing, looking for someone to deliver a pay-day, some way to cruise a job while he was in this neck of the galaxy.

Flicking through entries from various travel-guides he saw one that drew his attention.

Man, did that need expanding!

He brought up some holo-schematics and started looking for a likely landing spot, he noticed there was no space-port. He'd have to piggy-back on a buzzer. Not ideal, but not the end of the world.

As he was scanning through the maps, checking local manifests and departure times, trying to find a way he could dodge a ride, he was nudged by the person sitting next to him at the bar. He mustered a polite smile and turned to see who was trying to get his attention.

A short, scruffy man clutching a battered old satchel was smiling at him. The man's grin made Barfax fidgety.

Barfax was struck by the fact that this little man was at least as toasted as he was.

The man managed to widen his manic grin, “hi, yes, couldn’t help notice, you know, the map… you thinking of checking that place out?”

Barfax kept it close, not divulging until he knew what this guy wanted, “sure, you know, maybe, was thinking it could be cool…”

“It’s not… trust me, it’s not cool… not in the least bit froody… spent some time there… it was terrible…and now it’s even worse, a real, what’s the word…”

“I don’t know…” Barfax said guardedly.

“Anyway, just saying, wouldn’t bother if I were you… terrible place… and now it’s a grey-zone, so, y’know…” the strange little man fell forward on to the bar, his head resting on his folded arms.

“A grey-zone eh? Well, I’m not after trouble,” Barfax said as a closer.

“Yeah… gonna be a long time before that place approaches anywhere near its potential hoopiness… terrible place… did I say that?”

“Yeah, sure, anyway, thanks for the heads-up. Happy travels!” Barfax offered a friendly smile and left.

Drunk people at space-ports, as inevitable as Farquil suckers on a Grurin Hound. But take it where you can get it, intel is intel.

The disheveled traveler ordered another cocktail and sauntered over to a table, collapsing in to a sumptuous chair.

He smiled to himself, “terrible place… but it had its moments…”

There are no ends, only middles.

Thank you for reading SoulDice.

The sequel, ‘Mind’s Eye’ is in the works.